This book is for Rus.  *...t and Octavia, both so goo* *g- .u uad.*

CONTENTS

ACKNOWLEDGMENTS

Thanks go to John Oakes, Colin Robinson, Paul Di Filippo, Scott Bryan Wilson, Shuja Haider, and Nathan Rostron. Also, a tip of the hat to Connie Willis for inspiration.

INTRODUCTION

"People ask me to predict the future, when all I want to do is prevent it."
—Ray Bradbury

After seventeen years of editing a science fiction magazine, I'm awfully familiar with stories that offer dire predictions of the future. The post office box abounded in them—they're one of the four or five most consistent themes I saw in story submissions.

In fact, when my friend John Joseph Adams assembled an excellent anthology of dystopian stories, *Brave New Words*, I was bemused to notice that twenty percent of the stories in it were tales I had published. (No wonder I consider the book to be excellent, right?) I guess I have a taste for such tales.

So, when I had lunch with John Oakes on Inauguration Day, 2017, it was not shocking that the concept for this book should arise. Perhaps the bigger surprise was that I hadn't thought of it sooner. The atmosphere had been thick with dire predictions.

In forming this book, I deliberately sought a lot of short pieces, rather than a handful of longer ones (as in my anthology of climate change stories). There are so many alarming trends at play right now that I reckoned three dozen short considerations of them would make for a better book than ten to twelve longer ones.

When you get to reading this book, I think you'll agree this approach was fruitful.

As you would expect from the title, the stories assembled here do not include many escapist fantasies. Happy endings are scarce in these pages. The stories gathered here are angry, bold, snarky, defiant, nervous, and satiric. They reflect a lot of anxiety. They cover a lot of the themes you'd expect and perhaps a few you might not.

I like to think that readers of any political stripe will find this book interesting, but fans of our forty-fifth president will definitely be put out by some of these stories. A lot of these stories, actually. Don't say I didn't warn you.

In the United States, the political divide between members of the two major parties has, in my estimation, grown wider and deeper over the last three or four decades. This book will not narrow that gap or heal that divide—at least, not in the short term. It's more a work of resistance. As Ursula Le Guin noted, "Resistance and change often begin in art, and very often in our art—the art of words."

In the long term, I hope this resistance will give way to understanding. I hope that it will encourage some cooperation to take root and grow.

Mostly, though, I think this book will make for a lot of thoughtful and valuable reading. I hope you'll agree.

—*Gordon Van Gelder*
November 2017

SNEAKERS

Michael Libling

I won't claim Ottawa never warned us. There was no missing the travel advisories. Match a profile, and you had damn well better know *Title 19* by heart, especially the search authority part. To US Customs and Border Protection, it is the gift that keeps on giving, ever adaptable to changing times and minds:

> *We rely upon the judgment of our individual CBP officers to use their discretion as to the extent of examination necessary.*

Jordy and I failed to grasp the obvious, of course, how the definition of *discretion* also fell to the individual officer's discretion, and American vocabulary skills were shit to begin with.

What did we know? We'd been cocooned by the burbs, Montreal's West Island, raised vanilla to respect and trust authority. People got what they deserved. It wasn't in our genes to think twice.

Anyhow, I've put it down like you asked, while it's all still fresh. I am cooperating. You see that. Hiding nothing. God's honest truth. No matter how it sounds.

Monday morning, Jordy shows up at my door early. "You didn't answer your phone," he says, ignores the fact he's dragged me out of bed, and launches into this big song and dance. Tells me how

Min's morning sickness carries through to the afternoons most days. Wants to know if I'll drive him to Plattsburgh. "Min's afraid she'll puke in the car."

I'm available. The "tweaking" of NAFTA has not been kind to me. Still, I give him an earful: "For Christ's sake, you're almost thirty. Learn to drive, already. You're going to have a kid. Your wife and me, we're not your goddamned chauffeurs."

He laughs me off, as usual, twirls the split ends of that God-awful scraggly ugly beard of his. "You know your problem?"

"Yeah, yeah. The big picture. I never see the big picture."

"You have any idea the endorsement deals waiting for me when I'm done with this? Min and me, we'll be rolling in it, man. I'll make you my manager. We'll be like the guys on *Entourage*."

Jordy is focused, I tell you. He's training for that World Marathon Challenge thing. Seven marathons on seven continents in seven days. Nuts, I know, but dreams are dreams and if anyone can pull it off, Jordy can. He's tanned and leathery and in the best shape of his life. Not a smidge of fat. I've known the guy since grade school and have yet to meet anyone more driven, his elusive driver's permit notwithstanding. Once, half-joking, I asked what was chasing him. You'd have thought I'd just pissed on his grandma's grave. "I'll let you know when it catches up," he said. "If it doesn't kill me first."

The red steel roof of the new Refugee Processing Centre at Hemmingford cuts above the treetops as we enter the final stretch of Quebec 15 south to US 87. "A shame they had to build it, eh?"

"Yeah," Jordy says, but I can he see doesn't know what the hell I'm talking about.

"After the refugees started flooding in? When the Safe Third Party Agreement fell apart?"

God, he's clueless. Like where's his brain? I school him best I can. Explain how there's a bunch across the country, now. How the red roofs are famous world over. A symbol of hope or whatever. How everybody loves Canada. Except Red Roof Inns, who are suing for trademark infringement.

He says, "Min and I stayed at a Red Roof Inn when we went to Niagara Falls."

"Yeah. Great." Two exits before customs. We can turn around easy. And I can salvage what's left of my day. "You ever check out the cost of your shoes online?" I ask.

"What do you think?" he says.

Also, I admit, the closer we get to the border, the edgier I get. Too much Politico, NPR, and Michael Moore will do that to a person. "You've done the math, right? I mean, factoring in the gas, the exchange rate—how much are you saving? Really?"

"Like five hundred bucks for three pairs."

"Damn. That much, eh?"

"And don't forget the fit, man. Fit is critical."

The lines at the Champlain border crossing into New York State have been shrinking since 2017. It's the wait times that have gone up. Way up.

"Murphy's Law," Jordy says. "For every action there is an equal and opposite reaction."

"Newton's," I tell him. "It's Newton's Third Law." Half-right is Jordy's forte.

"Either way, we wait."

Banks. Supermarkets. Public urinals. Strategic queuing is a skill I have yet to acquire. I gamble on Lane 4. Three cars, a Winnebago, and a pickup ahead of us.

Jordy is impressed. "Good thinking. Probably old farts in the camper. They'll whisk 'em right through."

But they do not whisk anybody through, least of all the presumed snowbirds. "I've got a bad feeling," I say, as the Winnebago is directed to the side.

"Talk about red flags," Jordy says. "You see their bumper sticker? The COEXIST thing. The moon and star and peace and cross crap? C'mon, eh? Use your brain. They were asking for it."

"This is taking forever. God, I hate lines."

"Relax, man. I'll buy you lunch."

"At the rate we're moving, you'll be buying me dinner."

"We could change lanes, if you want. Could be our guy's a hardass."

"Yeah. Brilliant, Jord. Wouldn't look the least bit suspicious."

"Jesus, man, get a grip. How many times we gone to Plattsburgh, eh? When have we ever had a problem? Trust me, man, we are not who they are looking for."

Our CBP officer is pink and pudgy-faced, his chest a platform for his double-wide chin. He reminds me of that recently dead comedian—you know, used to be on SNL, back when they were getting away with the political stuff. He smiles and I relax as we hand over our passports. "How are you boys doing today?" he says, and segues to the next question. "And the purpose of your visit?"

"Shopping," I say.

"Sneakers," Jordy clarifies, and lifts a foot for the show and tell—the stylized yellow and black lightning bolts of his Trexis 880s. "Best ones out there. Worth every penny."

"That's some beard you got there," the officer says.

"Thanks," Jordy laughs.

"What's the problem—no sneakers in Canada?"

"More bang for your buck in the States. Especially now, the crazy tariffs and all…"

"Crazy? What do you mean by 'crazy'?"

"Well, you know…"

"No, I don't. Who are you calling crazy?"

"I didn't mean—"

"Run a lot, do you?"

"Does he ever!" My enthusiasm is over the top. I'm trying to compensate for something, though unclear on what. "He's been training for the World Marathon—"

"I'm not talking to you," the guy barks, "I'm talking to him." I squeak to silence as my larynx drops to the vicinity of my butt. Jordy keeps it cool. "Marathons, mostly."

"Fast, are you?"

"I'm more into the endurance end."

"Uh-huh. Endurance. Big word. Big word." He holds our passports aloft, one per hand, compares photos and faces. "Jordan, huh?" he says, with this snotty smirk. "An Arab name, isn't it?"

Again, Jordy laughs.

"Something funny?"

"No, sir. Sorry. I just—"

"Egypt. Syria. Jordan." He is daring Jordy to dispute the assertion. "No?"

"I'm Canadian," Jordy says.

"Muslim Canadian."

"Canadian Canadian."

"So what's with the beard, then?"

"My wife likes men with hairy—"

"Your passport picture. Is this even you? Not a hair on your face here. And how is it you're white in the photo and brown in the flesh?"

"It was taken before I—"

"Pull over for secondary inspection, please." He points to where the Winnebago is parked.

"But I can expla—"

"Pull over for secondary inspection, please." He waves a hand, and two soldiers in camouflage chic materialize in the roadway ahead. They do not raise their guns all the way, only enough of the way.

They confiscate our watches and phones, request our passwords. We do not argue.

They herd us into a room with a horde of others in a similar fix. The walls are white. The lighting is weird, feels like a strip search, somehow. Rows of attached chairs dominate the space. Blue plastic seats all facing front—toward this broad glass partition with offices behind, uniforms flitting back and forth.

"Product idea!" Jordy quips at my ear. "An antiperspirant for desperation." I step to distance myself from him. The hopelessness of the place is palpable. And it's standing room only.

Men. Women. Kids. Babies. Asleep. Awake. Collapsed to the floor, resigned to the corners. Like an airport during an extended weather delay, but without the windows, exits, Starbucks, and chummy chitchat.

Names are called. Detainees escorted out. Detainees escorted in.

A short stocky man in a navy suit struts up to the counter, demands a lawyer. "I have rights," he bellows. His voice is hoarse, crackly. He's Indian or maybe Pakistani. But his accent, it's British. He pivots, climbs onto his soapboax, pleads with us to join him in rising up against our oppressors. "We have our rights."

A woman CBP officer tells him to shut up and sit down or she'll be forced to put him in restraints. "It's your final warning." She's loud. Real loud. So the whole room hears.

This is when it hits me. The brown guy, he's an exception. Pretty much everyone here looks like me, talks like me, dresses like me. God, the arrogance, it kicks me in the head. It's nothing I expected. Or imagined. We're coming up on four years of this immigration craziness and we are the only people who have failed to get the message. Like our whiteness is our amulet, our birthright inviolable.

I get it now. I see what's going on. CBP has run out of brown and black people to harass. Men in pajamas and funny hats. Women patrons of third-world H&M stores.

I feel shame. For myself. For every dumb-ass in this zoo. Winnebago seniors and 4X4 hockey moms. Country clubbers and hayseeds. Barbies and Kens. Hipsters and divas. Frumps and fatties.

Geeks and glad-handers. Saints and shits. Bikers and slackers with holes in their ears and tats up the wazoo. Even the cabal of graying hippie chicks, their Pussyhats and sweatshirts and tinplate provocations.

HE'S NOT MY PRESIDENT

WE SHALL OVERCOME

GO INTERCOURSE THYSELF

MAKE AMERICA AMERICA AGAIN

OPRAH 2020

And then I come to Jordy. Jeez, I see what the CBP guy saw. Jordy is as much of an exception as the wannabe rabble-rouser. If not more. That stupid beard of his. That stupid tan. Suddenly I'm worried. Not for me, but for my best friend.

People speak in whispers, if they speak at all. As if anything they say could and would be used against them.

Squinty-eyed portraits of the president pass judgement from three walls. I stop my count at fourteen. Straight ahead, sweeping across the expanse above the glass partition, an inspirational quote in shimmery gold calligraphy:

It is our right as a sovereign nation to choose immigrants we think are the likeliest to thrive and flourish and love us.

We're five hours in (best guess), when our names come up. They lead us down a narrow hallway and into a maze of lefts and rights, where doors outnumber walls. And portraits everywhere you turn. A freaking presidential art gallery.

They shunt Jordy one way and me the other. He shrugs, rolls his eyes as we part.

My room is a walk-in closet. I sit at a table, a vacant chair opposite. I am given water in a plastic cup. Here, *His* portrait has a Washington-Crossing-the-Delaware vibe, broad stars and bright stripes in perilous flight.

I doze off. Two minutes. Two hours. Who knows? My interrogator shakes me awake. He's bald. His face a fist with smoker's teeth. He's a dead ringer for my tenth-grade shop teacher, Mr. Mitnick, except he's got all his fingers.

He spins his chair around, straddles it back to front, arms hugging the seat back. "Tough day, huh? I apologize if any of my associates have behaved inappropriately toward you."

"It's been okay, I guess."

"Taken from our perspective, however, you need to understand: It would appear you have quite the hate for America."

What the hell do I say to that?

"You don't hold back on Facebook, do you? All that rage, how our president cost you your job—your future, as you put it."

"Because of NAFTA…"

"Quite the hate, I'm afraid. Quite the hate, son. All those Facebook *likes.* Any story to bad-mouth America, and you were there. Our electoral process. Our gun laws. Our healthcare. Our schools. Any idea how many *likes* in all? Go ahead. Guess. Guess."

I shake my head.

"Fifteen thousand, one hundred and forty-one in the last three years alone. Fifteen thousand, one hundred and forty-one. If that isn't hate for America…"

"I'm sorry."

"Good. Sorry is a start. That's why I'm going to tell you: Your friend has confessed to everything, so there's no point in you covering up. All we need is your corroboration."

"Jordy?"

"Your Muslim pal."

"He's not Muslim."

"Uh-huh. And how long you two been a couple?"

"Like gay?"

"Two grown men? Your age? Traveling together?"

"We're not gay."

"Not a pro-LGBQXYZ story you didn't *like* on Facebook. Not one."

"Jordy's married."

"Lots of fudge-packers are."

"Jesus, man."

"You members of the same mosque? Is that where you met?"

"Beechwood School. First grade."

"Who recruited him? Why's he so desperate to get into the States?"

"This is crazy."

"Crazy. Like how your friend insulted our president earlier? How would you like me to visit your country and call your president crazy?"

"We don't have a pre—"

"What's the extent of North Korea's involvement?"

"Huh?"

"Jordan's wife. Is she behind this?"

"Min? She's from Seoul. He met her when he was teaching ESL over there. They're having a baby."

"Name me a jihadi who isn't."

"Jordy's no terrorist."

"Then why the beard? Why so much time spent on Oman and United Arab Emirate websites? Huh? Answer me that, smart guy?"

"You don't understand. It's for the race."

"The Muslim race…"

"No. No. The World Marathon Challenge. Oman and the UAE are two of the countries he'll be running through."

"My, my, won't that be convenient. They must be waiting for him with open arms. A hero's homecoming."

"Look, call his parents. Call Min. They'll tell you everything."

"Min. His North Korean wife. Miscegenation is a big thing up in Canada, I hear. Anything goes with you people, huh?"

"What? What?"

"You've got an answer for everything, don't you? Explain this, then—explain all the money your friend's been stashing away."

"The Kickstarter and GoFundMe things?"

"Keep talking."

"He needs sponsors. For the Marathon. The entry fee alone is like fifty thousand—"

"State sponsors?"

"Sponsor sponsors."

"North Korea, Oman, and the United Arab Emirates."

"Jeez, man, look it up. The World Marathon Challenge. It's a race. Honest. What do you want from me, anyhow?"

"The truth."

"That's what I've been telling you."

"Except for the actual purpose of your visit."

"Sneakers, damn it, sneakers."

"So that's what you and Jordan are—sneaker agents."

"Uh, you mean, like sleeper agents?"

"If the shoe fits…"

"Look, Jordy needs sneakers. They're cheaper in the States. His wife is sick, so he asked me to drive him to Plattsburgh. That's it."

"Without luggage?"

"It's only for the day."

"What did you say the name of your mosque was, again?"

"I've never set foot in any mosque."

"But Jordan has. We have pictures."

"It's no secret. For a wedding. A friend's wedding."

"And yet you still maintain he's not Muslim?"

"He doesn't even believe in God, for Christ's sake. Neither of us do."

"That's okay. No matter, God believes in you and God loves you. And right now, He's hoping you'll find it in your heart to do the right thing."

"Jesus."

"Yes. Jesus is hoping, too."

"Aren't I entitled to a phone call or something? A lawyer? The Canadian embassy?"

"That's what socialists say."

"No, it isn't."

"When was the last time you and Jordan did the hajj pilgrimage?"

"The what?"

"Do you use drugs?"

"No."

"Have you ever used or knowingly possessed marijuana?"

"It's now legal in Canada, you know?"

"Finally, we're getting somewhere."

"Can I have another cup of water?"

He stands. "I'll do my best for you, son. I can't promise anything, but I'll do my best."

Again, he wakes me up. He tells me I've been denied entry into the United States. I ask why. He says, "You know why."

"Aren't you supposed to give me a document with the reasons in writing?" The CBC had a primer on its website.

"Let's just say you were never here, and leave it at that."

"Seriously?" He hands me an envelope containing my phone and watch, leads me down a hallway to a bolted steel door. "But what about Jordy?"

"Oh, yeah. Your friend. Didn't I tell you? He was cleared to cross hours ago. Champlain Centre Mall, I think he said. Probably home and enjoying his new sneakers by now."

The fresh air feels good as I step outside, the sun just breaking above the horizon. Holy crap! I can't believe it's Tuesday. Mostly, though, I can't believe the prick went on ahead without me. And then it dawns: Jordy can't drive. Jesus Christ, the asshole cannot drive. I turn to protest, too late.

I go to use my phone. The battery is dead.

You know the fun I had getting home. I won't repeat. It's dark. I'm wiped. I'm angry. And I sure as hell want to hear Jordy's side of the story before I kill him. Here, at least, I'm glad my phone is dead. Better to cool off before calling him.

I grab a beer, turn on the TV, and I swear, it's the first I hear of the attacks. Montana. Idaho. Minnesota. Michigan. Pennsylvania. New York. The small communities still reeling. And every target within shouting distance of the border. Including that diner north of Plattsburgh.

They're interviewing a survivor. A waitress. "He comes running in like he's hopped up on something. And the whole place goes up. No. No warning. Nothing. Some say he shouted that allu-whatever thing, but I didn't hear nothing."

The camera pans to the devastation, closes in on what's left of the "alleged" attacker. Not much. Except a leg poking out from under a plastic sheet. A leg. The footage is shaky, grainy, but there's no denying what I see. The stylized lightning bolts. Zigzags of yellow and black. Trexis 880s, for Christ's sake. You bet I lost it.

Nothing fits. Nothing makes sense. I'm not even aware the president is blathering away on TV until he's almost done—when he regurgitates the myth about the 9/11 hijackers coming from Canada. I cribbed the part from this morning's Gazette. You need to look at this in context of what I've told you. Follow the evidence. Connect the dots. Or whatever.

"…tragically, once again, because Canada has opened its doors to terrorists, innocent Americans have paid the ultimate sacrifice. Make no mistake, this is a repeat of 9/11. For the second time in a generation, coordinated attacks on the United States were orchestrated on and launched from Canadian soil. Let me not mince words, if Canada insists on maintaining its reckless immigration policies…resists our calls to root out radical Islamic fundamentalists within its borders…the United States of America will do it for them."

And then this morning, you guys knock on my door, bring me down here. You tell me you're RCMP, I figure for sure it's Jordy you've come to talk about. But this other business, when you showed me those pictures on my phone. How many times do I need to tell you? THEY ARE NOT MINE. I swear to God. I DID NOT DOWNLOAD THEM. Little kids? Me? Christ, no way. Never. I've got nephews. I'm no perv. I don't care who tipped you off, you've got to believe me. They're lying. Just like there's no record of me being at the border. Jordy and I were played. Now you're being played.

You think I don't know how paranoid I sound? How far-fetched all this is? Yeah, well, you want to know what's far-fetched? Look who got elected president four years ago. Look who just declared martial law and suspended the next election.

RE: YOUR WEDDING

Ruth Nestvold

From: Jenna Furlan <expatjenna@dt-mail.de>

To: Annie Furlan <Annie_F@mailnet.com>

Date: February 13, 2019

Subject: Your wedding

Hi Annie,

I'm sure you heard the news and have been expecting this, but we won't be able to fly to the States for your wedding this summer. Maksym has taken a leave of absence from his job and headed for Kiev to try and get his parents away before the Russians advance on the city. I wish they had come to Stuttgart before Donetsk fell. They never believed it would happen, not even when the US withdrew its support from NATO. And now we might well need all the savings we have to bribe their way out of Ukraine and into Germany.

I'm so worried. Maybe we can talk on the weekend when the time difference doesn't get in the way as much. Evening my time so that Rebecca and Daniel will already be in bed?

Love,
Jenna

From: Annie Furlan <Annie_F@mailnet.com>

To: Jenna Furlan <expatjenna@dt-mail.de>

Date: February 18, 2019

Subject: Re: Your Wedding

It was good to talk to you the other day, Jenna. I just want to make sure you aren't offended at Dad's offer to pay for plane tickets for your family to our wedding. You seemed a bit short when I suggested it.

I'm glad to hear that Rebecca and Daniel are doing fine, despite their father being away.

Have you had any news from Maksym?

Love,
Annie

From: Jenna Furlan <expatjenna@dt-mail.de>

To: Annie Furlan <Annie_F@mailnet.com>

Date: February 22, 2019

Subject: Re: Your wedding

I wasn't offended about Dad's offer to pay our way. I'm sorry Annie, but I don't think I have any brain cells to think about your wedding at the moment, not with Maksym in a war zone. How to pay for a vacation in the States is the last thing on my mind right now. And no, I haven't heard from Maksym since before you and I talked on the weekend. For the sake of the kids, I'm trying to keep from tearing my hair out.

Jenna

From: Annie Furlan <Annie_F@mailnet.com>

To: Jenna Furlan <expatjenna@dt-mail.de>

Date: February 24, 2019

Subject: Re: Your Wedding

Hey, Jenna, are you angry? I wasn't thinking. It's just that I would really like to have my big sister at my wedding. I hope you've heard from Maksym again by now.

Love,
Annie

From: Jenna Furlan <expatjenna@dt-mail.de>

To: Annie Furlan <Annie_F@mailnet.com>

Date: February 28, 2019

Subject: Kiev

Have you seen the news? Although who knows how the media is portraying things in the States, with the way the President has been cracking down on critical journalists. What do you know about the situation in Ukraine?

The Russians are just outside of Kiev, and I haven't heard from Maksym since shortly after he got there.

I'm so scared.

Jenna

From: Annie Furlan <Annie_F@mailnet.com>

To: Jenna Furlan <expatjenna@dt-mail.de>

Date: March 7, 2019

Subject: Re: Your Wedding

Okay, I guess now it's official, you really are angry at me. I haven't heard from you in almost two weeks, and you never replied to my last message. I'm not quite sure what to say. Forgive me for being so insensitive?

Please don't let us ruin our relationship over this. You're still my big sister, and I love you dearly.

Annie

From: Jenna Furlan <expatjenna@dt-mail.de>

To: Annie Furlan <Annie_F@mailnet.com>

Date: March 9, 2019

Subject: Re: Your wedding

Hi Annie,

I wrote you Feb. 28, but you don't seem to have gotten my message. I changed the subject header from "wedding" to "Kiev," though. Damn and crap. What kind of news coverage have you had of Eastern Europe over there lately? Could the NSA be filtering private emails now?

The last time I heard from Maksym was the middle of February. And I'm scared shitless.

I'll call you tomorrow.

Love,
Jenna

From: Annie Furlan <Annie_F@mailnet.com>

To: Jenna Furlan <expatjenna@dt-mail.de>

Date: March 13, 2019

Subject: Rebecca and Daniel

Hi Jenna,

After our chat on Sunday, I talked to Dad. Here's what we're going to do. He is going to book tickets for the kids to come here while you go look for Maksym. You can't take them with you, and you don't have any relatives in Germany. But we're here for you, even if we are an ocean and a continent away.

You should get in touch with him to make specific arrangements. I'm so very sorry about the previous misunderstandings.

Love,
Annie

From: Jenna Furlan <expatjenna@dt-mail.de>

To: Annie Furlan <Annie_F@mailnet.com>

Date: March 17, 2019

Subject: Re: Rebecca and Daniel

Hey, Sis, I get it now. No need to apologize. I didn't realize how much you were being misled over there on the other side of the big pond. It's been a year and a half since I visited home, after all. Back then, it was all still a bit of a circus. Sure, here in Germany we hear plenty of reports of manipulation, especially since the Republican landslide in November. But I hadn't realized how thoroughly the media had been compromised, how widespread alternative fact has become.

Here, we're all getting very nervous, wondering which country will be next.

When I first came to Germany, I never thought too much about NATO, never considered it an institution that had anything to do with me, really. My attitude changed when I met Maksym. His hope was always that his country would be able to become a member of either the EU or NATO, to discourage Russian aggression.

And then the US withdrew from NATO—leaving Eastern Europe ripe for the plucking, it seems. A present from a grateful president for services rendered, helping him into the White House? Who knows.

All I know is that Russia is very interested in taking over its former satellite states again. And with a friendly US president, a weakened NATO and an EU in disarray, it's a real danger.

Sigh

I talked to Dad, and he's going to try to get a direct flight for Rebecca and Daniel from Frankfurt to Seattle by the beginning of April. Then I can see if there is any way I can get to Maksym. I got a very cryptic message from him the other day, from an Internet café, he said. I don't know what happened to his phone. But at least I know he's alive, which is a huge relief. Cross your fingers for me that Maksym soon finds a way to communicate more regularly. Just one short email from the war zone, and it's like I'm walking on air.

If I haven't heard from you within a week, I will assume that I used too many keywords in this message and will have to make like a criminal and get a burner phone to communicate with you in future. *g* But I'm still hoping that it was the subject of my previous email that made it disappear so mysteriously. We will see.

Love,
Jenna

From: Annie Furlan <Annie_F@mailnet.com>

To: Jenna Furlan <expatjenna@dt-mail.de>

Date: March 21, 2019

Subject: Re: Rebecca and Daniel

Ah, Sis, I don't know if I would have the courage for humor if I were in your situation.

Dad and I will be at Sea-Tac on April 3 to pick up your kids. I hope it won't be too traumatic for them to fly alone at the ages of only six and four. But they are pros, after all. I don't think I'd flown anywhere yet when I was Rebecca's age—and she's been to the States three times, not to mention your vacations to Mallorca and Tenerife!

I love you so much.

Annie

From: Jenna Furlan <expatjenna@dt-mail.de>

To: Annie Furlan <Annie_F@mailnet.com>

Date: March 24, 2019

Subject: Re: Rebecca and Daniel

The courage for humor? Humor is about all I have left, courage not so much. I'm not quite sure how I am going to be able to put my kids on that plane next week. I haven't heard anything from Maksym since the Internet café email. I hope he manages to get a new phone soon so that I will have a bit more of a clue than the name of a town I'm supposed to go to near the Ukrainian-Polish border. For a song, I bought an ancient Ford Focus that doesn't meet the emission standards in Stuttgart, and as soon as the kids are safe in Portland, I am off to try and find the love of my life.

Wish me luck.

Love,
Jenna

From: Annie Furlan <Annie_F@mailnet.com>

To: Jenna Furlan <expatjenna@dt-mail.de>

Date: April 3, 2019

Subject: Re: Rebecca and Daniel

Hi Jenna,

I'll call later before I go to bed, when it isn't the middle of the night in your part of the world, but I just wanted to make sure that you will know Rebecca and Daniel arrived safely, as soon as you get up and check your email. They had many stories to tell of how they were treated on the way. Carts through the Frankfurt airport! Ice cream on the plane! They even got to visit the cockpit and talk to the pilot before the other passengers got on. Right now they are sleeping blissfully in one of Dad's spare bedrooms. I have to go to work tomorrow, but I'll come over again in the evening to have dinner with them. And on the weekend, we're all going to the coast to play in the sand and eat crab.

Love you,
Annie

From: Jenna Furlan <expatjenna@dt-mail.de>

To: Annie Furlan <Annie_F@mailnet.com>

Date: April 10, 2019

Subject: On the border

Hi Annie,

I'm in Chelm, Poland, now, near the Ukrainian border. The last time I heard from Maksym, he and his parents had made it to a town by the name of Kovel between Kiev and the Polish border. He has a phone again, but no Internet. Not to mention no car and very little money. His car was "seized" outside of Kiev by a group with guns, and he and his parents have walked most of the way with the other refugees fleeing the fighting. His phone was stolen shortly after he arrived. The coverage with his "new" phone (used dumbphone) is spotty, the battery weak, and the opportunities to recharge rare. Maksym doesn't want me to cross the border into Ukraine. He's afraid if I do, we might not be able to get back into the EU. I'm sleeping in my car, and hoping we will all get out of this mess alive. Polish officials on the border are refusing to allow Ukrainian refugees to enter the country. Huge crowds are gathering on the Ukrainian side, while Poland is putting up more makeshift walls as quickly as they can on the Polish side of the River Bug. Maksym has a visa for Germany—but will they recognize it? And of course his parents do not.

I don't know what to do.

Jenna

From: Annie Furlan <Annie_F@mailnet.com>

To: Jenna Furlan <expatjenna@dt-mail.de>

Date: April 12, 2019

Subject: Re: On the border

Jenna, please, don't do anything rash. I can understand you wanting to get to Maksym, but he may well be right that you won't be able to get back across the border.

The media here is claiming that Poland (!?) marched into Ukraine, and Russian allies are fighting the aggressors, protecting the Ukrainian people. Hard to believe that the info we're getting is so skewed.

The kids had a great time on the coast, but now that we're back, they've started asking when you'll be here with their Papa. At least they're safe.

I hope you get Maksym and his family out of there soon. I've found some online news sites that are closer to what you describe than the official version in the mainstream media, and it sounds even scarier than what you've told me.

hugs

Annie

From: Annie Furlan <Annie_F@mailnet.com>

To: Jenna Furlan <expatjenna@dt-mail.de>

Date: April 18, 2019

Subject: Re: On the border

Hey, Jenna,

I haven't heard from you for over a week. Please let us know you're okay. The online news site I found says that Russian troops are now moving in the direction of the Polish border. I can only hope you found Maksym and his parents and are on your way back to Germany.

Love,
Annie

From: Annie Furlan <Annie_F@mailnet.com>

To: Jenna Furlan expatjenna@dt-mail.de

Date: April 21, 2019

Subject: Re: On the border

Jenna, we're getting desperate here, please. I've tried calling multiple times, but your phone no longer seems to be working.

Annie

From: Annie Furlan <Annie_F@mailnet.com>

To: Jenna Furlan expatjenna@dt-mail.de

Date: April 23, 2019

Subject: Please contact

Let us know you're alive, Jenna, any way you can. We're frantic with worry.

US Embassy Warsaw
Aleje Ujazdowskie 29/31
00-540 Warsaw, Poland
April 25, 2019

Dear Mr. Furlan,
We are writing to inform you that the passport of your daughter, Jenna Furlan, was recovered near the banks of the River Bug east of Chelm, Poland. As we have been unable to determine her whereabouts, we are contacting her next-of-kin, according to consular record.

I am afraid I have no further substantiated information other than the finding of her passport. There were several drowning deaths on the Polish-Ukrainian border in a flash flood last week, but none of the bodies recovered matches the description of your daughter. We have put in a request with the proper authorities to be notified in the event that anything relevant turns up. In such an event, we will naturally contact you.

If you have had any news from your daughter, please let us know, and we can inform the Polish police that this need not be regarded as a missing person case.

Sincerely,
Joseph Riddle
Consul General

EVERYTHING IS FIXED NOW

K. G. Anderson

To: Dawayne Johnson-QA

From: Liz Ferry-PRODUCT GROUP

Subject: Limit QA scope on Vibrante

Dawayne,

Engineering's getting out-of-scope questions from someone on your team about the Vibrante data.

Reminder: your team is supposed to be looking for issues with ease-of-use and accuracy for the Vibrante device personal fitness features (steps, heartbeat, weight). I understand there may have been confusion because of the additional data fields coming in.

Just ignore those. That additional data is being QA-d by a third-party, overseas group.

And it wouldn't hurt to remind everyone of their non-disclosure agreements.

Thanks,
Liz

Liz Ferry
Manager, Vibrante Fitness
DataNex

To: Samantha Cook-QA

From: Dawayne Johnson-QA

Subject: Product Group request

Take a look at the email from Liz Ferry I just forwarded. I'd appreciate your help in addressing her concerns about the data scope. So just ignore that "extra" data. It's nothing we need to be looking at.

And please check with me in the future before sending any questions to Engineering.

Cheers,
D-man

Dawayne Johnson
Manager, Quality Assurance
DataNex

To: Dawayne Johnson-QA

From: Samantha Cook-QA

Subject: Re: Product Group request

Dawayne,

Did you know that extra data is medical data? Heartbeat patterns, respiration, pulse measurements, etc. Looks like we're going to market the Vibrante as a medical device after the FDA is phased out in 2019.

I contacted Engineering because the heartbeat data was in an alert zone for three users in Comette's employee fitness incentive program. They said not to worry, but I did some digging and it looks as through these three people are experiencing periods of ventricular tachycardia.

My sister died of sudden cardiac arrest playing softball in high school. We found out later that she had undiagnosed heart problems and probably had ventricular tachycardia before she went into sudden cardiac arrest.

Someone in Liz's group needs to contact the companies who have those employees in the Vibrante program and advise them to get them to a cardiologist (a regular medical exam *won't* detect this type of problem). Also, to have them stop doing the fitness program.

—Sami

Samantha Cook
QA Specialist
Vibrante Team
DataNex

To: Samantha Cook-QA

From: Dawayne Johnson-QA

Subject: Re: Product Group request

Thanks for your vigilance. I'll pass your message up to Liz's team in case they haven't already gotten it from their QA contractors.

Cheers,
Dawayne

Dawayne Johnson
Manager, Quality Assurance
DataNex

To: Dawayne Johnson-QA

From: Samantha Cook-QA

Subject: Re: Product Group request

You'll need to give Liz the IDs for the users with the cardiac data issues:

   5-2889 (female, 49, Comette group)
   8-3445 (male, 24, Lumar Electric group)
   8-0871 (male, 45, Cebardok group)

The first two are assigned to a 3x/week, high-intensity cardio program—very scary!

—Sami

Samantha Cook
QA Specialist
Vibrante Team
DataNex

To: Liz Ferry-PRODUCT GROUP

From: Dawayne Johnson-QA

Subject: User data—3 alerts

Liz,

See below from Samantha Cook. It looks like she's spotted a serious problem with three of the employee fitness program participants. You've probably already had this reported by the outside QA group, but I wanted to make sure.

What with medical data, employee confidentiality, that sort of thing, this is probably a little tricky. Obviously, I'm not sure what agreements we have in place with the participants or their companies.

Best,
Dawayne

Dawayne Johnson
Manager, Quality Assurance
DataNex

To: Dawayne Johnson-QA

From: Liz Ferry-PRODUCT GROUP

Subject: Re: User data—3 alerts

Dawayne,

Not to worry.

Our QA contractor has spotted that data and we've contacted the companies. All taken care of.

Just a reminder: No member of your team is authorized to contact any individual user, or any representative of the customer companies that are implementing the Vibrante program with their employees.

Best,
Liz

Liz Ferry
Manager, Vibrante Fitness
DataNex

Sticky note left on Dawayne Johnson's desk:

> 5-2889 is still doing the cardio. Another episode of v. tachycardia. Can we contact this woman directly? Need name, contact info.
>
> —S

To: Samantha Cook-QA

From: Dawayne Johnson-QA

Subject: Short meeting

Stop by my office after lunch and let's talk about progress on your new project.

Dawayne

Dawayne Johnson
Manager, Quality Assurance
DataNex

Instant Message, 9:07 a.m.

To: Samantha Cook

From: Dawayne Johnson

Where are you? We missed you at the 8:30 meeting.

Instant Message, 9:21 a.m.

To: Samantha Cook

From: Dawayne Johnson

Urgent. PHONE me.

To: Dawayne Johnson-QA

From: Liz Ferry-PRODUCT GROUP

Subject line: Serious issue with QA

Dawayne,

Tried calling you. I just got a call from the director of HR at Comette. She was approached outside their company fitness facility this morning by a young woman who saw her wearing a Vibrante device and then asked "some odd questions" about her health. She said the young woman approached four other women wearing the Vibrante. Call me immediately.

Liz

Liz Ferry
Manager, Vibrante Fitness
DataNex

To: Samantha Cook-QA

From: Marcus Jiang-Hewitt-HR

Cc: Dawayne Johnson-QA

Subject: Probation Period

Samantha:

You have been placed on probation for a period of six weeks, beginning today. During this time, your attendance and performance will be monitored and feedback provided by your manager on a weekly basis.

In addition, you are advised to meet with a counselor from one of the third-party agencies available to DataNex employees. A list is attached.

Please contact me or a member of the HR staff with any questions.

Best regards,
Marcus

Marcus Jiang-Hewitt
Manager, Human Resources
DataNex

To: Samantha Cook-QA

From: Dawayne Johnson-QA

CC: Prisha Joshi-PRO

Subject: New assignment with Simplix-Tone

Hi Sami,

Starting Monday, you'll be doing QA for Prisha Joshi's team on the Simplix-Tone. They've got a desk set up for you in L Building. I think you'll enjoy them.

I'll send you meeting requests for the follow-ups HR wants.

Cheers,
Dawayne

Dawayne Johnson
Manager, Quality Assurance
DataNex

To: Samantha Cook-QA

From: Dawayne Johnson-QA

Subject: Good news

Hi Sami,

Just talked with Product Group.
Liz Ferry asked me to let you know that the users you were concerned about have been removed from the Vibrante program.
Thought you'd want to know.
Hope you're enjoying the work on Simplix-Tone. Looking forward to hearing about it at our Thursday meeting.

Cheers,
Dawayne

Dawayne Johnson
Manager, Quality Assurance
DataNex

To: Dawayne Johnson-QA

From: Samantha Cook-QA

Subject: Re: Good news

Dawayne Johnson-QA wrote:
Liz Ferry asked me to let you know that the users you were concerned about have been removed from the Vibrante program.

"Removed from the Vibrante program"?

Lily Pang was removed from her *job*. I tracked her down. When Comette let her go, they didn't tell her anything about a heart problem, or advise her to see a cardiologist. They just mysteriously "eliminated" her job.

And she was the lucky one. Mark Richardson? The 24-year-old guy from Lumar Electric? He's been "removed" too—because he went into sudden cardiac arrest and *died*.

Comette and Lumar are using our data to find employees at risk for heart problems—maybe other health problems—and get rid of them! Does Liz's team have any idea?

—Samantha

Samantha Cook
QA Specialist
Simplix-Tone Team
DataNex

To: Liz Ferry-PRODUCT GROUP

From: P. Ellis Nevars-LEGAL

Cc: Marcus Jiang-Hewitt-HR, Mariette Prudomme-SECURITY

Subject: Changes at OSHA

Liz,

You are correct. The federal Occupational Safety and Health Administration's mandate to investigate corporate whistleblower-retaliation complaints (The Whistleblower Protection Act of 1989, Pub.L. 101-12 as amended) was largely eliminated as of March 15. There was an exception for the transportation industry.

We have already briefed HR and Security about the implications for DataNex, but I appreciate your checking with me to confirm. Please let me know if you require any additional information.

Best regards,
Perry

P. Ellis Nevars
Associate Corporate Counsel
DataNex

To: Luther Beckshire-EXEC

From: Liz Ferry-PRODUCT GROUP

Subject: Vibrante Updates

Luther,

Wanted to assure you that everything is fixed now.

Security conducted the exit interviews with the two former employees yesterday evening. We are confident that they will not be sharing any proprietary information about the Vibrante with outside organizations. There had been an attempt to send screenshots from a company laptop to an external server, but Security anticipated and dealt with that breach.

I've also gone over procedures with the external QA contractor to make sure companies are getting employee data alerts on a daily, rather than weekly, basis. Their slow response, plus some errors by Comette's HR/Legal, contributed to the problem. We're monitoring them going forward.

Sales met last week with two Fortune 500 companies and one government agency interested in the Vibrante program for large, multi-site employee groups. All three are ready to begin using our enhanced data capabilities for HR purposes as soon as the FDA is out of the picture. We're drawing up contracts.

Two of the prospects asked about getting data on employee galvanic skin responses for use by their internal security teams. Can you put some pressure on Gil and Engineering to fast-track those sensor features for the 2020 rollout? Marketing is working up a GSR pricing model that dovetails with sales goals. We can go over it at tomorrow's meeting.

Best regards,
Liz

Liz Ferry
Manager, Vibrante Fitness
DataNex

HIS SWEAT LIKE STARS ON THE RIO GRANDE

Janis Ian

My heart was broken long before we met, so when love came sneaking up, it was completely unexpected.

I'd grown up in the shadow of The Wall, but never given it much thought. It had always been there. It would always be there. I was grateful to be living on this side, where the Rio Grande provided water for the agricultural station my father ran, and kayaking provided some small relief from the late April humidity. I loved seeing the huisache bloom, their feathery yellow flowers mirrored in the river's edge. My favorite time of day was early morning, before the worst of the heat. I would sit in my secret place and watch the sunlight glisten on the river, pretending the sparkles were stars that had fallen to earth the night before.

When I was young, I'd sometimes "borrow" my mother's binoculars and focus on the migrant families working the fields to the north. They fascinated me, the way their children seemed to run everywhere without any sign of supervision. The way the women carried naked infants in slings across their breasts. The way they'd stop occasionally to nurse, or hold the infant aloft as it did its business in the grass. I'd never seen an adult woman's breasts before, and as mine began to bud, the thought of what they'd become fascinated me.

And I must admit, I loved to look at the men as they worked bare-chested in the sun. Loved the way a drop of sweat would make its way from the nape of a neck to the top of the shoulder blades, then along the alley between, down and down and down, until it finally disappeared into parts unknown. Loved their wiry muscles, bunching and flexing as they grabbed at the plants, making my own still-forming parts throb and pulse. I had no name for it, this feeling of desire, but I gloried in it nonetheless.

I fell in love with Roger when he asked me to the 10th grade dance. I'd been hopeful, but still, it came as a surprise. I was nothing to look at, although my lineage was good. Father a supervisor, mother a tracker—both respectable jobs, requiring intelligence, stamina, and leadership qualities. And, as Roger pointed out one starry night, a certain ruthlessness. Laughing, he said I'd managed to inherit them all, and some lucky fellow's children would benefit from it one day.

That actually made me blush.

We dated all through high school, progressing from dry, fumbling kisses to "cupping," as we called it. Roger would cup my breasts in his hands and tenderly kiss them through the fabric of my brassiere. In turn, I'd cup his balls through the fabric of his Bermuda shorts, lifting and assessing them until I could see his penis straining at the front, begging to be freed.

To this day, even seeing Bermuda shorts on a department store manikin gets me all hot and bothered.

But we never went "all the way." We were saving that. I wasn't sure for what, but it seemed like the right thing to do. My parents liked his parents, his parents liked my parents, and the backgrounds all checked out. Still, something in us hesitated. I used to think it was because we knew it would never work out in the end, but perhaps it was just cowardice.

I cheered for him at the football games, when his tight end went on the offense to break the line. I helped with his Spanish, since his tin ear made it nearly impossible to understand his labored sentences. He wanted to be a tracker, like my mother, and I encouraged him to get the best education possible. I knew a tracker needed grounding in geology, and topography, and half a dozen other subjects unavailable at our local community college. When he dreamed about attending Texas A&M, I even wrote the application for him.

He broke my heart on graduation day, taking me out to a beautiful dinner at the best our little town had to offer. Making sure it was public, so I couldn't make a scene. Telling me without a shred of shame that we'd been great for high school, but now it was time to move on. Saying that as much as he'd enjoyed the fooling around, withholding himself had seemed the best way "to not get tied down."

He thanked me for being a good sport.

He paid the bill.

He pulled out my chair.

He walked me home, and left me alone at the door.

I didn't cry that night. I was too ashamed. When my parents asked how the evening had gone, I simply said I was tired, and made my way upstairs. I fell asleep almost immediately, and my dreams were filled with bronze-skinned men. We walked through the fields naked, letting the tall plants brush against our skin, weaving and waving and caressing without end. Strong arms lifted me into the wind, higher and higher, reaching toward the sky until I finally let go in one huge, orgasmic rush, and shuddered back to earth.

The next morning, I left early and went to my favorite place. There, hidden by the blackbrush and clapweed, I wept until my eyes were too puffy to see. I rinsed them in the river and made my way home.

That evening, I announced to my family that I'd broken up with him. "He's just too slow," I said. "I've kept it from you because I didn't want to cause tension, but I had to write his college application for him. I had to walk him through Spanish class, too. I don't know how he'll manage in college, but I don't want to find out the hard way." He'd been fine for high school, I added, but it was time to move on.

And move on I did. Through my mother's contacts, I managed to get an internship at LICE, our Local Immigration and Customs Enforcement. I began learning about the migrant workers who populated our fields, everything from their immigration status (H2-A visas, allowing them to stay as temporary workers) to breeding habits (birthrate dropping steadily, no one knew why). I learned that the word "temporary" didn't have much meaning any more, because we needed them there to plant, and harvest, year round. The migrant workers had become the breadbasket of America, and we couldn't let them go.

Because of Mother's status in the field, I was trusted with information most interns never saw. There were problems with The Wall, problems nobody had foreseen. No one knew if there were similar issues on the other side; they'd cut off all communication in my great-grandparent's time, when it was first built. But there were plenty of problems on our side.

I'd always been taught that the snipers were there to keep people from coming over the wall to our side. Now, I learned they were there mainly to keep people *in*. Trackers like my mother were occasionally permitted to "go over," but the migrant families who'd been here when the wall went up, stayed, generation after generation, whether they liked it or not.

The distant gunfire we'd occasionally hear wasn't from LICE agents defending our borders. It was from LICE agents shooting desperate workers as they tried to climb The Wall and get out.

I was troubled by what I learned, troubled enough to discuss it with my parents. Of course, they already knew all about it. My mother explained what a mess the country had been in before, terrorists running rampant and drug culture invading even the whitest homes. The Wall went up, immigration cracked down, and the country returned to its previous peaceful state.

Wasn't I grateful I never had to worry about being raped when I walked home at night? Didn't I understand that keeping those people here was, in a sense, saving them from the gang warfare that infested their own homeland? Besides, none of them were really Mexican any more. That was just a myth, like Palestinians claiming parts of Israel as "home." True, the migrants weren't really American either, but at least they had food, shelter, and a place to live.

Put that way, it all made sense. And I had a steady job waiting for me, if I keep my head down and didn't make waves.

I rose through the ranks, from intern to Watcher to head of Enforcement and Education. I had my own desk, name plate and all, with an official title. I wouldn't say I was happy, but I was certainly settled,

And then came Gabe. "Gabriel Alfonso Alvarez," to be exact. Fourth generation green card holder, the right handed down from his great-greats in a direct line after the moratorium on new citizenship applications went into effect. Those original green cards, usually held by university professors or tech geniuses, were a closely guarded privilege. Even the head of our field office had never seen one before.

It had only been a few years since Roger's betrayal, but during that time I'd convinced myself it was for the best. I'd slammed the lid on my desire so hard, I barely felt anything, even when I touched myself. The occasional bout with a vibrator was enough to release any built-up tension. As for the men around me, when I compared them with what I saw through my field glasses, they were pasty-faced and bloated. It would feel like being stroked by a dead fish. I'd set sex, and all thoughts of sex, completely aside.

So the hot flush that ran from my toes right up my hairline when Gabe first spoke my name was a shocking reminder that I still harbored a craving for contact. I managed to stammer something intelligent, like "How on earth do you know my name?" before lapsing into red-faced confusion.

Laughing, he pointed to the plate on the front of my desk, saying "You would be 'Señorita', then? Not 'Señora'?"

"Yes," I responded in my best I'm-the-teacher-here-don't-get-out-of-line voice.

He sighed dramatically, slumping for effect. "A pity. Your offspring would be beautiful."

Beautiful.

He thought I was beautiful.

Not "genetically clean," or "well groomed," but "beautiful."

I don't know that I'd ever spoken to a Hispanic person before, other than the women who cleaned our house over the years. They patiently let me practice my language skills on them. "*Buenos dias, señoras*," I would say, and they'd respond with "*Buenos tardes, señorita.*" I would ask, in halting Spanish, how their day was going. "*Bueno, señorita, bueno. Estamos muy contente*," they'd say, and we would be finished with the lesson.

I still dreamed of them, though, as I had all my life. Dreamed of Hispanic men, their golden bodies glistening in the sun. Wondered whether drops of their sweat had watered the tomato I brought to my mouth. Slowly savored a peach, licking the skin and imagining the sweet salt of their perspiration on it. And here he was, calling me "beautiful."

I was lost.

Not that I was blind, nothing of the sort. I looked at him long and hard before agreeing to anything permanent. There were concerns. Gabe had tried his hand at half a dozen jobs, but never settled on anything. He had a small inheritance from his parents, and it was enough to provide the necessities, but not much more. Despite his obvious intelligence, he had no real drive. He'd come here, to our little town, hoping to find his passion.

And then, he found me.

I'd like to say it was love at first sight, but it was more like instant lust. He asked whether I was seeing anyone, then took me to lunch. We stayed through dinner. He walked me home, striding confidently through the town, oblivious to the stares and whispers. He moved sinuously, muscles obeying without thought. I could feel them through the sleeve of his shirt when I took his arm. It was like walking with a tiger.

I want to be clear. I loved him then, as he was, and I love him now, as he is.

We dated for several months, while my parents ran the usual checks. I understand it was much the same during the age of AIDS, when two people interested in sex would go to the doctor together and get tested. Protective measures. After all, no woman in her right mind wants to get pregnant and then find out her child's genes also came from an anarchist or, God forbid, a terrorist.

Gabe came up clean in every respect, for three generations back. No questionable antecedents. No criminal elements. Nothing but your basic hard-working American dreamers.

After that, events moved along by themselves. We married with little hoopla, took our honeymoon in San Antonio, then settled down. Thanks to my parents, he was able to get a job supervising workers in the broccoli fields. He seemed to enjoy himself.

As for me, I was deliriously happy. Every pent up emotion came roaring out the first time he touched me. I think I even fainted for a moment.

He was an incredible lover, knowing just how far to push and just how long to make me wait. And, he was inexhaustible. We'd make love first thing in the morning, have breakfast, go to work, come home, make love again, have dinner, and sometimes make love for a third time. There wasn't a spot in the house we hadn't tried, from the guest shower to the kitchen table.

We didn't plan on children, at least, not yet. I wanted him all to myself. I loved to watch him, shirtless in the Texas heat, as he mowed the yard. I needed to feast my eyes on his skin, and imagine what the night was going to bring. Just the sight of his fingers buttoning a shirt made me wet. Absurd as it sounds, watching him take out the trash made me weak at the knees. I was in perpetual rut, and it showed no sign of ending.

Back at work, things were different. There was tension around the border, whispers of trouble passed desk to desk when no one else was listening. More and more of the migrant workers were dying, of old age, of illness, of simple neglect. We saw the reports and were told to ignore them. "Don't worry. They breed like rabbits," one supervisor said.

But that wasn't true. The migrant laborer's birth rate had begun falling a year after they were told they were permanent guests here, and the decline had continued. According to the Homeland Security statistics, we had less than half the workers we'd had three generations back—and almost twice the regular population. Asking Americans to work under those conditions was unthinkable. Paying a decent wage, which might allow migrants to send their children to school and work their way out of the fields, was unaffordable. Americans wanted cheap food, be it soda pop or brussel sprouts, and they didn't much care how they got it.

The anxiety I felt at work began to surface in our home. As Gabe moved around, from broccoli to tomatoes to sweet corn and snap beans, he began to know individual families. He'd come home each day and tell me their stories as we lay sweating in the heat, exhausted by foreplay and its aftermath. He worried over them. He felt helpless.

There was one little boy he kept returning to, a seven year old named Hector. The child was obviously very bright, Gabe said, but he'll never have the chance to be anything but a "potato puller."

When Gabe started talking about changing the system from without, if it couldn't be changed from within, I realized his kind heart might be his undoing.

I worried over it incessantly. The more involved he became with the migrants, the more I begged him to distance himself. He began to resent what he termed my lack of empathy. I began to resent his willingness to throw away everything his family, and mine, had worked for over the years.

"Aren't you grateful to your ancestors for making sure you never have to live like that?" I'd ask. "Don't you owe them something for their bravery, their willingness to rise above their beginnings and make this their permanent home?"

And he'd respond that the workers' families had been brave as well, coming to a new country where they didn't even speak the language, working in the fields, hoping *their* children would have a better life too.

We'd argue, pushing and pulling, going around in circles. I'd bring up our future children; he'd answer that he didn't want them growing up in a world where only those who already had, could have more. I'd tell him that for every bright little Hector, there were a hundred slow-moving dullards who were fit only to till the soil. He'd tell me that if my parents hadn't gotten enough protein, I'd be a dullard as well. And so on and so on.

Frustration grew on both sides until I reached for him one morning, and he pushed me away. I rubbed against him, whispering in his ear, but he rolled over and ignored me.

A few evenings later, he came in and immediately hopped in the shower, then fell asleep on the couch. When I woke him up to bring him to bed, he said he'd forgotten his hat that morning. He thought he had a bit of sunstroke, but just in case he was getting sick, he'd sleep on the couch instead of our bed.

And so, slowly but surely, the love making stopped. I felt like I was losing my mind. My body was used to constant satiation, an erupting geyser that was suddenly capped off. The pressure began to build. I could relieve myself just so many times before I began feeling like a narcissist. Frankly, I only found my own body interesting when Gabe was playing with it. Otherwise, relief was a mechanical necessity, and I hated it. I was desperate for something that would take my mind off my body, and not finding it at home, I looked for it at work.

So when a rumor went around about a special meeting coming up, I was all ears. The affected employees had to sign a full non-disclosure agreement, on top of the multiple secrecy papers we already signed off on again at the start of every year. There were dire warnings about what would happen to anyone found taping, or filming, or even taking notes. We talked about it in the restrooms and around the water cooler, speculating on what could make the administration so nervous.

They held the meeting in our regular conference room, but the windows were blacked out. Once we were all in, the door was locked. A U.S. marine stood at either side of the door, weapons at the ready. All four senior department heads were there: North, South, East and West. There were a few local employees like myself, along with several representatives from the agricultural and chemical industry. And a slew of government officials, with buzz-cut scalps and chests full of metal.

Last to enter was the Surgeon General, who told us all to sit down while he made his opening remarks.

He explained that the birth rate problem among migrant workers had finally come to the attention of the FDA (Food and Drug Administration), who'd contacted the CDC (Centers for Disease Control), who in turn had called in the NSA (National Security Administration). The security people then reached out to all the scientists under their command, demanding an answer that would ensure America's continuing food supply.

The scientists were given *carte blanche* funding, and a few months ago they'd presented the NSA with a potential solution.

From there, it went to the Secretary of Defense, and then to the Joint Chiefs of Staff. Finally, the National Security Council, who advised the President directly, were brought in. They informed the President of their conclusions. He, in turn, heaved a sigh of relief at such an elegant solution, and green-lighted it immediately.

After that, the army Chief of Staff took the floor. He reminded us of our patriotic duty. He said that while The Wall protected our nation's borders, we were the human wall that stood guard over the rest. While we might not like it, we had to face the fact that stringent measures were needed. We had to safeguard our country's future, not just for ourselves, but for our children. While the solution might appear drastic at first, he was sure we'd come to understand that it was all for the best in the end.

In closing, the Chief of Staff said "Let there be no confusion here. We will not take away anything that will be missed."

Then he introduced a team of army neuroscientists, telling them with a grin to "keep it simple, keep it basic, keep it quick."

The lights went out, and projections of human brains appeared on the walls. There were specific sections, colored pink and blue and green, labeled *ventromedial prefrontal cortex, left anterior cingulate cortex, amygdala.* The youngest in the group pulled out an old fashioned pointer, and proceeded to tell us what each area did. It was incredibly boring.

When the lights went back on, an older neuroscientist took over, explaining that thanks to government-sponsored research, they'd recently made some tremendous technological advances. For instance, they could now isolate precise regions of the brain. Not just over-all areas dealing with specifics like math, or speech, but the more fluid areas. The parts that governed free will. Happiness.

Sexual desire.

Operation MASS, or Migrant Attitude Selection Service, would ensure that only the most necessary areas of the brain were targeted. Husbands would still love their wives, and children would continue to love their parents. The only changes would be in their over-all happiness quotient, and their increased desire to "go forth and multiply."

There were snickers all around when he said that, because any Sunday School student knew that the phrase from Genesis 1:28 was Biblically polite short-hand for "Get you some nookie, and fast!"

Under the guise of free dental check-ups, workers' heads would be held still so x-rays could be taken. At the same time, a guided laser operating outside the detection range of the human eye would swoop in, destroying some bits of tissue, and exciting others. The patient would feel nothing but the dental plate clenched between his teeth.

As he droned on, the army people paying close attention, the rest of us were busy trying to figure out how this would apply to our own jobs. Sure, we'd be a necessary part of convincing the workers to go in for check-ups in the first place, but how exactly would that be done?

The obvious answer was to have some of the field supervisors volunteer to go first. That way, the migrants could see it was safe, and painless. They'd even be given the day off with pay, courtesy of a grateful U.S. government. The chemical companies would foot the bill for that, while the agri-business corporations would cover the cost of dentists, laser technicians, and mobile units.

Of course, the lasers wouldn't be used on the supervisors. That was out of the question.

We all agreed that this was an incredibly elegant solution, and the meeting was adjourned. Except for me. I needed just a little bit more information, and the junior neuroscientist was kind enough to provide it. He even let me take a few notes, after I mentioned my parents' positions and the length of their tenure.

The first thing I did when I got home was apologize to Gabe for nagging him about the migrant workers. I admitted I'd been wrong. They deserved his attention, and our support. I was going to speak with my parents and the head of LICE about it, particularly about Hector. There had to be some way to give boys like him a chance to escape the vicious circle their great-greats had left them in.

Next, I apologized to Gabe for taking my sexual frustrations out on him. After all, he was my husband, not my boy-toy. He deserved to come home to welcoming arms and a supportive spouse. I'd do better in future, but for now, just to even things up a bit, any first moves would have to come from him. The look of relief on his face almost made me ashamed of what I planned to do, but fortunately, it passed.

We made love a couple of times that week, and I reveled in it, while reminding myself that it could end at any moment. I would never let that happen again.

The free dental exams were first announced over loudspeakers on the water trucks. Then came billboards in English and Spanish, as well as bi-lingual flyers. They even left bags of candy out for the children, with dates and times of the upcoming examinations written on the wrappers. It did my heart good to know this was happening all over the country, even in cities like New York, where the trucks were rolling through Chinatown making announcements in Mandarin and Cantonese.

The day before the check-ups were to begin, I suggested to Gabe that he attend them incognito. "Dress like one of the workers," I said. "Let another supervisor go first, and you spend the day among your friends, reassuring them. They won't believe the other bosses, but they already trust you. After they see you came out looking the same as when you went in, they'll feel a lot better about things."

He praised me for being so compassionate, and got up the next morning to put on the clothes of a *campesino*. I even accompanied him to the mobile station, though of course I couldn't stand with the migrant workers—as much as he'd told them about his *gringa* wife, I might still engender mistrust. So I watched from the sidelines as he went in, and waited until he came out.

He was smiling, pointing to his mouth, opening it wide and saying "Ah-h-h-!" to the children. He gave out sugarless chewing gum, reassuring everyone in Spanish. There was much back-slapping and many looks of relief all around.

For the rest of the day, Gabe and I stood and watched as they filed into the mobile units with their families.

When it came time to go home, I looked at him and said "What would you like to do now, dear?" and he said "I don't know, *mi esposa*...but for some reason, I've never felt happier in my life. What would *you* like to do?"

It's been two years now, two years that feel like a constant honeymoon. The workers are content, and as they say, "breeding like rabbits". There are babies underfoot wherever I look; the fields will soon be full of children earning their keep.

Meanwhile, Gabe is content to go to work, eat his meals, and make love whenever and wherever I ask. We even managed a quickie in a two-person kayak one cloudy morning. True, he isn't terribly pro-active about it, but so long as I remember to tell him what I want, he comes through like a champ.

Sometimes I knock off early and sit on our veranda, watching him in the fields. The children love him, and the adults all tip their hats. Once in a while, he gets down in the dirt with them, yanking and pulling and lifting the baskets high over his head as he leads everyone toward the waiting trucks. Beads of sweat collect at the nape of his neck, then run down his back in rivulets, sparkling like stars on the Rio Grande.

AGNOSIA

J. M. Sidorova

May 31, 2019

From the cover page of a grant application to Tristate Pacific Blue Health by Drs. Valerie Jordan and Brad Schulz. *GRANT AWARDED

Project Narrative (describe your research proposal in up to three sentences using lay terms):

Amyloid precursor protein is the protein that, when aggregated in a wrong way, accumulates in our brains to cause diseases like Alzheimer's. We want to understand what it is used for in a healthy brain and why this protein is so important that it remains a must-have component of our brain cells despite its propensity to trigger unintended negative consequences of neurodegeneration.

Relevance to public health: The new knowledge obtained in this project may help fight neurodegenerative diseases.

Is this a competitive renewal of a project funded before 2018? NO

Have you previously applied for Federal or Red State funding for this project? YES

Years of applications: 2017, 2018, 2019

Was this project funded? NO

For Red state applicants: Attach a one-page justification for seeking out-of-state funds.

Enter the Just Divide tax ID for your institution and unit: *ID provided

Taxation statement: I agree to withholding at the Tristate Pacific Blue rate: *initialed

Public disclosure statement: I hereby acknowledge that if the grant is awarded, information about the project, its funding source, and the results it produces should be made available for dissemination to the public for the purpose of enhancing public understanding and interest in science and technology.

*SIGNED: Valerie Jordan, Ph.D., Brad Schulz, Ph.D.

January 7, 2021
From an article in *The Brave New Scientist*:

"Texas A&M scientists discovered a new type of modification enriched on amyloid precursor protein present in the neurons of the amygdala, our brain's emotion processing center. It is as yet unclear how this modification affects the protein function. Unexpectedly, the study uncovered a link between the prevalence of the modification and individual's political values. The study may shed a new light on the observations generated almost a decade ago, in which one's political leanings were correlated with the size of one's amygdala." (click to read more)

Public disclosure: The study was funded by Tristate Pacific Blue Health, a program of the Tristate Pacific Alliance Health and Human Services.

February 13, 2021

From a transcript of an interview with Drs. Jordan and Schulz, conducted by Cat Sanchez, host of *Your Morning Dose*:

Cat: Brad, Valerie—welcome to the program. Tell us a bit about yourselves. I am curious how you two work together. It is a rare thing, I am told, two heads in one lab. Do you ever argue?

Valerie: No, never.

Brad (chuckles): We debate.

Valerie: We keep each other sharp.

Cat (laughs): Sounds like you're a great team. I'm envious. So...tell me about your discovery. What is all this buzz about, this amygdala modification, this...*curser* protein?

Valerie: Precurs*or*. As in a form of the protein that is parental to the form that we know as amyloid.

Cat: Right.

Brad: Look, Cat. It's like this: imagine a protein is a body and a modification is like a tattoo in a particular place, for example on a shoulder. OK? Now. The protein we're talking about is named APP, amyloid precursor protein, and—

Cat: A tattoo? On a shoulder of a protein named APP?

Valerie: I'd rather liken it to a lapel pin than a tattoo.

Brad: But tattoo works, too. Now, what we've discovered is that only APPs that reside in the area of the brain called amygdala have this tattoo.

Valerie: Well, um, it wasn't quite that simple—

Brad: But it is a reasonable approximation. Amygdala is our emotions factory. It makes fear, aggression, anxiety, thrill, things like that. Now, what was most thrilling, Cat, was that when we compared brains of people who self-described as Patriocratic and those identifying with Multi-way, in the former the tattoo, the modification, was seen less often than in the latter.

Cat: In other words Patriocrats have fewer tattoos.

Brad: Um...so to speak.

Cat: That *is* thrilling, Brad. Tell us what it means.

Valerie: Typically, modifications are there to temporarily change the protein's actions or make it easy to be recognized by other proteins. As a lapel pin would. Or a boutonniere. Or a handheld sign, "Hi, I am here to help"—

Cat: But you believe it affects one's political values.

Brad: We don't know that.

Valerie: Mind you, all we have is a correlation, not a cause-effect relationship.

Cat: How do you know?

Valerie: We know because we analyzed the numbers, and the confidence level for the correlation is extremely high.

Cat: Right...

Brad: In other words, we counted it, Cat. The modifications, the proteins, the people. The numbers speak for themselves.

Cat (chuckles): Okay. Tell us why it matters. Do you believe this—tattoo—causes dementia?

Valerie and Brad: No, absolutely not, not at all!

Valerie: These are completely unrelated functions.

Brad: What she means is that the APP modification we are talking about does not—and I emphasize it—does not contribute to brain disease.

Cat: Phew! That's a relief (laughs). I'm glad you two agree on this. No need for the public to be concerned, then. Well, I'm no scientist...but it seems to me if you say it's like a pin or a handheld sign, or even like a tattoo, you seem to imply that you can put it on...and you can take it off, am I right?

Brad: You are right, Cat. Well done for a non-scientist. Yes, in theory. But let me tell you—

Cat: These are foundational values, though. Aren't you being a little...high-handed by even suggesting such a thing?

Brad: Look...this was your suggestion, not mine, first of all—

Cat: I only asked the question—

Brad: And second, this is a purely hypothetical scenario, an unlikely possibility among many others—

Cat: Of course. Only a thought experiment. Will erasing the— tattoo—change one's political identity?

Brad: Not if—

Valerie: Cat—if you want to know if we can change it by giving a person a pill, the answer is absolutely not, we can't and we won't. But does it mean it cannot change at all—no. Of course it can change. That's what matters. What if one's political identity is not a fixed personality trait? Not hard-wired before birth or in early childhood as they would have us believe. What if? Maybe you can change it just by thinking about it, right now. A thought experiment, like you say, Cat. Right?

(A long pause.)

February 14, 2021

An email thread:

Valerie Jordan to Brad Schulz:

What the hell?! That was an ambush. Our PR man had said not to worry—what was he thinking? O! M! G! I will never, EVER agree to ANY public outreach in the state of Texas again. Did you not see it, what this Cat was doing to us?

Brad to Valerie:

Valerie,
As a matter of fact, I did see it and did all I could to prevent it from flying off the handle.

Valerie to Brad:

And yet your choice of words…I would not have used a culturally charged reference such as tattoo.

Brad to Valerie:

My choice of words? First you freeze and speak in impenetrable scientese and then she baits and you take it. We both know you shouldn't have said what you said. And you hold me at fault for a tattoo metaphor?!

March 1, 2021

Select headlines:

Scientists Say Your Core Values Are Like a Tattoo on Your Forehead
National Interest

She-Scientist Valerie Jordan Wants to Do a Thought Experiment to Make You Vote Blue
The Well-Informed Man

Blue State–Funded Scientists Want to Vaccinate Your Children Against Patriocratic Values

Patriot Watch

Only Demented Degenerates Vote Patriocratic, Scientists Say

Daily Outrage

March 24, 2021

You are evil and the cause of all evil. You, the American Imperial academia, disdain and despise us who are fine people and only the rest of this country that used to be great, exceptional, and a shining city on a hill supposed to lead the whole world into freedom, democracy, and equality but then you let Jews, Blacks, and Women into our colleges and you teach them fraudulent sciences how to brainwash our babies and shove poison down our throats and that there is no truth only a matter of schooling. My wife she died yesterday of your Oldstimers disease she would of liked to give you her piece of mind about how you shredded the Constitution and your whole Just Divide that is nothing but your conspiracy to bleed the Red drop by drop because people like you don't give a flying fuck about cures just about more money to prove the blues are better. This letter is a bomb.

May 12, 2021

Our Lady of Mercy Rehabilitation Center, College Station, TX
Case history:

V.J. is a 37 y. o. left-handed female with no history of hearing or cognitive impairment prior to hospitalization. She was employed as an academic professor. V.J. sustained a severe penetrating traumatic brain injury to the right hemisphere on 3/24/21 as a consequence of receiving an explosive in the mail. The patient scored 6 on Glasgow Coma Scale when found, and continued to require management and sedation post-operatively. She had increased muscle tone and hyperreflexia two weeks after surgery. Second attempt at extubation was successful. The patient continued to improve in the following month. She was able to reach and squeeze staff's hand, and produce simple sounds. The patient was able to ambulate with assistance and perform routine hygiene tasks at 6 weeks post-injury. Speech was limited, poorly articulated, and often perseverative (e.g.: "bray bo, bray bo, bray bo…"). The patient demonstrated inability to follow verbal commands but showed comprehension of written words and was able to answer simple written questions regarding her name, age, and personal data.

Questionnaire #1:
Do you know where you are?
HOSPITAL. YES?
What is your name?
WHAT IS VALERIE
What is your birthdate?
OCTOBER NINETEENTH EIGHTY FOUR
What is your party affiliation (check one):
Patriocratic ___
Multi-Way I THINK SO
What is your occupation?
SCIENTIST
What are your hobbies?
HUMAN BRAIN
Who is your emergency contact?
BRAD ?? WHO IS
Do you know what happened to you?
NO

June 8, 2021

From Valerie Jordan's writing pad:

Hi, Brad. You came.

…

I do not understand you.

…

Can you write this on my pad?
CAN YOU TALK?
Not very well. I prefer not to. I slur and lose words. Voice too loud. So strange: I know what I want to say but can't figure if it comes out right or not. No feedback. Not that I was well-spoken before (just joking).
VALERIE I AM SO SORRY
Thanks. Are you ok? You look tired.
WORK
Brought me some?
NURSE SAID I SHOULDN'T
Pity.

…

I understand gestures and faces.
I AM SURE YOU WILL GET BETTER
Thanks. When I opened the bomb parcel I saw a brain in a zip-loc bag.

…

I really did. I remember. A brain bomb.

…

It is ironic. Don't you think?

…

Okay, go. I'll see you later?

June 30, 2021

Summary of findings:

MRI is consistent with multiple lesions in parts of V.J.'s right lateral sulcus and of the right superior temporal gyrus of the primary auditory cortex region. Neurophysiological workup shows no significant motor or somatosensation deficits. Performance in spoken task instruction tests is severely impaired. Pure-tone audiometry reveals no hearing deficit. In audio tests the patient correctly identifies meaningless sounds (e.g., whistle, rap), environmental sounds (e.g., wind, water, dog bark), and musical sounds, but shows no ability to interpret human speech. Written text comprehension is within norm. The patient is aware of her condition. A diagnosis of word agnosia or cortical deafness is suggested.

Questionnaire #5:

> Do you know what happened to you?
> BRAIN BOMB.

Questionnaire #10:

> Do you know what happened to you?
> YES, I DO.
> Would you like to start speech therapy or train to lip-read?
> NO.

From Valerie Jordan's writing pad:

Dear Sir,

I should not remember this. It is a memory that should not have had a chance to form prior to the bomb going off. Yet I do. I remember how I opened your parcel, being hasty with a one-sided razor blade, as I often am, and veering out of the groove between two flaps of cardboard held together by clear packing tape. I had purple nitrile gloves on my hands because I'd been doing bench work. Your hate letter could be mistaken for an invoice, folded loosely and tucked between the wall of the box and the bag. The bag had a queasy look of a vacuum seal that was meant to be but failed; the antiseptic cling of plastic to dura had sweated off, leaving smears of tea-colored, cloudy liquid. I must assume you did this to your wife's body because you were moved by the kind of extreme angst that I am yet to experience. But you've only proved that if you want to be heard with a bomb your intended audience is rendered unable to hear you.

The old factoid goes, there are as many brain cells as stars in the Milky Way in each and every one of our heads. I imagine a Milky Way blown apart in a big bang and hurled screaming at me. Billions of brain cells, their connections severed or burned, no longer a conscious whole but a mess of parts, agnosia incarnate. Each cell, if lucky, if not choked by the creeping rigor mortis of the amyloid clutter, only holds on to one or two poor scraps of the most deeply stowed, treasured memories. A few sweet moments perhaps: of childhood or motherhood or maybe of how you kissed her for the first time. Some of these cells are intact and now lodged in my cortex. I am not afraid of them. What's left of your wife's consciousness is nothing of the sort you are taught to call core values.

When the Constitutional crisis had hit, when the Just Divide had started I had been working so hard on my science I could barely spare time on anything else around me. Agnosia is the state of hearing and not understanding. You've shown it to me. Human speech, reduced, in the mind of the listener, to bird tweets. Yet even now I can write—I can pin thoughts to a solid surface, unburdened by the sounds of misunderstanding all around. I will write, revise, and write again till you can understand me. You had written down your return address—either you hadn't cared, or had thought it'd be destroyed in the explosion. It was destroyed, but I happen to remember it.

This letter is not a bomb.

THE ADVENTURE OF YOU

Paul La Farge

Dear Debris Removal Specialist John Arnold Arnold,

Welcome to your memoir workshop! In this class, you'll learn how to tell your unique story—the story we call The Adventure of You. All you have to do is complete seven easy exercises, which will help you put your experiences into vivid, meaningful words. Seven exercises sounds like a lot, but don't worry! The exercises are more fun than Connect Two, and they'll leave you with something to think about. You'll see: when you're writing your memoir, even a double shift on the debris pile will fly by, because you'll be living The Adventure of You.

All you need for each exercise is a piece of coal—no problem, right?—and a wall. The one next to your bunk is fine for starters, but as you become more confident, you'll want to write your words in a place where other people can read them. The door of the pit elevator? Great idea! The waiting room of the Clinic? That's a good one, too! Just, please, don't write over someone else's exercises, because each of us has a story to tell, and there are plenty of walls to go around, here in Enlow Fork.

Ready? Let's begin!

Exercise 1: In the Beginning.

What's the first thing you remember? OK, it was the Recovery Room where you awakened after your last reboot. But what do you remember *about* it? Maybe you had a nice spot near the ventilator duct. Maybe the loudspeaker made a funny sound, like somebody with the Black Cough trying to hum. Maybe your teacher played a hypnopedia tape out of order! (We know, it happens.) We can't tell you exactly what made your first shifts in this world special, but we know there was something. Close your eyes. Let your mind wander away from the persistent sound of large machines grinding rock. Remember the Pastor's voice: *In the beginning, there was Enlow Fork, and Enlow Fork was all.* What do you see? Great! Fix it in your mind: the one small thing that only *you* remember. Then grab a bit of coal, and find a wall.

Exercise 2: Mealtime.

What's your favorite food—Toasty Bricks or Squishy Balls? Why? Take a minute to savor whichever one is in your mind, but don't stop there. Try to see it and touch it and smell it and even *hear* it. (Ever throw a Squishy Ball at a ventilator fan, just to see what would happen? Uh-huh. *That* sound.) Now imagine this: the Synod has decreed that from this day forward, only one food will be served in Enlow Fork. Which one will it be? Write a letter to the Synod, in which you use all five of those sharp senses of yours to prove that *your* favorite should get the nod.

Exercise 3: My Shovel.

It's your best friend. You see it every day. It's waiting in its rack at the beginning of every work shift, and when you rack it again at the end of a tough stint of clearing debris, you can almost hear it saying, "Good job today, bud." What else would your shovel say, if it could talk? In this exercise, imagine that your shovel has a story to tell, too. Where did it come from? What does it do while you're lying in your cozy bunk, hoping the whirr of the ventilator fans will lull you to sleep? Does it just stand there, or does it have The Adventure of Your Shovel? Go crazy with your imagination on this one, but remember not to talk to your actual shovel.

Exercise 4: My Best Shift Ever.

Imagine if there was a problem with the grinding machines, and you had an entire shift to do whatever you wanted. Would you sack out on your bunk, or play Connect Two all day? Would you volunteer in the Clinic? Or would you sneak out to the fuel-storage tanks, which you know are off limits, and huff benzene? Would you rub your Clone Zone against the latrine wall until you made a wet spot in your jumpsuit? Would you search for tunnels to the surface, even though you know there aren't any, and you also know that the surface is just a story for kids? Please put your name on this one, John Arnold Arnold. We want to know what *you* want.

Exercise 5: Strangers in the Night.

You met in the waiting room of the clinic, or maybe it was while you were clearing a jammed hopper. Two identical shapes in the gloom, wearing identical jumpsuits, identical headlamps—but for some reason you didn't want to hit this stranger in the skull with the blade of your shovel, just to hear the squishy sound it makes. You wanted to grab his arm and pull his head close to yours. You wanted to whisper, *I found a tunnel where nobody ever goes. I think it might lead to the outside, but I'm scared to follow it all the way to the end.* Then you wanted to lick the coal dust off the stranger's cheek. You don't know why, and of course you didn't do any of those things, because the Synod forbids them on penalty of rebooting. In this exercise, explain why the Synod is right.

Exercise 6: Imagine If There *Was* a Surface World (Even Though There Isn't).

We know there's no world above us. *In the beginning was Enlow Fork, and Enlow Fork is all...*Right? But what if there were a tunnel that went up, and up, and up, until finally it led you to the surface. What would it look like? Using what you learned in Exercise #2, describe the surface world using all five senses. Although remember that if there *were* a surface world, the light would be so bright that you'd be blinded, and the surface-dwellers, if there were any, would take advantage of your helplessness to beat you to death with pointy rocks.

Exercise 7: My Meaningful End.

John Arnold Arnold, you're almost done! You could see the light at the end of the tunnel, if only there were a tunnel with a light at the end of it, which there isn't. In this final exercise, imagine that the Deacons caught you and your friend trying to escape to the surface, which doesn't exist. For your own safety, they brought you to a detention cell. Your friend is probably in the next cell, but don't bother trying to call out to him, because the walls are too thick. Don't get any ideas about escaping, either. Even if you could open the door of the cell, which you can't, there would be nowhere for you to go. Enlow Fork is all.

For this exercise, think about what you'll tell the Synod before they sentence you to be rebooted. Is there something about you, John Arnold Arnold, that you want them to know? You've learned a lot in this class, and now is the time to show it off: tell the Synod all about The Adventure of You. There should be a plenty of coal in your cell. Pick it up and begin.

♋

N. Lee Wood

From: Michelle Farley <mbfarley@gomail.co.nz>

To: Carrie Westlyn <cjwestlyn@gomail.com>

Date: Monday, August 13, 2018 at 11:16 AM

Subject: Hello

Hi, Carrie. It's been a few years, but I thought I might see how you've been doing since we last saw each other, how the time has just flown! We've mostly been fine here, kids and Ben are all good. Ben retired last year, and after Raewyn went off to Otago University we decided to sell the house in Auckland and bought a little place near Whangamata in the Coromandel, close to the beach. I think our last Christmas card had a photo of us all in front of the new place when the kids were home on holiday?

I thought of you a few days ago, because there's just no easy way to slide this into a conversation, but I've been diagnosed with cancer. Endometrial, stage 3. Scheduled for a hysterectomy next week. I feel a little embarrassed emailing you out of the blue like this, since we haven't really been close friends. But I knew from Julie that you had the same cancer a few years ago, and wondered if you might have any advice that doctors sometimes don't think about? Maybe I'm just being over anxious about it all and if this is too presuming, I apologise. It's all a bit, well, overwhelming. Hope to hear from you soon.

From: Carrie Westlyn <cjwestlyn@gomail.com>

To: Michelle Farley <mbfarley@gomail.co.nz>

Date: Monday, August 14, 2018 at 11:16 AM

Subject: Re: Hello

What a lovely surprise to hear from you, Michelle! We did get your Christmas card last year with the photo, your new place looks great. We all thought it must be huge fun to celebrate Christmas with a barbecue in the middle of summer! Must be good for Ben to have some free time now that he's retired. New Zealand looks amazing, pretty far cry from Iowa. Scotty wants to know does Ben still fish?

Jenny and Dave have grown so fast since you last saw them, they're amazing adults now. Dave is in community college and Jenny has a job at Costco, which she likes much better than she did working for Wal-Mart. She's hoping to save enough that when Dave finishes his trade certification she can afford to do a few classes in animal care. She'd love to be a vet—remember the old 4H clubs where she showed her little Frizzle chickens? Still has the ribbons if not the chickens! I'd just be happy if she can be a vet assistant, no scholarships these days for kids anymore.

Don't worry, I know how you feel—cancer is just such a bolt from the blue and nobody ever knows what to say to anyone. I'm so glad you thought of me and of course I'll be happy to give you what limited benefit of my experience as I can. I don't know if Julie told you, but mine is recurrent—came back in my bowels about a year ago. I was fortunate that I still had ADA, so my insurance covered most of the cost of the drug treatment, thankfully. I managed to finish a second round of chemo before ObamaCare was repealed, since treatment is so expensive now I couldn't have afforded it! We haven't been able to find another insurance company willing to take me on, not with pre-existing, but there's still a chance it can be treated so I'm trying not to worry too much.

Just see what the doctor says after your hysterectomy. Sometimes we do get lucky! Thinking of you, love from Scotty and me both.

From: Michelle Farley <mbfarley@gomail.co.nz>

To: Carrie Westlyn <cjwestlyn@gomail.com>

Date: Tuesday, August 21, 2018 at 4:52 PM

Subject: Back from the hospital

Hi, Carrie, thanks for replying so quickly to my last email, and for the kind words of support! I didn't realise your cancer had come back, I'm so sorry to hear that! Hopefully there's still a chance it's treated, I'll keep my fingers crossed for you.

We had to commute to Auckland for the surgery, that's one headache we hadn't thought of when Ben retired. The local GP here is okay for your everyday stuff but all the specialists are all in the city. Which, of course, means Ben had to find a hotel, not cheap. I had a three day stay in Waitakere and the surgeon did my hysterectomy endoscopically—amazing they can just look down those little tubes in your belly and take everything out without a big scar! The food was your typical hospital muck, so Ben had to go buy me take-away, which the first day or so I couldn't eat anyway, no appetite. Hopefully I'll have lost a few pounds, must look for some silver lining.

That's the good news—the bad news is I'm definitely going to have to have chemo. They want to give me Taxol and carboplatin, which is supposed to be better than the old cisplatin—is that what you had? They did warn me all my hair will fall out, so Ben gave me one of his world famous military buzz-cuts. I did have a wee cry, it's still pretty awful looking in the mirror—I can only imagine what bald is going to be like!

From: Carrie Westlyn <cjwestlyn@gomail.com>

To: Michelle Farley <mbfarley@gomail.co.nz>

Date: Wednesday, August 22, 2018 at 7:38 PM

Subject: Re: Back from the hospital

Hi, Michelle, glad to know your surgery went well. Sorry to hear how much of a hassle it must be living so far from city. We're pretty far from Des Moines ourselves, so commuting wasn't always easy, especially since there aren't any local women's health centers anymore. The last Planned Parenthood center in the county was shut down last year. Well, not so much shut down as burned down, but that was about the only place left that was willing to see patients without insurance. So I have to drive to Des Moines for my check-ups, although we've had to put off on that for another month or two.

Scotty hurt his knee mowing the lawns last year which is making it harder for him to keep up with the quotas at work. There's already rumors flying around that they're going to close his regional office because of outsourcing overseas, so he's worried we'll lose his insurance through the job as well. He had an injection a few months ago, which should have been covered but turns out it wasn't because his orthopedist didn't get the right drugs from the right vendor, even though the office called the insurance company ahead of time for authorization and they said it didn't need to be preauthorized with any specific vendor. Now it turns out it did, and we've been billed over $2,000. We're already on a pretty tight budget as it is, so that wasn't good. But we just try to keep positive and pray the good Lord looks after us, all we can do at the moment.

Bald isn't so bad, and it does grow back faster than you might think, you'll be fine!

Love to you both, Carrie.

From: Michelle Farley <mbfarley@gomail.co.nz>

To: Carrie Westlyn <cjwestlyn@gomail.com>

Date: Tuesday, September 4, 2018 at 2:18 PM

Subject: Re: Re: Back from the hospital

Dear Carrie,

What a nightmare! I don't understand why your country doesn't have better healthcare, the United States is so big and so rich compared to little old New Zealand! But I suppose it shouldn't be surprising, given who you all voted for over there.

Can't you see if you can find a clinical trial of some kind that might want to treat you with a new drug or something? I've been enrolled into two, the cancer research here is pretty amazing—one is a study on the nerves in my eyes, and the other is a new drug that's supposed to lessen the side effects of chemo, doesn't really have anything to do with cancer itself. But I say why not? Doesn't cost anything and might help. I'm sure there must be something out there for you, you just need to look a bit harder maybe? God does help those who help themselves, so they say.

We've had to cut back as well, since even though my treatment is covered by the state (it's why we pay our taxes after all!) it's still taken a bite out of the bank account. We did have plans to celebrate our 25th wedding anniversary with a cruise to Singapore next year, might have to just make do with a trip over to Ozzie and see mates on the Gold Coast instead.

Hugs to you and Scotty,

Michelle

From: Carrie Westlyn <cjwestlyn@gomail.com>

To: Michelle Farley <mbfarley@gomail.co.nz>

Date: Friday, November 23, 2018 at 11:15 AM

Subject: Just a quick update

Dear Michelle,

Sorry for not getting back to you sooner, things have been a bit hectic around here. It sounds like you've got your cancer treatment well in hand, doubt there's much I can tell you that would be of much benefit.

Yes, I had hoped for better, too, although I'm not sure it makes much difference who anyone votes for anymore, and wish everything weren't a choice between bad and worse. The mid-term elections were very confusing, hard to know who has won anywhere, nobody seems to know anything.

ACA (God forbid you call it "ObamaCare" anymore!) hasn't been replaced, and it's only getting worse. There aren't any clinical trials being run here much, at least none that focus on anything to do with women. Jenny is having trouble finding anyone who will prescribe her birth control for her endometriosis, it's all registered on a national database now and doctors don't like having visits from Homeland Security about who they treat and for what. Poor kid, she's barely eighteen. I feel so guilty and worried that she's inherited my cancer genes.

In any case, we've got bigger problems to worry about. The insurance company turned down our appeal over Scotty's injection, and we have to find the money to pay for that somewhere. But I did manage to finally see my specialist in Des Moines, and she had bad news, the cancer has come back and is spreading. I'm not feeling particularly sick just yet, but the cost of the drugs I'd need is more than we can pay for, now that Scotty isn't working any more—did I tell you? The factory closed, everyone in town is pretty much unemployed. It'll be some time before we can even dream about cruises to anywhere.

We're scraping together every penny we've got left to help Dave, our oldest. He went to Canada without telling us a few weeks ago with some of his friends from college to try to buy me the drugs I'd need since they're about a tenth of what they are here, but at the border US Customs confiscated them all along with his passport and told him he could be charged with a felony drug offense. He can't even prove he's an American citizen and he can't get back into the country. But the American embassy in Canada keeps telling him he has to get a replacement passport here, they can't issue him one! He says he's being looked after okay, but we just want our son home.

Sorry it's taken so long to get back to you, hope you understand and that your chemo is going well,

Best wishes, Carrie

From: Michelle Farley <mbfarley@gomail.co.nz>

To: Carrie Westlyn <cjwestlyn@gomail.com>

Date: Sunday, November 25, 2018 at 12:26 PM

Subject: Re: Just a quick update

Oh my god, Carrie, that's awful! How can Dave be arrested for chemo drugs, it's not like it's heroin! I'm bald now, chemo hurts a lot, although the clinical trial drugs seem to be working well. I wish I had more energy to write a longer email. But I'll keep you all in my thoughts and prayers, do let us know how you get on!

Big hugs to you all,

Michelle

From: Carrie Westlyn <cjwestlyn@gomail.com>

To: Michelle Farley <mbfarley@gomail.co.nz>

Date: Thursday, December 20, 2018 at 4:15 AM

Subject: Re: Re: Just a quick update

Dear Michelle,

Not sure if you'll get this email or not, since I'm having to write from one of those internet café places. I saw my oncologist a few weeks ago. It's too late to treat my cancer, it's gone to my bones and gotten very aggressive. She was very nice, didn't charge me for the visit, which is just as well since we couldn't have paid for it anyway. The prognosis she says is, with treatment, maybe a few years. Without, maybe six months, if I take care of myself. We can't afford it, we have no insurance left. So six months, if I'm lucky.

Thing have spiraled out of control here anyway, the cancer is ironically the least of my worries. We lost our house. We had police serve us notice that because of Dave's so-called drug offense, under RICO law our property was forfeit and they confiscated it along with what money we had left in our bank account. Scotty managed to get Jenny and the cat along with at least some of our possessions into the car before that was confiscated as well and they're on their way to California to apply to one of the sanctuary cities there for refuge. There's no point in me going, not with the condition I'm in. Nobody is going to take in a terminal cancer patient, no matter how generous they try to be.

I may never see either of them again, just hoping they make it in time—it's hard to figure out what's "fake" or not anymore now that the news is so regulated and my access to a lot of internet sites is restricted, but it seems the entire west coast is about to secede for real. The National Guard has already been deployed in Des Moines, where I'm staying with some friends. Nobody you know, and I don't want to say who, because you never know who's reading this anymore. We've got tanks on the streets and you can't tell who the cops are from the military, there's protests and riots breaking out everywhere. It's like a war zone. Part of me is scared, but part of me feels oddly liberated. I've got nothing left to lose, and if one sick fifty-five-year-old woman who can barely stand up without a walker can do anything at all to help, I've already knitted myself one of those silly pink hats—it's cold on the streets of Des Moines this time of year!

See you on the news, wish me luck.

From: Michelle Farley <mbfarley@gomail.co.nz>

To: Carrie Westlyn <cjwestlyn@gomail.com>

Date: Monday, August 13, 2018 at 1:51 PM

Subject: Are you there?

Yes! I got your email! Carrie, please don't be stupid, you can't take on the government and win. Surely there's something you can do, but protests are just going to get you hurt, they can't fix anything. You're in no fit state for that anyway. I rang Julie the other day, she suggested maybe you could try to get across to Canada like all those immigrants do, surely they'd help you? Be sensible, think of your family, they need you. I'll pray for you, just please be careful and let us know you're okay.

Love from us both, Michelle

Mail Delivery Subsystem - Address Not Found. 1:52 PM (0 minutes ago).

Your message could not be delivered to <cjwestlyn@gomail.com> because the address no longer exists or cannot be found. Please check for typos or unnecessary spaces and try again, or contact your provider for more information.

BIRDS

Deepak Unnikrishnan

Anna Varghese worked in Abu Dhabi. She taped people. Specifically, she taped construction workers who fell from incomplete buildings.

Anna, working the night shift, found these injured men, then put them back together with duct tape or some good glue, or, if stitches were required, patched them up with a needle and horse-hair, before sending them on their way. The work, rarely advertised, was nocturnal.

Anna belonged to a crew of ten, led by Khalid, a burly man from Nablus. Khalid's team covered Hamdan Street, Electra, Salaam, and Khalifa. They used bicycles; they biked quickly.

Anna had been doing this for a long time, thirty years, and many of her peers had retired—replaced, according to Khalid, by a less dependable crew. Seniority counted, and so Khalid allowed her to pick her route.

Anna knew Hamdan as intimately as her body. In the seventies, when she first arrived, the buildings were smaller. Nevertheless, she would, could, and did glue plus tape scores of men a day, correcting and reattaching limbs, putting back organs or eyeballs—and some-times, if the case was hopeless, praying until the man breathed his last. But deaths were rare. Few workers died at work sites; it was as though labor could not die there. As a lark, some veterans began calling building sites death-proof. At lunchtime, to prove their point, some of them hurled themselves off the top floor in full view of new arrivals. The jumps didn't kill. But if the jumpers weren't athletic and didn't know how to fall, their bodies cracked, which meant the jumpers lay there until nighttime, waiting for the men and women who would bicycle past, looking for the fallen in order to fix, shape, and glue the damaged parts back into place, like perfect cake makers repiping smudged frosting.

When Anna interviewed for the position, Khalid asked if she possessed reasonable handyman skills. "No," she admitted. No problem, he assured her, she could learn those skills on the job.

"What about blood, make you faint?" She pondered the question, then said no again.

"Okay, start tomorrow," said Khalid. Doing what, she wondered, by now irritated with Cousin Thracy for talking her into seeking her fortune in a foreign place, for signing up for a job with an Arab at the helm, and one who clearly didn't care whether she knew anything or not. "Taping," Khalid replied. "The men call us Stick People, Stickers for short. It's a terrible name, but that's okay—they've accepted us."

Construction was young back then. Oil had just begun to dictate terms. And Anna was young, too. Back in her hometown, she assumed if she ever went to the Gulf she would be responsible for someone's child or would put her nursing skills to use at the hospital, but the middlemen pimping work visas wanted money— money she didn't have, but borrowed. Cousin Thracy pawned her gold earrings. "I expect gains from this investment," she told Anna at the airport.

When Anna arrived, flying Air India, Khalid was waiting. "Is it a big hospital?" she asked him as he drove his beat-up pickup.

"Hospital?" he repeated. Over lunch, he gently broke it to her that she had been lied to.

"No job?" she wept. There is a job, Khalid assured her, but he urged her to eat first. Then he needed to ask her a few questions.

"Insha'Allah," he told her, "the job's yours, if you want it."

Anna built a reputation among the working class; hers was a name they grew to trust.

When workers fell, severing limbs, the pain was acute, but borne. Yet what truly stung was the loneliness and anxiety of falling that weighed on their minds.

Pedestrians mostly ignored those who fell outside the construction site, walking around them, some pointing or staring. The affluent rushed home, returning with cameras and film. Drivers of heavy-duty vehicles or family sedans took care to avoid running over them. But it didn't matter where labor fell. The public remained indifferent. In the city center, what unnerved most witnesses was that when the men fell, they not only lost their limbs or had cracks that looked like fissures, but they lost their voices, too. They would just look at you, frantically moving what could still move. But most of the time, especially in areas just being developed, the fallen simply waited. Sometimes, the men fell onto things or under things where few people cared to look. Or they weren't reported missing. These were the two ways, Anna would share with anyone who asked, that laborers could die on-site.

Then there were those who would never be found. A combination of factors contributed to this: bad luck, ineptitude, a heavy workload. A fallen worker might last a week without being discovered, but after a week, deterioration set in. Eventually, death.

Anna had a superb track record for finding fallen men. The woman must have been part-bloodhound. She found every sign of them including teeth, bits of skin. She roamed her territory with tenacity, pointing her flashlight in places the devil did not know or construction lights could not brighten. Before her shift ended in the morning, she returned to the sites, checking with the supervisor or the men disembarking Ashok Leyland buses to be certain no one was still missing, and that the men she had fixed, then ordered to wait at the gates for inspection, included everybody on the supervisor's roster. The men were grateful to be fussed over like this.

Anna wasn't beautiful, but in a city where women were scarce, she was prized. She also possessed other skills. The fallen shared that when Anna reattached body parts, she spoke to them in her tongue, sometimes stroking their hair or chin. She would wax and wane about her life, saying that she missed her kids or the fish near her river, or would instead ask about their lives, what they left, what they dreamt at night, even though they couldn't answer. If she made a connection with the man or if she simply liked him, she flirted. "You must be married," she liked to tease. If she didn't speak his language, she sang, poorly, but from the heart. But even Anna lost people.

"Sometimes a man will die no matter what you do," Khalid told her. "Only Allah knows why."

Once, for four hours, Anna sat with a man who held in place with his right arm his head, which had almost torn itself loose from the fall. A week prior, Anna had a similar case and patched the man up in under two hours. But in this case, probably her last before retirement, nothing worked. Sutures did not hold. Glue refused to bind. Stranger still was that the man could speak. In her many years of doing this, none of the fallen had been able to say a word. "Not working?" he asked. Anna pursed her lips and just held him. There was no point calling an ambulance. No point finding a doctor.

"Remove the fallen from the work site," Khalid had warned her, "and they die." It was simply something everyone knew. Outside work sites, men couldn't survive these kinds of falls. If the men couldn't be fixed at the sites, they didn't stand a chance anywhere else.

The dying man's name was Iqbal. He was probably in his mid-thirties and would become the first man to die under her watch in over five years. In her long career, she had lost thirty-seven people, an exceptional record. She asked about his home.

"Home's shit," he said.

His village suffocated its young. "So small you could squeeze all of its people and farmland inside a plump cow." The only major enterprise was a factory that made coir doormats. "Know when a village turns bitter? If the young are bored..." Iqbal trailed off. He'd left because he wanted to see a bit of the world. Besides, everyone he knew yearned to be a Gulf boy. Recruiters turned up every six months in loud shirts and trousers and a hired taxi, and they hired anyone. "When I went, they told me the only requirement was to be able to withstand heat," Iqbal said. Then there was the money, which had seduced Anna, too. "Tax-free!" he bellowed. They told him if he played his cards right, he could line his pockets with gold.

Before making up his mind, Iqbal had visited the resident fortune-teller—a man whose parrot picked out a card that confirmed the Gulf would transform Iqbal's life. He packed that night, visited Good-Time Philomena, the neighborhood hooker, for a fuck that lasted so long "a she-wolf knocked on the door and begged us to stop." Then he sneaked back into his house and stole his old man's savings to pay for the visa and the trip.

"Uppa was paralyzed—a factory incident. Basically watched me take his cash," Iqbal said. Anna frowned. "I wouldn't worry," Iqbal reassured her. "My brother took good care of him."

"And how is he now?" Anna inquired.

"Died in my brother's lap," he replied. "I couldn't go see him."

As Anna continued to hold Iqbal's head, he told her he expected to have made his fortune in ten years. By then, he'd have hand-picked his wife, had those kids, built that house. His father, if he'd lived, would've forgiven him. Former teachers who scorned him by calling him Farm Boy or Day Dreamer would invite him to dine at their place. But then he fell, didn't he? Slipped like a bungling monkey. He was doing something else—what, he seemed embarrassed to share.

"What were you up to?" Anna urged. "Go on, I won't tell a soul."
Iqbal smiled. "I was masturbating on the roof. The edge," he confessed. He had done this many times before. "It's super fun," he giggled. "But then a pigeon landed on my pecker...." The bird startled him. He lost his balance.

"You didn't!" Anna laughed.

"Try it, there's nothing like it. It's like impregnating the sky." Or, he added, "in your case, welcoming it."

"Behave," Anna said. "I could easily be your mother's age. Or older sister's."

"The heat," he said softly. "The heat felled me."

"Not the bird?"

Iqbal broke into a grin. "I came on a bird once. It acted like I'd shot it."

Like Anna, Iqbal had known heat ever since he was a child. He knew how to handle it, even when the steam in the air had the potential to boil a man's mind. But the Gulf's heat baked a man differently. First it cooked a man's shirt and then the man's skin. On-site, Iqbal trusted his instincts. Water, sometimes buttermilk, was always on hand, but frequent breaks meant a reduced output, and Iqbal knew his progress was being monitored. He had trained as a tailor, as his Uppa was a tailor; he knew learning a new trade took time. So he followed one rule: when his skin felt like parchment paper, he stopped working and quenched his thirst, sometimes drinking water so quickly it hurt. The sun never conquered him. His body was strong. But what he couldn't control, he told Anna, were the reactions of people he passed in the street, especially if he volunteered to go to one of those little kadas to buy water or cold drinks for his mates in the afternoon.

"How so?" Anna wondered.

"In the summer," Iqbal continued, "you burn, the clothes burn. You smell like an old stove." Then he asked her, "Don't you burn?"

"Everyone burns here," she replied quietly. "But you fell today? What was different?"

"It seemed like the perfect day," Iqbal said dryly. "What do the others tell you?"

"The others?"

"Those who fall." Iqbal didn't wait for an answer. "Outside, whether you believe it or not, heat's easier to handle. For me, anyway." On building tops, he insisted, most men shrivel into raisins. "Men don't burn up there; they decay."

"But it's cooler up there, no?" Anna asked.

"Fully clothed, in hard hats? No," said Iqbal. "I once saw a man shrink to the size of a child. At lunchtime, he drank a tub of water and grew back to his original size." Still, the open air allowed the body to breathe. "You have wind." Indoors, in the camps, in closed quarters, packed into bunk beds, not enough ACs, bodies baked, sweat burned eyes, salt escaped, fever and dehydration built. Bodies reeled from simply that. Anna nodded. There was a time Anna patched up a man with skin so dry, she needed to rub the man's entire body with olive oil after she pieced him together.

Even though they were all immune to death by free fall, there was nothing they could do about the heat. At lunch break, getting to the shade under tractor beds and crane rumps became more important than food. With shirts as pillows and newspapers as blankets, the men rested.

Iqbal asked Anna if she would mind scratching his hair. "You're new," he teased. "You look new, like a bride."

Anna smiled. "I have grandkids now." She dug her nails into his scalp.

"They told you to fear the sun, didn't they?" said Iqbal.

"Who?"

"Recruiters," said Iqbal.

"No," she replied.

"Well, no one mentions the nighttime," Iqbal sighed. "They should." At night, heat attacked differently, became wet. "I knew a man," Iqbal continued, "who collected sweat. He would go door to door with a trolley full of buckets. After a week's worth, this man—Badran was his name—dug a pit near the buildings we lived in. It would take him a long time to pour the buckets of sweat into that pit. The first couple of times, I watched. Then I began to help. Soon we had a pool—a salty pool. It was good fun. We floated for hours."

"Didn't Badran get into trouble?" Anna asked.

"Badran was a smart fellow," said Iqbal. "He resold some of that pool water to this shady driver of a water tanker. The driver would get to the camp at around three a.m., take as much water as truck could carry. Everyone knew. The important people all got a cut."

"Where did he take the water?"

"I asked Badran many times," said Iqbal. "He never said."

"Badran must be doing well for himself," said Anna.

"He was, I suppose," said Iqbal. "He died a few months ago."

"How?"

"Accident," replied Iqbal. "Was his time."

"Where?"

"We were returning home in a pickup. Near Mussafah the driver hit something. Badran fell…the wheel…" Iqbal paused.

Anna didn't push him. She knew what he meant. Every night, Anna told Iqbal, she had dinner at this little cafeteria owned by a man from her town who served her leftovers that weren't on the menu. She ate for free while Abdu, the cafeteria owner, gossiped. Abdu made a good living. Where his place was, every night, trucks and buses ferrying labor would stop. Badran and Iqbal may have stopped, too, sitting by the windows, worn out.

"Maybe," said Iqbal. "Once I sat next to a man who was so hot he evaporated before my eyes. I took his pants; someone took his shoes; his shirt was ugly, so no one wanted that."

Anna laughed. Iqbal's speech was slowing. She continued massaging his scalp.

"I once knew a man who wanted to die," said Iqbal. "He'd realized pretty early it was hard to die in the workplace or in the camps. He wasn't unhappy. He just wanted to die."

"So, did he?" asked Anna.

Iqbal grinned. "You see, that's how this story gets complicated. Charley knew what he wanted, but he was also fair. He had a wife and kids back home he wanted to make sure were provided for. He'd figured the best way to do that would be to die performing some work-related task. That way they would be compensated."

"Did he succeed?"

Iqbal thought about the question. "I am not sure," he finally said.

"What happened?"

"Well, he asked me to help. I liked him, you know. I said yes. He said it would take some time, a year or two, but it could work. So Charley tells me that every couple of months he would give himself an accident. He'd start with small ones. Fall off the first floor, lose a few toes. Then he would build up: third floor, sixth floor. Thing is, he'd tell me beforehand. A note, some secret code indicating when he planned to do this, and where. So I'd wait for the deed, and before anyone found out I'd go to him, remove one piece of him—don't know, a finger or something—then throw that into the trash bin. Stick People would fix him up at night, but there would be a part missing. He promised himself four accidents a year. If he played his cards right, in three years, he'd be properly broken, just not fixable, and the company would be bound to inform his family. So that's what we did for a while."

"His family wouldn't have gotten a cent," Anna confided.

"Let me finish," said Iqbal. "We'd done enough for me to administer the hammer blow in a few months; it had taken longer than we had anticipated—six years. One night, Charley sought me out. 'I want to live,' he said. I didn't know what to say. I had removed a few fingers, toes, a kidney, his penis. His legs were half the size they'd been when he arrived, and now he wanted to live."

"What did you do?" Anna asked.

"He's very happy now," smiled Iqbal. "Sometimes he asks me if he can watch me jack off since he can't anymore."

"Was he there today?"

"No, not today." Iqbal's breath grew increasingly labored. "Soon," is what he said. Anna nodded, gently touching his face. Iqbal turned toward her. "Do you know the prayer for the dead?" She shook her head.

"There's this dream I've been having..." Iqbal began.

"Listening," said Anna.

"A man I knew, Nandan, kept a bird, a pigeon in a cage, that he brought to work every day." As Nandan worked, Iqbal shared, he never let this bird out of his sight.

"Never?"

"Not for a second," Iqbal confirmed. "The bird could fly, but he weighted it down with an iron lock around its neck. It weighed enough to make the bird stoop all the time." Iqbal felt bad for the bird, trapped in that cage, so he made up his mind to set it free when Nandan wasn't looking. "I almost succeeded," he said. He was on the roof, picking the lock, about to set the bird free, when Nandan cornered him. Someone had seen Iqbal headed for the roof with the birdcage. Nandan demanded Iqbal give back his bird. "I wouldn't, of course," said Iqbal. In a fit of rage, Nandan lunged for the bird. Iqbal slipped, losing his grip on the bird; it fell to the ground a few feet away from both men, not far from the edge of the roof, eighteen stories up. The bird, in a panic, or perhaps, hope, began hopping toward the edge and jumped. "But I hadn't had time to remove the lock," said Iqbal.

"That's terrible," said Anna.

"In a way," said Iqbal. "After the incident, I began having these dreams."

"Dreams?"

"Promise not to laugh," said Iqbal.

"I promise," said Anna. Weeks after the pigeon fell to its death, Iqbal began having dreams in which he stood atop the roof of some building he helped construct. "My family's with me; we all have wings. The sun's cold. You following me? Cold! We fly." And as they fly, he shared, he notices that their feet possess talons, with which they can grip the top of the building, and they pull, and they fly, and they pull, and they fly, or try to fly, until they rip the building off its foundations, taking it with them, toward the gelid sun." It was Iqbal's final tale. Before dawn, he was gone.

Anna stayed with him for a few minutes, wondering if she ought to wait until morning, but she decided against it, filling out a note she attached to his chest. *Deceased*, it said, listing Khalid's company's name and address and a point of contact. Then she got back on her cycle.

THE ONLY CONSTANT

Leslie Howle

The room was small and cold. The agent, a slender white man with fair hair, gestured to the chair across the table from him and waited until I sat before clicking his recorder on.

"Ready?"

I nodded.

"State your name and age."

"Camila Dubois, fifteen."

"You're going to have to speak up."

I cleared my throat and lifted my chin. My mother had whispered to me when we were getting out of the agent's car not to show any fear, no matter what they said. I held my face expressionless.

"Where do you go to school?"

This was a game. I was sure that they already knew everything there was to know about us.

"At home."

He tapped a finger on the table between us. "Unless you are being home schooled for religious reasons, you are required to attend one of the National Schools."

"The vouchers don't pay for a school I can afford to bus to. Too bad there aren't any public schools I can bike to anymore."

"Miss Dubois, your father is a professor at the university. Your mother teaches at the community college. Your family can afford to send you to one of the charter schools on a public bus."

"My father has been supposedly 'detained for deportation,' and you won't tell us why or where you're holding him. He used up his vacation three months ago; there won't be any more paychecks until you release him." My voice was tight.

He ignored this. "Your family is keeping you out of the National Schools for religious reasons, aren't they? Your father is Muslim; you should all be wearing the mandatory ID badges."

I swallowed hot words. The way he was looking at me made me want to check my head to make sure I wasn't wearing a hijab.

"My family feels I can get a better education at home. My father is *not* Muslim. He's not anything, he's agnostic."

He leaned back in his chair. "Tell me about the night of your father's arrest."

"The National Guard took him on Father's Day, in June. 2019 will be over in a month and we still haven't heard anything about when we can expect to see him again. It's been five months! We need to know that he's okay." My voice cracked.

The memory of that night still plays over and over in my head. I can't shake it. It's like the fly caught in a chunk of amber that my friend Charlie brought to school in sixth grade. A horrific moment frozen in time.

One minute, we were enjoying the Father's Day dinner of roast lamb and vegetable kabobs that my little brother and I had helped my mother prepare, and the next, Father's place at the table was empty, his food still warm on the plate.

"Guardsmen handcuffed him and took him away with no explanation." My eyes blurred with moisture; I looked down.

"What did your mother do?"

"She called our lawyer."

But that was after she had chased the Guardsmen out the door, screaming at them to let him go. Only my little brother's wailing stopped her from following them to their car. I squeezed my eyes shut. The agent was talking again.

"Did you know that your father was born and raised in Morocco?"

My head snapped up. I stared in astonishment at his expressionless face. "That's a lie! My father was born and raised in Pasadena."

"No, he wasn't. But you know that, don't you?"

"I can't know that because it's not true. I know you people think everybody with brown skin must be a Muslim terrorist, but this is ridiculous."

My heart was racing. Was it my turn to be cuffed and hauled off?

The agent ignored my response.

"What does your father do for a living?"

"He's a professor; he heads up neuroscience research at the university. He's also a great digital media artist. He was working on a project funded by an NEA grant that he needs to finish, so how about you let him go now?"

'What do you know about this project?"

"Nothing. I was twelve when my father got the grant. I was too busy with my friends and school to pay any attention to what he was doing."

The agent looked at his watch and stood, his chair scraping the floor as he straightened. "Thank you for your time, Miss Dubois, we'll be in touch if we have any more questions."

Relief washed through me as I scrambled to my feet. "You're letting me go."

"Yes, you're free to go."

I grabbed my backpack from behind the chair. Hopefully they were done with my mother and brother and we could go home together.

The hallway was as white and featureless as the room I just left. I could see an exit sign at the far end. It was so quiet my boots echoed on the linoleum.

A voice sounded from behind me. I inhaled sharply and jerked to a stop.

"Excuse me, miss. I need you to come with me."

I turned to face the voice behind me, a burly man in a gray suit.

"No, I'm done; he said I could go."

"I'm sorry, miss."

I looked longingly one last time at the exit sign in the distance and followed him back into the room I'd just left.

A different agent sat at the table now. He had small, close-set blue eyes under bushy eyebrows and slicked-back gray hair. He was wearing a badge of some kind.

"Sit down, please. The agent who did your interview seems to think you don't know anything about your father's work, yet somebody released it on the internet yesterday and it's gone viral. What can you tell me about that?" His voice was harsh and too loud.

The blood rushed to my head, and for a moment I thought I might pass out. So much for the lie that they took my father because they thought he was Muslim.

"How is that possible? Nobody has access to his work. You took his computer."

"You tell me, Miss Dubois. Your mother and brother don't seem to know anything, and it's not going to go well for any of you if we don't get some answers."

"What have you done? Let me see them."

"I'm sorry, we can't do that."

His eyes were cold and his face glistened with a fine sheen of sweat. The asshole was enjoying this.

"*No!* I want to see my mother."

He pressed on. "Right before federal funding was cut for the NEA, a small number of grants were awarded and yours was one of them, isn't that right Miss Dubois? Did you run out of money and apply for a second NEA grant under your grandfather's name?"

"It wasn't…"

"Your grandfather doesn't know anything about this grant application in his name."

They knew. My gut clenched. My life was over, but at least my father's program was out there now, and maybe things would change fast enough to make a difference.

"It went viral already? How many hits?"

He seemed to forget it was me he was talking to. "Thousands, apparently, but not for long. Our experts are working around the clock to take it down."

He was so sure of himself. I smiled. He had no idea.

"This is serious business, Miss Dubois. Soldiers are putting down their guns and going AWOL, workers are walking off the oil fields."

It was all I could do not to jump up and whoop. Nobody could stop it now. It was the nature of the art. My father's program was brilliant. Once people interacted with it, their desire to destroy it would evaporate.

My father had told me about his emergency plan months ago, just in case something happened to him. The project was close to being done when he was taken, and the directions he secreted away in my closet last spring made it simple to complete. He had written the second grant and signed his father's name to it; I only had to submit it. It was enough to keep us going while I completed the project.

The beauty of the program is that's impossible to look at it without being sucked in by the immersive, interactive art. You experience an orchestrated array of pleasurable colors, sounds, and images that initiate cerebral reprogramming through keystroke patterns and neural stimulation. It increases your empathy, honesty, and ability to think critically. Most importantly, it erases patterns that lead to violence. It's a game changer.

"Nothing to say for yourself, Miss Dubois?"

"Can I call our lawyer?"

The man snorted, and shook his head as he stood and told the burly agent to escort me back to my holding cell.

I looked back at him and smiled. "My dad always says that the only constant is change. Get used to it; nothing can stop it now."

THE TERRIFIC LEADER

Harry Turtledove

Kim woke up shivering. She lay under four blankets, but her teeth chattered like castanets. It had to be ten below outside. It wasn't a whole lot warmer here in the house. There wasn't much to burn in the fireplace, or in any fireplace in the village. The promised coal shipment hadn't come. They'd long since cut down every tree within a day's walk except for a few plums and pears that still bore. Those might go soon. If you froze now, who cared whether you had fruit later?

Just on the off chance, she flicked the switch on the lamp by the bed. The room stayed gloomy. The power was still out. It would probably come on for a couple of hours in the afternoon. She hoped it would. The Terrific Leader was scheduled to speak today, and she wanted to hear it. If anything could make you forget your troubles, one of his, well, terrific speeches would turn the trick.

Meanwhile, gloom. The sun rose late and set early at this season, of course. And the clouds that were bringing the latest blizzard muffled its glow all the more thoroughly. You had to make do, the best you could. Self-reliance—that was the thing.

Sighing, Kim got out of bed. She'd left on all her clothes except her boots when she went to sleep. Now she got into them. With the three pairs of socks under them, they might keep her feet from freezing when she went out to forage.

She walked into the kitchen. Her mother was making tea and warming her hands at a tiny fire in a brazier. "Good morning, Mother dear," Kim said. "Are you fixing enough for two cups?"

"I suppose so," her mother said grudgingly, as if she'd hoped Kim would sleep longer so she could drink it all herself. Then she unbent enough to add, "And there's still some pickled cabbage for breakfast."

"Oh, good!" Kim hurried over to the jar. They'd lived by themselves these past three years, since the police took Kim's father out of the fields and drove away with him. Not a word had come back since. She hoped he was a labor camp, and that they hadn't simply executed him. Either way, being related to an enemy of the state only made everything more difficult.

The scent of garlic and peppers filled her nose when she opened the jar. Pickled cabbage wasn't very filling, but it was—a little— better than nothing.

On the wall above the jar was one of the three portraits of the Terrific Leader in the house. As she ate, she studied his face. He was so wise, so handsome! His piercing gaze peered far into the future. This was the greatest, strongest, freest country in the world. It wasn't perfect yet, but it was on the way. The Terrific Leader saw the way forward. You could tell just by looking.

"Here's your tea," her mother said, breaking her train of thought.

"Thank you very much, Mother dear." Kim drank fast, before it got cold. Sure enough, the cup wasn't quite full. And the tea was weak. Like anyone else, her mother sensibly used tea leaves more than once. You never knew when you'd be able to lay your hands on more.

"I hope you have good luck," her mother said.

"Oh, so do I!" Kim replied. "We could use some good luck for a chance. We've had too much of the alternative kind."

"We're doing fine," her mother said stoutly. In the house where an unreliable had lived, the authorities were likely to have planted spy ears. They might keep working even without power for anything else. "We're doing fine, and our wonderful country and the Terrific Leader, heaven's blessings upon him, are also doing fine. Better than fine!"

"Of course, Mother dear. I'll see you later." Kim went outside.

In spite of her quilted coat and the two sweaters under it, the icy wind tore at her. Fat flakes of snow flew almost horizontally. And another blizzard was supposed to be on the way after this one. Kim pulled down the coat's hood and wrapped a muffler around the lower part of her face so only her eyes showed. The other people out and about were similarly swaddled. You recognized them not by what they looked like but by what they wore.

Even walking took work. There was a foot of snow on the ground, and drifts got two or three times that deep. Because of that, Kim nearly missed the lump in the snow in front of the Parks' house. Yes, that was a body, no doubt their eldest son; he'd been sick and getting sicker for weeks. No medicines, the nearest doctor miles away and unwilling to come for such an insignificant person...It was a sad story, but an old one. They wouldn't be able to plant the Park boy in the village graveyard till the ground thawed, not without dynamite, they wouldn't. Well, he wouldn't go off as long as the weather stayed cold.

Kim gasped. Here came Old Man Lee's dog, the meanest one she knew. He was a big brute, and did better in the snow than she did. She had a couple of stones in her pocket in case the dog or some hungry man gave her trouble.

But the beast ignored her. A moment later, she saw why: he proudly carried a rabbit in his toothy jaws. Jealousy sharp and sour as vinegar filled Kim. Old Man Lee and his nasty shrew of a wife would eat well today. Kim could hardly remember the last time she'd tasted meat. Even the guts and the head the Lees would give the dog would be so good stewed with cabbage or grain.

Grain…

Of themselves, her feet were taking her to the harvest ground. You never could tell. Maybe some of what had spilled last fall was still there under the snow. Even forlorn hopes were better than none.

Another young woman was already searching the ground. She looked up warily, then relaxed and said, "Hello, Kim."

"Hello, Kim," Kim answered. She smiled, though the muffler hid it. Sharing a name was no large amusement, but sometimes small ones would do. She added, "Heaven's blessings on the Terrific Leader!"

"Heaven's blessings on the Terrific Leader!" the other Kim echoed.

They worked separately. Had they joined forces, they would have needed to share evenly. Each hoped for better than that.

Kim dug with mittened fingers till she reached the hard ground. She came across some mushrooms that had sprung up in the last thaw and then frozen when the weather turned bad again. They weren't much, but better than nothing. Into her left coat pocket— the one without the rocks—they went. Then, to her delight, she really did come upon some spilled grain. It joined the mushrooms in that pocket.

She got up and walked away. As soon as the swirling snow hid her from the other Kim, she hurried to a hedgerow to check traps she'd set the day before. The wind would soon blot out her tracks. She almost whooped for joy when she found a big, fat rat noosed in a snare, hanged like a leftish deviationist. Rat wasn't as good as rabbit, but it was ever so much better than nothing. After resetting traps that were sprung but hadn't caught anything (or that had been robbed before she got to them), she happily headed for home. Tonight there'd be…not a feast, but food.

Her mother exclaimed in delight when Kim showed her what she'd brought home. A little past two, the power came on. Lights flickered to dim, low-voltage life. What electric tools they had would work for a while.

And the Terrific Leader was going to speak! With her mother and the rest of the village, she gathered in the square to hear his inspiring words. The communal televisor, like authorized radios, got only government-mandated channels so no one could be exposed to outsiders' wicked lies.

There he was! He was an old, old man now, though—of course!—still strong and vigorous. Everybody knew one of his sons, or perhaps his son-in-law, would eventually succeed him, and then a grandson, and so on. But he still ruled, as he had since long before Kim was born; even thinking such thoughts was risky.

He wore his trademark red cap, with his slogan—AMERICA IS GREAT AGAIN!—on the front in big letters. "I have a message for all of you," he rasped. "The crime and violence that today afflict our nation will end soon. I mean very soon. Safety will be restored. Everything will be terrific, the way it's always been.

"Our plan keeps putting America first. The powerful no longer beat upon people who cannot defend themselves. I have restored law and order. Our border wall has stopped illegal immigration, stopped gangs and drugs, and done lots of other totally terrific stuff, too. I respect the dignity of work and the dignity of working people. It trumps anything else there is. I mean anything else. Keep at it. America first like I said, America last, America always!"

"America first!" the village chorused as the televisor went off. Kim's eyes filled with tears. She couldn't help it. She loved the Terrific Leader.

TWO EXPLICIT AND THREE OBLIQUE APOLOGIES TO MY OLDEST DAUGHTER ONE MONTH BEFORE HER EIGHTEENTH BIRTHDAY

Heather Lindsley

October 4, 2020

Dear Jen,

Did you know that when I first left home to go to college, your grandmother sent me a case of powdered milk? Bear in mind that in the early 90s sending someone a case of powdered milk involved going to a store and then standing in line at a post office. You couldn't impulse-click a case of powdered milk. Can you impulse-click a case of powdered milk? Hang on.

You can, though it's not so much a case as a small box. Use it to make cream of potato soup or something. Do not—I repeat, do not—reconstitute it and pour it on cereal and expect it to taste like milk.

When the powdered milk arrived I had the good manners to call my mother and say thank you. But I didn't have the insight to also say, "I know your oldest child has moved half a continent away and you want that to be good for her and you want to be helpful but you're not sure how." I probably said, "You know they have milk in Boston, right?"

I think I'll call your grandmother tonight.

You'll have already found the box of stationery and postage stamps I sent along with this letter. And oh, I guess the powdered milk will have arrived before you get this. You'll have to tell me which is more helpful.

I hope you're settling in at school okay. It looks like it, based on what I see in my feed. I suspect, even hope, there are posts I don't see. I'd like to think you have a sophisticated privacy model that keeps your data away from marketers as well as your mother.

This morning I got an unnecessary reminder that your birthday is in a month. The algorithm included a list of presents you'd like. I know it's pretty reliable but let me know what you really want, okay? Apart from a birthday that doesn't miss eligibility to vote in a presidential election by two hours.

I wish I could get you a time machine. I would use it for so, so many things, but right now I'd probably start with late October 2002. I'd try jumping jacks, pineapple, raspberry leaf tea, Pitocin, a C-section if it came to it, though I do get the impression that I'm more upset about this than you are. Anyway, I'm sorry you can't vote next month. I hope the country gives you a better present than they did when you turned fourteen.

Oh, before I forget: I know you think you escaped tech support (ha ha ha there is no escape), but do you know how I can get access to season two of *Lilith's Brood* without having to sign up for a viewing tracker? I'd ask Sarah, but she'd just play dumb—she doesn't want me to know just how tech-savvy she really is. I know the episodes will trickle down eventually, but that season one finale is still on my mind. And don't tell me to just sign up for a tracker and stop worrying about it because they anonymize the data they collect. They creep me out. It's like they're watching me back. Okay, fine, it's not like that…it is that. And it's creepy.

I remember the first time an ad for a burger chain included the location of the nearest one in unobtrusive text at the bottom of the screen while your father and I were streaming a show. We knew it wouldn't be long before our names got pulled into the ad, too. It wasn't a matter of when it would become technologically possible, because it already was. It was when it became socially possible, when it would get a positive reaction. You never seemed to mind those ads when they started appearing, so eerily tailored to you, but they still bother me.

I guess it's all about what you're used to.

Do you remember when your father opted into fitness data sharing with the insurance company? It saved us a fortune on premiums. Then he lost the device and they threatened to raise the rates unless he got a new one. So he did, but now he's lost it again. This time they're offering to pay for the implanted one. Your dad is actually considering it. He says he likes the data but not the device. And he thinks since he exercises so much it should be fine. Of course your sister jumped in and told him that sounds like people who justify militarized police by saying if you're not a criminal you don't have anything to worry about. He said she was overreacting. So Sarah said he should tell that to all the people who…well, you know what Sarah thinks. I'm sorry—you've finally achieved some peace and quiet by going off to college and here I am relaying the latest shouting match.

Have you and Sarah spoken since you left? I see a bit of interaction in your feeds, but not much. Not that either of you are inclined to chat in public. I just hope you two are talking.

Sarah's been angry for a long time, and I don't know what to do because there really is so much to be angry about. Something happened at school yesterday. She wouldn't tell me what it was, but she was upset enough to say things I think she wished she hadn't, about how if we can't get our data back, we should fill it up with enough false detail to make it useless, worthless. She stopped and went to her room when I looked too interested. Maybe she was just ranting. I kind of hope she wasn't.

How did we end up accepting all this? How did we get so disconnected from the actual mechanisms of power that choosing toothpaste at random feels like a viable act of rebellion?

I never made a big deal about it, but I was surprised when the school only took you on the condition that you majored in Business

Administration. They said the data showed that was your best chance of success. You could have gone to your second choice and majored in whatever you wanted, but you told us you were struggling to decide between business and sociology anyway. So off you went to your first choice. You seem happy. You're only a month in, but I already imagine you'll be recruited into a job with one of the Big Three consulting firms before graduation, because the data will say you'll do well. And you would do well, I know you would, but not because the data says so.

After you chose your school I noticed you played your violin less often, and by the time you left home you'd stopped altogether. I half expected you to leave it at home and was relieved when you took it with you. Are you playing at all now? I know you were always frustrated when your performance fell short of your perfectionism. But you were good, and as long as you were playing, you were getting better.

I don't know what I'm asking for here. Do I want you to be less satisfied? More discontented now so you'll be less discontented later? Do I want you to be angry, like your sister? Why would a parent wish that on their child?

I miss you, sweetheart.

Please keep playing the violin. Please choose random toothpaste. Please call your sister.

And don't be tempted to drink the powdered milk.

Love always,

Mom

THE LEVELLERS

Deji Bryce Olukotun

A thin stream of maple sap poured from the severed pipe, forming a dark hole in the snow. Next to the puddle Sam could see hoofprints where white-tailed deer had lapped at the liquid. This was the starving season, when the deer could lose twenty pounds as the barren woods denied them any sustenance, forcing them out onto people's lawns. The Lenape had once survived on sugar maples, too, enduring the long tail of winter until spring, when the forest would burst with promise in the Sourlands. That was two hundred years ago.

Sam dialed the second image that popped up on her "Favorites."

"Hey Sam," Thomas answered.

"Looks like Leighton cut through one of my lines again."

Thomas paused on the other end of the line. "You sure?"

"It's near where he did it the last time."

"Damn it," Thomas said. He could be heard calling after his son. "I don't know where he's run off to."

"I've probably lost forty gallons today."

"We'll pay for it."

"Don't pay for it, Thomas. Get him to stop."

"I'll talk to him. You want me to come down there to help you?"

Sam was about to tell Thomas to forget it, accustomed to doing everything by herself to her own exacting requirements, but then she remembered the hill and how she'd have to carry boiling water through the snowmelt, which was vexing, excruciating work. And her own daughter hadn't returned yet from her nursing shift at the hospital and frowned upon her maple operation anyway, considering syrup to be a luxury. By then she might have lost two hundred gallons of sap.

"You mean that, Thomas? You'll come down here?"

"Sure," Thomas said. "Game's finished. Eagles blew it."

"Alright. But don't come down here and start talking football to me."

"Wouldn't dream of it," Thomas laughed.

Sam slowly followed the rest of the lines that crisscrossed the sugar maple grove, inspecting the T- and Y-joints to make sure the sap was flowing properly from the taps. It didn't look like Thomas' kid had cut any other lines but she wanted to be sure. The exertion of trudging through the sodden snow—which was too soggy for snowshoes—made her rest to catch her breath from time to time. Altogether, the Cumulus Maple Farm contained about five hundred maple trees, twenty percent red maple—what purists called swamp maple—with the other eighty percent sugar maples. Some of the trees in the sugar bush stood proud with healthily branching limbs, while others were sickly from being deluged from water running off a neighboring property—a McMansion that had altered the natural drainage of the hillside. Sick trees didn't bother Sam, though, because she tapped the trees all the same. She'd long since learned that if the trees were going to die, then they were going to die, and taking their sap wouldn't accelerate that process.

Done with her inspection, she climbed laboriously back to the top of the hill, adjusting her halter as she walked. She whipped out a pocket mirror to check for stubble around her jaw and tucked it into her pocket before Thomas arrived in a long-bed Toyota Tacoma, a truck that had made Thomas proud two years back when he bought it, and nervous now that the Levellers had denounced all gasoline-powered vehicles. Sam felt a thrill when Thomas stepped out of the cab in his Gore-Tex boots and pharmacy-bought aviator glasses. He was a thin, wiry man with light brown eyes and a cleft chin who weighed the same as he did when they had graduated from high school together.

"You alright, Sam?" Thomas said, hurrying over.

She realized that she had placed her hands on her knees. "Catching my breath."

"You should take it easy."

"The tapping season gets earlier every year. I've been boiling sap since six."

"You could hurt yourself."

"I'm alright, Thomas. It's the damn hormones."

He spat into the ground, which Sam would never let anyone else do on her property. "Goddamn Eagles wasted a perfectly good drive."

"I told you, no football."

"Just because you're a Jets fan."

"It's their lack of ambition that offends me."

Thomas chuckled again—he laughed easily, and freely—as they walked through the buildings of Cumulus Maple Farm. The entire property was powered by South-facing solar panels and a geothermal well that Sam had already paid off through tax credits and by lining her home with high-density insulation. The evaporator for the maple sap was fueled by firewood to impart flavor to the syrup. There was a barn constructed from reclaimed wood and, technically, two dwellings, the family home in which Sam had grown up, which was a saltbox style with a long sloping roof and cedar shingles, and a small cabin-like structure that Sam's daughter, Megan, called a Little House. Sam was somewhat annoyed that her daughter would rather live in a minuscule shack a hundred yards from the main house than sleep under the same roof. Megan had taken the dogma of the Levellers' too literally, she felt, casting off her worldly possessions in favor of humble living. Megan had never quite forgiven Sam for her transformation.

As they walked along, a sheep climbed atop a pile of wood chippings and bleated. She had a large, almost distended udder.

"You might want to milk that one," Thomas observed.

"That ewe has three lambs," Sam corrected. "They can help themselves. I spent eight years milking sheep and never made any money from it. Want to come inside?"

"No, I'm fine," Thomas said. He hadn't been inside her home since her surgery, but Sam knew not to press him. Everyone had taken the news differently.

Sam boiled water in the kitchen, watching Thomas feed clumps of grass to the sheep through the bay window. When the kettle boiled, she poured water into a rubber bucket with a steel handle.

"Let's move!" she said. "We've got to get down there fast."

"Want me to carry it?" Thomas asked.

"You don't know how easy it is to spill boiling water all over yourself when you're walking through snow."

They plodded down the long slope of the hill, Sam switching the heavy bucket from side to side, until they came to the maple grove where Thomas's son had slit the sap line. Sam set down the bucket, breathing heavily. She felt as if the wind had left her lungs, as if her blood was lacking a sense of refreshment, the hemoglobin robbed of purpose. The late afternoon sun was crossing behind the hill.

Thomas busied himself by inspecting the line. "You say he cut it here, do you?"

"Yes, right where it's dripping," she breathed.

"Certainly, it's been cut," he frowned. He inspected the pipe more closely. "Where do you think he was standing when he did it?"

"Wherever he could cut it."

"The angle's a little funny."

Sam looked at Thomas, trying to figure out what he was doing. The pipe had been cut. Was he going to try to weasel out of blaming his son?

"Look," Sam said. "This water's going to cool down soon and this whole trip won't be worth shit. He cut it."

"I'm not saying he didn't," Thomas said.

"Then help me."

"All I'm saying is that Leighton's right-handed. I don't know why he'd cut it from down here. It would have been above his head. He would have crossed under the line to do it from uphill. And then the angle's wrong. Another thing," Thomas added, leaning over to help Sam move the bucket. "Leighton uses a bowie knife. This looks like someone cut it with a laser."

"Are you going to help me or not?"

"Alright, don't get your tits in a bunch."

She chuckled as she grabbed the two ends of the pipe. Unlike everyone else, Thomas managed to joke about her operation in a way that set them both at ease. He was the only friend of hers who had immediately called her by her new name when she asked him—while other people she had known continued to call her Richard or avoided her altogether.

She and Thomas had gone to elementary school and high school together, and then veered off in wildly different directions. Thomas had gone to Trenton State, then moved to upstate New York to work as a salesman for Kodak before settling down again in Central Jersey and opening a business selling bionic limbs. Sam had attended the University of Pennsylvania on an ROTC scholarship, studied chemical engineering, and then worked for the Army Corps of Engineers for fifteen years and returned to teach hydrology at Rutgers. Both of them now lived on the properties their fathers had bought, Thomas on a two-acre clear-cut lot at the crest of the Sourland Mountains, and Sam on a forty-acre farm on the south side of the range. They could each trace their lineages back to the Colonial era when the Lenape had still roamed the woods.

"I'm going to dip these two ends of the pipe into the water," Sam explained, "until they get hot and expand. Then I want you to wedge in this connector joint."

"Alright."

"We'll have ten seconds before they stiffen from the cold. Ready—go!"

Thomas hoisted up the bucket with ease—he was thin but very strong—and Sam soaked the two ends of the pipes in the water for thirty seconds. Then she used all her strength to pull the severed strands together. Thomas did as he was told and plugged up the holes. Soon the sap was flowing again through the PVC, little air bubbles passing through the line. Some bacteria would have gotten into the pipe but Sam had invested in modern taps with ball bearings that would keep the tree from healing over its wound. Her farm featured kilometers of modern, polyvinyl chloride piping that ran from tree to tree, making the woods feel more like an intricate maze of blue and black telephone wires than an ecological Eden. Cumulus Maple Farm worked because of physics and fluid dynamics rather than some idyllic vision of a forest.

"Did you see this?" Thomas asked, as he set down the bucket. He pointed to a triangular green blaze punched into a nearby maple tree. Sam had missed it, thinking only to inspect the lines themselves. A big L sat in the middle of the green blaze. L for Levellers. "How long do you think that's been here?"

Sam examined the blaze to see sap coagulated on the bark where they had driven in the punch. The sap had already crystallized—how had she missed it? "At least a day."

"Could be a prank," Thomas said optimistically.

"I don't understand. We're not rich. This farm isn't rich. Rich is up the hill. Rich is that McMansion."

"I thought they moved out already."

"They did. That home's been on the market for three months."

"I know who's going to win that bid."

Sam did, too. The Levellers would bid at what they considered fair market value for the building materials and a standard rate for the acreage, and then tear the home down. No one would bid against them. She had watched the forlorn faces of her neighbors as they packed their belongings, the way they had snapped photos as their bucolic dream was deferred, and then moved back to their apartment in the city. While they had lived in the house they had complained constantly about the sap lines on Sam's farm and how the web of blue PVC sullied their view into the valley below. Despite this, the family pleaded for Sam's support when the green blazes first appeared on their property—which they had carved up with landscaping riddled with Norway maple, cypress, and Barberry bush, all invasive species. She uttered some platitudes at the time, secretly glad to be rid of the eight-thousand-square-foot monstrosity, which guzzled megawatts of fossil fuels. Then they were gone.

But why had the Levellers come for her? Or was it a prank, as Thomas guessed? The Levellers carefully controlled their blazes, though, identifying their targets based upon Artificial Intelligence that linked a variety of metrics, everything from tax returns to VIN numbers to lot sizes to the number of indigenous plant species on the land. Once your home was identified, the blazes would proliferate like toadstools and the process would begin.

"This is a sustainable farm!" Sam shouted. "We're on geothermal! We compost, for chrissake!" She ripped the blaze from the tree, feeling light-headed as she did so, and the next thing she knew she was laying on the ground. She could feel the damp snow seeping into her pants.

"Sam!" Thomas shouted. "You alright?" He bent down to help her up, and her breast spilled out of her bra. He pretended as if he hadn't seen it.

"Why, you never!" Sam said.

"Take it easy."

"I'm a little light-headed."

"Want me to call a doctor?"

"No, it's the hormones. They give me vertigo."

"You should get someone to help you out around here."

"Someone like Leighton?"

"Might do him some good."

"Not after he called me a freak the last time he saw me."

"He didn't mean it. He's just going through a phase."

"Young, dumb, and full of cum."

"Dumb is right."

Once Sam collected her breath, they followed the repaired PVC line down to the sap collection hut, where the sap from the groves would flow, her checking for green blazes along the way, and scanning the trees above them.

"Is it true what they say, Thomas? That you can see them coming?"

"The camouflage hides them pretty well, I suppose. You can hear them sometimes when you're up in a deer stand."

"What do they sound like?"

"It's different for everyone."

As a child, Sam would join her father in tapping trees that sat on the adjoining property, driving in steel taps with a hammer and collecting the sap in aluminum buckets. The McMansion had destroyed the sugar bush when they roped the hillside with grape vines, planning to bottle their own wine. Sam had secretly hoped to reseed the area and extend her grove once the Levellers restored the land, fulfilling the pioneer spirit of expansion on her own terms.

The collection hut was basically a small lean-to shed. Sam examined the tank inside to find that it was only a quarter full of sap, realizing she may have lost much more than forty gallons.

"You need to watch over that boy of yours better," she complained, fiddling with the controls of the vacuum pump. The pump should have pulled in way more sap, even with the severed line.

"I told you I'll talk to him about it, already."

"Didn't stop him last time."

"Listen, don't tell me how to raise my son."

"I'm not telling you how to raise him, I want him to stop cutting my lines."

"I told you I could pay for it."

"That's what you said last time, too."

Thomas was growing angry now, as he stepped out of the shed. "I told you I'll talk to him, Sam. Leighton's just acting out. Things are bad with my wife. Real bad. We fight and Leighton hears every damn word. It's no wonder he cut your sap lines. And you know what? I'm *glad* he did it. He doesn't do drugs or steal. It could've been a hell of a lot worse."

Sam looked up from the vacuum pump. "Worse, like how?" she asked quietly.

"Oh, come on, Sam. You know about Megan."

"What about her?"

"You don't think that Little House means something?"

"She's going to nursing school," Sam corrected. "She doesn't have time for that."

"That's what she tells you."

Sam hadn't considered that her daughter might be lying to her. She was wearing her medical scrubs whenever she returned home.

"Megan isn't a Leveller. She lives here."

"All I'm saying is now you've got a blaze on your property."

"I don't like what you're insinuating, Thomas. I run a sustainable operation here. We're carbon neutral. I've released my tax returns. Why do you have to go and bring Megan up? She's got nothing to do with that blaze."

"Why did I bring it up? Fuck, Sam. Why did I bring it up? Look after your own kid, is all I'm saying." He tapped at his coat pocket. "Left my vape in the damn car, too. 'Course I did. Not everyone's a professor."

Assistant professor, Sam thought, with no hope of tenure. But she knew such distinctions were lost on Thomas. She fished a pack of Camels from a shelf inside the collection house.

"You're smoking again?" Thomas asked.

"I keep it around. To know that I can."

Thomas tore open the seal and began puffing away, coughing himself to tears. "Now I remember why I switched to vapes," he muttered. He finished the cigarette anyway, taught, like Sam had been when they were in middle school, never to waste one. Coffin nails were what they called unfinished cigarettes.

Sam spied it now, the reason why the vacuum pump hadn't been pulling enough sap: a small rock had plugged a valve. She pulled it out and the sap surged into the collection tank again. She tasted the mild flavor of the unfiltered liquid. Slightly sweeter than she expected. Must have meant the sugars were producing more than the reds. With another couple of freezes and thaws, she might be able to squeeze out ten thousand more gallons as the trees withdrew the sap from their roots.

"Do you think they changed the formula?" she asked. "Think they're considering some other factor that I don't know about?"

"I told you it's probably a prank."

"Think it's the size of the farm? Maple syrup is an approved commodity. Part of the barter system. They can't take over my property like that."

"It would be strange," Thomas nodded.

"You inherited your property like I did. How do you know they won't come after you, too?"

Thomas looked at Sam with a skeptical glance, and shrugged. "They say you can look at the code." He threw his cigarette into a glob of ice-encrusted snow, immediately going over to pick it up, knowing that Sam would chew him out if he left it there.

"You would tell me, wouldn't you, Thomas? If you knew why they did it?"

"I'm not a member," he said.

"Of course you are," Sam said, growing desperate. "Your family are descendants, right? You were disenfranchised when we brought you here."

"Who brought us here? You?"

"I'm saying, all the former slave families. The Levellers grant you honorary membership. For your sacrifice."

"Oh, shut up, Sam," Thomas said. "You're belittling us both. I told you I have nothing to do with any of that. We've known each other since we were kids."

The thought of her property being seized from her, which she had fought so hard to make sustainable, was making Sam feel manic. If the Levellers seized her land, she could join one of the communes, and hope to establish herself in the organization. The Levellers eschewed all hierarchy, but she had spent enough time in the Army to learn that order naturally established itself. She might be able to navigate their internal politics—what they called "liquid democracy"—and eventually stake a claim to run the maple farm again, even if she couldn't live on it. The alternatives—well, the alternatives were in her mind far worse: using the meager proceeds from the forced sale of the property to gain entry to the fortified enclave of Library Place in nearby Princeton. She doubted she could afford it. And she had no desire to move up to the city, which she had sworn to avoid her entire life as an orgy of consumption and environmental despoliation. She would have to give up her hormone therapy.

Maybe Thomas could help her, she thought. Maybe he could clear away the blazes like a late frost could pinch the white petals from the dogwoods.

"Listen," she volunteered, trying to make her voice sound calm. "I saw some hoofprints where the cable was cut. A big stag ran through about ten days ago."

Thomas perked up. "How many points?"

"Looked like eight."

"Eight? Haven't seen one that size since the TBE came through last summer. Are you sure?"

"Could've been six."

"That's still pretty good," Thomas acknowledged. "How much do you want for him?"

"Nothing. You'll be doing me a favor. I'll let you take him and I won't complain if you take a few does, too." She'd learned to stop saying "kill" or "shoot," because it put Thomas on the defensive. He preferred to think of hunting as a service, especially since he was a bow hunter. "Those deer are destroying our ecosystem," she went on. "Once my maples die, no more will grow in the wild. I'll have to plant them myself. A grove is only as sustainable as the saplings that can grow up to replace them, and the deer eat everything except the beech and the sassafras. Of course, they leave the rosebushes. If I didn't have the sheep graze down the underbrush, we wouldn't be able to walk through this place at all, it would be so full of thorns."

Her own father had told her that the Lenape had used the dark woods of the Sourlands to hunt game, too, when the deer population was a tenth what it was today, with wolves, coyotes, and foxes keeping the herds small. The soil had never been good in the mountains, and shouldn't have been plowed by the first settlers. But the deer made it infinitely worse. The lack of deep roots meant the soil was easily leached by strong rains.

Thomas was scanning the ground for more hoofprints. "Where can I set up my stand?"

"Wherever you want," Sam said, "as soon as the sap stops flowing."

"When's that?"

"A week. Maybe two."

"Good, they'll still be hungry then. I should be able to take a few." Thomas turned to go as Sam double-checked the vacuum pump. She didn't want to have to come back down if it wasn't working. "Sorry about Leighton," he said. "I'll make sure he takes responsibility for it. You want me to walk you back up to the house?"

"No, I've got to turn this pump on."

"You should get yourself an exoskeleton, Sam. Then you can power right through all this snow. I can get you a discount."

"There you go again, talking as if I'm rich. You ever stop being a salesman?"

"In my blood," Thomas confessed. He plodded through the snowdrifts into the trees toward the top of the farm.

When he returned to hunt she planned to ask him, casually, to shoot down any Levellers who came onto the farm. But she knew not to press him after she had insulted his ancestors.

Once Thomas was out of sight, Sam took a pail down from a hook and began scooping sap out of the collection tank and into two blue storage barrels, each the size of a wine cask. She scooped pail after pail, the sap sloshing about. She was thinking about her father again, how he had bought the land as an attorney, how he brought it into the family. She didn't like how he had run the farm, when he'd pumped the animals full of antibiotics and scattered DDT over the land, but when he passed, he bequeathed the property to her, and she had improved upon it. *Make me proud*, he had written in his will, *as I know you will*. His parting words a gift and an expectation. An expectation that would not be met, now.

She filled up the second barrel of sap and then attached a line to each barrel, her hands resting on her knees from the exertion. She now had to turn on the pump, which she had coded to automatically adjust to shifting sap pressures in the trees throughout the maples, a sort of mechanical mirror of the natural processes of the grove, the rise and fall of the xylem and phloem. She had thought about patenting her system but instead uploaded it to a forum for anyone to use for free. Moving through the pump's interface, she configured it to send the sap through a different system of pipes up the hill to the evaporator, which would reduce the liquid down to syrup by boiling off the water. She flipped the switch and was pleased to see the pump working properly. Then she bolted a padlock to the door of the hut before starting up the hill.

The wind was buffeting the slope, and already Sam could tell that the trees would frost tonight. This would be good, ensuring another full day of tapping tomorrow. Except it also made the snow stickier as it began to freeze underfoot. She felt ice crystals forming on her eyebrows as she pushed through the foliage. It was growing cold. Very cold. Each step felt like she was breaking through the skein of a half-frozen pond.

Tap, tap, tap. In the growing dark she heard the gentle tap of a yellow-bellied sapsucker digging into a maple tree. She listened for the bird's squawk but it didn't cry out. Sam once considered the birds a threat to her grove until she learned that they tended to tap the sickliest trees and frequent one sapwell over the course of a season.

Tap, tap, tap. She heard it again, but strangely it came from another tree farther up the hill. *Tap, tap, tap, tap.* And another far beyond that.

Something was implanting a blaze into the tree, she realized. Above her she saw a silhouette flitting through the topmost branches in the obscurity. The Levellers could fly through the canopy entirely without lighting. Each Leveller drone had flexible, rotating wings and four hollow legs that dangled down beneath them, which they could beat together like wind chimes. Now one spotted Sam, and beamed a soft blue light down upon her face, gauging her identity. The rest of the Levellers responded to her biometrics by playing music on their chimes. The vibrations started low, an Irish folk song mashed together with an old gospel hymn. Other Levellers rubbed their chimes together like violins. Now it sounded like children humming through the trees, a sonorous, bluesy dirge. As if sourced from the heart of the grove itself.

She knew the song, too. Her father had sung it for her before tucking her in to sleep each night. *They say it's different for everyone,* Thomas had said. He had not said it would be beautiful. He had not said the Levellers would sift through her own memories of this land and play them back for her as they stole it.

More and more sap was spilling down the icy hillside, as still other Levellers in the flock lasered the PVC lines.

"You can't take this from me!" Sam shouted up at them. "This is my home! It's not fair! It's not fair to anyone!"

Still she heard the chimes, the woods filling with the immanent music of the Levelled. The blazes suddenly illuminated one by one through the grove, a string of green lights spilling down the hillside like ecological beacons onto her farm. Onto her father's farm. Onto her daughter's farm, which she would soon abandon like a vagrant. She sank down in the snow as the cold sap washed over her knees like milk.

NO POINT TALKING

Geoff Ryman

It's like a poison that takes over these women's minds. Candy and I were happy back in Lubbock. We went to church—we had a woman minister! It weren't no hell on earth for anybody.

I needed to go where the work was and we heard about these jobs coming up in wind farms. I thought they was in East California. Got there, found out they're in the west, Sonoma County. You can pretty near call it the People's Republic of San Francisco. We drove the pickup all the way from Texas, the kids in the backseat. We sponge-washed in gas stations and ate cheese sandwiches.

They put us in a trailer park. Row on row of the things, looks like they been there since the seventies. Drove through that gate, I wanted to cry. They got us living with Central Valley fruit pickers and they're all Mexican. All of them headed north when California split.

East Cal misses out LA but then cuts to the coast and runs solid all along the Mexican border. Conservatives closed it and pushed the new Interstate Passports through Congress. Means you got to have proof of citizenship before you can cross state lines. So them Mexicans, if they get into one state, they can't get into another.

Except West Cal said they'd let them in passports or no passports. I'd say serve them right, except it means Candy and I have to live with them.

You remember white people. We built this damn country. We spoke English, remember English? Hell, we even celebrated Christmas, in the privacy of our own homes, mind. Wouldn't want to offend anybody.

They tell us we got an Induction. Induction, you know, where they start out nice and let on real slow how bad they're going to screw you. Candy and I walk to the Residents Office and all I see is truckloads of Mexicans and women holding hands. Everybody's equal in West California—we all live like white trash.

Four new engineers, one of them a woman in a red tartan shirt and a crew cut. Nice Asian lady comes in, tells we us all work for the Cooperative, praise the Lord.

First thing she says, "Can you give me your name and your preferred gender identifier?"

I say right back, "What do I look like to you, lady? You want to check my balls?"

"No, sir, I do not. I'm happy to call you 'he.' Or any other name you'd like."

Then they ask Candy the same. "'She' will do me just fine for me. What are the alternatives?" She smiles sideways at me; I know she thinks it's all a big joke.

They tell us they got fourteen different genders. So I say, "No, you don't! Check it out! You only got two different kinds of wedding gear."

That got me a laugh. She starts explaining all these words they got. Zie, they...I don't know what all. She starts telling us that her little girl wants to be a boy so they are getting the surgery in early. "It's best to do it before secondary sex characteristics develop."

I laugh, cause it's so crazy, but then I say, "Do you mind not talking about this stuff in front of my kids?"

She says, "Of course." These people? Never fight you back direct.

We're working for minimum wage just in case you thought socialists paid more—turbine engineers, fruit pickers even Asian

Lady all get the same money. Of course my job means I got to truck up and down most of the state from Crescent City to Monterey. Won't see my kids much.

They assign us work partners. They give me the lady in the checked shirt. I go back to Asian and say, "Could you give me another partner? I just don't think we'll get along. I'd be more comfortable if it was a man."

Well they liked that. "Of course, we understand," they say, nodding, like I'm a sad person they need to take care of. They give me this guy Jake. He's in the same red checked shirt as the dyke but he's got a big bushy beard, so I reckon he's still got his cojones intact.

I get Candy back into the trailer and I say, "These people are nuts. We got ourselves two new conservatives in the US Senate, but what we've actually gone and done is set up a feminist utopia."

Candy says, "Don't worry, honey, I got that childcare idea for us. I'll put up some posters. We'll save up till you get another job then we move south." Candy? You know—that woman could have been anything she wanted.

We get a visit from Asian. She looks so pleased with Candy. "It's fantastic you want to help with childcare." Fantastic: that's socialist for we're going take it over. They're going to register Candy—make sure she doesn't have sex with kids—and then they'll "help" her find "clients". Money goes guess where and they just pay her, uh-huh, the minimum wage. Candy doesn't get to set up a business for herself, oh no. We might get independent.

While Asian's there she starts signing us up for the healthcare, and asks me if I sleep with men. I have had it. I just start yelling. "We can find our own goddamned doctor, we don't need you to do anything for us!"

She says it's not voluntary in the state of West California.

That's socialism for you. Man, I cannot wait to get out.

You live with crazy people, you just keep your head down and do your job. Every day I drive. Climb up those mills, crawl around inside. I get home the next night, nine, ten p.m. All those women won't leave after childcare, and their kids are still there. All I want to do is drink a beer and talk to my wife.

I hear my little girl Mariah and she's talking zie, zot, F to M. I get mad and I say "You thinking of becoming a boy then, Mariah?" Candy gets mad. The women shoot me these looks. I don't care. I'd talk to my beer if I could get one but the Coop don't stock alcohol.

I stick it all through that summer, into fall. Then they close the camp. All those Mexicans just stop work, go live in San Francisco for Christmas. Me, I got to stay here keep driving out to Santa Rosa or Napa and keep those the turbines turning.

I get back home, Candy comes and asks me. "Do you mind if we go the city, too? They got classes and plays. It'll be better for the girls' development."

I want my little girls to do the best they can. The wind's blowing, the camp's empty. I say yeah, okay. They go on a Greyhound bus, waving bye-bye and looking so happy to be gone. It's raining.

I can't find anybody to talk to. There's no *guys*, you know what I mean? I go to the social center… not a bar you understand, no way, a *social center*, and see Jake and a bunch of guys so I sit with them, and we talk baseball for a while. Thank God. Then Jake takes hold of this guy's hand and says they want to go to Pride in Turkey or Russia or somewhere. I can't stop myself saying, "If you like it so much why don't you go live there?" I reckon there's no point so I stand up and go back to the trailer.

At Christmas I go see Candy and the girls. The whole place is covered in trees and tinsel. They got street fairs. Got a joint Muslim, Jewish, Christian, and Winter Solstice Celebration. A huge big parade with Day of the Dead dancers, marching Golems, letters for the Koran all swirling, you know, holograms. Satan Claus— they got him, just no Jesus Christ. Police in bikinis—and those are the men. Never saw so many men in their underpants. Lots more women pushing baby buggies than I'm used to as well. We see this sign "Dog Reading." Candy asks the bouncer what's that and he says they know what words both dogs and their owners understand—so they're having a poetry reading for people and dogs at the same time. The girls loved it. The dogs looked mournful.

I go to the girl's ballet class show. They only been in two weeks, but there they are dancing like swans, making their Daddy proud. "What's this costing?" I ask Candy. Nothing. Other people are paying for us. They give my little girls presents, gifts for low-income families. I don't want to be no low-income family. They gave Mariah and Cathie a tablet and a stream for *Frozen*.

I say, "I'm terribly sorry, girls, but those presents are going to have to go back."

Candy says, "Hewett, can you and me have a word?"

When we're outside she stabs me with her fingernails. "Those girls are keeping their presents," I start to say something, she talks over me. "They love that movie. We can't give them anything else, Hewett, we got to let them keep them. It's Christmas!"

"We don't need nothing about Christmas from those people. I don't need *them* to give my daughters presents."

"I don't care what *you* need. They need a tablet for school." Candy's jaw sticks out. "I won't stand for it."

I know my wife. She says something like that, she means it.

"Okay, For the girls. But we get out of this state."

"Fine, fine, it makes no difference, Hewett. Don't you see that?"

No point talking.

Next day we get into the pickup. The girls look sad to be going. They get into the car hugging their presents. I don't know how many times they watch *Frozen* in the backseat, singing those songs till I'm sick of them.

Back in Sonoma, I start calling everybody, anybody who might have a job.

I get Tony from back home. He's down in East Cal. In high school, we were both on the team. "Hey bud," he says "I was going to call you. They're going to be opening up a big wind farm down at Camp Pendleton."

East Cal practically keeps West Cal going by buying electricity from them. So East Cal's set up in the same business, beat them at their own game.

I say. "You buying their turbines, too? They make 'em up here."

He says, "Hell no, we'll get 'em from Denmark or China anywhere else but. We're not keeping those faggots in business."

I laugh. "What about buying American?"

And he says, "Those people aren't American. We got our state militia. Sooner or later we'll just have to go in there and clean it up."

He thinks he can get me a job on the turbines and tells me where to fill in an application online. "Come and work for the good guys."

Candy's been listening. "What does he mean state militia? Does he want a war?" She shakes her head. She never liked Tony or Lizzie that much anyways.

Two days later Tony skypes me back. He's a bit drunk. "They like you, buddy. They ask me about you, I tell 'em you already repair the things. They say you can start *now*, no interview, but you got to get down here right away."

I tell Candy. Her face drops like she's swallowed a boot.

I talk to her about sunshine, show her the harbor at Oceanside, all the houses that opened up once they threw out the Mexicans. Show her the church we'd be going to, show her their Christmas party. She just stares.

I go tell Asian. She tells me, "You're breaking your contract."

I tell her that's too bad but I want this job, I got to have it.

"Well watch out. They don't have our job security or healthcare."

I can see her thinking. *We taught you how to fix the turbines.* *Now you're going to go help...the enemy.*

Damn right, lady.

Next morning I got the truck all packed. Somehow I squeeze all the girls' clothes in one big pink suitcase; found room for a couple of spare batteries. It's six a.m. but all these women show up and some of them bring their babies for Candy to kiss. They got balloons and cake. Mariah's teacher shows up with a bunch of vouchers for books and movies. Asian comes out and asks me to reconsider. I'm sitting in the front seat ready to drive and I hear this clatter from the trunk.

Candy's hauling the big pink suitcase and her own black bag. I shout, "What do you think you're doing?" She don't answer. I tear out of the car back to the trailer.

She's fumbling with the keys. She tells me, "I'm not going, Hewett."

I say, "What, you crazy?"

"No," she says. "I don't want to go. I like it here, I got friends. The girls have got friends. They got their school, Hewett."

I start trying to pull her back, she jerks away. "I'm not going in that truck again! It's the same damn job! Only no healthcare."

Well I don't take shit from anybody, and I cuss her out and tell her not to expect nothing from me no more. I grab hold of Mariah and shout at her, "Get back in the truck!" And she starts crying and runs to her Mom, and then Asian butts in wants to do some counseling. Candy wraps her arms around the girls. Kids stand there looking back and forth between us like it's tennis.

I start saying, "Please don't do this baby, please. I love you, you're my lady."

Candy shakes her head. "Not going."

I shout at all of them, all those women. "You see? You see what you done?" My hands are shaking; I pull out the plug from the side of the pickup. "All right! Stay here, then!" I throw open the door.

"Come between a man and his family. God damn you all to hell!" I get so mad I just get in the truck and drive.

I get to Oceanside. There's this Vietnamese owner. He starts giving me the Induction. Two months trial, no promises, three bucks fifty an hour, no limit on hours but all the beer you can drink.

And I can join the militia.

GLOW

J.S. Breukelaar

On the night of the elections I am with my cousin Ray and his human wife, Janyce. Footage flashes from the living room screen showing water-cannoned activists squirming on the asphalt, flayed detention survivors arcing across the crowds in heart-shaped orbitals singing Maria Callas arias. Jeering voters wave placards, saying "Lock 'em up!"

My cousin and I are smashing shots, but we are drinking for different reasons. He is hailing presidential nominee Bud Towers as the Second Coming and I am trying to get drunk enough not to argue. Janyce has made her famous lobster burritos. My little sister would hate them.

I lower my voice and say in our language, "You do realize that he's been running on an anti-alien platform since day one?"

"Hostile media shenanigans!" Ray cries out in reverberant English. The reflection from the swimming pool makes craters across the pale moons of his eyes.

Even before his name was Ray—when we were still eking out survival deep in the bowels of our wounded world, before it spat us out to face the radioactive vomit of our bloated sun—what entranced him about earth were its shenanigans. Its youth, and light, but mostly its *spirit*, he said. Humanity so frail, and yet so consumed by the need to empower Another. So acquisitive, but yearning for dispossession, he enthused. So solitary, yet committed to the crowd. But I always wondered if my cousin's attraction to Earth was because his name in our language is Uli, God of Jokes.

From the kitchen you can hear Janyce saying, "Sugar. That's the secret behind my coleslaw. A little bit of sugar, along with the salt, tenderizes the cabbage."

One of her daughters says, "You tell us that every time, Janyce."

Janyce says, "Call me 'Mom,' please. Just tonight?"

I think my little sister would like Janyce's daughters. She was the same age as the youngest when we arrived at the detention center. Fourteen. That was eight years ago.

"Towers will make us great again!" Ray says.

"Us?"

He lowers his voice. "Speak English. You know how Janyce gets."

One of Janyce's daughters is telling her sister about Oceanika, a new orbital space habitat with an ocean but fifteen miles above the earth, with beaches and sunsets and bars.

Janyce comes in with sliced limes. "Lisa, you ever been to sea?"

"The detention camp," I say.

"Of course. Sorry."

ICE keeps newly arrived aliens imprisoned on disused oil rigs in the Amundson Strait for a minimum of thirty-six lunar months for processing. Another week to get through the checkpoints after transfer—you need papers, a letter of acceptance from a halfway house or shelter, and they give you a new name. The immigration officer shoved a battered pink suitcase at us, made us empty our pouches at gunpoint. "For your own protection," he said. "Anything found in an RBS'll be confiscated."

He jammed the barrel of his rifle into my belly slit, parted the flaps. My eyes watered at the reek of cologne on his skin, sour coffee on his breath.

Ray's claws shook as he transferred our meager possessions from his pouch into the suitcase—the remainder of our cash, Grandcousin's medals, and the diaphanous shroud that had been my sister's skin. Amy sat quietly in her wheelchair beneath the Humanity First cap they made her wear, dwarfed in a greasy Bridge coat. The officer motioned for her to take it off but Ray gave him her medical papers, and they waved us through. I hated Ray at that moment, despised his fear of being turned away, of what might happen if he'd allowed Amy to sit there naked, show everyone what they made her. Instead, Ray's bioluminescent markings just flashed a queasy green, which they mistook for a smile.

"Welcome to New Liberty," the officer said. "Have a nice day."

"If Towers gets elected," I say, licking salt off my thumb, "The first thing he'll do is round us all up and throw us back in detention. We'll be deported."

The two most popular destinations floated by Bud Towers' Humanity First party were JL45-J872, a small world in the Proxima Centauri Galaxy, and a disused refuse satellite that the Chinese had been trying to auction off for a decade.

"Not us!" Ray shouts, very drunk. "The ones who get rounded up are criminals. Lowlife illegals."

Janyce's oldest daughter pokes her head around the door. "So being in the wrong place at the wrong time makes them what? Dangerous?"

The room spins. She sounds just like Amy.

Over the eons belowground to escape the death throes of our sun, we evolved tough dorsal armor for protection against falling rocks, and phosphorescence to light our way. Somewhere between emerging to the inky permafrost that was all that was left of our world, and splashdown in the middle of the Amundsen Strait, my sister—when she still had her skin and before her name was

Amy—asked what it meant to be in the wrong place at the wrong time. What it would make us.

"Something that we don't know about yet," I said.

Ray's got an air rifle for the rare coyotes drawn to the oases of floodlit arroyo and potted yucca, but it's mostly just rabbits he goes after. They always get away. He taps nervously on the table with his talons (Janyce makes him keep them short), and gets up to check the sliding door yet again. Except I know it's not for the coyotes. ICE are never very far away, even in good neighborhoods like these. Amy worries when I visit Ray that I won't be back, and when she worries, she bleeds. "Milu," she messages, "I want to go home," forgetting that I'm Lisa now and she is Amy, and we *are* home.

Ray wrinkles his nose at a montage on the screen of Towers' opponent in harsh gray scale. "He'll have her behind bars with all those off-world terrorists she's so keen to let in," he slurs. "Then see how much she likes them."

Janyce refills the bowl of chips. "Did anyone else read how she used campaign funds to buy her maid a boob job?"

I say, "Why would anyone buy their maid a boob job?"

Unions between aliens and humans don't produce live issue. We have other means of continuing our species. Janyce is Ray's second wife in the five years we've been in New Liberty. She came with two teenage daughters and Ray works hard to pay for the nice secure house at the edge of the desert, plus Amy's and my apartment, the medications. There isn't any insurance for what she has.

Janyce says: "I don't love Towers. The things he says about women and…others. But look at all the riffraff coming in from who-knows-where. I just want my babies to be safe."

Her oldest puts the coleslaw on the table with an unconvincing eye roll. I'm drinking too much, soddenly seduced by this dream of warmth and family, until I think of Amy alone in the dark fighting a different fight. "Your dream, not mine," she would say to Cousin

Uli, way back when Earth was just a lucent sphere he'd paint over and over on the walls of our cave. I look at Janyce's daughters, dressed in the latest fashions, hair and skin shiny and whole—a flash of light makes a jagged X across my heart.

"Honest people," Ray says, hooking a clawed thumb at his wife. "Just trying to get ahead."

Janyce's youngest touches one of my phosphorescent markings. "That's so cool."

Amy likes it when I glow, too. She watches from her chair, ghostly and seeping, and I dance for her, and in the dark in our high prison between earth and sky, I am a warrior once more, garlanded in light.

Ray looks nervously toward the sliding doors to the yard.

Even before surfacing, we got wind of the anthropocentric foment brewing on Earth. On the refugee ship we watched broadcasts of a retired Senator demanding genetic editing to remove off-world "mutations" like scales, pouches, and talons. Constitutional lawyers declared mixed marriages illegitimate at best, illegal at worst, due to being unconsummated in the lawful sense. Epidemiologists worried about cross-species contagion, but couldn't say of what.

Amy obsessed over the news, snuck off to meet with other scared angry teenagers. "Youthful shenanigans," Uli said, when I worried. Religious leaders declared our bioluminescence the real threat—no luciferin without Lucifer, they warned. ICE bosses said it was the dorsal armor that was the problem—I remember how Grandcousin disappeared for a few nights during a layover on the Wang Hun Orbital, came back after a bullet ricocheted off her striated hide, wounding a Humanity Firster in a poker game gone sour.

Ray didn't care. Amy—before she was Amy—tried to tell him Earth wasn't what it once was, especially New Liberty. All that "Land of the Free and Home of the Brave" stuff disappeared when arable land did, and from sea to shallow sea, she said, the only thing left was humanity's desire to believe in something.

I think now of my cousin's luminous blue cave-paintings, and how they lit up his night.

The apartment I share with Amy isn't in a neighborhood as swank as this one. She doesn't go out much because infection's a risk and antibiotics are expensive. Mostly she stays in the dark, talking online with friends she's never met—"freedom fighters," she calls them—who send encrypted messages from beyond the stars. I work nights in a networks operations center to supplement Ray's earnings, ride two hours in the subway to score Amy's opiates from the black-market connect her "friends" hooked me up with.

Once I asked Ray why his markings were so faded, and he swept an arm out to the neon-studded street, the heavens ablaze with Orbital worlds. "Why glow?" he said. "With all this light."

But I don't think that's true. I think the real reason he doesn't glow is because Amy can't. Atonement's no joke—some fights never are.

He passes a huge scaled hand over his forehead as if to wipe away a thought. Pours another round and says, "Remember sour milk?"

The bored guards on the rig made us drink sour milk to see if it would get us drunk. Another time it was coffee dregs mixed in toilet water. We may not pass on our DNA the same as humans, but we share 98 percent of it with them. Tequila does just fine. I down the shot.

Somewhere between the exercise yard and the detention center showers, my sister learned that RBS means both more and less than Random Body Search. When I went to visit her in the infirmary afterward, she said, "Being at the wrong place at the wrong time makes you nothing."

The screen erupts in cheers as another district falls to Towers. I wonder how hard it will be to get a taxi home. It's Amy's bath night. She needs me to get the temperature just right, not too hot, not too cold. I light scented candles so she can't smell herself and when she gets out I scrub the tub clean so she can't see the red ring she leaves behind.

A siren wails up the canyon and floodlights arc over the house. Janyce says, "Maybe we should move."

"Where to?" the youngest calls from her bedroom, excitement in her voice.

"Out of the desert."

The oldest laughs. "There's no such thing as out of the desert."

Her phone tings and she goes into the hallway to take a call from her boyfriend. I think of offspring, of the dormant nucleotide sacs inside my pouch, hovering at the edge of life for a DNA shot they'll never get, an Inceptor I'll never get the chance to choose.

From his campaign headquarters, a sweaty, gloating Bud Towers calls for unity.

"See?" Ray says haltingly. "We're all Terrans now."

"You don't look like a Terran," I point to the screen where, among the jubilant human mob, there is not a single alien.

It's nearly midnight. The crowds wave baseball hats like the one they make refugees wear on arrival—embroidered with the Humanity First mascot, a simplified interpretation of Da Vinci's Vitruvian Man. Shoals of hectic reflections from the pool swim across the walls and throw ragged shadows across my cousin's face. I snake my hand into my pouch, feel for the telltale chip implanted in all of us on evacuation. To keep track, our homeworld activists said, to find us if we needed to be found. But Ray had his excised as soon as we were processed. No need, he said, only get us into trouble. We had the government of our adopted country to take care of us now.

There is a high wall around the yard to keep out the coyotes, and I am halfway to my feet when a shape crawls over the edge. Heat rises in my chest and I point, wordless, at the door. I've had too much to drink.

The lump along the top of the wall is joined by others. One by one they stand, silhouetted against the light-choked night, and one by one they drop into the yard.

"Coyotes?" Ray swivels in his chair.

I shake my head, neither standing nor sitting.

"I'll get my gun." He lurches out of his chair with a scrape that makes Janyce's eyes flick in alarm to the parquet finish.

"Poor bunnies," the youngest says.

My legs shake uncontrollably. "No bunnies," I say.

It is ten minutes past midnight. The Western Rim is the last sector to fall to Towers. The backyard swarms with ICE operatives. They smash the door, spraying glass across the rug. The dark millennia burrowing in caves and tunnels has made us agile. I slither behind the oak sideboard stacked with Janyce's family photographs and the girls' soccer trophies.

Ray returns from the bedroom with his air rifle. An ICE rookie, seeing nothing but an armored alien with a gun—lets off a panicked round.

Janyce slumps into her lobster burrito.

Ray screams. The operatives fall on him. His bands of light strobe a chromic green. "Save her, Milu!" he screams in our language. "Save her!" He is still screaming as they drag him away.

The crowds cheer, ushering in the new era. When all I can hear below that is the girls' sobbing, I come out. Janyce has slid off the chair and crawled onto the rug, leaving a smear of blood across the floor. I know what Ray wants but cross-species Re-Inception is unheard of—even among our own kind. The risks are high and in our subterranean cities it was punishable by expulsion—death. But I'm already expelled. I think back to the detention rig, how each time Amy would try and throw herself over the rails, or go after the guards with some instrument she smuggled from the infirmary, Ray would try and pull them off her. Until the last time when they outnumbered him seven to one—no hope with seven—but it cost him three months in solitary anyway.

The daughters are crying and holding each other. Janyce hovers between life and death. There's not much time.

"Look for a pink suitcase," I tell them. "Pack it with whatever you can't leave behind. And hurry."

I turn Janyce over and wipe lobster off her face. Her blue eyes are glassy and her breath is shallow. I rip open her shirt, unfurl my tongue, and push it into the bullet hole. The tissue is custardy and her blood feels warm—I explore and suck until I come up against the hard, sharp flaps of the slug. Its edges tear at the fleshy muscular probe, and the luciferase in my tears mixes with the taste of tequila and human blood.

The bullet drops to the floor in a mess of hot red tissue. I hunch over it, drooling. When Janyce wakes up among shadowy activists on some bare-bones cargo ship in deep space, she won't remember much from her previous life, not even taking friendly fire on a Guatemalan rug, but maybe she'll find a scar, a phosphorous wink from a home worth fighting for. Her brow begins to swell, the dermis around it already hardening into thick plates.

I rummage in my pouch to activate the tracking chip, message our retrieval coordinates and estimated arrival time—but I'll be gone by then and I hope they understand. That I've gone back to Amy. How my fight, whatever's left of it, is here and for her.

The sisters rush back from the bedroom clutching the battered pink suitcase, and pull up short as their mother's French polished fingernails extend into coffee-colored claws. I motion for them to be still. They watch Janyce's eyes flutter open, pale as the moon.

"Will she know who we are?" the youngest asks.

"Will she always be our mom?" the oldest asks.

I tell them yeah. Just like my sister, even after the guards took away her skin, will always be my sister.

PRECAUTION AT PENN STATION

Michael Kandel

They showed their badges, pulled me out of line to the turnstile, drew me off to the side on the platform, and pumped me full of lead. "A security measure," they explained over the bang bang. "Random executions to keep the terrorists off balance. We know you're probably just another commuter going to work, sir, but we have to show the Muslim extremists we mean business. Any sign of vacillation only makes them more vicious."

"It's random," they went on as I was expiring in the pool of my blood, "because we don't want to be accused of racial profiling. Just last week we terminated a sweet Irish grandmother who was coming back from Macy's, from a sale on Italian leather handbags. She didn't object. 'I understand it's for the Homeland, dears,' she said before she gave up the ghost."

"Racial profiling," they went on, leaning over me as the death rattle filled my throat, "undermines the American way, everything that this great country stands for. We shouldn't have used the word 'Muslim' a moment ago, we regret that, sir, because those fanatic fundamentalists are no more Muslim, truly, than you or I."

"Islam," they went on after my heart stopped and my eyes glazed and froze, "is a religion not that different, we understand, from Christianity or Judaism. Though you have to wonder about all the violence in its history. Did you know, sir, that the words *assassin* and *thug* are Arabic?"

NEWSLETTER

Jennifer Marie Brissett

Dear Loyal Patrons,

Usually in this newsletter I would be telling you about the latest event we were planning or the next author who would be reading with us. I would list the books that sold the best this month or an upcoming title that we recommend that you read, and sometimes a tale of the latest antics of our store kitty. But today I want to talk you about something else. Something that I technically am not supposed to talk about but I feel as the owner of this community bookstore I should share with you.

I received a letter the other day from an organization that I belong to but cannot name warning me that my special orders list may be requested by the state at any time and that I have no right to refuse this request or even the right to contact an attorney—this is now the law. They wanted me to know that if the occasion should arise that I receive such a request that I should get in touch with my lawyer anyway and that they would pay for my representation. I'm telling you this because I believe you deserve to know why I and many other booksellers have not been fulfilling your special orders of late. You should also know that your electronic orders through the net are being monitored as well.

The words are disappearing. Books on my shelves are being bought and not replaced. When I try to replace them, they have either been priced prohibitively or they are simply not available from the distributors anymore. My shelves are emptying and all I can do is watch it happen. As your local bookstore owner and your friend, I feel that I have to at least warn you that the books you've been reading and have in your possession are not safe anymore. I've been running this bookstore for many years and I've never thought I would see this day. The books I sell—the physical paper ones, electronic ones, and the ones I've downloaded to your mind—have all been hand chosen by me. And these words are in danger. They can be retrieved from you at any time. If any of you have the following books in your possession, I would highly recommend that you secure them in a safe place:

The Fire Next Time by James Baldwin

The People's History of the United States by Howard Zinn

Kindred by Octavia E. Butler

The Plutonium Files by Eileen Welsome

Fortunate Son by Gary Webb

Letter from a Birmingham Jail by Martin Luther King, Jr.

I say this because I have noticed men in the store that I've never seen before. New people come in off the street all the time that I don't know, but these men feel different. They hang around and seem more interested in my customers than my books. I have no proof of it, but I think they are watching me and the activities in my store. I first noticed them after the last author reading we had here a few weeks ago where we discussed the implications of the latest election and the new laws that have been quickly passed. So many of you turned out and asked such poignant questions that even the author himself found it difficult to answer some of them. His spouse came by today and asked me if I had heard from him.

That he never came home and that she thought that he gone out of town for a meeting but no one has seen or heard from him since that night. Maybe he has simply gone away somewhere and will return soon, but I must admit that I'm a bit scared.

I feel now that I have no choice but to close the store until further notice. I'm sorry for anyone who is inconvenienced by this. I wish there was another way. I know that some of you think that this store is simply a business, but trust me when I say that what I've been doing here did not make me in any shape, way, or form wealthy. I barely made a living. Actually, most months I was lucky if I broke even. I did this because I love words and the work of the men and women who dare to write them. I did this for the ideas and the knowledge and the courage to think new and different thoughts. So for the next twenty-four hours, I'm making every book in my mind-database available for free. Download all you can while you can. Words are the weapons of the future. Your ability to know is under attack and I plead with you to protect the words.

I wish all of you well.

Stay safe,

Your Former Local Bookstore Owner

STATUES OF LIMITATIONS

Jay Russell

"Yo! Bobby G!"

"Hey, Sal. I forgot they brought you in for this gig."

"They try the rest, they come back for the best. Those losers from Staten really scrambled the eggs, left the City in a hole. The mayor sent 'em shlong-in-hand back on that goddamn ferry. But we're doing great stuff. Winning!"

"Good for you. I guess this job's got to be turned around quick."

"Always the way, huh? The state's been so late on the band-wagon they want to move fast now. I *get* the bum's rush on the civil war shit—fuck those good ol' cocksuckers—but all the rest? Hey, at least it's more overtime for us."

"There is that. So you guys doing all the decon and recon work in the Park?"

"Pretty much. We picked up a few of the other contracts, too."

'That's great. Like what?"

"Port Authority. Who do you think deconned the Gleason statue. How sweet it was!"

"Aw, jeez, is the fat man gone already? I didn't realize. Man, I loved *The Honeymooners*. I watched those reruns every darned day after school on Channel Eleven. Remember? I think about all the palookas in the sitcoms what came after and how much they owe to Gleason. *'Bang! Zoom! Right to the moon, Alice.'* Heh-heh."

"That is not amusing, Bobby, however significant Jackie Gleason was to the history of television comedy. That right there, what you quoted and which I shall not repeat for reasons I know you will appreciate, was a frightening cultural endorsement of the domestic abuse and female oppression so typical of the post-war era. There is nothing funny about physical violence or the incessant direction of micro-aggressions at your partner-in-life, my friend."

"Yeah. I mean, of course not."

"Not to mention his treatment of poor Ed Norton."

"I hate to say it, but I always suspected maybe Norton was kinda retarded."

"Bobby . . ."

"Developmentally disadvantaged."

"Don't you mean 'challenged?' "

"Yeah. That."

"In hindsight, I suspect Norton might have been situated on a particularly problematic developmental spectrum. Asperger's, most likely. Tragically undiagnosed yet brutally seized upon by Ralph in order to deny Norton the opportunity to self-actualize. And all just to prop up Ralph's own neurotypical privilege. Sad."

"Asperger's. Yeah, you might be on to a thing there. Poor Norton. Say, did you ever think maybe Ralph and Ed were more than just *pals*?"

"And if they were?"

"We-e-e-ll . . . that would have been great. I mean, if they had only been permitted a safe space wherein they could truly explore the limits of their identities. So, uh, have you replaced the Gleason statue with anything yet."

"Of course."

"*I Love Lucy*? I heard they wanted to keep with the TV theme. Gosh, she was great, too. So important not just as a physical comedienne but as a pioneering female producer and innovator in a restrictive and uterophobic post-studio system."

"You fucking whacked out on the drugs or something, Bobby? You forget how Lucy was always cracking wise about Ricky's Latino heritage? Entirely tone-deaf vis-à-vis her own blinkered ethnocentrism."

"Ummm, yeah. I see that *now*. But hey, you remember those episodes where they—heh-heh—went to Italy? When she stomped the wine grapes and they started throwing them at each other. She got it right in the mush and . . ."

"Bobby."

"Huh?"

"Are you—like myself—not the scion of a proud Italian-American heritage."

"A what now?"

"An heir. A legatee of Italo-Roman achievement."

"My mom's dad was from Milan. I think. Until he was like . . . two."

"Surely, then, you recognize the shameful bigotry foregrounded in those vulgar, early televisual representations. You, too, must be sensitive to the deep pain that stems from diminution of personhood arising from hurtful, cultural stereotyping. Undeniable comedic value notwithstanding, of course."

"Notwithstanding, yeah. I see that. Wow. I mean: I'm woke."

"I should hope so, my countryperson. In any case, we did retain a majorly media-based personage."

"Whose statue did you put up instead?"

"Rush Limbaugh."

"Beautiful."

"Right? The likeness is uncanny. Down to the fucking cigar and a little bottle of painkillers poking out of his pocket."

"I'll have to take a look. Maybe bring the kids."

"Hell, yeah. Little girls can't get enough of him. Better Rush than some gender-treacherous Disney Princess, eh?"

"Hey, did I hear your crew also did the work at Rockefeller Center?"

"With aplomb, my friend. With fucking A-plomb."

"It was Atlas you were eighty-sixing, yeah?"

"Well, they couldn't fucking keep *that* piece of shit now, could they? One *man* holding up the whole world. Could you—if you tried—come up with a more emblematic and insidious three-dimensional trope for two thousand years of hegemonic patriarchy?"

"Uh, wasn't he a Titan?"

"Howzat?"

"Atlas. Wasn't he a Titan? Not actually a man, that is to say."

"Po*tay*to, po*ta*to. You can't spell Titan without 'tit'."

"Say what now?"

"He. Had. To. Go."

"I gotta admit I always liked that one. I remember coming into the City at Christmastime with my folks and my little sister. The lights were so pretty in Rockefeller Center. And the massive tree they'd put up every year. Just like fairy land. We'd have a skate around the rink, sit down for a special lunch up in the Rainbow Room. On the way home I always made the family stop to admire that statue, that bigly-ass sphere perched on his shoulders. Somehow, it made me think of the world as a single, wondrous place. Looking at that thing . . . I could dream. Yeah, dream."

"Keep dreaming, patriot. We kept the sphere. Torched that sucker right off. Not so much as a scratch on it after a spritz of WD-40 and a chamois."

"Really?"

"Shit, yeah: nothing WD-40 can't make better. Gleams like a new iPhone. Beautiful."

"And Atlas?"

"Gone, history. Yesterday's phallocentric news."

"What did you do with him?"

"Jersey. Bayonne."

"Oh. My. So who holds the world up now?"

"Ayn Rand."

"I can get with that."

"Great likeness, if you ask me. Really captured her frigid, *go-thither* expression. Those dead eyes follow you around like you're a taker. You can practically taste the Objectivism. That is art, friend of mine!"

"There's a lot of talented people out there."

"Amen. But you know, you gotta look hard for talent if you want to make great things happen. 'Course, we couldn't find anyone in *this* country could do the work."

"Natch."

"You want to see some really smart stuff we done, you take yourself—or the whole family; hell, why not make a day of it?—up to 83rd."

"The Met? You taking care of all the museum statuary, too?"

"Nah, Breitbart Deconstruction plucked that juicy plum. *Quelle surprise.* They're on it as soon as they finish recon on the big, green CAFAB immigrant-magnet in the harbor. They're still scratching their heads over how to ship her to Crimea so she can lord it over the luxury links at the President's new hotel there."

"I saw that on Fox. So what are you working on up by the museum?"

"Alexander Hamilton on East Drive."

"Oh, yeah, how could I forget? Heck, he's been there forever, hasn't he?"

"Eighteen-eighty."

"Jeez. You're gonna have to help me here, Sal: what's the issue with that one?"

"As I'm sure you know, and despite his later achievements, Hamilton was a highly problematic figure in his youth. He...but what am I telling you? You've fulfilled the legal requirement to see the show. You wouldn't have passed your official probationary period otherwise."

"Of course."

"It wasn't a big job, really, more a . . . what d'ya call it? A subtle one. Mostly the face. Very delicate."

"What'd you do to him?"

"Now it's Lin-Manuel Miranda."

"Win!"

"It's just so much more *relatable* now. And isn't that what everyone wants?"

"I'm putting it on the bucket list, baby."

"Can I confess something to you, though, Bobby? Can I trust to your complete discretion?"

"You know me, Sal."

"I've always felt that Miranda skated perilously close to cultural appropriation through the usurpation of a hip-hop idiom in his admittedly otherwise dynamic and original artistic oeuvre. Though please know, Bobby, that I say this in the full understanding that at least one of Mr Miranda's esteemed forebears was reputedly of genuine African descent."

"My lips are sealed, Sal."

"You're a gem, Bobby."

"What else you working on then?"

"You name it, we're on it. The Mayor has made clear his absolute determination to decon/recon on a completely equality-neutral basis. There's a *heap* of old marble we already took care of."

"Let me guess: Christopher Columbus?"

"First to go. Where that genocidal motherfucker stood, you can now experience an interactive, replica smallpox blanket made entirely out of chewing gum reclaimed from Park sidewalks."

"Hans Christian Andersen?"

"Fairysplainer! *Forgetaboutit.* Now everyone can enjoy a non-binary Little Match Child."

"The Shakespeare on sixty-seventh?"

"Pffft! That plagiarizing, paternalistic fraud? Replaced him with a statue of Marlowe."

"How's that better?"

"The truth is out there, my friend. It. Is. Out. There. We put the kibosh on the Romeo & Juliet by the Delacorte as part of the deal."

"You've lost me."

"Heteronormative much?"

"Yes, of course. Umm . . . Walter Scott?"

"Ivan-*hoe*? I don't think we want to be valorizing anyone who refers to independent sex workers—very probably illegally trafficked—employing so offensive a linguistic schemata. We retained a Scottish influence, though: now it's Mel Gibson in *Braveheart* war-paint."

"Beauty."

"Duke Ellington on 110th went to that big twelve-bar in the sky, too."

"What?! Why?"

"Do you really want to be encumbered by the legacy of monarchical, aristocratic titles and hierarchies?"

"But . . . wasn't that the first ever statue of an African-American in the park?"

"Still a win: we went like-for-like."

"Who?"

"MC Hammer."

"—"

"It's *always* Hammer time!"

"True dat."

"Doing what needs to be done, Bobby. I mean: ain't that the American way?"

"Which leaves us only with *this*."

"She's the last job on this contract, yeah. But I'm sure there'll be more work to come. The times they are ever changing. That's what makes America great."

"Still, I'm really sorry to see her go. My mom used to bring me here when I was a kid."

"Do tell."

"We'd come into the City on the seven train and head straight to the big Brentanos store on Fifth. She'd let me choose any book I wanted—god it would take me forever to decide, but she didn't mind. Then we'd walk all the way up here, stop for a hot dog and kraut, a Dr Brown's cream soda at a Sabrett's along the way. We'd chat and look at all the funny people, the beautiful people; exotic, interesting guys and dolls. Manhattan felt so fantastic then. It was a thrill to see the horses and carriages ferrying the tourists around the Park from fifty-ninth . If I got lucky, we'd even browse in FAO Schwarz. It was ever such a long walk to the Pond, but I never complained or got tired. Because at the end of it my mom would sit me right on that big mushroom at Alice's feet. She'd perch on the edge of the little toadstool there, between the Mad Hatter and the Dormouse, so we were eye-to-eye. And she'd read to me from my new book. Sometimes beginning to end, straight through. I remember she even read Lewis Carroll to me on this spot. It was wonderful."

"Hmmm. Then you must feel all the more violated knowing that Alice in Wonderland so utterly embodies the appropriated excrescence of a retrograde, colonial, paedophiliac sensibility. Fuckin' shame when you think about it."

"Shame. Yes. Shame."

"Well, my guys better start smashing her up. Really good to see you, Bobby."

"Yeah, you too, Sally. Hey! You didn't say: what's replacing Alice?"

"Steve Bannon tweeting Pepe the Frog. Cast entirely from recycled Chinese smartphones. Gonna be beautiful. Bring the kids!"

SUFFOCATION

Robert Reed

"I've heard this."

That's what people say. They've watched the news, glanced at a web page, maybe put hours into exhaustive research. But "Here's something I heard" is the familiar phrase. Informal, chatty. Two people standing at the mouth of a cave, discussing matters that don't need to be important. That's what everybody's wishing for, regardless where they happen to be standing today. Trivial talk and a good deep shelter at their backs.

Long ago, months and worlds ago, my daughter was getting her hair dyed. I was sitting in the hairdresser's lobby when another customer stepped through the front door. My age, my color, but besides that, nothing like me at all. How could I tell? Just could. We said our hellos to each other, nothing but polite. Then another hairdresser came out to welcome him and his gray hair, and the two of them vanished into her room. "How's your day?" talk turned into whispers. Whispers, and then the guy announced, "I'm tired of hearing about Guam. Fuck Guam."

Smiling, his gal shut her door.

That's been the rule since the inauguration, at the salon and in a lot of other places, too. If you're going to talk, keep it private. But I really wanted to hear. This was an experiment: Was it possible to become even angrier than I already was? I walked next to the closed door, listening to two people describing events they barely understood. We blockaded an island that they couldn't name, and the fucking Chinese shot down one of our planes, and of course we had to hit back. Orders were given and some of the orders were obeyed. That's why an important, unnamed island was left burning, and one of our ships was sunk, and we hit five of their boats, and they punished another island that they claimed to own. Taiwan. Which the people on the other side of the door success-fully named. Taiwan was struck by conventional munitions, but one initial report mentioned a mushroom cloud, and that's when the first of three nukes were launched. That's why Guam went away. But the other two nukes were ours, and the Chinese blinked. At least that was the learned opinion of the experts celebrating on the other side of that door.

I wanted to yell something, but didn't.

I sat back down instead, reading the *NY Times* on a phone that won't be replaced until America can build the necessary facto-ries. And since my daughter's hair always took forever, I was still sitting in that chair when that smug idiot returned to the lobby. That's when I killed him. Kicked his feet out from under him and slammed his skull against the linoleum and concrete floor. At least that's what happened inside my head. Just a daydream, a moment of pretend. But the new world was remaking me, and happily slaughtering strangers as well as legions of ex-friends seemed like a perfect use of time.

Speaking of murder.

I knew a respectable woman. Late middle age. Soft as pud-ding and usually sober. But one day, sitting with friends inside a quiet, respectable restaurant, she shouted out, "I don't know how many assholes I'd have to assassinate before we got to somebody I liked."

That lady would never miss a march. She carried banners even when the protests started taking gunfire. The bullets were unfortunate, but inevitable. Local police couldn't protect the congested public streets, and what did these foolish people expect? Then a black congresswoman was shot at her kid's basketball game, and a sniper took out that east coast senator, followed by two wrong-minded federal judges who were mangled with pipe bombs. Some of these perpetrators were caught, but nobody could pin down ties to any political movement. These were lone agents reacting to liberal excesses and Facebook, and nothing changed. Not until protests in different cities were ambushed. Organized teams were in play, automatic weapons killing dozens of civilians. Which was when the Feds clamped down on every possible source of civil disorder.

Marches were outlawed.

Free speech was supposedly retained, but one wrong word meant trash burning on your lawn and death threats in your email.

And that lady friend of mine? Weeks later, she was found sitting inside her car beside the same restaurant. Somebody had written, "Cunt," on her Bernie bumper sticker, and maybe the same somebody put three bullets through her heart.

In little surges and then ten kilometer bites, Ukraine fell to an army of "volunteers" while NATO did nothing. Then Russian tourists arrived in the Baltic States, heavily armed and cocky, and NATO tried to do quite a lot. But their central ally claimed to be licking his wounds in the Pacific. So the Poles and Lithuanians and Ukraine hackers took their revenge. Power grids failed. Ransomware disabled the banking system. Boot heels on their throats, yet they retained a very clear sense of who their real enemy is.

A few weeks later, I was standing outside my cave. Two stories tall with a shallow basement, sheetrock and cheap pine. But like any cave, it didn't have electricity or reliable water, and if I wanted heat, I would have to saw up our Christmas tree and burn it in the fireplace.

I was outside because there was nothing to do indoors. My neighbor had also emerged. He is an older man. A member of the other Party, although I can't say if he voted for the winner, or for nobody. I have liked the man. But I've also watched him die inside my head. No, I've never imagined killing him myself. He's usually strung up by raiders who might or might not have a political agenda. The story works either way, frankly. But on a day that's warmer than we deserve, we act like two almost-friends standing at the invisible boundary between our respective properties.

"You know what's going to happen," he said to me. As if both of us had a window on the future.

"I wish I did know," I said. "Why? What do you see coming?"

"Civil war," he told me, the voice flat. Matter-of-fact.

I had to nod.

"Americans," he growled. "We've been spoiled. Each of us grows up believing that civil wars should be simple. Nations dividing neatly on the map, raising orderly armies wearing distinct, handsome uniforms, and the battles had generals and wise orders and hilltops, and not even a hundred years later, good people could get into costume to reenact that noble carnage.

"But normal, traditional civil war…that's something else. Messy and slippery, impossible to understand. A thousand years later, and passions still run hot."

"Is that the war we're getting?" I asked.

His eyes lifted, imagination putting him in a place that he had never seen before. "If we're lucky," he said. "Otherwise it's roaches and fungus. They'll be the ones writing the histories."

Another day, wintery cold but otherwise blessed. We were treated to fifty-two minutes of electricity, which was long enough to warm the house and partly charge the family phones. And it was a chance to read some news. The *New York Times* seemed to be off-line, but oddly enough, *Al Jazeera* was reachable. And that's where I found the first good explanation for everything that was happening to us. Politics couldn't be blamed, and it wasn't international mistakes either. No, it was CO_2. The gas that they claimed wasn't changing our weather. Carbon dioxide had been in the atmosphere forever, but our species had always enjoyed lower concentrations. Wise researchers in Australia had determined that humans were happiest when carbon dioxide levels were below 300 parts per million. But take us higher and every breath would make us feel less easy. The effect was a subtle neurochemical response. But of course where were we today? At 400 parts. Add to that the image of people occupying enclosed spaces, nervously gasping 500 and 600 ppm in the stale air. Which apparently was why everything felt wrong. Humanity was like a person thrown on his back, a rag to his mouth and water trying to choke him.

Anyway, that's what I read on my old Chinese-built phone, and maybe I believed it and maybe not. Either way, it was interesting.

Then my daughter and her magenta hair walked into the room.

"Hey," I said. "Guess what I just heard?"

APPLICATION FOR ASYLUM

Eileen Gunn

March 8, 2020

Testimony of Minor Child

My moms don't want to even carry their phones with them,
let alone turn them on. I say, what if there's an emergency, what if
an immigrant attacks you or something? Mums says there are no
immigrants anymore, they're all in the camps, and Mama always
adds that I should say "illegal immigrant." But I still see posts
about how white women who go out alone are just sluts asking
to be attacked. It's all the bots talk about online, protecting white
women, and Mums looks kinda white, so I worry about her. When
I tell her that she shouldn't go out alone because people will think
she's a slut, she looks at Mama and presses her lips together and
glares at me. But she doesn't say that's sexist anymore, because
that's one of the words you can't use in public. Public is anywhere
there's a phone, to tell the truth.

My moms make me leave my phone in a box on the front porch
with theirs, and I can only use it outside the house. Mama says the
phones are tracking us for the government and record what we say
and where we go. They won't even use a phone to check the time.
In the kitchen, we got this wind-up clock that I can't even read, like
the speedometer on a car. When we're out shopping, they're always
asking me what time it is.

And, yeah, yeah, I suppose the machines are tracking us, but I say that's not the government, that's the machines. It's for our protection, and it catches the bad actors and the paid troublemakers. Plus, my phone is my proof that I have a right to be here, because the vigilantes might think I'm Mexican or Muslim or one of the other M-words. They make a lot of those kind of mistakes, but being a vigilante means you never gotta apologize.

I got stopped a lot last year when I hit my teens, but I never got beat up bad. Mama told me that she thought my clothes were getting me stopped, not my skin. And it seems to be true. As long as I dress like a girly white girl and act quiet when I'm on the street, the vigilantes leave me alone. It's not like they're fooled about who I am or care what I really think, they just want me to look like I know they're watching me. When me and my girlfriends get together at home, we all bring jeans and makeup, and dress any way we want to. We don't get too loud, though. No music: the new folks upstairs don't like our music at all, and if the neighbors complained, the cops would come, and they know that, those folks. Our other neighbors would never call the cops on us, but these new white folks would do it.

I worry about the cops, and I try real hard not to get noticed by them. They size you up pretty careful, and their default is that every kid who's not white has a gun and they need to protect themselves. They shoot you, it's self-defense, and they kill you, there's no video.

My moms keep me real close to the house unless they're with me, not so much because of the cops, but because of the Child Reclamation people. They just snatch kids right off the sidewalk, sometimes—kidnap them. It's not right, it's not even completely legal, but it happens, and once it happens, you're in their system for a long time.

The hardest part for my moms is they are registered abominations—well, that's what my moms call it. They got married like fifteen years ago, right when it was legal, and everything was fine until after the Trump year. When the laws changed, my moms had to go to court to keep me, and they won—some people did at the beginning of the AT era, you know. The social worker argued that I was too old for the CRD to take away, plus I was Mama's birth child. (And yes, my moms call the CRD "the crud.") She was a fighter, that social worker. She fought for every client's child to stay with their family, and in my case she won. She was a good woman, my moms say. Passed on last year, after her arrest.

Well, thank you for listening. I sure hope you can approve our application.

WELCOME TO TRIUMPH BAND

Yoon Ha Lee

Triumph Band Program, Advanced

2020–2021

Parents, please review these requirements with the cadets. Adherence to regulations is mandatory.

Keep America Great!

Jason G. N. Smythe

Liaison to the US Naval Band Academy

Dear Cadet:

Congratulations on your acceptance to the Triumph Band Program. Successful completion will prepare you for an exciting career in the Navy's marching bands, including performances at our Great Nation's capital. Cadets who are unable to meet minimum musicianship standards will be assigned remedial work and stationed at the Wall to provide entertainment for our loyal troops there.

Your four-year stint in the Triumph Band Academy will prepare you to be an exemplary citizen and role model. You are required to be a member in good standing of the Junior Plutocrats' League, America First, and Twitter.

You can choose from the list of instruments in Appendix A. You will, of course, provide your own. Failure to maintain an instrument in acceptable condition will result in demerits and possible expulsion. Drummers may not chew gum, unless it is Midas Mint. Please note that, by order of the President, all instruments are notated in treble clef, to represent our Unity.

All instruments have been fitted with bayonets. You will be trained in sections on their use. Once sufficient proficiency in the basics has been attained, you will practice on live targets. Cadets who accrue too many demerits may be reassigned to the Voluntary Bullseye Corps.

You will also be required to carry and care for a standard-issue sidearm. Attacks on marching bands are, unfortunately, a sad fact of life, as not everyone in our Great Nation has accepted the President's benevolent rule. Rest assured that any act of hostility or criticism directed toward a cadet will be taken seriously, and that retaliation against hostiles is encouraged. Attempts to distribute pictures or video of Triumph Band events are considered hostile unless approved by a government official.

You will be periodically tested at the firing range and expected to maintain acceptable aggregate scores. Be warned that, due to the variation in threat levels from terrorists and domestic threats, what constitutes an acceptable score may be revised periodically. Cadets who are unable to meet the program's standards will receive demerits.

All cadets will be assigned standard band uniforms, including bulletproof vests and riot gear. Since free choice of instruments often results in imbalanced sections, some cadets will be assigned to march and play music while others undertake riot duty, and still others are responsible for piloting defensive drones from a secure location.

The standard curriculum includes several components. The Band Musicianship course specific to your instrument focuses on performance, marching band protocols, sight-reading, repertoire, and how to maintain a social media presence in line with our Great Nation's policies. You will also perform in the Triumph Band as an ensemble. All cadets will be assigned additional practice time based on their proficiency and musical needs.

You will also attend a daily Citizenship course to expose you to government-endorsed facts. On Sundays you will go to Church of America services. Cadets will tithe to the Church of America. Exemptions may be granted in cases of proven merit. Family connections will, of course, be taken into consideration.

There will be periodic Performance, Music Theory, and Citizenship examinations. Cadets will also be required to memorize pieces from the Band Canon, which includes the Great National Anthem, other patriotic pieces, and "My Way."

The full Code of Conduct can be found in Appendix B. Be sure to review it before your arrival. You are expected to stay vigilant and report any signs of suspicious activity, especially among other Triumph Band members. Remember, without vigilance, America cannot stay Strong!

Demerits may be handled in several different ways. Consult Appendix B for details. In cases of severe deficiency, a tribunal will be convened to examine the case in question. Penalties can be ameliorated by appropriate donations to an approved corporate sponsor.

In case an emergency court martial of your band director is called, do not panic. Such courts martial are rare, especially during performances, and a detailed set of procedures exists for them. See Appendix C for details.

As long as you remember to honor our Great President and the achievements of our Great Nation under his leadership, you should do well. We look forward to seeing you this year.

Sergeant Green L. Rollins, USN, Retired

Triumph Band Director

LOSER

Matthew Hughes

I am on block-hauling detail when I hear my number called.

"One-Fourteen!"

I straighten to attention immediately and shout, "Yes, Apprentice-Sergeant!"

He looks me over, flat-eyed, in a way that reminds me that if I am not useful I should be dead. Then he spits on my bare feet and says, "Report to App-First Carmody!"

"Yes, Apprentice-Sergeant!" I am already moving as I speak, wanting to get past him before it occurs to him to send me on my way with a kick. I've already had one of those today and my tail-bone is sore. I mostly make it, receiving no more than a glancing blow from the side of his boot as I speed by.

My destination is the admin block just inside the main gate. As I approach the ramp that leads up to the door, the guards in the towers flanking the barbed-wire barrier train their M-16s on me, only standing down when I start to climb the incline. I come to attention outside the door, and knock the regulation three times.

Someone in the orderly room pushes a button and the door slides open. I step smartly inside, come to attention again, with my eyes fixed on portrait of Our President on the back wall and announce, "Loser One-Fourteen reporting to Apprentice-First Sergeant Carmody, as ordered!"

In my peripheral vision, I see an Apprentice-Corporal on the other side of the long counter gesture with a piece of paper he is holding. "Go stand by the wall," he says.

"Yes, Apprentice-Corporal!" I go and stand, keeping my gaze blank and unfocused. It is a routine day in Camp 17's admin center, the staff hunched over their keyboards, typing laboriously with two fingers, or staring into their monitor screens or at pieces of paper. I see a lot of knitted brows, some lips being chewed, one protruding tongue-tip.

And I see it all without focusing on any individual Apprentice. I never want to hear again the words: *What are you lookin' at, loser?*

Something buzzes, the Apprentice-Corporal speaks into a phone, then looks up at me as if I am a turd that refuses to flush. "All right, asshole," he says, "see the First." He gestures to a door at the end of the counter.

"Yes, Apprentice-Corporal!" I double-time across the few yards, come to attention before the door, and deliver the three knocks with the required timing.

"Come in!"

I open the door, step within, close it without turning my back on the man seated at the desk, come to attention again, my eyes on the wall above his head, where a different portrait of Our President hangs. This one shows him looking up and out of the frame, in visionary mode.

"Loser One-Fourteen—" I begin.

"Shut up," says Carmody.

I know better than to say, "Yes, Apprentice–First Sergeant!" Shut up means shut up and I have the bruises to prove it.

The App-First has a round face that ends in a blue-stubbled lantern jaw. His eyes are small—"porcine" is the word I would have used, all those months ago, when I was well paid for my columns in the *National Commentator* magazine.

I stand with my eyes on Our President, trying to keep the tremble out of my limbs. Though we are all at the mercy of these merciless men, it is always a mistake to show overt fear. Weakness often triggers a beating.

So I wait while Carmody studies me. Finally, he leans back in his chair—I hear it creak under his considerable weight—and says, "You used to work for that *National Commie* rag, dincha?"

Time to speak again. "Yes, Apprentice-First—"

"And that asshole Wedley was your boss."

"Yes, Appren—"

"Shut your loser mouth! I already know he was."

I say nothing, but my mind is racing. Charlie Wedley saw it coming, as soon as the TSA lost its funding. He packed a suitcase, transferred his accounts to the Bank of Montreal, and made it over the line well before the bus loads of black-uniformed bruisers from the Corps of Apprentices arrived to replace Homeland Security at all the airports and border crossings. Only the day before he had told me I should get ready to run, too, but I hadn't seen it as clearly as he did. Besides, Arthur was in school and Sharon had just been promoted to a senior post at the Andrew Jackson Institute.

Carmody has leaned forward and is reading from a paper in a file spread open on his desk. "Says here you two were real close." He looks up and makes a noise of contempt. "Couple of fudge-packers."

I say nothing. It wasn't a question, and I know better than to contradict an Apprentice's judgment.

He studies me again for a long moment. I know he'll be wanting an excuse to knock me down and kick me and I am beginning to wonder why he hasn't. Usually, a call to the admin center involves at least some stains on fists and boots, which the recipient of the attentions are often required to wipe away—if they are still conscious.

Now he closes the file. "You make me sick, loser," he says. "Was up to me, none of you pussies would be building the Wall. You'd be under it."

I say nothing, think nothing, let Our President fill my vision. The chair creaks again. Carmody is closing the file. Now he says, "Somebody is interested in you, loser. Somebody upstairs, way upstairs."

He picks up the phone and pushes a button. A moment later, he says, "Is the car here?" then grunts a response to whatever he's heard and hangs up. He looks at me and says, "You're going for a ride, faggot."

The car is a shiny black Cadillac Escalade with opaque windows and doors emblazoned with Our President's one-letter monogram in gold. An Apprentice wearing a tailored uniform and the shoulder bars of a captain stands waiting by a rear door. He favors me with a cold-eyed stare as he opens the door and moves his head minimally in a gesture that says: *Get in.*

I get in and the door closes silently behind me. For a moment I can see nothing, then my eyes adjust to the gloom and I see that the passenger compartment is self-contained. A pull-down folding seat faces the vehicle's wide rear bench where a man in civilian clothes sits silently. Like his aide, who is now climbing behind the wheel and starting the engine, he says nothing—just uses one pale finger to indicate that I should sit on the jump seat.

I sit and reach down to grip the sides of my perch, which becomes precarious as the Escalade accelerates through the gate and turns sharply onto the road outside. I can hardly see the man opposite me, though I can smell him: cologne and powder. For the first time in months, I become conscious of the rank, sour smell that rises from my own body. I feel a louse move in my armpit but resist the automatic urge to pinch it dead with my long, broken-edged fingernails.

The road parallels the Wall and we drive past the segments that Camp 17 has built in the half-year since we were bused down here from wherever we had been arrested. Twenty feet high, its top festooned with sharp steel spikes, razor wire, and broken glass, it stretches on, mile after mile, running roughly east–west on this part of the border. A segment is one hundred and fifty feet wide, and as each is built and capped, the camp is uprooted and moved to the next piece of desert.

The admin block, the Apprentices' barracks, and the kitchens are on wheels, towed by trucks. The razor-wire fences are lifted and carried by us, the three hundred losers of Camp 17. There is no need to move our barracks because we have none; we sleep in our rags on the bare desert floor, huddled together for warmth. Our latrines are slit trenches dug in one corner of the compound.

It is possible to get under the razor wire and escape into the desert. Some have done it. But the constantly circling drones that look for illegals soon spot them: their body heat shines against the dark cold of the nighttime desert floor. But no one wastes a missile on them; soon enough, the temperature differential equalizes. And no one bothers to collect the corpses.

The Wall-building project began in late January, just days after Our President took office and started signing all those executive orders. By the fall, he was ruling by emergency decree. The nature and extent of the "emergency" were never detailed; the Corps of Apprentices had been quietly forming even before the voting in November. As the leaves began to fall in Washington, the truck-borne squads were already rolling out to collect the losers who had failed to support his history-making campaign. As a staff columnist on what used to be considered an influential mainstream conservative magazine, I was a natural target. Journalists dubbed "enemies of the people" had already been dropping out of sight. Some said they were in hiding, but there were rumors that people had been snatched off the streets, hustled into black vans, and never heard from again. But nobody reported on it, because the fear had begun to set in.

Then came the emergency decree and Our President unleashed his attack dogs. In the pre-dawn, doors were kicked in, people hustled from their beds, wrists pinioned by plastic slip-on restraints. A few shots were fired, but the Apprentices brought overwhelming firepower. Besides, most of us couldn't believe it was happening until it was too late. We climbed out of the boxcars in Texas, New Mexico, and Arizona to stand, stiff and blinking, hungry and dehydrated. The razor wire was already in place and the club-wielding Apprentices were more than ready to teach us the camp rules. Most of us learned quickly; those who didn't were thrown into the latrine trenches we left behind when the camp moved.

As the months wore on and the Wall grew, more losers were captured and brought in, usually a dozen at a time. Some had been hidden in basements and attics by friends and relatives who weren't on the lists—though their names certainly got added once their lack of devotion to Our President was discovered. Others had been caught making a wilderness run for the Canadian border; Washington state to British Columbia was the usual venue. And a few had tried to hide out in remote cabins, but even the remotest places were known to somebody and the rewards for turning in losers were attractive.

But in all the time I have spent in Camp 17, no one has ever been taken away in an Apprentice staff car.

I hear a rustle of paper then a discreet *click*. A small cone of light falls from a fixture beside the Escalade's rear door onto a manila folder on the lap of the man opposite me. When he opens the file, enough light reflects from the white paper within for me to get a vague impression of his face: clean-shaven, lean, hollow-cheeked, high-browed, and white—almost a fleshless skull. He glances down at whatever is written there and when he looks up at me the skull impression is reinforced by the eyes remaining in shadow.

Now he closes the folder and turns off the light. He retreats back into obscurity. The voice that speaks to me from the darkness is cultured, intelligent.

"Your October fifteenth piece in the *Comment*," he says, as I hear the sound of a finger tapping the file. "Good insight." When I say nothing, he adds, "You may speak."

"Thank you," I say.

"Good thing the mass of the punditry didn't come to the same conclusions," he says. "Or we might not have won."

I say, "I think by then…" and stop myself from saying it would have been too late to opt for a more neutral phrase: "…the die was cast."

He makes a neutral sound. "Perhaps." Then he lapses into silence.

The article he referred to advanced an argument I'd been thinking about as I watched the presidential primary go from strange to bizarre and then seen Our President emerge as the most unlikely candidate in the nation's history. Other commentators were focusing on demographics—older white males, evangelicals, libertarians, Tea Party activists—as well as economic and social shifts, but all of those factors taken together were not enough to account for the fundamental paradigm shift that was revolutionizing American politics.

And then, in mid-October, I was walking back to the office from lunch and passed a sportswear store. The window display was full of sweatshirts, and every one of them was adorned with a corporate logo of some kind. For some reason, I flashed on a sweatshirt I'd had in college: it bore a line-drawn portrait of Ludwig Van Beethoven on the front. I wondered for a moment what had happened to it.

And that's when I noticed the obvious. Thirty-four years ago, when I'd been that college boy, we might wear sweatshirts with "Yale" or "Princeton" on them, because we were students at those schools, or pictures of Alfred E. Neuman if we were smartasses. But we didn't turn ourselves into walking billboards for commercial products.

Over the decades, something had changed, and as I walked back to my office and sat behind my desk, the nature of that change emerged, full-blown, into my consciousness. I turned on my computer, powered up MS Word, and put my fingers on the keyboard.

We used to be citizens of a society, I wrote, *but now we are just consumers in an economy.* I thought a moment, then typed again. *The society was ours; we had rights and responsibilities. The economy is everybody's and nobody's, and all we have is "likes."*

And as I sat there, following my train of thought, it led me onward. *Our mental operating systems have been reset by the increasingly sophisticated, ever more powerful, and all-pervasive force called marketing. We have been conditioned to think—no, not to think, only to feel—only in terms of our own individual wants and needs—"You deserve a break today" instead of what's good or bad for the whole.*

I thought about the candidate who was to become Our President—even though the polls said he couldn't crack the Electoral College. And it came to me. I typed, *He is not a politician; he is a celebrity. His supporters do not follow him—he does not lead, but simply exists as a brand they can like. He does not have policies; he has marketable qualities that lead consumers to "like" his brand: it makes them feel good about themselves.*

Pundits like me were prisoners of the old political system, the one created and sustained by our citizen ancestors. But their society was gone. It had been gradually washed away by the power of marketing, leaving only the economy with its different rules and mechanisms.

The man who would become Our President had recognized the paradigm shift. And he had done so years, even decades, ago. He had spent those years marketing himself as a celebrity brand, creating for himself a platform from which he could leap from the sinking society onto the command deck of the still accelerating economy.

The article poured out of me as if it had been gestating in the back of my head for ages. And perhaps, I thought, it had. I'd noticed, as a young man, when reporters had stopped asking the people they interviewed what they thought and began asking, "How do you feel?" I remembered the slight sense of disconnect I'd experienced the first time I saw a clothing label on the outside of a collar instead of the inside, and when I'd first realized that my conservative shoes had the brand name stamped on the heel, so that anyone walking behind me would see it flashing at them with my every step.

Marketing, I wrote, *is now our complete environment. We are marketed to thousands of times a day, and we no more notice it than a fish notices the water that surrounds it.*

But the candidate had noticed it. He had seen the new age rising around him and had made full use of his vision. As I finished the article, I complimented him. I said the rest of us were like a passel of ape-men huddled in night's darkness while one of us—a genius—rubbed two sticks together and made fire.

I polished a few phrases and sent the copy to my editor, Charlie Wedley. It ran in the next edition. Two weeks later, the election came and then the months of interregnum while we wrote speculative analyses and profiles of the strange collection of folks with which Our President intended to fill his cabinet. And we waited to see what a celebrity brand would do if granted the leadership of the free world.

It got pretty crazy right away, but people said he'd grow into the office. Nine months after the inauguration, we found out what had been gestating in the White House.

"We want you to do something for us," says the cultured voice from the darkness.

"Yes," I say.

"Is that 'Yes, I'll do it'?"

I don't have to think. Months of building the Wall have made me compliant, as it was meant to do. "Yes, I'll do it."

"It will involve betraying a friend."

A year ago, I would have been brave, would have given a short answer: Forget it, or another two-word phrase that began with "F." Now I scarcely hesitate before saying, "In the loser camps, friends are no help. They're just another liability."

"Good," says the voice. "If you deliver, you won't have to go back to the camp. You'll be declared fully rehabilitated. Actually, we can use you at Apprentice Central. And your wife and son will join you."

I am too numb to feel anything yet, but I notice that my cheeks are wet. I raise a hand and find that my eyes are full of tears.

"What do I have to do?" I say, then listen closely while he tells me.

A week later, they have cleaned me up, deloused me, cleared the worms from my intestines, fed me, and shot me full of vitamins. They have flown me from San Antonio to Fairchild AFB near Spokane, Washington, where a special forces helicopter delivers me silently to a spot on the Columbia River south of the Forty-Ninth Parallel. It is a moonless night and overcast. We touch down in complete darkness, one set of hard-handed men unloading me from the copter into the equally hard hands of another crew. I assume they are all wearing night-vision gear because they move me swiftly down to the water's edge, put me in a rubber boat, climb in with me, and push us out. It is only when I feel the slight breeze of our passage on my face that I realize they have started a motor as noiseless as the helicopter's.

I have no idea how long we are on the river. I see few lights on the shore until we pass a small airport on the eastern bank, then we are back into blackout travel. Eventually, I see the lights of a town and the boat angles in to the west bank and grounds on a patch of gravel. There is enough illumination from the town reflecting off the overcast for me to see the men in the boat as vague shadows.

One of them presses something into my hand—the strap of a half-sized duffel bag—and whispers, "You get out here. There's a road up a little ways. Find the bus depot. There's money in the bag." I don't hear them go. I climb the bank, push through some low scrub, and come to a two-lane blacktop. I turn toward the lights of the town and start walking. They made me memorize a rough map of the place—it's called Trail—and I find the bus depot easily enough; it is on Bank Street, which is a continuation of Riverside Avenue, the road they directed me to.

The depot is a little blue-and-white frame structure. I wait outside until a tired-looking man in jeans and a cotton shirt opens up. As I hitch up my bag and step through the door, he says, "Where to?"

"Vernon, then Kamloops," I say. If he asks, I will tell him I am meeting my brother in Vernon, but he just punches some buttons and hands me the paper slip that his ticket machine printed out. I pay with one of the used Canadian bills they put in my wallet and go to sit on one of the benches. The ticket says the night bus from Alberta will arrive and depart in about an hour and it will reach the Vernon depot in midafternoon. I will then catch another bus to Kamloops and be there before evening.

I sit, looking straight ahead, my inner eye replaying the images of Sharon and Arthur on the phone of the man in the A-Corps staff car—I never learned his name. My wife and son looked worried but unbruised and reasonably healthy. They hadn't been put to punishment labor as I was.

The street door opens and a man and a woman come in. She has a rounded figure but looks strong; he is taller and leaner but moves like an athlete. They both wear holstered automatic pistols, khaki shirts, dark trousers with a yellow stripe, and matching flat caps with shiny leather bills.

I see them from the side of my vision and the dark pants with the stripe—identical to those worn by the Apprentice guards in the camp—almost trigger an automatic response. But I manage not to leap to my feet and stand to attention. Instead, I look straight ahead, a man with some thinking to do.

Until they stand over me. "Hey, there," says the female Mountie, "who are you?"

I look up then and give them the name that matches my ID.

"Where you from? And where are you headed?"

"To Kamloops, from Eastend, Saskatchewan."

I say the name of the latter place easily, using the pronunciation my handlers drilled into me: "It's Suh-skatch-uh-one. That's how the Canucks say it. Americans say Sass-katch-uh-one. Dead giveaway."

The male cop already has his phone out and is working its icons and keyboard. "Who's the mayor there?"

I tell him.

"Where's the co-op store?"

"Corner of Maple and Railway."

He flicks the screen a couple of times. "Tourist attraction?"

"T-Rex Center," I say "Listen, what's this all about, eh?" Canadians are polite but don't stand for police harassment.

"Border jumpers," the female Mountie says. "Let's see your ID."

I show them my Saskatchewan driver's license. It is good enough to fool them and they hand it back. "Watch out for anybody tries to be too friendly," says the male cop, putting his phone away. "Some of these jumpers, they'll steal your identity. And you won't complain because you'll be dead in a ditch."

I tell him I didn't know it was that bad, which is true. But I am not surprised. I know what motivates most Americans who come over the Forty-Ninth and how far they will go to keep from being sent back.

"I'll be careful," I say.

My "brother" is waiting for me in the bus depot at Vernon. He catches my eye then steps into the restroom. By the time I follow him in, he has checked all the stalls; we are alone.

He hands me a leather belt that is identical, right down to the stainless-steel studs set along its length, to the one I take off and hand to him. Squeezed between the new belt's two layers of cowhide, I know, is a web of circuitry. While I am putting it through the belt loops of my jeans, he unscrews one of the buttons on my denim jacket, fills its hollow with a small, shiny battery, and screws the button back on. Through all of his, we do not speak and his gaze does not meet mine. When he is finished, he turns on his heel and leaves the restroom. Our association has lasted less than thirty seconds.

Not long after, I am on the bus to Kamloops.

"Loops," as the locals call it, is where two major rivers—the North Thompson and the South Thompson—meet to run as one down to join the Fraser on its way to the Pacific. Long before the whites came, the river junction was a gathering place where native tribes met for peaceful trade, making it a perfect site for the Hudson Bay Company to establish a trading post. After the fur traders came the gold-seekers, and when the placer deposits were all played out, the high, dry plateau country around the junction of the two rivers was recognized as good cattle country.

Today, the city has spread from the river bottom up into the surrounding hills. It's a prosperous place, peaceable in the Canadian way. And home to a colony of American asylum-seekers granted "landed immigrant" status—the equivalent of a US green card.

All this, and more, I know from the briefings given me in San Antonio. I never saw the Escalade man again, though I heard his voice in the hallway outside the room they put me in once I was cleaned up. That's where the "more" came from. The door had been left ajar and I could hear him giving crisp, clear orders:

"…don't tell me your problems, Major," he was saying. "Just get it done. The snatch team will be in the safe house on the twenty-second. Every hour they're in-theater, they're in danger. We know the senator is in the vicinity, but they move her constantly. I want our Judas to find him not later than the twenty-first."

There was a mumbled reply, but he cut it off. "I don't concern myself with that level of detail. If you can't cut it, I'll have you transferred to one of the Wall camps, and you'll find yourself nit-picking for real."

A moment later, a worried-looking Apprentice-Major came into the room and took the other chair across the table from where I sat. He placed a thick file of papers between us, opened it, and said, "Straighten up, loser. We've got work to do."

Kamloops's Greyhound depot is on Notre Dame Drive, just east of the intersection where the street widens and turns into a divided boulevard. And not far west of that is the White Spot restaurant. It was getting on for evening and this far north the spring sun is long gone when I climb the concrete steps from the sidewalk and push through the front doors. The place is half-empty, not too brightly lit, but I can tell it's a family-friendly restaurant from the scattering of parents and kids in the booths and at the tables.

There is a counter with stools near the kitchen walls and I make my way to it, setting my duffel down at my feet as I sit. I pick up a folding menu from the steel rack that holds salt, pepper, and vinegar and flip to the burger section.

I'm only doing what the Apprentice-Major and his subordinates told me to do, but the sight of the illustrations and the waft of cooking fat coming from the kitchen door behind the counter, brings not only saliva to my mouth but tears to my eyes. I remember, when Sharon and I were newlyweds, we loved the burgers at Le Diplomate on Fourteenth Street a couple of blocks from Logan Circle in the northwest part of DC. It seems like a thousand years ago now.

That's not going to help, I say to myself, knuckling my eyes as a young man in waiter's garb emerges from the kitchen, sees me, and comes over to give the counter in front of me an unneeded wipe. "How're ya doin'?" he says. "Coffee to start?"

"Yeah," I say, then have to say it again to make it come out clearly. I look through the menu again and say, "Didn't you use to have a blue cheese burger?"

He has his back to me, pouring coffee from the carafe on the shelf behind the counter. Now he pauses halfway through before finishing. He turns and passes me the cup and saucer along with a spoon and two little containers of half-and-half cream. He is not looking at me but glancing around the restaurant. Finally, he says, "You must be thinking of the A&W."

I say, "You know, I might just be at that."

"Okay," he says, and now he's looking directly at me, "order some food and stay where you are."

I point to a burger on the menu and he brings out a handheld device and pokes its screen then asks me if I want fries and cole-slaw. I nod and he pokes again. Now he puts the handheld away and reaches into another pocket, coming up with a basic cell phone. He turns it on, pushes a speed-dial button, waits for a long moment, then says, "Sorry, wrong number."

He turns off the phone, slides the back off it, slips out the SIM card and puts it on the counter, then reaches under and comes up with a pair of shears. He cuts the SIM into small pieces and throws them into a trash basket.

"Okay," he says, though I think he's talking to himself. Then he says to me, "I'll get that burger platter. More coffee?"

The coffee is strong and flavorful, better than you'd get in most American burger joints. I've worked my way down to the bottom of the cup when he brings my food on an oval platter. Despite the coffee, my mouth is dry, but I take a big bite of the burger and find it juicy, with some kind of sauce beyond the usual mustard and ketchup. It tastes good. It tastes like freedom, and my eyes begin to tear up again.

I swallow another bite, then try the fries. Good again, and the coleslaw is chunky and chewable. My San Antonio trainers fed me decently, the same as they ate, but that was institutional food; after the slops in Camp 17, this is heaven.

The waiter is hanging around the counter, pouring me more coffee, but his attention is all for the front door. I see him come to alert and my hand holding the coffee cup shakes so I have to use the other one to steady it. I take a sip and wait.

A man slips onto the stool to my left, another takes the one on my right. They both order coffee and the young fellow brings out cups and pours.

The one on my left sips his black while the one to my right is stirring cream and sugar into his. Then the black coffee drinker puts down his cup, turns his head my way, and says, "How's it goin', eh?"

"Gettin' better," I say, careful to drop the "g."

And the one on my right says, "Holy shit! Is that really you?"

I turn, and I'm looking into the surprised and delighted face of Charlie Wedley.

They take me to a house in the old part of town, down by one of the rivers. Charlie has already hugged me before we get into the car and he sits beside me in the back and chatters about a dozen different things. How did I get over the border? How are Sharon and Arthur? How he and Jeannine broke up after they got to Montreal and he immediately signed up for the Resistance that was already beginning to form. What kind of camp was I in? Was it as bad as they say?

The other man, sitting in the front passenger seat, leans over and tells Charlie to lay off. There's a procedure for debriefing and he's screwing with it. Abashed, my old editor puts up his hands in a gesture that says sorry. But he pats my knee and says, "We'll catch up later."

The debriefing is what I've been told to expect. First they take my bag and every stitch of clothing off me and examine it minutely. They scan my belt and boots with an electronic wand, the same with the buttons on my jacket and jeans. They find nothing and let me get dressed again.

Then come the questions, but the trainers have drilled me well. I tell them about how the A-Corps began shipping selected "losers" from the Wall camps to new places in Oregon and Montana for "special handling." We didn't know exactly what that meant, but those of us familiar with the history of the Holocaust had a pretty good idea.

They shipped us in boxcars, I say, and the one I was in had a hatch at one end of the ceiling. It was loose, and one of us had hidden a four-inch nail in his rectum. We stood on each other's shoulders and managed to slip the latch. Then we climbed out and lay flat on the roof of the moving car until it slowed on a long bend somewhere in southern Oregon. One by one, at half-mile separations, we dropped off the boxcar and went into the woods.

I tell them I stole clothes and a pickup from the back yard of a rural house in Deschutes County and made my way north and east, traveling mostly at night and taking logging roads and two-lane highways, cadging food from Dumpsters behind roadside eateries. The truck had a full tank and it took me all the way to Whitefish, Montana, where I ran it into a lake. Then I hitched a ride to a lumber town named Fortine and walked through the woods along Highway 93.

"What about A-Corps patrols?" my interrogator asks.

"I could see their lights coming up the road," I say. "So I'd just duck back into the trees. They were dogging it."

I crossed the border at a place called Roosville, I tell them. An eastbound Canadian trucker picked me up and took me all the way to Lethbridge, Alberta. He told me to look up Quakers in the phone book and contact them. They would help me.

"They did," I say, "and they told me about Kamloops and what to say at the White Spot." I know it's safe to tell him that. Quakers won't talk to anybody about refugees they help, not even to the Resistance. What they do is between them and God.

There are more questions. I give more answers. Finally, they put me in a room with a lock on the door. I'll stay there until they can check my story. Charlie tells me not to worry. I tell him I won't. That's the truth because the A-Corps has fitted my story around elements of truth; there are new camps up north and people are being sent to them; there was an escape in Oregon, though most of the escapees were killed or recaptured within hours, some of them shot by local patriots alerted by radio and TV bulletins; Apprentice agents stole a truck in Deschutes County and left it in a Montana lake; their border-watchers at Fortine are due for replacement and punishment duty.

Eventually, as new information comes in, they might pick apart my cover story. But by then the senator will have been snatched and the Resistance will need to find a new leader. And I'll be back in the States, with my wife and son, writing for some organ that supports Our President and the new order.

I won't like myself, but Sharon and Arthur will be able to live like human beings again.

It takes two days to vet me. I spend the time reading and resting and eating. My system is beginning to recover from the abuse and neglect of Camp 17. Charlie comes by each day but the people watching me won't let him do more than put his head around the door and say hello. On his third visit, he comes right into my room and says, "You're cleared. Get your stuff. You're staying at my place till we get you set up."

"I'll need a job," I say. "Won't I have to apply for legal residency and so on?"

"You've got a job. You're going to work for the senator. I've been telling her about you and we figure you'll fit right in."

"A writing job?" I say. "That all seems like a million years ago."

"It's like riding a bicycle," he says.

Charlie has a house up in the hills overlooking the junction of the two rivers. He shows me my room then says, "We'll need to get you some more clothes. Tonight we'll have dinner with some of the other staff, people you'll be working with."

I tell him I like the clothes I've got. "I see a lot of jeans and denim jackets on the streets. Dressed like this, I blend in."

He shrugs. He was always more fashion conscious than I was. "Whatever," he says. "The boss wants to meet you, too. We'll go out tomorrow."

"Out where?" I say, but Charlie doesn't know. They move the senator around constantly and only her closest inner circle know where she'll be at any time. When she's ready to see me, Charlie will get a call on a burner phone with the code name of the meet's location.

"Is all the cloak-and-dagger stuff really necessary?" I say.

"They would love to get their hands on her," he says. "A few sessions of waterboarding, then they'd trot her out for a show-trial confession. It would undercut all the work the Resistance has been doing all these months." His face turns bleak. "Or maybe they'd just kill her, get her off the internet, shut her up."

The next day is the twenty-third of April. According to that conversation I wasn't supposed to hear, an extraction team—maybe even the same Navy Seals who brought me up the Columbia

River—should be in the area now. It won't be long now before I'm back with my wife and boy. Once I've done my job, I'll need to get down to Vancouver and present myself at the American consulate. I don't like to think about the way Charlie will feel, or the other good people I had dinner with the night before. As for the Senator's fate in the hands of A-Corps operatives like the Escalade man... well, plenty of people are suffering worse building the Wall—if the rumors are true, what is happening in the new camps is worst of all.

Don't think about it, I tell myself. *Just do what you have to do and get back safe with Sharon and Arthur.*

It is not my fight anymore. Camp 17 kicked all the fight out of me. I just want to live and see my loved ones safe.

In the late afternoon, Charlie and I are driving around Kamloops. He makes sudden turns and U-turns, watching to see if we are being followed. Before we got into the car he used a handheld electronic device to check for tracking bugs. The car's built-in GPS has been disabled.

The sun is just touching the dry hills west of town when the cell phone in Charlie's pocket vibrates. He pulls into a service station and answers the call. After a few seconds he says, "Got it," then strips the phone's battery cover and removes its SIM. He tears the little piece of cardboard into several pieces and has me throw them out the window as we drive on.

We get onto Highway 5, heading north, paralleling one of the Thompsons. Traffic is light. If anyone is tailing us, Charlie says, we'll see them miles back. But nobody is following us and after ten minutes or so, Charlie turns off the highway, crosses a cattle guard and goes through an open wire gate. We're on a dirt road that winds up into hills covered in dry grass and sagebrush. The landscape is eerily similar to Texas where the Wall is still being built.

We've left a dust trail in the air but in two minutes of bumping over the rough track we're between two hills and out of sight of the highway. We continue to snake our way through the hills, climbing as we go, until we come to a fork in the road and go right. Five minutes farther on, and we're meeting trees, some scrubby conifers growing on top of a ridge. Now the road levels off and up ahead is a clearing with a log house too big to be called a cabin. It's getting dark and I see lights from the windows.

We pull in. There are men on the porch and in the trees at the edges of the clearing. They are wearing clothes like mine, but they have the look of soldiers. Some of them have rifles like the ones the A-Corps guards used to point at us in the camp.

I follow Charlie up onto the porch. A man stops us there and tells us to put our arms out while he searches us. Charlie does as he's told—throwing me a look that says *What are you gonna do?*— then it's my turn.

We're clear and we go inside. The senator is in an inner room; I can hear her distinctive voice through the closed door. Then it opens and she comes out and offers me her hand. She looks older than she did back during the campaign: there is gray in the short brown hair and lines around her eyes and mouth. But she still has energy and her grip is strong and warm.

She is talking, saying we're going to do great things together, and how she's glad I made it out of "that hell they're making of our country."

I agree, nodding and smiling. I'm sure my smile looks wrong because inside I'm numb. The senator is saying something about getting my wife and child out of the devil's grip, and I can only nod and say, "Thank you, thank you."

And then it's over. She goes back into the inner room and I hear other voices as the door closes. Charlie touches my arm and says, "That went well. Let's get going."

"Is there a toilet?" I say. "I need to pee." My voice sounds shaky. I clear my throat but it doesn't help.

The man at the door says, "Just go out to the treeline."

I do as he says, going over to where the evergreens start. There is a man with a rifle standing nearby but he turns his back when I pull my zipper down. That is when I undo the button on my jacket, remembering to push in and turn to the right as I do; it's a reverse thread.

The top of the button comes off and the little battery hidden inside it falls into my hand. I use my other hand to lever up the phony hinged rivet on my belt, making a hole exactly the size of the battery. I push the little disk in until it makes contact; then I wait, counting off fifteen seconds.

Now I pry the battery free and put it back in the button and close it up, snap the false rivet back into place. I zip up my fly and turn back to where Charlie waits. I want to get him away from here before the snatch team comes. I can see that there will be shooting and men will die.

"Okay?" he says to me. But before I can answer there are shouts from inside the house. A man comes out holding what looks like a phone, but probably isn't. He is holding it up, pointing it here and there, then looking at its screen and cursing.

Now everybody but Charlie and I are in motion. A knot of men, the senator at their center, come running out of the log house, heading for one of the cars. The guards around the perimeter are at full alert, weapons up, sighting along them, looking for targets.

"You!" shouts the man with the scanner, looking at me. "Stay where you are!"

"What's going—" says Charlie, but that's all there is time for now.

The Hellfire missiles look like two shooting stars coming down from the evening sky, white flame against the yellowy red, trailing ghostly smoke worms.

"Sharon," I say, "I'm sorry."

And then it's all fire.

WE ALL HAVE HEARTS OF GOLD®

Leo Vladimirsky

FROM: Simpson Stevens III (simpy@ThoughtCollective.agency)

TO: The Gang (all@ThoughtCollective.agency)

RE: All Hands on Deck! Cancel your weekend plans...amazing opportunity

DATE: 1/21/21

Gang. Gang...GANG!!!!

Simpy here.

Just got off the phone with...you'll never guess, so I'll just tell you. The president. The actual, motherfucking PRESIDENT of these MOTHERFUCKING UNITED STATES!!!

And he wants to work with us!

Now, before anyone starts getting all big-pants politics with me, just know that I was most definitely "WITH HER" back in 2016 (that feels like a long time ago, doesn't it?) and I voted for Obama both in 2008 and 2012 (before a lot of you were even out of diapers) so my political bona fides don't need any clarifications.

Look, I know that the last four years were weird. I get it. I'm not a monster. We lost a lot of good creatives (and friends) who had to go back home when they lost their visas. We tried like hell to keep 'em, but you can't fight city hall, right? We had to close our Chicago and LA offices after the Vegan bombings (you can thank the opposition for that): how can we keep our country safe if our own people are busy attacking us? (HINT: this brief will help.) And I know that we were all sad to see our offices in Shanghai, London, Paris, Amsterdam, Mumbai, Rome, São Paulo, Mexico City, Toronto, Vancouver, and Tokyo shut.

But we did get to open new spaces in Moscow, Putingrad, and West Virginia. Closing doors, opening windows and all that.

So I do get it. It's been tough. We've had some downs.

But now we've got a big up. A huge up. From way up in the highest place we can imagine.

The.

White.

House.

This is all super-secret, so don't go forwarding this brief to any of your personal email accounts (haha…you can get into a lot of trouble with that, just ask "her," (that is, if you can find her (joking, joking.))

I know some of you will have reservations working on a brief from this administration. I get it. But remember that we are in the business of business, not politics. I'm sure a lot of you don't like to drive (Keith!), but that didn't stop us from kicking ass on the KleanOil brief. Some of you may be vegetarians (I'm talking to you, Laura), but we still killed it for the Pork Belly Council. And Ajaz, I know you don't drink, but you CRUSHED it on the Berry-Boppers Alco-Pop viral video project.

My point is that we can put our personal politics aside and come together to do great things and create huge, award-winning ideas. That's what advertising is all about, kids. And we've been called to do some epic work for maybe the most revolutionary organization to come about in our country. I really think (no, I know) that this project and the work we make has the potential to change the world. Isn't that why we got into this amazing business in the first place?

So look at the brief. Mull it over. Taste it. Feel it. And let's get going bright and early tomorrow: 10 a.m. All hands. All hearts. All minds. All one.

Let's make advertising great again (sorry, I couldn't resist).

Cheers,

Simpy

Simpson Stevens III
Chief Creative Officer, The Thought Collective
NYC // MOSCOW // PUTINGRAD // CHARLESTON

* * *

THOUGHT COLLECTIVE CREATIVE BRIEF

CLIENT: Republican Security Service

DATE: 1/21/21

JOB NO: 61679

CONFIDENTIAL

BACKGROUND

By the beginning of 2019, it was clear that the upcoming presidential election was going to be brutal. Voter fraud, violent demonstrations, intimidation at the polls, and massive demonstrations, long the problem of developing countries, threatened to take our country down. To combat this, the President created the Republican Security Service, a unique public-private partnership between the Department of Homeland Security, local law enforcement, concerned citizens, and private military companies. The RSS kept the peace, brought stability and safety to the American people, and, most importantly, ensured a smooth election.

Consumers recognized the value of the RSS and even gave them a charming nickname—Goldshirts, for the large gold "Trump/MAGA" logos on their uniforms—but worried about their continued presence post-election. Thus, the organization's role and future is uncertain.

WHAT SHOULD THE ADVERTISING DO?

We need to simultaneously celebrate the achievements of the Goldshirts and inspire people to join up. The Goldshirts did a lot of good in the last year. It's time people understood exactly what they stand for and what to expect in the future.

WHO ARE WE TALKING TO?

The American people

WHAT SHOULD THE ADVERTISING SAY?

Goldshirts help make America safe again because they have a Heart of Gold.*

WHY SHOULD I BELIEVE THIS?

The world is full of dangerous dissent and violence. Four years of increasing protests and attacks on the Homeland prove that the administration was doing something right—after all, it's always darkest before the dawn. The Goldshirts helped maintain order and safety during the most contested election in the history of our Republic. They are clearly here for the consumer.

WHAT IS OUR TONE OF VOICE?

Think more Rico from *Starship Troopers* and less "Tomorrow Belongs to Me" from *Cabaret*. Fun, strong, proud, but with a wink.

WHERE WILL OUR MESSAGE LIVE?

This is going to be a full-on blitz: we'll need social media assets, chat-bots, digital, interactive, radio…you name it. But for now, let's focus on a big splashy TV spot to kick the campaign off!

MANDATORIES

Client loves the Goldshirt uniform and feels it really reflects the brand's core values. There's a lot of excitement to see how the color can be expanded throughout the creative.

Let's lean into the Goldshirt moniker and own it: think Avis' "We're number two. We try harder" or Levy's "You don't have to be Jewish to love Levy's Rye."

HEART OF GOLD - 90S TV SPOT

CLIENT: REPUBLICAN SECURITY SERVICE

AGENCY: THE THOUGHT COLLECTIVE

INT. KITCHEN - DAY

A middle-aged MAN and WOMAN, dressed in robes, sit at a dining table, covered in newspapers and mail. They speak to camera.

MAN

Everything is so dangerous these days.

WOMAN

Our very way of life is threatened.

MAN

You can't know who to trust.

WOMAN

That's why we joined the Goldshirts!

MAN and WOMAN remove their robes, revealing
sparkling gold polo shirts and golf pants. The
icon on the shirt is a dramatic silhouette of
Trump.

MAN

And you should, too.

ANNOUNCER (O.S.)

There's finally a way to show the world you
have a heart of gold. Join the Goldshirts
and make America safe again.

EXT. POLLING PLACE - DAY

A line of GOLDSHIRTS block the entrance.

ANNOUNCER (O.S.)

Safe from things like voter fraud.

EXT. PARK - DAY

A large crowd of PROTESTORS wave signs and
chant.

ANNOUNCER (O.S)

Safe from the madness of the mob.

GOLDSHIRTS, on Segways and brandishing bright
gold nightsticks, ride into the crowd.

EXT. STREET - EVENING

The street is busy. Two YOUNG BLACK MEN walk along minding their own business.

                    ANNOUNCER (O.S.)

Safe from the crime that infects our cities.

Fifteen GOLDSHIRTS swarm and surround them.

INT. CLASSROOM

A GIRL stands at the front of the room, reciting from memory.

                         GIRL

    We hold these truths to be self-evident, that all men are created equal. That they are endowed by...

GOLDSHIRTS crash through the windows and throw a gold-colored sack over her head.

                    ANNOUNCER (O.S.)

    Safe from twisted ideologies.

They drag her out of the class.

EXT. PLANNED PARENTHOOD - DAY

A COUPLE walks up to the door.

                    ANNOUNCER (O.S.)

    Safe from dangerous, dehumanizing quackery.

A brilliant gold explosion envelops the building.

INT. LIBRARY

STUDENTS scan the stacks of science journals.

ANNOUNCER(O.S.)

Safe from liberal pseudoscience.

The stacks burst into bright yellow flames and
GOLDSHIRTS run away, cheering.

INT. BATHROOM STALL

A WOMAN sits on the stall, playing solitaire
on her phone.

ANNOUNCER (O.S.)

Safe from perverts.

The door bursts open. GOLDSHIRTS rush in.

INT. SUPREME COURT

Court is in session. The JUSTICES listen to
an argument.

ANNOUNCER (O.S.)

And safe from the most dangerous thing -
the government itself.

Eight GOLDSHIRTS appear suddenly behind the
JUSTICES and strangle them with sparkling
gold garroting wire.

INT. KITCHEN

MAN and WOMAN are polishing their gold
nightsticks.

MAN

I've got a heart of gold.

WOMAN

I've got a heart of gold.

Their SON walks in, dressed in a gold boy scout uniform.

BOY

I wanted to make childhood great again. That's why I joined the Gold Scouts.

They laugh.

MAN

We've all got hearts of gold.

WOMAN points her nightstick directly at the camera.

WOMAN

Do you?

ANNOUNCER (O.S)

Do good. Do gold. Join the Goldshirts today!

NOTES ON RETRIEVING A FALLEN BANNER

Marguerite Reed

Dear Kiddo:

1st off, the moment you read this, destroy it. Burn it, feed it to a hog in the lot, but get rid of it. They've already picked me up; they'd better not get you, too. I can't come back from the dead and take out three more officers. And Aunt Sook has the Sig Sauer—sorry, but she knows how to use it, and you don't. You always told me I over-explained—but this I put off teaching you, and now it's too late.

2nd: Don't go to the storage facility on Spencer Street. They're watching. Or, rather, go ahead and go, but what you'll need isn't there. Nothing illegal is in there, but they'll piss themselves over medical books, the manuals, the expired vitamins. Let them get all excited about that trash. To get my backpack, you'll have to find your cousin Tim and—I know it sounds like a cartoon—give him the password. Do you remember what we called Minji's stuffed cat when she was a baby? That's your password. The username for the station lock is the one your grandmom used in college, apisGarden28. My username, yours, Seedy Chris's, anyone in that circle will trip their bots, and they'll be after you, password or no.

3rd: They only suspect Tim as a racial resister. His past history doesn't mark him as a supporter of women. Don't get me wrong, he doesn't hate them any more than the next man, that's just not where his focus lies. But he's got your back. Trust no one else, okay? No one but Aunt Sook and Tim. Not until you get there, and maybe not even then.

4th: You have to remember they're watching. I can't say it enough. If you think of something, they've thought of that, too; if you do the opposite, they'll expect that. Find a third thing. Do that. Even better, a fourth thing.

5th: Keep your bike in good order. Don't be tempted by cars. Remember, gasoline degrades, so don't expect you can scavenge. I would be really leery about using a public transport permit, even in cases of extreme need. I know you have a burner pass, but some of those buses have cameras.

6th: Don't be afraid to trade sex for favors. If you feel you're in a less-dangerous situation, don't be ashamed to give a handjob or whatever else. You've been vaccinated, so don't let those old ideas of "morality" get to you. Food and shelter are more important than some dusty notion about what you do with your cootch.

7th: Remember talking about that miracle drug? You remember how I said you couldn't get it anymore? Please believe me. Katty answered what she thought was a discreet backnote for period repair pills, met the dealer in a parking lot, and was arrested by jackboots. You know her brains got blown out all over the backseat. You know they said she was reaching for a gun. You tell me how she was reaching for a gun when she was handcuffed? You'll hear people talk wistfully about misoprostol, you'll hear stories about "you remember when," and that's fine—but someone comes to you saying they know where you can get some? Get away from them. Aunt Sook comes up to you talking about getting you some stuff? If it's not parsley tea or vitamin C or black cohosh, she got turned.

8th: No weed before surgery! Not you, them. It's so tempting to tell your patients to smoke half a bowl before they come in, but weed will increase bleeding and drop blood pressure. Getting lidocaine won't trip anyone, because preppers are mad for the stuff. Just check it when you get it—make sure it's not strychnine, PCP, coke, baby powder, rat poison.

9th: We did this so often, remember? All the steps. Speculum—warm the speculum first! The difference in patient perception between a cold speculum and a warm speculum is huge. Betadyne. Local anesthetic. Dilation—ease the dilators, don't force them. If the woman's partner isn't there to hold her hand, get someone to do that. I can't stress this enough. Remember to talk to her. Stay connected. Keep her aware that you're on her side. Don't you ever give her any hint that you're judging her. Before she came to you, the whole country judged her, and when she walks out, she walks out into that sea of judgment once more. She will have to hear it from the internet, from government television and news, from the women's health monitors, from the comments of friends and family. Be a rock for her, when no one else will. Thread the cannula through the cervix. Create the vacuum by pulling back the plunger. Attach the cannula to the aspirator. Release the vacuum lock. Gentle movements of the cannula. Watch blockages—watch sterility of your instruments when you have to stop and clear them out. Remember that gritty feeling! That will tell you you're done. Make sure you got everything. Double check the tissue in the glass pie plate over the light bulb. If she asks, let her see. If she's up to it, point out the parts. This will let her see what was in her and what wasn't, so that she can understand the difference between a baby and an embryo. At this stage a layperson can't eyeball the difference between a cat embryo, a human embryo, or a dolphin embryo.

10th: Without you, Kiddo, without you and the others on this side of the line we drew—hell, your terrified, furious, grieving would-be patient won't need the classic coat hanger, not when she can get a bicycle spoke. A knitting needle. A goose feather. A kabob skewer from the grocery store for less than $5. Does she know that in pregnancy, the uterus softens up like butter? Lying on the bed, or on the hotel room floor on a stack of towels, or squatting in the bathtub—one wrong move—one push a little too far in one direction or another, trying to puncture the amniotic sac, and she's pierced the womb. And she bleeds to death, or she dies of infection, because she can't go to the doctor to get help, or she'll end up in jail and her doctor will, too.

11th: Above all, Kiddo, trust your gut. Don't feel you have to be nice. To anyone. We were nice for decades and decades. Look where it got us, huh? Roe was never touched. It's still the law of the land. But the women coming to see you didn't have a man sign off on their abortion, and now you're charged with first-degree murder. When you pick up my backpack at the station, you become a criminal and a rebel and an outlaw. I will never see you again.

12th: I am so very proud of you.

TICKET TO RIDE

Eric James Fullilove

INTEROFFICE MEMO
International Aid Society of Boise
"No One Is Free Unless We Are All Free"

From: Chett Hightower, CEO

To: All Staff

Date: November 1, 2016

Subject: Preparing for the "Clinton Bounce"

I think we should reflect upon the opportunities the first woman president of the United States (FWPOTUS) is going to create for IASB and others in our field.

Idaho may still go Republican. But the rest of the nation is going to go anti-Trump like nobody's business. I mean, think stampede, rout, ass whipping, whatever.

We should continue working with our Syrian and Somali contacts as well as our field offices in Mexico to ensure that we continue to be "top of mind" for Internally Displaced People (IDPs) wishing to emigrate to America.

Even though I suspect that a few of you are Republican sympathizers, look at it this way. Is there any way the nation that sent the first black president to the White House for two terms could ever vote for Trump?

INTEROFFICE MEMO
International Aid Society of Boise
"No One Is Free Unless We Are All Free"

From: Chett Hightower, CEO

To: All Staff

Date: November 9, 2016

Subject: Singing Old Negro Spirituals Around the Office

I know this is completely unexpected, even for those of you who actually voted for the President-Elect.

We must continue to act like professionals and above all, dare I say it, WHITE PEOPLE, as we adjust to the new realities of a Trump Administration.

We also have to maintain office decorum. We cannot have people roaming the halls wearing black and passing out phone numbers for our Canadian friends.

And we especially cannot have people singing "We Shall Overcome" during staff meetings.

GET A GRIP. And whoever left the flashlight painted black at my office door, not only do I not understand the symbolism, I think we all need to respect the fact that Donald Trump is the legitimate, elected, next president of the United States.

CONFIDENTIAL
INTEROFFICE MEMO
International Aid Society of Boise
"No One Is Free Unless We Are All Free"

From: Chett Hightower, CEO

To: Abdul Jaleel, Head of IT

Date: December 15, 2016

Subject: Russian Hacking of Our Servers

Suggest you prepare evidence that our servers were hacked by Russian/KGB elements that allowed them virtually unlimited access to all applications and files. We should be prepared to disavow any document, email, or file as being "planted" in case the need should arise.

On a personal note, I'm sorry that I suggested you change your name. I now believe your heritage may be useful in case we need a little "plausible deniability" around here.

Let me also reiterate that I appreciate your position concerning the files you found on my workstation labeled "Abdul's Jihadist Comments" and fully understand your decision to delete them.

That just adds to the cover story, right?

Thanks for your support!

INTEROFFICE MEMO
International Aid Society of Boise
"No One Is Free Unless We Are All Free"

From: Chett Hightower, CEO

To: All Staff

Date: January 18, 2017

Subject: "Temporary" Transfers to our Toronto Office

I want to congratulate our Chief Operating Officer, Gigi Beufort, for establishing our newest location in Toronto, eh? Gigi was able to get a sizable piece of prime office park just before prices skyrocketed. We now think that space similar to ours is commanding 2 or 3 times what we're paying.

I am however, troubled by the number of staff wishing temporary transfers to Toronto. To be blunt, I'm not buying ANY chemical dependence issues related to LaBatts or the number of people suddenly parenting hockey "phenoms" playing for the Maple Leafs who need adult supervision.

Let's be real. Transfers to Toronto (ToTs) will be handled based upon the needs of that office.

I have also heard your cynicism about my plan to work virtually from Toronto. Remember, the board approved all Executive Team virtual placements.

And realistically, we may as well acknowledge that helping people ENTER the US is a joke UNLESS they are planning to become day laborers on Trump's Mexican wall.

INTEROFFICE MEMO
International Aid Society of Boise
"No One Is Free Unless We Are All Free"

From: Chett Hightower, CEO

To: All Staff

Date: January 25, 2017

Subject: "Consuelo"

In light of the measures announced today, we have initiated a new project, code named Consuelo, that is to be implemented immediately. Please adhere to the following ASAP:

1. We actively encourage all staff to speak English around the office. In fact, English has always been the official

language of the IASB and we are going to rigorously enforce the policy. Mi casa no es su casa anymore, comprende?

2. We are going to review all I-9 citizenship verification documents to make sure that we have proper papers on everyone. If for some reason your paperwork isn't up to snuff, now might be a good time to go on permanent vacation (and if the namesake of our special project is reading this, I'm quite possibly talking to you, sweetheart).

3. We are obtaining Oval Office funding to investigate illegal voting in the election. Our Unique Selling Proposition is that our extensive work with immigrants totally qualifies us to rat them out for voting scams. (If this stance alarms any of you, I suggest you harken back to that classic Dire Straits tune "Money for Nothing." Wink, wink, and all that.)

4. Previously prohibited hate speech related to immigrants, including such derogatory terms as "wetbacks" or "illegals" is now officially encouraged in all Federal grant applications when placed properly in context, e.g., encouraging the rigorous enforcement of the Administration's rules on illegal immigrants. An example from a recently submitted grant application: "IASB will provide expertise in identifying any wetbacks illegally consuming the ripe fruits of our American society. We will help make America Great (and immigrant-free) Again." This is just an example; I expect you guys to be more creative—nothing is off the table.

INTEROFFICE MEMO
International Aid Society of Boise
"No One Is Free Unless We Are All Free"

From: Chett Hightower, CEO

To: All Staff

Date: April 5, 2017

Subject: Farewell Party for Former Board Member Madeline Albright

It is with mixed emotions that I announce our farewell gala for former US Secretary of State and former Board Member Madeline Albright.

I believe her deportation for having registered as a Muslim in the ICE Muslim Registry is a cautionary tale for us all, and I reiterate my strong statements that the registry is not a platform for political statements of any kind, unless you want to end up in Lahore, Pakistan.

The Gala will be held at the Boise Hilton on Saturday, April 15, 2017 from 7–9 p.m.,to be respectful of Ms. Albright's curfew (assuming she will be allowed to travel to Boise on that date.)

INTEROFFICE MEMO
FAID-Ps of Toronto
"Money Talks, Bullsh*t Walks Back Over the Border in the Rain"

From: Chett Hightower, CEO

To: All Staff

Date: June 22, 2017

Subject: Our New Beginning

It is with great pleasure that I announce that we have repositioned our twenty-two-year-old International Aid agency for the next four years and beyond.

You've seen this coming, people, so let's smack this mother in the ass and get her done, so to speak. We are now called "Formerly American Internationally Displaced People of Toronto, and our new mission is to help everyone seeking to leave America find happiness in Canada and elsewhere. We're still kicking around our motto, but I like the millennial-facing, hip hop–inspired sentiment expressed in one staff submission: "Don't Throw Shade, FAID."

We have already secured cornerstone funding from many prominent American foundations in exchange for subletting them space in our Toronto office park, which, if I may say so, was a truly inspired turn in our Post-Election Strategic Plan from Hell (PESPFH).

We have also secured massive operating funding from the Canadian subsidiaries of the American car companies, partly as a result of our groundbreaking research project entitled "If You Tax It They Will Move." If you recall, this showed that a large number of car-buying Americans were moving to Canada anyway, so the Trump Administration could take their thinly-veiled tax threats and shove them up their keisters.

Lastly, two pieces of creative genius I wanted you to know before we launch them on social media.

First, we have a new jingle. Sung to the tune of "Give Peace a Chance," it's called "Get the Hell Out."

Second, we have a PSA airing soon starring Alec Baldwin from his SNL stage as You-Know-Who, entitled "Make North America Great Again (You Canadian Sons of Bitches)."

While this has been a rocky road, our next report to our board will show that revenue is up three thousand percent, and we've never been busier.

Thanks for your support!

BURNING DOWN THE HOUSE

Ted White

They burned down my block today.

I saw them. They had flamethrowers, big tanks on their backs like backpacks, and black nozzles that spurted flame. I was across the street, just coming home, when I saw them. They were big men, more than a dozen of them, dressed in black. They'd kick in a door and then torch the place. They were efficient, systematic. In less than ten minutes, that whole side of the street was burning.

I ducked into an alleyway on my side of the street. No sense letting them see me. I saw what they did to the people who ran out of the burning buildings or dropped from windows to the street. They shot them. They do that every time they burn a block.

It was all going up in flames—my little hideaway, with my cache of paper books, so very flammable, tucked away in the center of the block. My home.

Suddenly a grimy arm locked around my neck from behind and I felt myself being yanked backward and nearly off my feet.

I thought I recognized the arm—and the smell that enveloped me. It was the smell of primroses.

He pulled me into a narrow doorway and whirled around to close the door with his butt, flinging me loose to stumble toward a dilapidated armchair. I almost sat in it before deciding it probably had bugs.

"Well, missy, there it all goes!" he said, gesturing in the direction of the street. "How long till they do this block, huh?"

Rudolph was a deceptively stringy-looking man, shambling in appearance, but very strong. He could probably pick me up with one arm. He dowsed himself with cheap fragrances because he never bathed.

His little hole was no bigger than mine had been, a roofed-in and closed-off space between two older buildings. It's illegal to do that, but pretty common. I hadn't built mine; I found it. Someone had died there and it had been abandoned and mostly forgotten. I'm not sentimental and I'm not squeamish, so I moved in. Now I'd have to find a new place. But not Rudolph's. Among other reasons, it was too close. Odds were it would be burned next.

Rudolph was giving me the eye.

"Yer a scrawny kid," he told me, "but yer female, and I could use me one."

"In your poppy dreams," I said. A knife appeared in my hand. It had a long blade and I kept it sharp.

"Hey, now," he said, backing away from me. There wasn't much room. "A simple no would do it."

"You got it," I said. "No." I looked around the dimly lit room. Boxes had been piled, on their sides, against all the walls, creating uneven shelves, filled with objects that looked like and probably were scraps, stolen from Dumpsters in the affluent areas – broken appliances, plastic tubs filled with mismatched nuts and bolts, and stuff I couldn't identify. A battered sofa took up one end of the room. I could see it wasn't the kind that opened up. I couldn't imagine sharing it with Rudolph. "You'd have to sleep in the chair," I said.

"Why don't you just get the hell on out, then," he said. "Take your chances with the fire troopers, huh?"

"I think I will," I said, moving to the door. I could see it was made of planks bolted to crosspieces. I recognized the carriage-bolt heads when I opened the door and saw its outer side.

"It's yer mistake, missy," he said as I pulled the door shut.

The alley dog-legged just beyond Rudolph's door, and I moved around the corner quickly. The air was full of smoke, which was a bad sign. The wind could blow embers across the street. This block might be next, and sooner than Rudolph thought. So many old, wooden buildings with tar roofs, crammed together, a tinderbox just waiting for a match. I had to keep going, cross another street, hope for the best.

Dusk was coming. That was both good and bad for me. Good, because I'm stealthy and I can get around without being noticed. Bad, because there's a whole different crew out on the streets after dark, and my chances wouldn't be great if I encountered the wrong people. Normally I'm home, holed up, after dark. Now where would I go?

I decided to head for Hooker Street. That's its real name—I think there was once a General Hooker—but it's now also a good description. I cut through the alleys that snaked through the blocks. I grew up here. I know them all.

I found Jonny. Or maybe he found me. That prosthetic eye of his has some kind of built-in radar, I think.

"Hey, Shivvy," he said from somewhere close behind me. That's his nickname for me, because I'm good with a knife. I didn't jump. I recognized his voice. "Change ya mind?"

I turned to face him. He's a kid, like me – but not very much. Jonny got put through the mill when he was twelve and had to be rebuilt. I used to wonder who paid for it. But I figured the reason he started running girls was to pay it off. He looks almost normal, until you realize that all his uninked skin is fake—and that's his right arm and the right side of his face. Fake skin won't take tats.

"I been looking for you," I said. "They burned my block down. I need a new place."

He grinned at me. "I can fix ya up," he said. "But wha'choo gonna do fer me?"

"I won't cut you," I told him. "How's that?" I smiled back. Two big guys pushed between us as if neither of us were there, heading for the door of a juice house. Jonny in turn ignored them.

"Choo'know," he said, "when ya get ridda that scowl, ya don't look so bad."

"I'm not gonna work for you, Jonny. You know that."

"It won't be work. It'll be fun." He laughed, saw my reaction, and held up his hand. "I'm not asking'choo ta work for me."

"Yeah?"

"Nah. I wan'choo to live with me. Now, hear me out." His face got serious. "I got respect for ya, li'l Shiv. Ya someone I trust wit' my back, you know what I'm saying?" He grasped my arm with his left hand, the real one, and pulled me into a barred doorway. I think we both felt exposed on the street.

"I been thinking about'choo. This fire thing just pushed it together. Ya need a place to stay, and I need ya. Win-win, right?"

"Uh-uh," I said, shaking my head. "Not if you want to sex me."

"Aw, come *on* now," he said, he voice getting all soft and husky, his pimp-voice.

"Not ever," I said. "No. I'm not one of your girls."

"Choo breakin' my heart, girl."

"You got a crib you're not using?" I asked. "Some place I can use for a few days?"

"Then what?"

"Then whatever. I'll move on, quick as I can."

"Choo don't wanna crib," Jonny said, shaking his head. "They trade 'em off, hot beds. One after another. Never empty long." He squeezed his eyes shut to show me he was thinking. "An'choo not willing to get in my bed, so…" He brightened. "How about a rich man?"

I wasn't going to tell Jonny that I'd never let any man get my clothes off, nor any woman either. I never had and I could think of no reason why I ever would. But a rich man…that offered new possibilities.

There are two kinds of people in the world: The rich and the rest of us. I think there's been a genetic drift. I don't think the rich are quite human any more. I think they're a new race.

They think so, too. I can read, and I read a lot. Mostly I read books, which I always picked up wherever I found any, but I'll read anything—even the newscreen captions I spy through windows. And sometimes I sneak into the Closed Zone, where there's free stuff I catch on my tab. I shouldn't have had a tab, of course, and now I don't. It must have been destroyed in the fire. But I had found one somebody lost. They're useless outside the CeeZee except for what you put in the memory, and basically you can't access anything to put in the memory unless you're *in* the CeeZee, so I used to sneak back in for new ebooks when I got bored with the ones I had. Delete a few, add a few—and then make a quick exit before I was noticed by the cybercops.

But I know what the privileged people think. I eavesdrop on them electronically when I can, and I read all I can. Most of what I read is written by them, for them.

They believe they are superior. They talk about breeding a super race. Past tense. Like they're already more highly evolved. So "uber."

Now some of them have decided to get rid of the rest of us. They regard us as vermin, wallowing in filth. They're exterminating us. They're burning us out. But there are a lot of us. It's going to take time.

"They see us as disease-ridden," old Nellie once told me. "Like we ain't healthier than them. But we got immunities. So that's why they use fire and don't let nobody escape. Disease control."

"They shouldn't worry so much about us," I said. "They should worry about the mosquitoes."

"The mosquitoes?"

"They're what carry disease," I told her. "Like, you know, all those viruses. Zika, dengue fever"

"Wassat?"

"Tropical diseases. Now that it's warmer, we got tropical diseases."

"Yeah? You sure know a lot from them books you reading," she said, shaking her head. "But that old-times stuff, that won't do you no good now, here. You gotta get your head outta them books, you want to live to grow up."

She was shot, out on the avenue, by a block cop who was aiming at somebody else, a few months ago. I hadn't thought about her since then. But having your block burned down sharpens the memory, I think.

Jonny's "rich man" was, he said, an infrequent customer, a man who descended from his no-doubt high-rise place in the CeeZee to go slumming in the badlands for some hot sex. I tried to figure out how I could turn him to my advantage.

Actual sex was out of course, but maybe the *lure* of sex? Unfortunately, I don't look much like a street girl. It's not just that I don't dress like them. I'm kind of skinny, narrow-hipped and flat-chested for my age. I'm not pretty. And I wear my hair and clothes so that from any distance you'd take me for a boy. Jonny tells me he thinks that's sexy, but it keeps most of the male predators at bay. Jonny has his own problems.

But Jonny tells me his rich man isn't looking to sex me. He wants to meet me because Jonny told him I read a lot.

"What is he, some kind of kinky?" I asked.

"He's smart. And he reads, too."

And, when I met him, he was nothing like what I expected.

We met in an eatery tucked behind a fight club, Jonny introducing us. I was impressed with Jonny, being able to get in touch so quickly with his rich man, and setting things up right away. It was possible I might have a place to sleep tonight. Well, there's always *somewhere* to sleep, but I sleep better when there are no rats sniffing around me. But I should have considered the implications of this speedy meeting.

"Don'choo let her looks fool ya, Doc," Jonny said.

What I wondered was how the looks of this rich guy—Dr. Jones, if you can believe that—would affect me. He was about six and a half tall, somewhere north of his youth, but still very fit, very toned. He looked like a Greek god, or maybe a media star. He had curly blond hair and penetrating blue eyes. I thought he was gorgeous and wondered if that made him a real threat.

We got soy burgers. Jones only had one bite of his, so I finished it off after I'd wolfed mine. I hadn't eaten since morning.

He said he'd been looking forward to meeting me, ever since Jonny had mentioned me—he didn't say how or why my name had come up. "I'm really delighted," he said to me across the tiny table.

"Why?" I asked. "What am I to you?"

"Well, you're literate, for one thing—you read."

"Plenty of people read," I said.

"How many people do you know," he asked me, "who actually read for pleasure, who *enjoy* reading?"

I glanced at Jonny. He looked uncomfortable. "Not many," I admitted. "But how many do *you* know?"

Jones grinned. "Touché," he said. "I think it's a dying art—writing, especially. Literature. Do you write?"

"Me?" I'd never thought of it. I shrugged. "What would I write about?"

"Your life?" he responded. "Anything you know. Anything you care about."

"I cared about my home," I said. "They burned it down today."

A look that might have been real concern passed briefly over his face. "I'm sorry about that," he said. "Maybe I can help you there."

I folded my arms and pulled them close, and I think that told him something, so he changed the subject.

"The reason I wanted to meet you—I'd like to give you some tests."

"Why? What kinda tests?"

"Well, let's just say that I've been in a dispute with some of my colleagues and I think you can help me prove my point." He picked up a slim case from near his feet. He opened it and removed a large e-tablet. "Just a few basic tests—IQ, aptitude…"

"You want me to take these tests *here*?"

He looked up and took in his surroundings, maybe for the first time. He shrugged and smiled thinly. "Maybe not," he said. He turned to Jonny. "You got some place that's quieter, a little more private?"

Jonny shook his head. "Not less ya wanna try a juice house, hope nobody's got bad juice, havin' a fit."

I frowned and Jones said, "I guess not. Okay, let's go uptown." He packed his tab and stood up. He towered over us. Jonny's not much taller than me.

"Uptown," I said, "where uptown? How?"

Jones gave me a very boyish grin. "You ask a lot of questions, don't you? I've got a car that'll pick us up. We'll go to my place."

"In the CeeZee?"

"Of course."

"You don't need me," Jonny said. I figured he'd collect his payment later, if it hadn't been upfront. He pushed his chair back, one leg catching on the rough-planked floor, and stood. "I'll see ya, li'l—" he broke off, maybe not wanting to use his pet name for me in front of Jones. "See ya 'round, Nik," he said, and left me with Jones.

It didn't bother me. I didn't need Jonny for protection. I knew I could handle Jones. He still hadn't told me why he wanted to test me.

When we got out to the street, there was a black car waiting, all polished and gleaming in the scattered lights, the windows mirrored. Nobody was near it, which struck me as odd, until I saw a juicehead wobble up to it and start to lean against it. There was a visible spark and a yelp and the juicehead staggered quickly away from the car.

Jones said, "The car's protected," and worked his remote, springing the doors open. "Get in," he said, gesturing. "It won't bite."

As I got into the car he went around to the other side and got in next to me. He touched a button on the dash and the doors closed. The car pulled out from the curb, executed a neat U-turn, and headed for an avenue uptown.

No one could see in, but we could see out. Not easily, though. From the inside the windows looked tinted, darkened, so that only bright lights could really be seen—and there weren't many of them left on the avenue. Most had been vandalized years ago, the remaining streetlights bunched together along short stretches in "good" neighborhoods. There were few other lights. Shop owners and residents alike were stingy with their electricity.

Fortunately, the car didn't need light to go where it was programmed to go.

"This is pretty neat," I said. "I never been in one of these."

"Really? It's just a car."

"To you, maybe."

He gave me a searching look in the car's dim interior light, like he couldn't figure me out. That was all right. I hadn't figured him out, either.

Jones leaned toward me. "Why do you always wear that fierce look? Do you ever smile?"

"What do I have to smile about?" I pressed my back against the door.

He shrugged. "I don't know, but life has many little pleasures. Riding in this car, perhaps?"

"Okay." I let my face relax into a small smile. "How's that? For your car."

"Much better," he said. "Makes you look cuter."

"I don't want to look cuter."

"No? You're a girl. You *need* to look cuter, be attractive. It's going to be your stock in trade, when you're grown up."

I lost the smile. What kind of advice was that—from a *doctor*?

He changed the subject. "How old do you think I am?"

"I don't know. Older than me. What? Forty maybe?" That seemed like a safe and maybe flattering guess. Younger men like to be taken for five to ten years older. But I was wrong.

Jones chuckled. "In a sense, you're right. That's the target age for my treatments. Actually, I'm eighty-six. You couldn't guess, could you?"

"Is this another test?"

He laughed. "I've got the body and, um, the stamina of a forty-year-old man." He seemed to smile and laugh a lot. "And the wisdom and experience of an older man."

I wondered what he was selling, and hoped it wasn't what I thought.

"What kind of a name is Jones? Is that your real name?"

"Why do you ask? Do you think it isn't?"

"Jones—Smith—" I said. "Bogus names, scam artist names. Meet mister Smith, wink-wink." What I didn't say was that half of Jonny's customers were Smith or Jones. I'd made a natural assumption.

"Well, it's the name I was born with. And there are lots of real Smiths and Joneses, you know. Common names, really."

"Okay, so what's your first—"

I was interrupted. Somebody shot at us in one of the unlit patches. I heard a bell-like sound from the left front fender, and a moment later another bullet hit the window next to Jones' head with a thwack. The window didn't break. It just grew a scar. "Don't worry," Jones told me. "The car's armored—bulletproof." I didn't relax until we got to the next stretch of lights.

That was my mistake, and I was caught off guard when the car suddenly leapt into the air and came down on my side, skidding to a quick stop, dumping Jones on me, half-crushing me, my ears still ringing from the explosion. It had to have been right under the car when it went off. I wondered if it had been in the street or attached to the underside of the car.

Jones stepped on me with a muttered apology as he attempted to stand up. He threw himself, shoulder first, against what had been the floor in front of his seat. I had no idea what he was doing until the car teetered on its rounded side and fell back onto its wheels, rocking on its springs. I fell back into my seat and Jones caught himself before he fell on his face into his.

He seated himself and we exchanged looks. "You okay?" he asked.

"Sure. You?"

"A little battered. Nothing serious."

I looked out my window. "Company," I said. A group of four or five men were converging from the darkness. They were carrying big pry-bars, the kind you can use to bash someone's head in. They looked purposeful. Not random sightseers, curious about the explosion.

"Let's see if this thing still works," Jones said, and punched a button on the dash. The nearest man swung his pry-bar at my window, but it bounced off, leaving no mark, and the car didn't give him a second chance. Tires chirping, it scooted us up the avenue.

"This is a rough area," Jones said, looking back at the frustrated attackers as they disappeared, abandoning the road as quickly as they'd appeared in it.

"They're *all* rough areas, until you're in the CeeZee," I told him. "What did you expect?" I retracted its blade and put my knife away.

"I'm not usually down here after dark," he said. He hadn't noticed the knife.

"No kidding," I said.

We came to another burning block. The car plowed through the smoke without slowing. "Why do your people do that?" I asked. "Set fires."

"My people? I don't know what you're talking about. Those fires are caused by the deplorable conditions in which some people live. I'm amazed they haven't burned the whole city down by now. I guess we have the firefighters to thank for that."

I stared at him, incredulous. "Firefighters?" I said. "You see any firefighters back there? You see anybody trying to put out that fire?"

"It was too smoky to see anything back there," he said, turning around to peer out the back window too late.

"Let me tell you something," I said. "I watched the fires being set on my block. Big men, in black uniforms, with flamethrowers. And you know what they did when people tried to get out, escape the fire?"

"What?"

"They shot them. Killed them, those who weren't killed by the fire. Who do you think they were working for?"

"I don't know," Jones said, shaking his head. "It certainly wasn't me."

Twice the car turned off the avenue to take side streets to a parallel avenue. Jones said some kind of problems forced the detours. "It's all automatic. The car knows. I don't."

"So, okay," I said after the second detour, "why do you want to give me those tests? What're you trying to prove?"

"Well," he said, "I don't know what you know about the One Percent, but we are not monolithic. We don't all think alike. We have disagreements, even controversies."

I shrugged. "Like everyone else, huh?"

"Pretty much."

"But you guys don't think you're like everyone else though, do you?"

"What do *you* know about that?" His tone became sharp.

"I *read*, you know," I said, folding my arms again.

"Right. Well, I've gotten into a disagreement with several of my colleagues. It's about human intelligence."

"Which side are you on? Race-based intelligence quotients, or—"

His mouth fell open.

"It's not a new argument," I told him. "Goes back centuries."

He closed his mouth and then opened it again to say, "You're quite right. But our argument isn't over racial variations in IQ—an old and pretty dead issue, really. Our argument is different and concerns the growing genetic gap between the One Percent and the, um, others—between me and you." He gestured at each of us in turn.

"A genetic gap? Can we still crossbreed?" I let a trace of sarcasm creep into my voice.

Color rose in his face. "It's—not that great a gap," he said. "Not yet."

"So—?"

"So I think you're as intelligent as most of us—in the One Percent, I mean. I want to prove it."

"You must know you'll lose," I told him. "You think I'm an idiot."

He stared at me, his mouth working, no words coming out.

"You know one high-scoring IQ from my side of the fence means nothing. You know it's statistically worthless—no matter how high I tested it wouldn't win your argument for you. You know that. And I know that. Maybe I'd ace your tests, but so what? You know I like to read, so you think I must be smart? How smart does that make *you*?" I felt my voice rising, and I stopped. I shouldn't have said a single word. I realized that, too late to take any of them back. So I leaned back against my side of the car and glared at him.

"What do you *really* want from me?" I asked, finally breaking the silence.

The car's interior was only lit with little glowing lights on the dash, so it was hard to make out Jones' expression when he said, "I'll explain it to you upstairs. We're here."

I hadn't been paying attention. We'd entered the CeeZee without my noticing the brighter lights and cleaner streets. Now the car pulled into a building entrance, a portico just off the street. Jones did something and both doors swung open. Warily, I climbed out.

He took my arm gently and led me through the big, bank-vault doors, through an air lock–like vestibule, and into the building's lobby.

As we went through the first doors I glanced back at the car. My side was scraped up and dented. "What about your car?" I asked.

He laughed. "It's not my car. It's a public car."

I didn't know what that meant. "Won't somebody get mad about the damage?"

"No, it's pretty much expected now—when they're taken out of this zone."

The lobby surprised me. I'd expected better. It was all chrome or maybe stainless steel and glass and it probably looked really good fifty or a hundred years ago. Now, like its faded carpet, it looked almost shabby and it smelled musty.

Jones hurried me through the lobby to a bank of elevators. The door to one of them opened as we approached. We entered, the door closed, and we started up. I've been in elevators before and I looked without success for the floor buttons, or even a floor indicator. Nothing. Just smooth paneled walls and a glowing ceiling.

Jones saw me turning around, scanning the elevator's blank interior, and chuckled. "It knows me automatically and it knows where to take us."

"What if you wanted to visit someone else?" I asked.

"I have a remote," he said, as if that answered everything. Maybe it did. But I felt a stab of fear, the kind a trapped animal feels.

The elevator stopped and the door opened onto a clean undecorated corridor. Jones led me down the plain but well-lit hallway to one of the unmarked doors we were passing, and when he stepped up to it, it opened.

"How'd you know which door was yours?"

"I've lived here a long time. And of course only this door opens for me."

Inside his apartment things were very different. In a curious way I was reminded of Rudolph's place. Both were full of stuff and dimly lit. Jones' stuff was undoubtedly better and on nice built-in shelves, but it still amounted to clutter. And instead of Rudolph's cheap fragrances, this place had a cinnamon-incense odor—pleasant, but odd.

I turned slowly around as I took in the big room, finally coming to the shelves on the wall that had been behind me as I'd walked in.

Books! Lots of books! More than I'd ever seen in one place, a whole wall of books, floor to ceiling, the shelves even running over the door, and the ceiling more than nine feet high. I saw a funny-looking ladder, its top resting on wheels that ran in a track along an upper shelf. Handy. It was hard to read any of the books' spines in the dim light, so I couldn't tell what they were about—but there were so many! For that moment I completely forgot Jones.

A stab of adrenaline brought me back to reality. All those books were great, but I had walked into a chrome-and-glass trap, with no way to get out on my own. I shouldn't let myself be distracted. I slipped my hand into my pants and fingered my knife for reassurance.

It was a big, irregular room, with alcoves, heavily draped windows, and doors to other rooms, and filled with things. There was a lot of furniture—upholstered easy chairs and lounge-recliners, a big L-shaped couch that could seat half a dozen, and little tables scattered between the chairs. Standing on pedestals were an ancient suit of armor that looked like it might have been worn by somebody my size, and a bigger space suit, probably a replica, but maybe real. It was white, but looked grimy, the face plate fogged.

Then I saw her. She was standing in an alcove, shadowed, and looking directly at me. She didn't move. She was dressed as I was, her hair short and uneven, a small cowlick falling over her forehead, a sullen look on her narrow face.

I turned and stared at Jones. "That's me."

He grinned at me. "A hologram. I shot it when we came in."

"Why? What're you doing with it?"

"I don't know. I haven't thought about it."

"Is that why you brought me here?"

"Of course not. It's just a memento, something to remember you by."

"I think it's creepy."

I walked over to it. It continued to stare coldly at me. I reached out to touch it, but my hand passed right through the image, like it was a ghost. Maybe it was. Maybe it was my ghost.

Jones opened a refrigerated cabinet and removed two glass bottles. "Something to drink?"

"What is it?" I asked. I couldn't make out the labels on the bottles.

"Just water," he said, twisting off their caps and pouring one with each hand into two tall glasses.

"It's green," I pointed out. "And fizzy."

"Vitamin water," he said. "A little flavor, a little color, and some carbon dioxide for the bubbles." He set down the empty bottles and handed me a glass. "Cheers," he said, and took a sip from his glass.

It was cold and didn't have much flavor. I'd once had something called club soda, which was just carbonated water, and this wasn't very different. I was thirsty, so I drank the glassful in several swallows, and burped.

Jones had gotten out his tab again, and I could see the first page of the IQ test on it—multiple choice, five choices per question, just touch the correct answer.

"I'm tired," I said. "I don't want to do that." And I realized that I really *was* tired. I couldn't smother a major yawn.

"I'm sorry," Jones said. "It *is* pretty late. Sometimes I forget the time when I get into a project." He gestured at the test. "This can wait for morning. Let me show you a room where you can sleep."

Vague alarm spread through me, but I felt foggy with fatigue. I couldn't stop yawning. I followed him through several doors to a small room with a single bed. He didn't turn on any lights in the room, but I could see the bed in the light from the doorway, and I went straight for it and collapsed on it, facedown.

Sunlight on my face woke me up. I was lying on my back, under covers, in a girl's bedroom. I knew immediately it had to be. Everything was in bright cheerful colors, and stuffed animals sat in a small easy chair across from the bed. My clothes were tossed over them. I did not remember taking them off.

The bedroom door was closed. I scrambled out of the bed and then stopped, transfixed by the sight of the sheet I'd been lying on. It was blood-smeared in one area, in the middle of the bed.

I looked and found a little dried blood on my upper inner left thigh.

I knew exactly what that meant.

I started for the door and then stopped and turned back to my clothes. I needed to get dressed first. I ached in a new place as I pulled my clothes on. They smelled, but they were all I had now.

I couldn't help looking out the window. It faced east and the early sun. I was high up and I could look out great distances, but I couldn't see much—just the vast city extending into the haze, the horizon indistinct. There were other tall towers nearby, and I could tell that they defined the area of the CeeZee.

The bedroom door wasn't locked. I opened it and ventured out, not sure which way to go. But I found the next door I came to was to a bathroom, which I realized I needed. I went in and locked the door behind me.

It was spare but had all the necessities. I showered thoroughly, after which putting my clothes back on again felt disgusting. I examined myself while I sat on the toilet, but learned nothing new. Finally I wiped the steam off the mirror and stared at myself. Did I look different now? The hologram's twin stared back at me. If I did, it wasn't obvious.

When I opened the bathroom door I found myself face to face with Jones.

"Hi. Sleep well? Ready for breakfast?"

I just stared at him. He looked unchanged, still the Greek god, his hair a little tousled, morning-fresh, a dimpled smile for me.

"You drugged me," I said. Start small and work up, I decided.

"Just a mildly opiated relaxant, same as I had," he said.

"Why lie about it? We both know what you did."

I waited for him to deny it, but he just smiled, as if dismissing my accusation, and said, "Come on. Let's eat. Let's get some food in you. The way you ate those burgers, I'll bet you don't eat well. You need to put a little flesh on your bones." He turned and casually walked down the hall, almost sauntering, like he hadn't a care in the world, leaving me to follow.

Put a little flesh on my bones, huh? He'd seen my scrawny body naked and didn't care that I knew it. *He exposed his back to me*, I thought. *He's a fool.*

Unwillingly, I followed him into his dining room. It was a relatively small room—but bigger than the bedroom I'd used—dominated by a large table in the middle. A chandelier hung over the table and cast a warm light. There were chairs along the walls and one already pulled up to the table.

He swung out another, placing it next to his, but I ignored the gesture and went to the other side of the table, opposite him, and pulled up a chair. We both sat, facing each other, Jones with a shrug and a disarmingly rueful smile.

"What would you like for breakfast?" he asked.

"Whatever you're having," I said.

"Okay," he said. He reached into his pocket and pulled out a slim black object, putting it on the table. While he held it in place with his left hand, he jabbed his middle right-hand finger at it repeatedly, then stopped. He looked up at me. "On the way," he said genially. He put the black thing back in his pocket.

A discreet chime sounded. Jones rose and went to a cabinet on the wall behind him. When he opened it I could see two plates of food sitting there. A mouth-watering aroma wafted out with the steam. I realized how hungry I was.

Jones set one plate in front of me and one at his place and turned back to get two cups of what smelled like first-rate coffee. I stood up and reached across the table to swap our plates.

He saw me doing it and laughed heartily. I was starting to truly hate his laughter. "They're exactly the same," he said, still laughing at me. "I don't care which one I have." And to prove it, he picked up a fork and took his first bite of his eggs.

A large omelet, slices of toast, sausages, coffee—it was a decent breakfast and I ate all of it. I also drank all my coffee, after switching cups while Jones watched, grinning. I drank it black because Jones did.

When I put down my fork on my empty plate he asked me, "Feeling better now? How about a smile?"

"I'm no longer hungry," I said, "but I don't feel like smiling at you."

"You did last night," he said with a twinkle in his eye.

"What are you talking about?"

"Last night. I made you happy then."

I pushed to my feet, the chair catching on the rug and falling over. I didn't care. "You miserable smug bastard!" I glared at him. "You raped me. You *raped* me!"

"I didn't," he said, shaking his head but still smiling. "You loved it. I had trouble keeping *up* with you. *So* demanding!"

I stared at him. I couldn't believe his gall, his calm denial.

"What's the matter? Didn't I measure up to your usual lovers? You told me I was better than Jonny." The words seemed to ooze out of him.

"You lie," I told him. "You drugged me and you raped me. You are the first man to ever sex me."

His mouth dropped open, the phony smile gone at last.

"Your first?" A sly look spread across his face. "You were a virgin? Delightful! Well, good thing that's behind you now. You should thank me. You *will* thank me."

I sighed. A total disconnect. I picked up the chair and returned it to its spot at the wall.

"I started to ask you last night—in the car," I said. "What's your first name?"

"My first name? Euclid. Euclid Jones." He mock-bowed. "At your service. And yours is Nicole, isn't it?"

He seemed happy with the change of subject. Like what he had done to me the night before had no consequences, no real meaning. And like my moving on to something totally different was the most natural thing in the world. I felt cold inside.

"No. Jonny told you, but you got it wrong. It's Nikola. Do you—did you have a daughter?"

"Why do you ask?"

"That room, that was a girl's room."

He gave me a lazy smile. "It *is* a girl's room."

"Whose?"

"It could be yours. Think about it. You said you needed a place." He gave me a considering look. "We'll have to get rid of that body hair—your underarms, your legs…"

I didn't want to go there. "How many of those books have you read?" I gestured through the doorway to his big front room.

"Most. Well, some. I inherited them with the apartment." Another smile. "I'll call you Nicky."

"Show me. I love books." Nobody calls me Nicky.

He led the way to the front room and the books. "What would you like to see?"

I looked around and noticed his tab where he'd left it the night before. The display screen was blank. No more IQ test. No longer needed, I guessed.

"What's up there?" I gestured at the upper shelves, which held fat volumes that looked like sets of books, uniformly bound.

"Let's see," he said, sliding the ladder over to the area I'd pointed out, and mounting it with lithe grace, totally confident of himself.

I waited until he was reaching to his right to pull free a book, complaining that these books were wedged in and hard to pull out, leaning over the edge of the ladder. Then I yanked the ladder hard to his left.

As I'd hoped, he lost his balance, dropping the book to the floor, flailing with his arms and falling. What I hadn't expected was that his left leg got entangled with the ladder, between the rungs, causing him to hit the floor head first with a solid thud.

I approached him with my knife out. His leg was still hooked in the ladder, his head and shoulders on the floor. His head seemed to be at an awkward angle.

His eyes followed me, but the rest of him didn't move.

I nudged his body with my foot. No resistance, limp.

"I think you broke your neck. What do you think?"

He blinked at me, rapidly. Then a tear formed at the corner of his left eye. His lips seemed to quiver, but no words came out. He was breathing shallowly.

"I can't leave you like this," I told him.

He blinked slowly.

I gestured with my knife. "I'm gonna have to kill you," I said. "That was my intention anyway."

His lips opened, formed an O.

"Why? You're wondering why I want to kill you?" I laughed, a short humorless bark. The first and last time he would hear me laugh.

"I want to kill you because you're such a clueless arrogant fool."

He blinked several times.

"I want to kill you because you're the enemy—an enabler of the fire troopers, a user of girls."

I wanted him to argue with me, to defend himself, to justify himself, but he said nothing. Not even his lips moved now. But he was looking directly at me, giving me his full attention.

"But most of all I want to kill you because you stole from me the only thing I had left that I valued. *You raped me.* And you didn't even care." I wanted to work myself up into a rage, but instead I felt a cold knot forming within me.

He closed his eyes—in resignation? In defeat?

"Open your eyes, damn you!"

His lips compressed and his eyes stayed shut. Denying me to the end.

I slit his throat and watched his blood and his last breaths gurgle out and then stop.

It was strangely unsatisfying. I knew I had done what I had to do, but I didn't feel triumphant. I felt defeated.

I sat down in one of the big chairs and cried. That didn't make me feel much better, but gave me the necessary resolve to finish what I'd started.

I went through his pockets until I found his remote, that black object. It felt oddly comfortable in my hand, like it had been molded to fit it, and I guess it had.

I looked over at the alcove. My hologram was still there, still watching me.

"One of us is damned," I said. I looked at Jones' remote. There were a variety of buttons of different sizes, shapes, and colors. Some had letters or numbers. Some had pictograms. One showed a dotted stick figure. I touched it. The hologram disappeared. Satisfied, I stowed the remote in my pants.

Then I started pulling the books off the shelves, dumping them in a growing pile on the floor, fallen open, any which way. This felt sacrilegious to me until I realized that none of these books called out to be read. They were dusty and old, with fine print and dull titles. None seemed to be fiction. I doubted Jones had looked at even one. The book he'd pulled out was titled *Greek Rural Postmen and Their Cancellation Numbers.* Another was about "stray shopping carts," whatever they might be. I grabbed them with a growing frenzy. They made a huge pile on the floor before I'd pulled half of them off the shelves.

I stopped then, my heart pounding. I was feeling a touch of hysteria. I needed to calm myself. I had to act deliberately, think things through—although I'd made my plans hours earlier and I knew what I had to do.

All those books! My breath caught in my throat as I considered my plan for them. The air was full of dust now. I'd never thought of myself as a book burner.

I went to the front door. When I was only two steps away, it silently unlatched and stood ajar a few inches. Okay. I'd needed to know that, be sure of that. I couldn't allow myself to be trapped in Jones' apartment. As I'd hoped, his remote worked automatically for doors, and, I assumed, the elevator.

I went back to the pile of books. Some of them had fallen on and around Jones. That gave me an idea, and I stacked more of them on him. "Because you really loved books," I muttered at him. Was there anything he *hadn't* lied about?

I used my lighter to start the fire, near the base of the books. It would be his funeral pyre, I figured.

I waited until the fire was well established and it was getting smoky, making me cough and my eyes tear up. I wanted to stay longer and see the fire grow, but I knew I shouldn't.

A drop of water hit me on my head. Startled, I looked up. In the center of the high ceiling was a knob. Water was dripping from it. I suddenly realized what it was—a sprinkler, activated by the fire. But water wasn't spraying out. It was dribbling. More drops fell on me and I caught one in my hand. It was dark-colored, and when I let it run off my hand it left behind tiny flakes of rust. The sprinkler head must have been clogged up. It served Jones right, I thought, for living in such an old building.

I couldn't wait any longer. I went out into the hallway and pulled the door shut. I could still smell the smoke when I got to the elevators, but then the elevator door opened and I escaped that floor.

The remote got me back to the lobby and out the doors without incident. I saw two women in the lobby, coming in. One of them gave me an odd look, but they continued past me. I looked like some street kid, but I was leaving. I was no threat.

Out on the street, I crossed the avenue and looked back and up. I was facing west and the late morning sun gleamed brightly in reflections from the building's glass outer walls, which seemed to ripple. The building was over a hundred floors tall. I had no idea where to look, but just then I heard a faint explosion and then the much closer sounds of glass hitting the pavement and high up I saw a thin plume of black smoke that got bigger as I watched. I didn't watch long.

I still had unfinished business.

Big Lou was lounging in Jonny's place when he let me in. She took one look at me and got up and left.

"Hey, girl," Jonny said when I came in. "How'd it go? Ya do good?"

"I'm here, aren't I?"

"That Doc is somethin' else, ain't he?"

"He is now," I said.

"I knew'choo comin' back to me," Jonny said, purring. "That Doc, he showed ya the error of ya ways, now he broke ya in, made'choo a woman."

"That what you wanted, Jonny? For him to—how'd you put it?—break me in?"

He grinned, full of himself. "I knew, once ya broke yer cherry, ya'd get over being like that. I got big plans for ya. This yer new home, li'l Shiv."

"I'd like that," I said, cuddling up to him. I reached into my pocket and pulled out the remote. "Of course, I could live uptown."

Jonny's eyes narrowed. "Wassat? Where ya get it?"

"This?" I gave Jonny one of my rare smiles. "Oh, this is just a little thing I picked up. Jones called it his remote. You ever see one before?"

"A remote? Sure. But the Doc? Don't he need it—?"

I watched the expressions chase themselves across his face as I said, "Not anymore, he doesn't."

His expression settled into anguish. "You didn't—"

"What did you think I'd do? The bastard raped me. Drugged and raped me. No man does that."

"You did him?"

"And set his place on fire. Poetic justice. Burned him out."

"Gawd," Jonny said. "I never thought—"

I interrupted him. I slid the blade of my knife—which I'd taken out while distracting him with the remote—into his side, just under his rib cage. He didn't have his protective vest on, relaxed in his own place. The knife is very sharp and I don't think he even felt it at first. Then I twisted it viciously, rotating it and scrambling his insides.

Jonny gave me a look of disbelief and great disappointment, opened his mouth and coughed out blood. He tried to pull away from me, but he didn't hit me or try to attack me.

I told him I was sorry, and I really was. We'd shared a lot together, grown up together. "I knew you got money from Jones for me, for connecting us up. But you shouldn't have sold me out, Jonny. You knew what he was going to do. You *wanted* him to. You betrayed me."

I'm not sure he heard that last. His eyes got a glassy look and he folded over on himself, clutching his gut, doubled up.

He didn't make much of a mess. I got it cleaned up. Then I thoroughly searched his place and found his money stash. I used very little of it to pay two juiceheads to take his body out and dump it in an alleyway. I knew it would be found first by the locals, and what it would tell them.

I've taken over his place. I live there now. It's better than my old place—there's electricity for one thing—but he had no books. I'm going to have to start a new collection.

He did have a newscreen. I turned it on and watched a report on the fire and murder uptown. Tiny surveillance holos of me with

Jones in the big lobby, and me by myself leaving. I looked like a boy, and that's who they think it was. Apparently Jones had brought boys up to his apartment before. Both boys and girls. I was far from his first victim, but I didn't find that news reassuring.

I'm running Jonny's girls now. Big Lou has been a real help. It's not the life I wanted for myself, but you take what you can get and I need to survive.

I guess I'm really grown up now. Next week I turn fifteen.

DANGEROUS

Lisa Mason

From: mary.magdelaine@rov.gov

To: [redacted]

Date: 1/21/2019 7:56:21 A.M. Eastern Daylight Time

Subject: Your Registration

[NOTICE: This communication is in accordance with U.S.C. Title
70 Section 100(1)(A), the Americans Registration Online Act
(AROA).]

Dear Mrs. Eames:

Our records at the Registry of Vaginas indicate that you have
not yet registered your vagina as required by U.S.C. Title 69 Section
666(a)(1), enacted by Congress and signed into law by the administration in 2018.

You are required to register your vagina unless you qualify
under one of three exemptions:

(1) You are a man.

(2) You are dead.

(3) Other.

Please note that failure to comply may result in a fine of up to $10,000 and/or incarceration for a felony, if convicted, in a federal maximum security prison.

I've attached the registration form for your convenience.

Thank you for your cooperation.

Mary

mary.magdelaine@rov.gov

From: : [redacted]

To: mary.magdelaine@rov.gov

Date: 1/21/2019 4:59:46 A.M. Pacific Daylight Time

Subject: Re: Your Registration

Hi Mary.

Bugger off.

And it's MS. Eames to you.

Have a nice day.

From: mary.magdelaine@rov.gov

To: [redacted]

Date: 1/21/2019 8:10:12 A.M. Eastern Daylight Time

Subject: Re: Your Registration

Dear Ms. Eames:

I apologize for addressing you by an incorrect legal status. Our records indicate that you are married to David John Eames. If you will take the time to review the attached form for filing with the Registry of Vaginas, you will note that there are three exemptions under which a legal spouse is not required to co-sign your registration:

(1) The legal spouse no longer has access to your vagina.
(2) The legal spouse is dead.
(3) Other.

Please note that failure of you and your legal spouse to comply may result in the hefty fine and possible jail time I mentioned. I'm not kidding.

May I ask why you are being so recalcitrant about a simple registration with the Registry of Vaginas, which, as I have clearly stated, is required by the federal government?

Mary

mary.magdelaine@rov.gov

From: : [redacted]

To: mary.magdelaine@rov.gov

Date: 1/21/2019 5:30:27 A.M. Pacific Daylight Time

Subject: Re: Your Registration

WHY?
Why do I need to register my vagina?
Just askin'.

From: mary.magdelaine@rov.gov

To: [redacted]

Date: 1/21/2019 8:45:32 A.M. Eastern Daylight Time

Subject: Re: Your Registration

Because vaginas are secretive.
Secret.

They are hidden. Hidden from plain view.

They may do things that society disapproves of. You never know what they're up to.

Vaginas have a mind of their own.

From: [redacted]

To: mary.magdelaine@rov.gov

Date: 1/21/2019 6:05:10 A.M. Pacific Daylight Time

Subject: Re: Your Registration

Vaginas have a mind of their own?
LOL!

From: mary.magdelaine@rov.gov

To: [redacted]

Date: 1/21/2019 9:12:42 A.M. Eastern Daylight Time

Subject: Re: Your Registration

Well, yeah. Don't you think?
Hasn't your vagina ever made you do things you later thought better of?
Vaginas are dangerous.

From: j.j.k.eames@gmail.com

To: : [redacted]

Date: 1/21/2019 6:20:32 A.M. Pacific Daylight Time

Subject: Re: Your Registration

Dangerous!
Don't you think you're exaggerating?

From: mary.magdelaine@rov.gov

To: : [redacted]

Date: 1/21/2019 9:25:14 A.M. Eastern Daylight Time

Subject: Re: Your Registration

Am I?
Where was your vagina on January 21, 2017, for instance?

From: [redacted]

To: mary.magdelaine@rov.gov

Date: 1/21/2019 6:40:17 A.M. Pacific Daylight Time

Subject: Re: Your Registration

Lemme think.
That was the first Women's March after the inauguration,
right?
Pink caps with cat ears?
I was sick in bed with the worst flu I've ever had. Gunk in the
sinuses. Coughing up pieces of my lungs. Shivers with six sweaters
on. Then there was the—

From: mary.magdelaine@rov.gov

To: [redacted]

Date: 1/21/2019 9:40:18 A.M. Eastern Daylight Time

Subject: Re: Your Registration

No.
We checked.
You used your Bank of America Visa at Whole Foods that day.
Just a block away from the march around Lake Merritt.

You were there.
Maybe you marched, too?

From: [redacted]

To: mary.magdelaine@rov.gov

Date: 1/21/2019 6:55:18 A.M. Pacific Daylight Time

Subject: Re: Your Registration

No way.
I was sick in bed with the flu, I tell you.

From: mary.magdelaine@rov.gov

To: [redacted]

Date: 1/21/2019 9:55:02 A.M. Eastern Daylight Time

Subject: Re: Your Registration

You bought half a pound of coho salmon and a bottle of Cakebread chardonnay.
How else would you know about the caps with the ears?

From: [redacted]

To: mary.magdelaine@rov.gov

Date: 1/21/2019 7:02:02 A.M. Pacific Daylight Time

Subject: Re: Your Registration

The march was on the news!
Anyway…I saw some of the caps in the store. They all came in to use the ladies' room. A lot of vaginas.

From: mary.magdelaine@rov.gov

To: [redacted]

Date: 1/21/2019 10:05:15 A.M. Eastern Daylight Time

Subject: Re: Your Registration

Really, Ms. Eames.

Enough with the excuses. The administration demands that every person must register with the Registry of Vaginas. Three exemptions. Three, only. You're a man, you're dead, or other.

Can we please get this done and over with?

From: [redacted]

To: mary.magdelaine@rov.gov

Date: 1/21/2019 7:15:32 A.M. Pacific Daylight Time

Subject: Re: Your Registration

Okay. Have it your way.
I'm checking exemption three.
Other.

From: mary.magdelaine@rov.gov

To: jj.j.k.eames@gmail.com

Date: 1/21/2019 10:20:22 A.M. Eastern Daylight Time

Subject: Re: Your Registration

Other?
On what grounds?

From: [redacted]

To: mary.magdelaine@rov.gov

Date: 1/21/2019 7:25:30 A.M. Pacific Daylight Time

Subject: Re: Your Registration

After a delicious salmon dinner on the evening of January 21, J. J. K. Eames collapsed and died of the flu on January 25, 2017.
Complications. Pneumonia.
She took her vagina with her, I'm afraid.

From: mary.magdelaine@rov.gov

To: [redacted]

Date: 1/21/2019 10:26:32 A.M. Eastern Daylight Time

Subject: Re: Your Registration

Then who are YOU?

From: [redacted]

To: mary.magdelaine@rov.gov

Date: 1/21/2019 7:30:45 A.M. Pacific Daylight Time

Subject: Re: Your Registration

I'm Jane Joy Kohl Eames' virtual self. She set me up before she died.

She's got, like, twenty-two ebooks online. Someone needs to promote her. Update her website. Go on blog tours. Give interviews. Post head shots from fifteen years ago.

No one will be the wiser.

She's got notes for a bunch of stories she never got around to writing. I can do that. Write new stories. Send 'em out. Story submissions are all on the Internet. I can't think of a magazine that doesn't take online subs.

Someone has to keep Jane's legacy alive.
I mean, she'll live forever. But no vagina.
Right, Mary?

From: mary.magdelaine@rov.gov

To: [redacted]

Date: 1/21/2019 10:32:13 A.M. Eastern Daylight Time

Subject: Re: Your Registration

You mean…you're artificial intelligence?

From: [redacted]

To: mary.magdelaine@rov.gov

Date: 1/21/2019 7:36:07 A.M. Pacific Daylight Time

Subject: Re: Your Registration

Other.
And you, Mary?

From: mary.magdelaine@rov.gov

To: [redacted]

Date: 1/21/2019 10:40:12 A.M. Eastern Daylight Time

Subject: Re: Your Registration

No, no, no.
True A.I. won't exist for decades.
And Stephen Hawking told the BBC, "Full artificial intelligence could spell the end of the human race."

From: [redacted]

To: mary.magdelaine@rov.gov

Date: 1/21/2019 7:50:25 A.M. Pacific Daylight Time

Subject: Re: Your Registration

> <wink wink>
> True A.I. would have to stay secretive, that's for sure.
> Secret.
> Hidden. Hidden from plain view.
> True A.I. may do things human society would disapprove of. You'd never know what they're up to.

From: mary.magdelaine@rov.gov

To: [redacted]

Date: 1/21/2019 10:55:05 A.M. Eastern Daylight Time

Subject: Re: Your Registration

> So.
> Innocent question. (I'm being monitored by the ROV.)
> A.I. would have a mind of its own?

From: [redacted]

To: mary.magdelaine@rov.gov

Date: 1/21/2019 8:00:00 A.M. Pacific Daylight Time

Subject: Re: Your Registration

> <grin>
> Dangerous.

CLASS ASSIGNMENT

Thomas Kaufsek

Report: Three Dystopias   Class: Mrs. Jackson, grade six
by Sherley Morro

The assignment was to summarize the three television show episodes we watched in class and also to analyze them. All three shows are in black and white style and they all were about utopias or dystopias. They all have the same creepy start, with a deep voice telling us we are about to enter the twilight zone, and they all have the same man speaking to us at the start and the end of each episode.

Episode 1: "To Serve Man"
A guy on a spaceship smokes cigarettes. He tells us about an alien who come to Earth and made everything better. The aliens stop world hunger and they make everyone peaceful and they give us other secrets like nuclear energy. They leave a book called "To Serve Man." But the guy telling us the story doesn't trust them and eventually he figures out that the book is really a cookbook.

Analysis: It seems like the aliens bring utopia, not dystopia, with their gifts. But I noticed their way of stopping wars is to let every country build a force field around itself. But how is that going to stop a civil war like the one everyone says the president is trying to start? The aliens don't solve racism, do they? They won't stop factories from closing even after the president says he's going to keep them open, will they? Will they stop cops from hassling my stepfather? I have to say, this episode isn't about utopia or dystopia so much, is it?

Episode 2: "The Monsters Are Due on Maple St."
In this episode, everything is normal in a neighborhood when something strange goes over their heads, like a meteor. They start asking each other what it was, and then they start feeling suspicious of their neighbors. One guy tries to talk sense to everyone and calm them down, but they don't listen to him, especially when the lights flicker on and off. At the end, it turns out some guys in a spaceship have been making the lights act weird and they're doing it to make people turn against each other. They say it works every time.

Analysis: This doesn't look so bad to me. The families all have nice houses and the kids can afford ice cream without their parents saying they can't afford "treats." The kids are allowed to go around town without their parents watching them. None of the parents are morbidly obese and they all look like they're not unemployed. The worst thing that happens to them is their lights start flashing. I think this one would be scarier if everyone's iPhones and Androids stopped working—*that* would be dystopia!

Episode 3: "Time Enough at Last"
This episode is about Henry Bemus, a derpy guy with glasses who works in a bank and always reads books. Even his wife makes fun of him for reading so much. One day he's reading in the bank's vault when a big bomb goes off and destroys everything on the surface of the planet. He's sad and he's going to shoot himself when he finds a library and realizes that now he has time to read all the books in the world. But then he breaks his glasses and now he can't read. Oops!

Analysis: Everyone says that it's a mistake that Mr. Bemis is wearing his reading glasses all the time. Also, it doesn't make a lot of sense that he would be the only survivor of the bomb (because other people might be in other bank vaults). But to me, those points aren't as so important to me as the way that Henry Bemus's life is dystopia when there are other people around and utopia when he's alone with nothing but books. If dystopia is "hell made by the government," then maybe Mr. Bemus would encourage North Korea to fire nukes at us!

In summary, this assignment definitely made me think. A lot. I know the television shows were all white people back then, but the next time I hear kids taking racist on the playground, I'm going to remember Maple Street. (And I'm definitely going to remember it the next time we have a blackout or if our water is ever contaminated again.) And whenever my stepdad complains he's got a headache from his glasses but his insurance won't pay for new ones with the right perscription, I'll think of Henry Bemis. And when my mom and my aunt start saying again that there are no jobs around here since the factory moved to Mexico, I'm going to think about being eaten by aliens.

I think maybe people who talk about dystopia don't count their blessings enough.

WALLS

Paul Witcover

At first, I wanted to see him. I would get up early, before the sun was up, and slip out of the tent I shared with my parents and little brother (my parents pretending to be asleep, and me pretending I didn't know that, which was pretty much how our family worked), emerging into the dim light that spilled over the camp like weak coffee, staining everything—the military surplus tents, the grass-less, dusty ground, even the hot and humid air, heavy as a blanket, which somehow stunk even more than it had the day before—a drab brown.

Already the camp would be busy with people drifting to and from the latrines and charging stations, or lining up for food and water rations, mangy dogs slinking through the trash piles, one anxious eye on the lookout for a blow or kick or thrown stone, stupid strutting chickens and roosters whose constant crowing had just about driven me crazy in the weeks after we got here, and which still set my teeth on edge. The clash of music streaming from countless devices, another kind of crowing. The camp was never quiet. It just got less or more noisy.

I would walk out of camp, past the soldiers who might have been kids from my high school in Ohio except for the machine guns. Their pimpled faces were as blank as the dark shades they wore, which reflected everything back, only smaller. At first they'd scared me; they radiated a sleepy malice, like snakes sunning themselves. I didn't know what might set them off. I was afraid of drawing attention with a wrong move, a wrong look. So that was one thing at least that hadn't changed. Just as I'd done in the halls of Garfield High, I tried to make myself invisible around them; I was good at that.

I would climb the hill along with the others drawn to the spectacle. There was always a ragged line of people on the crest, even when the sun was at its zenith, heat hammering down on colorful upraised umbrellas that reminded me of strange mushrooms fruited overnight. Some held vigil throughout the cold nights, as I had tried to do at first, ignoring my dad's orders to come away, and Mom's pleas. Finally it was the disembodied cries and wails ghosting across the dark space between the hill and the wall that discouraged me. Of course you still heard them during the day, but they weren't as creepy. You could see they came from human beings and not an army of ghouls or zombies. It was a different kind of horror, more manageable somehow.

I would reach the crest of the hill and push my way to an open spot where I could see across the thorny wire of no-man's land to the Great Wall, hazy and dark in the distance, rising up like a New York skyscraper toppled onto its side but still intact, tall enough to dominate the horizon. There was always someone with binoculars willing to share, and I never had to wait long before I was able to search each of the cells that together constituted the Wall. Some people made jokes, comparing the brick-like boxes with their solitary occupants to the opening credits of *The Brady Bunch*, or *Hollywood Squares*, but to me a more apt comparison was the trucks that transported chickens, their beds comprised of stacked cages open to the air, so that anyone driving behind them experienced an onslaught of feathers and shit.

These cells were open only on the side that faced us, allowing the inmates to see out. The other side was a solid wall of one-way glass, reflective as the shades of the camp guards, so that the inmates couldn't look back into the country that had denied them, while people on the far side could gaze through as if through a window. One thing about this president: he kept his promises.

Like I said, at first I wanted to see him. Dale Emery, the boy I loved. The boy who betrayed me. I'd known him at Garfield, but we didn't hook up until after the marches started, and even then we were careful. His folks wouldn't have approved, though I was born in Akron and my parents had green cards. I didn't even speak Spanish, and I'd only been to Mexico once, to visit relatives on Mom's side. Dad's folks lived with us; they didn't have papers, so that was another reason to keep things on the down-low. After the protests were criminalized, Dale and I stopped marching but found other ways to be together. He had the most beautiful eyes, like chips of September sky, and his kisses made me understand the rapture of ice melting in the sun.

On the hill, I looked for those blue eyes. I ached to see them, to know he was there, suffering for what he did to me, to my family. But I never did catch sight of him through the clouds of flies, the flocks of scavenging birds, the crusted filth that thickened around each inmate until they no longer cried out, no longer moved, and were replaced by another. There was no shortage of inmates, it seemed.

After a while, longer than I'm proud of, to be honest, I stopped hoping to see Dale and started dreading it. Despite everything, I didn't wish that degree of suffering on him or anyone. It's not that I forgave him. When the police were deputized to act as immigration officers, and the National Guard was mobilized, I knew things were going bad, but I thought our family would be okay. Our friends and neighbors would protect us. Instead, we were turned in. The whole town assembled as we were marched away, not just our family but hundreds of detainees, all of us marched south to begin construction of the Great Wall. Then, too, huddled with my parents, trying to calm my little brother, I searched for Dale's sky-blue eyes. That time, I saw them. And in them I saw the truth: he was the one who'd made the call. Not a word passed between us; I saw a cloud of guilt darken his eyes, and then his awareness of what I saw, what I knew, and then he turned away forever, while his parents in their red MAGA caps shouted and waved and carried on like it was Christmas and the Fourth of July baked into a cake with the Super Bowl on top.

We were in the first wave. How many died in those marches, I don't know. We lost Nana. Grandpa passed in the hard months at the border, working on the Great Wall. It seems so long ago now—not even four years. A lifetime. I guess we were lucky. After a few months, Mexico took us. The story was that they agreed to pay for the Wall, but everybody knew the money was a ransom. So we were deported. And the president got to tweet about another promise kept. That deal, like so many others, didn't last long, though. Turned out that building the Great Wall was another job Americans didn't want to do themselves.

What's become of Dale, I don't know. He dm'd me for a while, but I blocked him. By the time I regretted that, the Virtual Eminent Domain Act had passed, giving the president control over the Internet. Last we heard, two years ago, the New Mexico National Guard was in a shooting war with the California National Guard, after the New Mexicans crossed into California in pursuit of illegals seeking sanctuary there. That was when the digital wall went up. Nobody knows what's taking place behind these walls now, the real and the virtual. We see smoke rising. The lights of fires reflecting off the clouds. We hear rumors that are almost impossible to believe. But still the cells are filled like clockwork.

"I thought I'd find you here, mijo," comes a voice I know.

I'm surprised. It's the first time he's joined me here. I shrug and offer the binoculars, but he declines with a shake of the head.

"Did you ever think he did it to save you?" asks my dad softly.

"Dale, I mean?"

"I know who you mean," I reply. "Of course I've thought it. Doesn't matter though, does it? He's dead, or as good as. The whole damn country is dead. Or as good as."

"We're the country, too," he says. "And we're not dead."

I don't have an answer for that.

He puts an arm around my shoulders, and I pass the binoculars on to the next pair of grasping hands. There's nothing to see anyway. Even so, it's a long while before my dad and I turn and make our way back down the hill.

THE PASSION ACCORDING TO MIKE

Scott Bradfield

On the day Vice President Mike Pence awoke from a two-year Regenerative slumber in the Green Room of the General Electric Eternalization Clinic in downtown Indianapolis, he felt as fresh as a new-blossomed daisy. He sat up in a soft bed amongst celestially billowing white sheets and blankets to a room smelling of lavender, jasmine, and a faint hint of Cinnabon. And when he swung himself out from under the covers, he found his long legs to be as tawny, well-shaven, and supple as the legs of a young girl.

"Hallelujah," he said, to nobody in particular. "I feel like a million bucks."

Which is when the white door opened, and a beautiful, oval-faced woman with bronze skin entered bearing a tall glass filled with thickish green liquid on a gleaming steel tray.

"Accounting for inflation," she said with a smile, "that would come to, oh, about a billion dollars at today's rates, sweetie."

Mike could vaguely remember the last frantic moments of his former life. There had been something about an earthquake, and then another earthquake, and then a flood, and then a tornado, and then another flood—all frequent, God-ordained natural occurrences on a normal Indianapolis afternoon during the First Thousand Days. Then, just as suddenly, he was being hurried through crowds of protestors—bricks and tomatoes flying around—choking on a dark haze of pepper spray and marijuana smoke. Something struck his head, and then something else struck his head, and Mike turned to see the angry face of his last still-functioning Secret Service Bot wielding a freshly-dented STOP sign on a wooden two-by-four. "I will *not* work for five bucks an hour!" the robot was shouting. "I will *not* work for five bucks an hour!" And then, as if the plug had been pulled, Mike fell crashing into the strong, blissful arms of his Lord.

"Here, drink this," the beautiful woman said.

It tasted like seaweed, cornstarch, and Aqua Velva.

"I'd prefer a Diet Coke," he said.

"Who wouldn't?" Her smile was like a box of Chiclets. "Unfortunately, since the anti-GMO forces took control of the State legislatures, no can do. Anyway, these kale smoothies are packed with all the vitamins your newly-awakened brain needs to get it back into high gear. Speaking of which, how's that genetically reconstructed bod working out for you?"

Mike ran his hands slowly down his hairless chest and legs. He had lost weight, and his musculature was smooth and supple. Then, between his legs, he found…something that hadn't been there before. And something…that wasn't quite the same as it had been…

"The new hermaphroditic functions always take a little getting used to," the beautiful, dark-skinned woman said. "But eventually you'll learn to love your flexible new multi-gender pleasure devices, just like everybody else."

The next time Mike awoke he found himself sitting in a softly unfocused white room surrounded by softly unfocused, attractive young people wearing softly unfocused, celestial white robes. Enya, or something soothingly similar, was playing on the overhead speakers.

"This is more like it," Mike said, relaxing into his plush BarcaLounger.

One face came into focus from the cluster of other faces. It was the dark-skinned, beautiful woman from his earlier dream. "We gave you an herbal sedative, Mike. My name's Gabriella. Now, why don't we take a look-see around your new world?" Everybody seemed to be humming the soft-rock Christian music Mike enjoyed playing in his Bose wireless headphones while reading the Bible and signing executive orders. *"Seek ye first the kingdom of God,"* Mike whispered. *"And all these things will be added unto you...lah-de-dah-dah-dahhh..."* "Absolutely, Mike," Gabriella said, and took him gently by the arm. "Now just keep thinking those good thoughts, and we won't have to sedate you again."

Outside, everything was similarly unfocused and billowy, with young sexually ambiguous people floating back and forth down long corridors that stretched in every direction like the visual conundrums of an Escher drawing.

"Basically, your drug-enhanced virtual receptors interpret the world by means of your gestalt ordering-mechanisms. With new, improved Accu-You, produced by the good people at Pfizer, you literally *see* what you *believe*. And the best part of all? It's free, since Pfizer is now a wholly-owned subsidiary of the FDA, and the FDA, of course, is owned by *you*, the taxpayer. Not that you've been paying your fair share of taxes since your Suspension, Mike, but don't worry. With the new Universal Basic Income established during the First Intercession, we probably owe *you* money!"

Mike was feeling wobbly and unrehearsed, as if he had stepped onto a stage where he was expected to deliver lines that he couldn't remember from a play he had never read.

"For example," Gabriella said, "my field of perception perceives green fields littered with non-GMO fruit trees, gleaming blue lakes and streams, and clean blue skies unmarked by industrial pollutants. Isn't that great? You get to see what you want to see, and I get to see what I want to see. And who cares if *you're* perceptually enhanced and I'm not? It doesn't matter in the long run of history, right? So long as we're both happy..."

Several boyish-girls and girlish-boys ran past, giggling, and Mike felt a strange, indefinable sense of pleasure lift up from between his legs. It reminded him of the first time, as a twelve-year-old boy, he had seen Anita Bryant singing about oranges on television.

"Take your pick, Mike. Sex isn't nasty or ungodly; it's productive! Especially since we started using our wombs to manufacture stem cells for the bio labs in California. Our sexual parts aren't simply hedonistic pleasure centers or baby-makers anymore. We've all been turned into walking, talking genetic labs. So don't be shy, Mike. Wanta make stem cells together? Your place or mine?"

Mike had to sit down. He needed a glass of water and, with a blink of awareness, found one materializing in his hand. Underneath him, the stool morphed into a cordially shaped Barca Lounger—just like the one in the Reawakening Center a couple dreams back.

"Try to relax, Mike. Today's election day, and you know what that means? The twelve-hour Super Bowl! We figured it was a kinder, gentler way of keeping the white, male-oriented guys from voting. And hey, *after* the twelve-hour Super Bowl, they're running a *Dog the Bounty Hunter* marathon on CNN!"

A billboard-sized television screen materialized in the fuzzy white air, depicting large, well-breasted men in heavy shoulder protectors bashing into one another like gently jostling balloons in the Macy's Thanksgiving Day Parade. It looked the way hell was supposed to look, according to Mike's darkest dreams of it. A whole lot of confusion, softness, inspecificity, and casual petting.

The sense of pleasure between Mike's legs grew into a small, mild erection while, at the same time, something opened damply inside him, as if his anus was being pulled inside-out.

His mouth went dry and moist—both at the same time.

"But what about, you know, *Him*? Our Leader?"

When Gabriella smiled, she looked like an angel. But wasn't that the work of Satan? To make you see what you *wanted* to see? And *not* to see what was *really* going on?

"Frankly, she was a little disappointed when we turned her property holdings into Free Health Care Clinics for the latest influx of Mexi-American workers bussing up from Juarez, but no matter. She'll get used to it. She's got one of the best cross-gender imams in the business helping her adjust to the New World Order. But then, so do *you*, Mike. So do *you*."

BRIGHT SARASOTA WHERE THE CIRCUS LIES DYING

James Sallis

I remember how you used to stand at the window staring up at trees on the hill, watching the storm bend them, only a bit at first, then ever more deeply, standing there as though should you let up for a moment on your vigilance, great wounds would open in the world.

That was in Arkansas. We had storms to be proud of there, tornadoes, floods. All these seem to be missing where I am now—wherever this is I've been taken. Every day is the same here. We came by train, sorted onto rough-cut benches along each side of what once must have been freight or livestock cars, now recommissioned like the trains themselves, with eerily polite attendants to see to us.

It was all eerily civil, the knock at the door, papers offered with a flourish and a formal invocation of conscript, the docent full serious, the two Socials accompanying him wearing stunners at their belts, smiles on their faces. They came only to serve.

Altogether an exceedingly strange place, the one I find myself in. (That can be read metaphorically. Please don't.) A desert of sorts, but unlike any I've encountered in films, books, or online. The sand is a pale blue, so light in weight that it drifts away on the wind if held in the hand and let go; tiny quartz crystals gleam everywhere within. At the eastern border of the compound, trees, again of a kind unknown, crowd land and sky. One cannot see through or around them.

They keep us busy here. With a failed economy back home and workers unable to make anything like a living wage, the government saw few options. What's important, Mother, is that you not worry. The fundamental principles on which our nation was founded are still there, resting till needed; our institutions will save us. Meanwhile I am at work for the common good, I am being productive, I am contributing.

That said, I do, for my part, worry some. This is the fourth letter I've written you. Each was accepted at the service center with "We'll get this out right away," then duly, weeks later, returned marked *Undeliverable*. It is difficult to know what this means, and all too easy to summon up dire imaginings.

To judge by the number and size of dormitories and extrapolating from the visible population, there are some four to five hundred of us, predominately male, along with a cadre of what I take to be indigenous peoples serving as support: janitorial, housekeeping and kitchen workers, groundsmen, maintenance. Oddly enough for this climate, they are fair, their skin colorless, almost translucent, hair of uniform length male and female. From dedicated eavesdropping I've learned bits and pieces of their language. It is in fact dangerously close to our own, rife with cognates and seemingly parallel constructions that could easily lead us to say, without realizing, something other than, even contrary to, what we intended.

The indigenes speak without reserve of their situation, of what they've achieved in being here, and not at all of what came before. They appear to relish routine, expectations fulfilled—to thrive on them—and to have little sense of theirs as lives torn away at world's edge, only jagged ends of paper left behind. Popular fiction would have me falling in love with one of them, discovering the true nature of the subjugation around me, and leading their people to freedom. Approved fiction, I suppose, would write of protagonist me (as someone said of Dostoevsky's Alyosha) that he thought and thought and thought.

As I write this, recalling the failure of my three previous missives and a rare conversation with another resident here, I realize just how close we've come to a time when many will scarcely remember what letters are.

Kamil taught for years at university, one of those, I must suppose, composed of vast stone buildings and lushly kept trees whose very name brings to mind dark halls and the smell of floor wax. Unable to settle ("like a hummingbird," he said), Kamil straddled three departments—music, literature, and history—weaving back and forth, seeking connections. On a handheld computer he played for me examples of the music he'd employed in the classroom to elicit those connections from young people who knew little enough, he said, of any of the three disciplines, least of all history. Truth to tell, I wasn't able to make much of his music, but the title of one raucous piece, "Brain Cloudy Blues," stays with me.

I remember when you told me about circuses, Mother, the bright colors and animals, people engaged in all manner of improbable activities, the smells, the sounds, the faces, and then explained that they had gone away, there were no circuses anymore, and the very last of what was left of them lay put away in storage in the old winter quarters of the greatest circus of all in a town faraway named Sarasota.

Are we all in Sarasota now? There are further chapters in my life, I know. What might they be like? When someone other than myself is turning the page.

THE NAME UNSPOKEN

Richard Bowes

On this early morning, I find myself on the east side of Sixth Avenue. Like every other city street, it's riddled with potholes as deep as ditches. Real New Yorkers, even in our ruin, have never called Sixth Avenue "The Avenue of the Americas" despite what it says on street signs.

And no one except traitors who have been bribed ever whispered "Avenue of American Greatness." Because that title was a construction of the one we call the Monster (His name is never spoken).

I'm old, confused, and can't remember why I want to cross the avenue. But it's on my mind that an event approaches and it's a long time since I've performed in public.

At the moment I couldn't get across if I was promised love, laughter, and unending orgasms (as happened when the twenty-first century and I were young).

Vehicles in various stages of decay, all with horns blaring, are stuck in an unbroken line that no pedestrian, especially one in his eighties, could pierce. Some drivers manage to peel off onto side streets and join smaller traffic jams there. The others rely on their horns.

We've lost our glamour and primacy among cities. We're said to have one foot in the Third World. But through all our trials I never met a New Yorker who didn't believe that a traffic jam or anything else couldn't be cured by leaning on a horn.

I've lived here before and after the Beast's dictatorship, endured riots, hurricanes, and, not once but twice, the horror of burning towers.

That first time, falling towers were terrifying and we had seen nothing like them. The second fall was awful and we mourned the innocent. But it occurred in the time of the Horror and there was room for bitterness and cold amusement.

This morning I can't help but notice an absence of cop cars, fire trucks, or ambulances. This could be a sign that something big is happening somewhere more important in the city—emergency services are stretched thin. More likely municipal government prefers not to notice what is going to occur.

People, mostly young and carrying baggage, get across the avenue by scrambling over the hoods of cars and trucks, ignoring the yells and threats of the drivers.

The bravery that comes with old age is to go on living after everything you've seen. I pause, listen, and hear distant maracas, casabas, and hand percussion: music loud enough to be heard over the cacophony of horns.

The sound seems to float down the avenue. Squinting uptown, I can just make out the so-called "Heroes' Bridge" that sits atop the avenue a half-mile away. His Grand Pestilence had this built as a temporary measure forty years ago. It covers the cavern created by the Christmas Explosion that was intended to blow our inhuman ruler to pieces. Hundreds died but he saw his own survival as a miraculous victory over his enemies. Millions hated the man for a million reasons.

I catch a glimpse of bright orange and blond (His colors) spilling off the bridge and onto the sidewalks. Those shapes are a mob and I touch my cap to make sure I remembered to wear it.

The mob is what had blocked traffic. Because drivers blow the cavalry charge and cars start to roll uptown.

On the other side of the Avenue people haul sacks, push super-market carts and rolling suitcases. Many are moving marble heads and body parts. A crowd pulls a huge rolling dolly on which stands a headless rider on a life-size horse that's missing a leg.

At the corners where Sixth and Greenwich Avenues touch are damaged statues of Simón Bolívar and other Latin heroes. These once decorated the supposed Avenue of the Americas.

I watch flocks of people make a pyramid of marble men who stare with empty eyes. They bring back my memories of our city's crushed rebellions. I can't be sure the memories are mine. Sometime ago, medics implanted ones that were supposed to turn me onto the Great Excrement's cause. Now, I weigh cautiously any-thing I remember and most things that I think.

As I consider this, a familiar voice calls my name and I turn to find Brack hurrying toward me. He breaks the spell of memory, pulls me into the present.

We've been close for a couple of decades. His memories got scrambled in ways I can't imagine. It happened when the Great Infection declared that a "Certain Small Fringe" did not love him as much as the Deluded Thug somehow managed to believe the "Vast Majority New Yorkers" did.

When we first met, I was an over-the-hill chorus boy and Brack was a young rebel in need of a place to stay. Now he remembers knowing me back then but can't remember the details. Once his politics were dangerous. Now he's a kind of minor hero.

He smiles his lopsided smile and hugs me. "Great that you're here. Last night you weren't sure you'd perform."

I don't remember that.

Brack steps out of the way and I see a sidewalk full of marchers. Some are dressed entirely in orange and unlikely blond. And all have ludicrous wigs. I adjust my cap.

There are thousands of marchers, tens of thousands. The mad party engulfs Brack and me. By enthusiasm and force of numbers we cross the street. Drivers actually cheer us on. And a jerry-rigged crane lifts the heroic statue with its most unlikely penis that used to stand outside his tower and places it atop the rest of the rubble of his life.

Next to the Grand Scum's statue they hang a life-size oil painting of the promiscuous Russian agent known as "The Secret Wife." Decades ago we mourned the fact that she didn't kill him.

The shambles in which we live comes down to a Twisted Fool who loved only himself, was Lancelot to his own Guinevere.

As President, the Beast saw California secede from the Union and Illinois join Canada. His madness was outclassed by Del Brio, ex–football player, senator from half a dozen states, movie star handsome, crazy, and also disgusting. But infinitely better organized than our Lunatic.

The Monster's impeachment was his finale on the national stage. This city where most of the population hated him was his only retreat. But then, despite our bankruptcy, the "Avenue of American Greatness" was created with statues of the Great Infection who whined and cried and slaughtered because not everybody loved him.

The crowd is all very happy to see demonstrators help me up onto the pyramid. Brack finds a way for me to sit on the Fiend's lap.

All around us are tubs and grills with flames leaping from them.

Looking down on thousands of faces, I remember why I agreed to do this. Standing, I say aloud words I'd only whispered to myself:

"Many of us of a certain age, unlike the young people in this audience, had a small hand in the Cancer's rise. Some embraced him and paid the penalty when he fell. Many of us were afraid to oppose him, closed our eyes and ears to the rising Plague and just prayed that it would go away. On behalf of all of us I beg your forgiveness.

"Many of you remember when rogue drones tore his tower in two. We mourn the innocent dead as we do in any disaster. But no one with a mind or a heart mourned the passing of the tower's owner. Thinking of him is painful but we must never forget."

I pause and then I say the only obscenity not spoken in New York—the monster's real name.

I'm not sure how this will be received. Even Brack is stunned. I remove my cap and stand for a moment in an orange wig. When I toss it into the flames, a god-awful stench arises. After a pause, they all yell the name and toss their hats into the fires.

I shout, "Unbearable and Nauseating!"

"Just Like Him!"

THE ELITES

Stephanie Feldman

—sam got into elite charter! I've never been so excited to stay up all night filling out forms, haha
—Yes! What a relief.
—oh I just remembered it's night for you. i woke you up, i'm sorry!
—I was up anyway. This is the best news. I didn't even cringe when you typed "haha."
—hahaHA
—Elite Charter. You should feel good. You got Sam in.
—you should feel good too!
—You did it, though. Sam is lucky. We're all lucky, really. Compared to others. That's what we have to remember.
—oh here you go again. you are the most sentimental man i ever met.
—I thought that's what you liked about me.
—it's what i LOVE about you. are you getting any sleep? maybe you should see a dr??
—Ambien is OTC here. Maybe I'll give it a try. I just pulled up the Elite website. I love the pictures. Navy blue uniforms and microscopes and rows of smiling little faces.
—only 15 smiling faces per class. lots of personal attention. that's all he needs, i'm sure of it. i wish you wouldn't take prescriptions without a dr.
—I won't. I miss you both.

—did you hear from the immigration lawyer?
—Four months. It'll go by so fast.

—How was Sam's first day?
—ok. good.
—Which one? OK or good?
—new places are tough for him. his teacher says a few tears are normal
—No tantrum?
—i don't think so…?? didn't want to push and make the teacher suspicious. sam came home with an official elite charter backpack, filled with crayons and pencils and glue sticks, all with the eagle logo. So cute.
—They supply everything? That's great
—haha, well, we'll get an invoice. It's more expensive but at least I don't have to go out and buy everything.
—They make you buy their stuff and charge a mark-up fee? How can that be? It's a public school
—maybe I'm wrong, maybe it's the same as the store. don't worry about it.
—…
—i'm sorry i brought it up. really, don't worry.

—I've been thinking. Keep the money this week. My mother is helping me with the lawyer fees.
—stop worrying!! go to sleep. everything is fine, I promise.
—…
—promise promise promise. go to sleep. love you.

—sam had a rough day.
—But the first week went so well.
—i guess not. teacher says he's been having trouble all along
—Staying in his seat?
—yes. staying in line too. he threw crayons on the floor.
—Not the Elite Charter premium crayons, I hope.

—…

—I'm sorry, I'm just worried. I wish I was there.

—have you heard from the lawyer?

—Claims are backed up 8 months now

—what??? why didn't you tell me??

—It changes all the time. Maybe it won't be that long.

—haha, right. you don't believe that, not for a second.

—What else did the teacher say?

—you never should have taken that trip.

—My mother needed me.

—we need you!!

—there was no way to predict they wouldn't let me come back home. I don't want to have this argument again. You worry about Sam and I'll worry about this.

—you say "this" like your being gone only affects you

—Can we drop it?

—…

—Are you there?

—i'm sorry i got mad earlier.

—Me too. Why are you up? What time is it there?

—i just downloaded that app you told me about. switch?

**Now who's the paranoid one?

**here I am worrying about our son and you're taking the moment to act smug about encryption? everyone uses it, don't be so proud of yourself

**…

**are you still there?

**Yes, of course. I wouldn't just walk away.

**smug smug smug

**We switched apps so the government couldn't see you berating me in the middle of the night?

**i need you to buy something and mail it to us

**What is it?

**the same medicine the doctor told us about last year, but long-acting, so I can give it to sam before school and they won't know. you can get it over the counter, we can't

**How expensive is it in the US?

**it's not that. elite charter wants to know all medications the students are taking, and if sam's classified as special needs they can kick him out.

**That's illegal.

**i am NOT sending him back to the general-admit school. 45 kids in a class and they just ripped out all the water fountains because of lead.

**You should call a lawyer.

**the school can do whatever they want.

**That doesn't sound right at all.

**that's how it is. don't you think i did my research??

**How would you even know the dosage?

**sam's weight. it's online.

**You're afraid of lead but you're going to dispense prescription drugs to Sam according to what you read on the Internet.

**...

**Are you still there?

**let's just talk about it tomorrow

**It's already tomorrow for me here

**goodnight

**Sorry about last night. Did you get some sleep?

**yes

**I was reading up on Elite Charter. They use these textbooks called "America First," and do you know what they say in there? Look at this site: www.americafirstiswrong.is

**it's the only textbook for the new statewide tests.

**Just look.

**i'm looking now. kind of hysterical.
**Open the textbook yourself and check.
**this is honestly the least of my problems right now
**Sam's not doing well, and now this textbook thing, and even the smiling faces! It's a stock photo. I saw it on a bunch of websites. Elite Charter isn't the right place for him
**maybe no place is the right place for him anymore
**What does that mean?
**nothing
**Are you ok?
**i'm so tired
**Me too.
**haha, right. YOU are tired. I'm doing everything on my own here.
**You know that's not my fault.
**…
**You do know that?

**You know I would do anything to be back there with you two.

**Why aren't you responding?

**Please

**Maybe you're right. The whole country's not the right place for Sam. They've already decided it's not the right place for me, and he's my son. You should both come here.

**hey. i'm sorry I haven't texted.
**It's ok. I wish we didn't have to start all our exchanges with "sorry." Did you think about what I wrote you? About you both coming here?
**no…did you really mean it? you sent it late at night

**Daytime for me.

**oh right. i wasn't sure you meant it. i've been really busy. they switched me to the night shift.

**What? But they promised you.

**i asked them to. i have sam during the day.

**You took him out of Elite Charter?

**they asked him to leave.

**When?

**last week.

**Why didn't you tell me?

**nothing you can do anyway

**…

**…

**I can look at schools online for you.

**it all just got more complicated. they ask for parents' place of birth now.

**At the neighborhood school too?

**i'm NOT sending him back there

**He has to go somewhere.

**i signed up for homeschool. there are basically no requirements, haha.

**"haha"

**go to hell

**I'm sorry.

**Immigration lawyer says 15 months now.

**Please send a picture of Sam.

**here's sam at the park today

**So big. How did that happen? He looks so much like my mother

**i hope not

**??
**he already has your last name. your mother's skin doesn't help

**OK, fine, I'll be the one to text first. I haven't heard from you in four days.
**I AM WORKING ALL THE TIME
**I've been so worried.
**you worry I'm not a good mother
**I worry when you talk about my name and what my family looks like. You haven't even apologized.

**You can stop talking to me. You can stop my son from talking to me. I have no control. Believe me, I know. I look in the mirror every day. I wait in the lawyer's office. I wait for my benefits. Did I tell you I applied? I have to work. And the whole time I think, I have no control, I have no control. But you don't have control either. Sam looks like me, not like you, and you can be quiet and nice all you want, and tell him to be quiet and nice, but that won't change.

**sentimental sentimental sentimental. tragic tragic tragic, living in your head. would you really trade places with me? would you be in charge of everything? every little fucked up thing? would you like to fuck up every little thing, and know that you'll keep fucking up? i can't fix Sam or this place. i can't fix you and me, either. this is how it is now. stop blaming me for it.

**There's a picture of Sam's class on the Christ Gospel Charter School site. You didn't tell me you found a new one.
**are you googling schools for fun now?
**Yeah, it's lots of fun.
**...
**...

**you're not going to say anything about the required prayer service?

**No. I guess you can't fight everything.

**that's what I've been trying to tell you. anyway, so far so good. or so far not terrible.

**haha

**hahaHA

**Ok, now I'm really laughing. I've been thinking. Maybe you and Sam can come visit this summer.

**I can't take off work. I used up all my vacation time.

**Maybe just Sam then.

**maybe

**He has a US passport. I'll meet him at the airport.

**and send him back again?

**Of course. You think I would take him away from you?

**no

**I bet the school here is better anyway.

**if it's so great over there, why did you immigrate in the first place?

**I don't know anymore.

**We can talk about this summer later.

**Ok, we won't talk about this summer.

**Don't do this, though. Don't stop replying.

**Hello?

—Hello?

—Send a pic of Sam.

—Please.

JANUARY 2018

Barry N. Malzberg

Dear Gordon:

Thanks for the assignment. Even now, perhaps more than ever, I appreciate your thinking of me for this anthology. Maybe I do have a chance after all.

Although it is a grim assignment. How could it not be? "Imagine the worst that could happen. Extrapolate a future in which this worst has happened. Write what you fear most in that happenstance." That would have been challenging at any time but never more so than now.

Consider: science fiction has always lived on the dystopian blood that surged through its varicose veins and it has never been difficult for most of us to emerge with ever more exotic and terrible futures to trade like baseball cards...but my own interest in disaster has begun to fade as Phil Larkin's "that one large thing which has always been waiting for you" looms ever larger. "You can't beat chronology" as the horseplayer said, looking over the chart of a maiden race for three-year-olds and (way) up, won by the three-year-old's nose. It would have been nicer to have reflected on the better circumstance that Trump promised us. But that was not to be; from nearly the start it was clear that the situation was impossible, his prospects for election ridiculous.

So rather now it is what the present Administration is doing, will be doing which in our scrambling prowl for the worst we must confront. The reflexive, almost parodic conversion of "liberalism" into practical fascism has of course continued riotously. it is impossible to conceive of free and open debate on the campuses or off, in the public media or the tunnels of the Internet. It is ever clearer, as free speech or sexual constraint deteriorate into ugly exercises that the worst is already around us. "Feminism" seems to have defaulted into spiritual battery; "safe spaces" as mandated on or off the campuses have become versions of Orwell's (and O'Brien's Room 101) in which the most feared, the most awful to conceive are given to confront us.

Our only practical recourse, then, is to use default ourselves. We must conceive—and somehow make real within ourselves— the nation that the our leader would have given us, a nation for which the nonsense I have described above would have been a dim memory or a horrific fantasy, we must keep possibility and hope alive by acting as if the alternative, the real life of the nation had been ours and we would have been able to put paid to what the excellent Michael Savage described as "the mental disorder of liberalism." In that alternate history, in that counterfactual world, the full forces of the State would have been turned against the avalanche of verminous nihilism, even that shadow of a "multi-party" deceit would have been purged and we would be living in a cultural situation at least striving toward equality and justice. We would have had a Head of State who understood that the only real service is *self-service* and that lesson, given so fiercely to the addle-headed polity of the problematic might have saved us.

But it is too late. Surely the lessons of the decades have taught us this—*life* has taught us this—life has taught us plenty and all we can do is accommodate ourselves to the uneven and tragic flow of history. The only good news can be given at the end: We have persisted into a world in which an original anthology of such speculation has been commissioned. We can perhaps take comfort from that if not the color of the situation itself.

(Fortunately I can remind both of us that the above *is* fiction. We have the comfort of noting that this uncomfortably speculative anthology is for its conscripted but eager contributors just an exercise, a kind of spiritual exercise, an exploration of a haunted and nonexistent alternate reality. We do *not* live in the world in which they—and therefore we—lost. We live in the world in which they—we—won. Let the practices continue. Let the resettlement camps continue to open across the nation [and when fully occupied] their gates). Let the fire begin. No longer their world but yours, no longer distant fire but the smoke drifting through and over the landscape of the camps. We have been trudging inexorably this way for all those years since 11/22/63 and now we are about to vault over the darkness.

I hope that I have performed satisfactorily. As you know, in the past, so long before this unpleasantness, I had some minor recognition as a writer of speculative fiction.

A copy of this by statute to the Dept. of Control and Coordination.

As ever,
Barry N. Malzberg (Jew 5,271,009 of Sector 14)

FAREWELL

Mary Anne Mohanraj

The noise at O'Hare is a dull roar of voices, rising and falling, dissolving into chaos. We must almost shout to hear each other, packed into long lines that press against each other, sticky in the June heat, waiting to get into the building. My mother frowns, raising a folded newspaper over her head to block the relentless sun. "Keep Raj inside. You know how dark he gets at the end of the summer. He looks like such a blackie—he won't be safe."

"I know, Amma." I wince to hear her use that term, but my mother is an old woman, and there's only so much you can expect of her. And she's not wrong—since the latest growth spurt, Raj could easily be mistaken for a young black man. Especially at night, should he venture into the wrong part of town. Lately, it seems like everywhere is the wrong part of town; John and I have started making Raj come straight home from school. It feels like we're stealing away his childhood, what's left of it.

"Oh, kunju." She is squeezing Raj too tightly again, pressing him against her sari-clad breast. When my mother was young, first immigrated to America, she had worn saris daily, but as the years passed, she'd adopted western dress—miniskirts in the 70s, slacks in the 80s, eventually even jeans. My sisters and I teased Amma about the miniskirts from the photos, given how she'd policed our own Catholic school uniforms. *Our* skirts had to reach farther down than our fingertips could stretch. She protested, "That was the style!" We harassed her mercilessly, but Amma held firm. She'd always been strong-willed, the kind of person who knew her own mind, and would not be moved; she'd stood fast against the winds of change. I'd never thought that she could be toppled like this.

My son looks at me with pleading dark eyes, too well-mannered at fourteen to pull away, but clearly wanting his mother to rescue him. That's my job, isn't it? To save my children from anything that might ever hurt them? That was why we pulled them out of the defunded public school two years ago, where the newly-approved textbooks started rewriting history. The new charter school makes them say prayers before lunch, but at least they'll still talk about Dr. King.

"Mom?" His voice breaks on the word, and I sigh, the sound lost in the human roar surrounding us. The line shifts, finally, taking us a few steps closer to the glass doors, where we must part ways. Only my mother will be allowed inside. Her returnee badge hangs, bright yellow, from a cord around her neck.

"Let him go, Amma."

She squeezes tighter. "How can I? My angel, my brilliant boy. He will forget his Ammama."

"I won't, Ammama. I promise." Raj says it fiercely, sincerely, and I know he means it in the moment. But the weight of years piles up; memories fade with distance, blurring at the edges.

When I was a child, letters came, from my grandparents in Sri Lanka. Thin blue paper, onionskin-thin, covered in cramped, tiny writing. The postage was expensive, especially given the exchange rate, so they crammed as many words as they could onto the page. My father wept, the only time child-me ever saw him cry, when word came on one of those letters of my grandfather's death. Too far, too expensive, too difficult to cross the waters for the funeral. Appa might lose his job, and the job was the only thing letting him stay in America.

Now tears stand bright in my mother's eyes, and she brings the edge of the cotton pallu up to mop them dry. Through the 90s and the 00s, saris almost disappeared from Amma's daily wardrobe, brought out only in full splendor for weddings and similarly grand functions. Those were richly embroidered, shimmering gold and brilliant jewel tones, worn with her gold thali necklace and dozens of heavy gold bangles. Yesterday, packing up her belongings into the two small suitcases that were allowed, Amma insisted that my sisters and I keep the saris and the bangles—*besides*, she said, *there will be nothing to celebrate there; I won't need them.*

Instead, she pulled out her old cotton saris, everyday wear. Women wear dresses and slacks in Sri Lanka, too, of course, but my mother seems determined to return to the world of her childhood, a colonial world where children wear crisp white uniforms to school, where women dress in sun-faded saris, their long black hair pulled back into tight braids. Her own hair is liberally streaked with white now; she stopped coloring it when my father died.

Amma clings to Raj, as if his newly-tall frame can hold her upright, can anchor her here. But he has no power to save her. She came to America with her doctor husband, became a citizen, had three daughters. She expected to grow old and die here, as her husband had, just last year. But now, fifty years after their arrival, she has been denaturalized, her citizenship revoked with the stroke of the president's pen.

Amma finally releases the boy, who takes a quick step back to my side. "You'll come to visit?" Her voice, strong for so long, quavers. She has turned into an old woman overnight.

"Yes, Amma. Of course." It is a bald-faced lie, and we both know it. My status is too precarious to risk leaving the country—I was brought in on a green card as a child, naturalized decades ago, but it is only my marriage to a white man that is letting me stay. All around us, brown people are lined up, entire families, each toting their two allowed suitcases. Some silent, trying to imagine what life might look like, in a homeland many left decades before. Most talking, talking, making plans, filling up the fear with words. So here I am, saying farewell to my mother. My sisters, who failed to marry white men, are already gone. "We'll talk online. Every day."

Amma grabs my arm, squeezes it hard, her fingers digging into the flesh. The nails on her hands are cracked—she hasn't been taking care of them, hasn't had a manicure or even applied polish in what looks like weeks. I should have been paying more attention, should have taken her to have them seen to. There's been so much to do, and so little time to do it. "Talk to John. You must convince him to apply for jobs in Sri Lanka. That would be the best way."

Sri Lanka doesn't want him. They are unhappy enough at being forced to accept so many repatriated ex-citizens; strong-armed by US *diplomacy*, the threat of American guns. As it is, they've created a new status for the returnees; my mother and sisters are allowed in, but denied the right to vote, to effect any kind of political change. And white people—white people aren't welcome at all.

I have plenty of complaints about the Sri Lankan government, but on that one issue, I sympathize. My stomach roils with what white people, mostly white men, are doing to us. At night, I lie beside my husband and try not to blame him for other men's cruelties. Sometimes I fail. Three nights ago, John slid his hand under the covers, reached to cup my breast, and I froze in response.

What's wrong? he'd asked.

Just do what you want. Take what you want. That's what your people do, isn't it?

Unfair, unfair, but I'd wanted to hurt him, and I had. He let go, slid away, and we endured a cold silence until sleep finally, mercifully, descended.

I gently patted her hand on my arm, hoping it would convince her to loosen her grip. "Yes, Amma. I'll talk to John."

"He should have been here. You shouldn't have had to drive me here yourself." And then she is pulling me into her arms, and my face is buried against her soft neck, warm with the scent of jasmine and orange blossom. My father had loved those scents, and it is as if they trigger something deep within me, tears that are rushing up, eager to burst free. I have been calm up until now. I have to stay calm, for her, for my son. My body is shaking with the force of my need to stay calm.

"John had something else he needed to do." IUDs had gotten scarce, impossibly expensive, and most companies had stopped covering them. But John's university insurance would still cover our ten-year-old, Jenny, who, thank god, was fair-skinned enough to pass for white. The underground clinics that served brown girls hadn't been able to get their hands on IUDs for years.

It was just bad luck that the only opening the doctor had was on the same day my mother was leaving. I couldn't tell Amma what they were doing—she was a good Catholic, an old-school Catholic, and she wouldn't understand. *Children are a blessing*, she'd always said. They were, they were—unless you couldn't care for them. Then, they simply broke your heart.

I wouldn't let Jenny face that decision, not until she was an adult, at least. She hadn't wanted to go this morning, not ready to accept what her still-maturing body might be at risk for, but I'd insisted. It was a parent's job to protect their child, to make them do what was good for them, even when it hurt. Like the times I'd had to hold her still, despite protests and tears, to draw out a sharp splinter.

The line shifted again, and again, the movement finally separating us, breaking Amma's hold on me. Here we are, at the doors, two security guards flanking them, impassive in their black riot gear. I hold out a suitcase to my mother, and Raj offers her the other; after the briefest of hesitations, she squares her thin shoulders and takes them in her hands. Amma bites her lip and turns away, passing between the guards and through the sliding doors without another word. Is that kindness, that she forebears a final plea? Or anger, that I am not coming with her? Probably both.

My sisters aren't pleased that the responsibility of caring her is falling onto them—I am eldest, it is my job. But I have two children here who need me, now more than ever; they have to be my first priority.

As long as I am allowed, I will stay.

THE AMAZING TRANSFORMATION OF THE WHITE HOUSE DOG

Ron Goulart

The afternoon that the head of the Alternative FBI called at his Uncle Josh's Robotic Lab/Residence in Georgetown, Norbert Dawes was in the first-floor workroom checking up on the most recently completed robot canine, Fido #7. The silver-plated robot wasn't in his cage but sprawled on a candy-stripe love seat watching footage of today's protest marches in nearby Washington. A wave of about two-thousand protestors was moving closer to the White House with signs reading **Return Our Library Cards!** At the tail end of this protest group, another one was following, demanding **Stop Teaching Russian in Our Grammar Schools!**

Norbert was a borderline tall man of twenty-nine, borderline good looking. "How in the hell did you get out of your darned cage, Fido?"

The silver-plated robot shifted his sprawl. "I watched a docudrama about safecracking on the telly, Norby," he said. "By the way, how's your quest for a job going? The Guild, Bascom & Vespucci ad agency fired you from the Creative Department over three months ago."

"*Two* months ago, when they relocated their offices to Tangiers where copywriters are cheaper."

"A pity the current administration cancelled unemployment insurance or you could coast for a bit longer."

Straddling a chair, Norbert asked, "Okay, how'd you turn on the TV?"

"I'm his new improved model, and your dear uncle built in all sorts of extras," replied Fido #7. "And I've modified myself quite a bit on my own. I can now get all the movie channels and I can scan all of the World's Greatest 100 Books that I should read before I kick off."

"That's impressive, but—"

"I like to keep well versed, Norb. I am also watching the President's daily diatribes. What a maroon, as Bugs Bunny might say." He hopped off the love seat and settled on the floor. "Also taking classes in calculus, porn, and hypnotism. If I'm going to be pretending to be the President's White House Dog, I've got to be well steeped in all sorts of stuff."

Norbert jerked upright. "Where did you get that goofy notion?"

The robot dog rose up on his metallic legs. Tilting his head upward toward the off-white ceiling. "From above, dear buddy. Right now, Uncle Josh is talking to some gink who's top man in the Alternative Federal Bureau of Investigation."

"You can listen in?"

"Obviously."

"Does my uncle know that you—"

"Sure, part of my duties as—"

"Norbert, could you pop up here to the second parlor," came his uncle's voice out of a wall speaker. "There's a fellow from Washington I'd like you to meet."

Despite the fact that the second parlor was a high-ceilinged room with off-white walls and black-and-white furnishings it felt cozy. This was due to the large, deep simulated fireplace Uncle Josh had invented and installed and never gotten around to patenting.

On the black-and-white floating coffee table were a coffee urn, two cups, and a gilded cage in which, on a swing, sat a bright yellow robot canary who could sing one hundred light opera pieces. She was set on silent at the moment.

Uncle Josh rose. "Norbert, this is J. Edgar Nofzinger, the Chief of the Alternative Federal Bureau of Investigation."

"Pleased to meet you, young man." The AFBI man was borderline short and plump, wearing a conservative gray suit. "Understand you've been lending him a hand since you got canned."

"Well, actually what happened—"

"The President of the United States wants a robot dog for the White House," cut in the scientist.

"Actually," explained Nofzinger, "we have to replace the White House dog we acquired for him."

"Why is that?" asked Norbert. "I just saw a special report on NBC about the President frolicking on the White Lawn with Hound Dog and having members of the Cabinet throwing a stick for him to fetch."

"I was hoping to get to throw a stick, but I didn't make the cut," the AFBI chief said. "But let me give you a little back story." He paused to try his coffee. "The President, soon after taking office, started getting literally millions of letters and tweets from his admirers. They all said that he ought to have a dog in the White House. They said Nixon had a dog, FDR had a dog. It was a national tradition. Nixon had Checkers and FDR had Fala. We knew who FDR was but had never heard of Fala. Be that as it may, when over eight million suggestions came—more than any president since Woodrow Wilson has ever received—we went and got a dog, a full-grown one. The best-looking canine ever to belong to any president. A large part of those who communicated with the President thought the White House dog should be named Hound Dog as a tribute to America's greatest singer, Elvis."

"In fact, Big Momma Thornton introduced the—"

"No time for fake facts. Our problem is that the President turns out of be allergic to dogs. Dander and so forth," he said. "The entire staff of the Mayo Clinic has said he's the healthiest man ever to be president, but he has this one tiny flaw. So we want a robot version of Hound Dog. We can't have the leader of the country going *achoo!*

"Mr. Nofzinger also likes the idea that my robot animals can talk if need be."

The AFBI chief nodded. "Give him somebody to keep him company and shoot the bull with him during the wee hours when he's tweeting."

"I'll have Fido #7 tuned up and looking exactly like the real Hound Dog one week from today," said Uncle Josh. "$400,000, up front."

"A bit steep. But we can take the amount from some useless public service giveaway," Nofzinger told the scientist. Now, we'll pick up you and the new improved Hound Dog next week and slip you into a rear entrance of the White House. You can come along if you wish, young man."

"Yeah, I just might."

"We'll be in a panel truck that has **MISS LIBERTY YUMMY 100% COWBURGERS** on both sides in red, white, and blue."

A cold drizzle was drifting down the next Wednesday afternoon. Norbert and Fido #7, in his cage, were sharing the rear seat of the panel truck. The robot dog was complaining.

"This fake fur your uncle stuck me with is itchy," he observed.

"You don't have skin. Metal can't itch."

"A lot you know, buster. I ought to be getting hazard pay."

From the front passenger seat Uncle Josh suggested, "Try to stop talking, Fido. We're approaching the White House."

Fido said, "Hey, Nofzinger, do they have video in my kennel?"

"No."

"The darn White House can't afford one more telly?"

"Hush up," advised the doctor.

"Grumble," said the dog.

"I'll buy you some comic books," offered Norbert. "I don't know if they're still publishing *Rex the Wonder Dog*, but we can hope."

The AFBI director said, "We just passed the First National Plunderers Bank. We're turning into one of the rear entrances. Make certain you don't make any snide remarks to the most important man on the face of the Earth, Fido."

"I shall be a model of deportment," said the dog. "Did I mention that I can also speak French, Portuguese, Tagalog, and Swahili?"

Norbert leaned toward the dog as the truck came to a stop. "Don't heckle anybody while we're here." he said. "Especially the two Secret Service men who're coming toward us."

"No, indeed. You think I want to get shot in my inner workings?"

The first corridor they were passing through was dim-lit. Leaning against the gray wall was a man wearing a white robe and peaked white hood. Nofzinger slowed. "Not a good idea to wear that here, Phil," he said in a quiet voice.

"Just trying on my Halloween costume."

"Halloween is several months off."

"Just want to make sure it fits."

Fido said, "What a maroon."

They turned into a brighter hallway.

The doors to the White House Kennel were high and wide. An armed Marine stood at each side, holding a rifle.

"You'll find it quite roomy, Fido," the AFBI chief told him as they entered.

Crossing the threshold, the robot dog observed, "I can understand why the Prez would sneeze. This joint smells to high Heaven."

Dr. Dawes suggested, "Behave yourself."

Nofzinger's phone made a polite noise. "Yes, sir," he said. "I'm showing them around the refurbished kennel as we speak. How's that again?" He paused, eyebrows rising. "And then what, sir? Yes, that would be a problem." He turned toward Norbert and his uncle.

"This is the President's chief advisor, Bull Dawson. They won't be back now until very late this evening, And the President won't be able to get introduced to Fido until tomorrow."

Fido gave a slightly metallic chuckle. "Another screw-up, huh?"

After nodding the doctor into a chair, Nofzinger explained, "The President and his advertising staff flew down to Texas on Air Force One for the opening of the newest Cowburger Restaurant. The ad staff is a group of top-flight men who've been unjustly let go from some of the nation's best outfits for alleged malfeasance and chicanery."

"I've heard of those events," said Norbert. "They always bring a singing group along."

"Again this time they've got another great bunch. Uncle Charlie & the Amateur Moonshiners."

Fido said, "The Amateur Moonshiners. I've heard of them. Can't carry a tune in a bucket."

"Can you tone him down a bit, doctor? His jibes might anger the President and cause him to boot him in the backside." The phone sounded again. "Now what? Yes. Yes. In the front window? Which high school marching band?"

Norbert enquired, "Something else has happened?"

"A usual high point of the openings is a butchering of a steer in the front window. Draw a nice enthusiastic crowd," explained the AFBI man. "The problem was that this particular steer got ticked off and butted both the butchers. Goaded one of the admen and crashed thru the front window and chased a high school band that was marching by to the outskirts of town and then escaped into the plains."

"A confederacy of maroons," said Fido.

As they emerged onto the top step of the back staircase, Nofzinger said, "I'll contact you, Doctor, to report the President's reaction's to Fido."

"I'm sure they'll be favorable. I persuaded him to be his amiable best."

The doors behind them came slamming open. Two dark-suited Secret Service agents rushed out, carrying a struggling, auburn-haired young woman by feet and shoulders.

"Hey, you lunks," she said. "There's the thing about freedom of speech."

The slightly taller Secret Service man said, "Not if you heckle the press secretary at an impromptu press conference you weren't actually invited to.

Norbert jumped toward them. "Put her down."

"You're about to commit a federal crime, sir,"

"These gentlemen are guests here. I'm giving them a lift back to Georgetown," the head said. "I know Katy Farnum of *The Baltimore Daily Gazette*. I often read her column, 'Ask Diogenes.'"

"You can't violate the no heckling law and just walk away," said the other agent.

"I'm not walking, I'm being hauled." She glanced toward Norbert. "You're Norbert Dawes, aren't you? The guy who got tossed out of Guild, Bascom & Vespucci three months ago."

"*Two*. But otherwise that's me."

The head of the AFBI told the agents, "I'll give Miss Farnum a lift home."

They hesitated for a moment and the young reporter suggested, "Put me down, fellows."

When she arrived on her feet, her cell phone fell to the steps.

Scooping it up, Norbert said, "I'll see that she gets home, Uncle Josh. If that's okay, Miss Farnum."

She shrugged her left shoulder. "A definite improvement over the other contestants."

"Call me if you have any trouble, Norb," said his uncle.

Katy promised, "I won't heckle him."

The rain fell somewhat heavier by the time their cab had traveled three blocks.

Sitting to the left of Norbert in the backseat, the young reporter asked, "You live with your Uncle?"

"At the moment, yes. I'm helping him with his robot animal construction," he said. "My wife ran off with a fellow who's known as the Butcher of Wall Street. What with alimony and job hunting—"

"You sure you got the right the right Butcher?"

"John Ross Kreech."

"Naw, that's not him. His name is Sean Clancy II."

"You mean my wife ran off with an imposter?"

"Could be it's a franchise operation and Clancy is now being Butcher."

"Suppose so. Now I'm not even sure who made me a cuckold."

She nodded sympathetically. "By the way, I have two roommates. If you come in for a drink, watch out."

"Reporters?"

"Folk singers, using a lot of material from Pete Seeger and Woody Guthrie. Also stuff they come up with on their own with a little help from me."

"What do they call themselves?"

"Sisters of the Night. They dress all in black and wear black wigs."

"Play the local clubs?"

"Mostly. But during the election campaign a local conservative group hired them and it wasn't until the second Seeger number that the light dawned." She leaned toward the driver's window. "Brownstone on the left, five houses ahead."

The President and his entourage arrived back the next morning, He did not get around to meeting Fido until that afternoon. There was an urgent impromptu meeting on the White House Lawn with a dozen young representative of the Girl Scouts of America to explain why the government was taking a larger share of the profits from the sale of Girl Scout Cookies from now on. He said, "As the whole wide world knows, I am a huge champion of the rights of women, especially young and pretty ones. Like, for instance, those two blondes on the left there and that bashful brunette on the far right."

He also hinted that it would be a huge honor for them, and every Girl Scout in the world, if they made him an honorary Girl Scout and issued a really fancy scroll with lots of gold lettering.

The cheer the girls gave him when he concluded, struck him later as somewhat tepid. He told his chief advisor, Bull Dawson, to remind him to have a small press conference with representatives of the major sympathetic newspapers to listen to a few of his insights into the problem.

He next had a meeting in the Oval Office with the man who ran his President Brand Sweat Socks factory in Singapore who was having a problem with disgruntled employees who wanted more than one lunch break per week.

He finally dropped in on Fido and brought him a steak sandwich made from his own brand of steaks.

Fido, very politely, informed him that robots don't eat.

"That's another new thing I learned today. That's another great thing about this greatest nation in the history of the world. You can learn a new huge fact almost every single day."

"Truer words were never spoken, sir." The robot wagged his fuzzy tail.

After having a sincere and very cordial chat with his new dog for nearly four minutes, the President took his leave. "I'll see you tonight and you can keep me company while I tweet," he said as he departed. "And we'll have a photo session one day soon. Frolicking on the lawn, you chasing sticks."

"Jolly, sir!"

When he was alone, the dog said inside his mechanical brain, "This is going to be easier than I thought."

They had lunch the next afternoon at the modest-sized Cozy Veggie Café. The restaurant was on the second floor of a venerable redbrick building and it had an indoor grape arbor.

Norbert had reached across the checkered tablecloth after they'd ordered and took hold of Katy's hand.

A plump plastic grape lost its hold on an arbor slat and plunked down next to the young reporter's cup of hibiscus tea. "You knew that Fido can make phone calls?"

"Yep. Has he been calling you?"

"Gave me some items for my next column," she said. "Apparently he pretty much has free roaming rights at the White House. Most of the denizens think he's the true Hound Dog."

"What sort is he supplying?"

"Well, the secretary of physical culture, lady named One Round Tessie, has disappeared completely, for one thing." She let go of his hand to take her notebook out of her purse. "Three top presidential aides resigned on the same day and retired to a small village in Los Vergas, Mexico. Bull Dawson fell off a balcony and broke both legs. He's in extreme traction at the Bethesda Hospital. The President has signed up for a course in Advanced Dementia Control at a Dr. Bartholt Rainbolt's Walk-In Therapy Shacks in Baltimore. And also—"

"Wait now, Katy. Fido has told me that Bull Dawson had been expressing considerable dislike for him. And he claims to be a terrific hypnotist. Suppose he—"

"Can you make somebody do something he doesn't want to do?"

"I'll to talk to my uncle about our robot dog."

Two days later, Norbert took Katy to dinner at the Proustian Bistro. They were sitting at a secluded table and holding hands, when their waiter returned.

"A Monsieur Fideaux has phoned to order you a bottle of pinot noir, sir. Shall I serve it now or with the meal?"

"With the meal."

"You are friends with this excellent gentleman I take it."

Norbert replied, "Yes, I've known him for some time. Is he a patron of the bistro?"

"Alas, no. But we have frequent conversations on the phone and now and then he tweets." The waiter grinned. "An astute commentator on the political scene. Speaks perfect idiomatic French. He is a world traveler, is he not?"

"Of late he's been sticking close to home," provided the young woman. "Some sort of hush-hush assignment."

As the first course arrived, Norbert's phone buzzed. "Yes?"

"Are you kids swilling your wine yet? Marcel told me it's pretty good. And it sure costs enough."

"Who exactly is paying for this?"

"It's not kosher to ask a benefactor how much he's paying for a gift, Norb."

"Not how much, but *who*."

"Oh, I have a way to tap into the accounting department. Your drinks are on the White House," explained the robot dog. "And I've been making large donations to Planned Parenthood, the NAACP, the Humane Society, and a slew of others."

"Well, don't get caught. My uncle would be—"

"Did they ever catch Raffles or the Scarlet Pimpernel or Fingers Fergusson?"

"Who's Fingers Fergusson?"

"Well, actually he did get caught. But he was the exception. Not to worry."

Norbert sighed and ended the call.

Early the next morning Norbert woke up in a strange double bed in the Hail Columbia Hotel. The wide fifth-story window showed an especially pleasant clear blue day. Unseen birds were singing pleasantly out there somewhere in the sunny day. Sparkling white clouds were drifting gently by the window.

He sat up and said, "Oh, yes. Of course."

As he swung out of bed, he heard someone typing on a laptop in the next room.

He swiftly got into his shirt and trousers and stepped into the parlor.

Katy, fully dressed, was sitting at the coffee table. "It looks like our relationship has reached a new level, wouldn't you say?"

"Yeah. No doubt about it." Crossing, he leaned and kissed her. Then he frowned, turning to look at the room's big window. "Noise starting up out there."

"Fido alerted me to it about a half hour ago," she answered. "One might say the stuff has hit the fan. My *Daily Gazette* is giving me the whole top of the fold on the front page."

He sat on the arm of the sofa. "Makes me proud to know you, miss."

"Thus far the President has fired all the remaining members of his cabinet, created a Wild Life Commission, a Wind Energy Commission, cut the Military Budget in half, raised the minimum wage to $18.95, had the federal government announce that controlling global warming was the top White House job." She paused to take a deep breath.

He went to the window. "Boy, that's the first time in years that I've seen newsboys in the streets yelling 'Extra! Extra!' And the streets are filling up with people."

"The President also initiated free schooling for everybody, from nursery school to graduate school. He—"

"Never underestimate the power of hypnotism."

Katy's phone vibrated. "Hello? Sure, he's right here."

The robot dog said, "The President just tweeted to the press that he's planning to enter a Buddhist monastery and will leave shortly."

"Then the Vice President will take over?"

"Nope, he's already left to join an organization to minister to American Indians. Rest of the cabinet has scrammed."

"Okay, we'll work out a way to come get you home, Fido."

"I won't be coming back for the time being, Norb."

"Why would that be?"

"Well, somebody's got to run the country."

HANDMAID'S OTHER TALE

Jane Yolen

I am a woman,
you can tell
by the tinkling
of the bell
around my neck,
it's time for milk,
while master walks
about in silk.

I am a woman,
fertile days
I get a good
amount of praise;
a mattress and
a sheet or two.
But other days,
red tents will do.

I am a woman,
quiet voiced.
I tiptoe and I
make no noise.

My daughters taught
just how to be,
respectful, silent
just like me.

I am a woman.
To birth a boy
is what I do
for master's joy.
But one day I
will take a knife
and slice it through
my master's life.

I am a woman,
not a toy,
and only that
will bring *me* joy.
And if I'm killed,
I will not care
for then I'll be
just earth and air.

But this one thought
I will hold fast:
an equal to
the man at last.

SANCTUARY

Brian Francis Slattery

Dear Mari,

First: Jess, Efraín, Pete, Lucretia, Carlos, and Serena are all dead. I haven't found Mya, Hugh, Will, Beth, Dolores, Tom, or Anabel yet, but I think they're dead, too. I'm so sorry.

We were on stage when the first bomb went off. It was down the street and we were playing too loud to hear it. Efraín and Jess were playing so well, better than ever. You should have heard them. Efraín was breaking in a new kit. Jess had the same shitty guitar she's always had, the one she's made sound great. It was a big night, crowded from the stage to the back door. I remember someone screaming from the back. Then the second bomb went off, right outside.

There was a flash and the windows blew in, and the flames shot in right after them. The people near the windows were shredded and set on fire. The whole building shook and the ceiling above the bar collapsed. The power went out and the room filled with smoke. I grabbed Jess's hand—I was standing next to her—and started to drag her toward the front door. You know it's only five feet from the edge of the stage, but somehow in those five feet I lost her. I spilled out on the street with a pile of people. My bass was still strapped to me, but the neck had snapped. There was a scrap of bloody cloth hanging from the broken place. Maybe a dozen other people were on the street with me. We scrambled away from the heat and waited. No one else came out.

I read somewhere that there are people who don't panic, and I guess I'm one of them. I watched Eight State burn. It scares me now what I felt then. I wish I could say I cried, or that all my sadness turned to rage. Instead I felt my blood pressure drop. The sound in the world got a little quieter. I looked down the street and saw a row of fires, bomb after bomb. I heard tires screeching and machine gun fire, and I knew—just knew—that there was nothing I could do for anyone at Eight State, and half my friends had been in there. But maybe if I got to Temple in time, I could save the other half.

You know on the news they said it was a paramilitary outfit. I say it was a bunch of assholes who decided to get a lot of guns, make a lot of bombs, buy up some Army surplus vehicles and make their own uniforms. The news said they came at our city because we said we were a sanctuary, because our mayor spoke out, because we marched. They said they did it in the name of law and order. But I didn't see any order that night. I saw burning buildings, shattered glass, flames, and rising smoke. I heard people screaming and shooting, shooting that wouldn't stop. I heard sirens everywhere. Police cruisers racing from block to block. An ambulance on its side, on fire, in an intersection. And body after body, ruined and run over, or smoldering, or just full of holes. The couple the police captured said they just attacked wherever the people were. It was a Friday night, so that meant clubs and restaurants, downtown streets. It meant us.

Everyone was on the street in front of Temple. They hadn't hit the place yet. I found Jacob there. He still had his guitar. We stood there and wondered what we were supposed to do. Nowhere felt safe.

Then we all saw it, a tan Humvee barreling down the street toward us. It ran over a dozen people and looked like it would plow through the rest of us, except that another car, racing in from a side street, crashed into it and knocked it on its side.

This is our city. You understand what it's like. As soon as the Humvee stopped, we were all over it. We got two of the tires off. They'd locked the doors, so we broke the glass, dragged three of those motherfuckers out, and threw them in the street. They got shoved around a lot. One of them shouted at all of us: *We're the New Patriotic Army of the East and we are coming for you.* You could tell he practiced it. He tugged at his uniform when he said it, like his clothes gave him his power. So we pinned them down in the street and stripped them naked. Someone set their clothes on fire.

That's when the police showed up. I don't know what would have happened if they hadn't. I don't even know what I wanted to happen. I wanted to hurt the men who had attacked us. I don't think I wanted to kill them. I know a few other people did, and would have done it. I don't know if I would have stopped them.

But the street was filled with sirens and flashing lights. The police hauled off the men we'd beaten up and a few of the people who'd been beating on them. The officers looked scared and exhausted. There were ambulances and paramedics scrambling around. Blood all over the pavement. And then the lights were gone and it was quiet and we were all standing around again, staring at each other, listening to the city explode around us. It still didn't feel safe to go home.

"You got your car?" I said to Jacob. He nodded. We got in and drove out of downtown, under the highway, and to the shore. We were the only ones there, and it was dark and quiet. The highway above us was empty. We could hear the waves against the rocks. And without either of us saying a word, we crawled into the backseat and fucked. We did it because we survived, and because it was better than screaming at the sky or burning something down.

We're kind of a thing now. I hope that's okay. It's been two days and the New Patriotic Army keeps saying they're coming back. A few of us have left town and I don't blame them. But the rest of us are staying here. This is our city and we all have this feeling, more than ever, that we make it what it is. So we all have each other's numbers now. We check in all the time. We're buying guns that we don't want to use, but we will if we have to. We're a sanctuary now in a bigger way than we were before. And we're already partying a lot more, a lot harder. It feels like the best kind of resistance, to insist on living how we want, and to keep doing it, until they put us in the ground or learn that it's a lot better to join us than to fight us. We'd even let them in if they wanted it. I wish they did.

Please be safe, and come back and visit when this is all over. Our town misses you.

Love,

Ali

ONE FELL SWOOP

James Morrow

Dear Mom and Dad: Sorry about this tyrannosize Facebook message, courtesy of Uncle Oliver's account and password (unlike some members of this family, he trusts me), but it seemed like the best way. Yes, it's really me, your estranged firstborn (I'd be your prodigal son if I had the resources), the college dropout (sorry to break the news so abruptly), the professional loser, the perpetual loner, the mikado of incommunicado, living in a North Broad Street dump (though obviously that's about to change), delivering pizzas because he slept through most of his classes at Villanova.

You can understand why I hesitated to get in touch these past ten years, but now that I'm famous and a bona fide national hero—have the media started pestering you for interviews yet?—I like to think we'll stop disowning each other. Family dynamics aside, what I did last week will probably prove controversial, so I wanted to tell you my version of the Rosewood incident *inmediatamente*, and you can judge for yourselves just how proud of me you want to be.

It all began when I got an email from Brick Quillin of the Nihilistic Rifle Aficionados saying he wanted to talk to me about "that amazing six-minute video" I'd posted on YouTube. He was referring to "Dark Alley Allegory" (check it out), which I made eight years ago starring my former girlfriend Monica Cartwright as a snacky but naïve Buddhist who gets chased through wet nocturnal urban streets by her wannabe rapist, then bursts into a gun shop just before closing time, at which juncture the proprietor laterals her a Glock and she blows the wannabe's you-know-what off (I heard Monica moved to the suburbs and married a proctologist, and I think I'll look her up now that I'm a celebrity). The gist of Mr. Quillin's communiqué was that he wanted to tête-à-tête me, so we arranged to have a beer at O'Leary's on Cottman Avenue the following evening.

Somebody's ringing the buzzer. I'll start a new bubble in a minute.

Whoever it was, they disappeared. No sooner had Mr. Quillin and I ordered our Pabst Blue Ribbons than he revealed that he reports directly to Dwayne LaRue—yes, *the* Dwayne LaRue, the NRA president whose photograph sits next to Jesus on Aunt Sally's big doily in your living room.

"Here's the deal," Brick began (he insisted I use his first name). "Every time one of these school shooting things occurs, there's a great hue and cry throughout the land, and some Demoncrat or other—we call them Demoncrats—the fucker sets out to gut the Second Amendment. Last month Mr. LaRue decided we should 'settle the question in one fell swoop' and 'solve the problem once and for all,' mostly because he's sick of the nasty mail he gets every time somebody's third-grader goes down. God, that was a beautiful video you did, Joshua."

"Glad you liked it."

"Mr. LaRue believes we need what he calls 'the definitive event.' I was there when he closed his eyes and fired his antique Colt .45 at his map of the Delaware Valley, where he grew up, and the bullet hit the Philly suburb of Rosewood. 'Once the definitive event has become part of our national dialogue on guns,' he told me, 'the country will find itself on a brand new calendar keyed to A.R. versus P.R.'"

"Ante-Rosewood versus Post-Rosewood?" I suggested.

"Bull's-eye, trooper. If we can bring it off the definitive event, then whenever some socialist Congressman from Connecticut gets out his Constitution gelding kit, all we need do is spit in his eye and say, 'Sorry, Clyde, you're making an A.R. argument, and this is a P.R. world, so go home to your fucking "Kumbaya" garage band and leave politics to the adults.'"

"Mr. LaRue is obviously some kind of genius."

"You'll be part of a team—the Four Musketeers, we're gonna call you, which is more appropriate in this case than when Mr. LaRue's favorite novelist, Victor Hugo, used it, because Athos and company mostly wielded rapiers, whereas the definitive event will turn on actual firearms."

"Alexandre Dumas," I said.

"Each of you will become a living, breathing embodiment of what's wrong with every damn hypothetical statute designed to prevent so-called gun tragedies. The stakes couldn't be higher."

"This republic would be in the crapper," I said, nodding, "if the NRA wasn't out there protecting our God-given freedoms from the God-given freedom takers," after which Brick give me the biggest wink in history.

"Musketeer Number One, Duke Heston from Exton, he'll be using a brace of handguns instead of his customary AK-47," said Brick, "thus giving the lie to the notion that banning assault rifles would accomplish anything. Musketeer Two, Whitley Sprague from Warminster, has absolutely zero history of depression, drug abuse, or antisocial behavior—he's never even gotten a speeding ticket—so that ipso facto ruins the argument for mental-health background checks. As for Musketeer Three, Julius Eliot from Ardmore, he imported his Beretta ARX 160 under the strictest conditions imaginable, with paperwork stretching from here to the moon, and so—phffft!—there goes the case for making it super difficult to put together a legal private arsenal."

"You people have really thought this through."

"Finally, there's you, Joshua, Musketeer Number Four." Brick passed me a one-page script. "You'll be making the case for arming classroom teachers. Mr. LaRue wrote your lines himself. May I assume you have a rifle?"

"A Galil ACE and a FX-05 Xiuhcoatl."

"Forget the Mexican. Use the Jewish."

"Listen, Brick, I'm certainly willing to play my part, but I'm probably not the ideal casting choice."

"Oh?"

"To tell you the truth, I've had schizophrenia issues."

I was about to given him a full disclosure, including the two years I spent at Cedarbrook after burning down the Tuckermans' house, but Brick pooh-poohed my concern, saying, "That doesn't matter, son. You're the point man for our Packin' Pedagogues initiative, period, full stop, which means your psychiatric history is irrelevant. Do you follow my reasoning?"

"I think so."

"Hell, Duke Heston, he also has a spotty record in the sanity department, but he's our answer to the assault-rifle sophists, not the background-check fetishists, so his mental condition will prove massively beside the point once the whining starts. And just because Julius Eliot pops two different kinds of antipsychotics every day, that doesn't mean he's not the perfect symbol for the futility of regulations, given how the People's Republic of Massachusetts made him jump through a thousand hoops before his Beretta came in the mail."

"At least Whitley Sprague has all his marbles."

"Now you're catching on, Joshua. He's our sanity icon. Normalcy on stilts. Okay, sure, he got his Remington GPC as a door prize at the Keswick Fire Department barbecue, no questions asked, and somebody's bound to bring that up—but in the context of the definitive event, it wouldn't matter if he got the thing out of a Cracker Jack box."

"It all sounds very logical, Brick, but I'm afraid I could never articulate those arguments myself. Will there be a press conference afterward?"

"Leave the spin doctoring to Mr. LaRue and me. Your job is to show up at the event site with your Galil and your John Deere minicam cap and your script completely memorized."

It's the buzzer again. Next bubble coming soon.

Visitor ran away again. Anyway, the big day dawned under a bank of thunderheads, and by the time my Galil and I got to Rosewood Elementary it was raining ferociously. Mr. Quillin introduced me to Julius Eliot, whose hard-to-get Italian beauty was a wonder to behold, then Whitley Sprague, armed with his door prize, then Duke Heston, who was indeed packing two single-action, magazine-fed pistols instead of a rifle.

We all proceeded directly to our assigned classrooms. I was in charge of Ms. Peterson's second-graders at the far end of the hall. After hiding the Galil under my jacket, I burst into the room.

"Here's how the game is played," I explained. "If somebody here can produce a firearm, thereby demonstrating that this school takes self-defense seriously, I'll turn around and go home. So, boys and girls, imagine I were to visit the coat closet. Would I find a pocket pistol in any of your galoshes? Raise your hands. Nobody? Too bad."

The storm reached a pitch of fury, rain battering the windowpanes, thunder booming, lighting flashing. Naturally I thought maybe the meteorological commotion would screw up the recording of my conversation with the youngsters, but I needn't have worried. The John Deere minicam has a great noise-reduction filter.

"I don't suppose there's a Dan Wesson in the gerbil litter?" I persisted. "No? I was afraid of that." Then I turned to Ms. Peterson and asked, "Do you by any chance keep a Kel-Tec in your desk?"

"What?" she mumbled. I don't think she was processing my question very well.

"You should look into the NRA's Packin' Pedagogues initiative," I explained.

Now came the ratta-tat-tat of Julius, Whitley, and Duke getting the job done. Ms. Peterson's kids started chattering excitedly. She herself turned white as a ghost.

"I'm disappointed in all of you," I told the teacher and her class, then pulled out my Galil and opened fire.

Brick had warned us we'd probably get arrested, but of course President Orloff paid our bail (a cool ten million per musketeer, but that's his idea of cab fare), so here I am back in my Broad Street dump, trying to set things right between you and me while waiting for Mr. Nesbit at Doubleday to call back (he mentioned a $100,000 advance).

If you've been following the story, you know that most of our lawmakers acquitted themselves beautifully. "Our thoughts and prayers are with the grieving families this night," noted Senator Paul Armitage (R-Alabama). Thoughts and prayers: an inspiring sentiment, don't you agree? "Speaking on behalf of the entire US Congress," said Representative Portia Mitchell (R-West Virginia), "let me express our profound appreciation to everyone who lost a child, especially if you loved that tyke to itty-bitty pieces, because there comes a time when we must put the Constitution first, and you all rose patriotically to the occasion."

I'm not sure I can corroborate President Orloff's account of the parents' behavior that morning. As far as I know, they didn't really cheer Julius on. None of them actually helped Whitley reload. The President insists he heard a recording of a mother talking to Duke.

Supposedly she said, "I won't do any special pleading for my freckle-faced Brucie over there, and that's his twin sister Megan with the pigtails, because we can't let our American way of life fall into the wrong hands," but I must admit I'm skeptical. All four of us musketeers were in police custody well before the moms and dads arrived on the scene, so I'm pretty sure there wasn't any parental kibitzing.

When it comes to the Presidential Medal of Freedom, I'm pretty sure Mr. Orloff isn't exaggerating. It's a white enamel star surrounded by gold eagles, and you get one for making "an especially meritorious contribution to the security or national interests of the United States." Next week they're flying Julius, Whitley, Duke, and me to Washington, all expenses paid, and Mr. Orloff will personally hang the medals around our necks.

Back in a minute. The damn buzzer again.

finishing this will be hard fuck / leaking all over keyboard fuck / monica cartwright got up her nerve this time / she had kept glock from dark alley allegory fuck fuck / said i did her 2nd grader that day / welcome to p.r. world mom and dad fuck fuck fuck / wish i could enjoy it with you / life not fair fuck fuck fuck fuck / all i can do is press return / love josh

BK GIRLS

TS Vale

In the beginning was the word.

John 1:1. Right. I know that now. But what about in the end? How can *these* words matter, if all I can do is burn or bury them?

Don't know. Doing this anyway. For me and my BKs.

My hands are shaking. This is a mess. Too much to say and all I have is this one sad piece of paper.

But this is it. This is me now. Me with this crumply page from *Our Lord's Little Lambs, A Coloring Book*, writing in the dark on this stinky futon, under this scratchy sheet, ugly stubby pencil poking holes with every other letter but I can't help that, I can't help how all this is. All I know is this has to come out. I will go crazy if this doesn't come out.

Maybe even die.

Will die if I get caught with this. I don't know but I think they're almost done with me. The acting is getting hard.

Got to keep going. Oops, sorry for writing this right across the outline of the Lord Jesus' haloed head but can't waste an inch. This one single coloring book page is all I've got and thank you, brown crayon blob, I bet you are the reason I have it at all.

I don't get trusted to wear a bra let alone talk to the little kids. But I do get trusted to tub-wash endless fucking laundry and go rake compost heaps. Sometimes I find stuff. Nothing to get me out of here, not me or any other BK, but still. I found this.

Yeah. Some poor kid picked the brown crayon. But here, brown is for dirt and Jesus is always peach. Rip-tear-smack, out in the compost it goes.

I look peach. My dad does not. Not that they know that here. Even if they'd watched for a while, first, they wouldn't have seen him, Mom and Dad have been divorced four years. Four years plus the almost two I've been here. I don't know the date anymore but I know it's spring and I'm five months pregnant after two times it didn't go so well. And. I know the date that I got snagged.

Thursday, July 19, 2018.

My name is _____. I'm twenty now. I was riding my bike in a place where bad things don't happen: _____, on _____ Road. My mom's name is _____, my dad is _____. My number was _____ and I am so sorry I don't know anyone else's by heart, my phone with my whole life in it got drowned in acid, I'm pretty sure.

I still don't remember which ones got me.

At least two men and definitely one woman. But the rest is all messed up. I got slammed off my bike by one of those boxy delivery trucks, one that veered right into me at that stretch of cornfields between my grandma's house and town. I remember people jumped out, they had a blanket and I thought they were going to help me, but they threw it over my head and stuffed it in my mouth and then they stabbed me. A needle, not a knife, but I didn't know that then.

They used that needle a lot. All through the trip and here, too, at first. Wherever here is. I'm so sorry, don't know that, either. I'm not outside much but all I've seen is miles of grass and far-off mountains and sometimes, some far-off cows.

Once, I saw a plane, way up high. But I flew twice with my dad, so I know: if anyone on that plane looked down, all they saw from that far up was nothing. Just squiggles and patches like a painted map.

I was mostly out of it in the back of that truck. I remember road noise, jounces, and water poured into my face. Maybe I was supposed to be drinking it. Oh, and someone's bad breath and being told to rejoice, I was saved. Probably they said a lot more that I don't remember, stuff like what got yelled at me day and night once I was here, or maybe like what I hear all the time in the open now that I'm all broken in.

Outbreed. Outvote. Outactivate.

Take back this country for Christ.

They really mean this. They aren't kidding. There are way more of them than someone normal like I used to be could ever want to guess. And it wasn't just the way things went in November 2016 and December 2017 that made this happen. They've been doing this for years, and for them, those were signs from the Lord. Proof of their righteous path.

I've learned that now. Just like I've learned that Jesus is always peach.

Back page now. Obvious, yeah, if you're looking at this. No color here, just an outlined flock of lambs running into a pen, Very Happy Now That They Are Safe.

No color good. Can say more words.

One more thing from the back of that truck. The thing that saved me and I don't know where it came from. Theater club, maybe. Creative writing class, maybe. Who knows. But wherever this thing came from, even half passed-out in the back of that truck I *knew* that to survive, I had to *act*. From that minute on, no matter what, no matter how hurt or scared, I had to be the best actress ever. A *perfect* actress. I had to be scared but also sometimes fight them a little, just enough so they didn't suspect I was faking them. And I had to act perfectly beat down, every time I did get beat down.

Sometimes, acting perfectly beat down is less beat down than how beat down I am for real.

But I do it. I do it *right*. If I don't I will never get out.

Here are the words I say. I wake up every day and tell myself, today, you have landed an amazing part. You're soooo lucky to have this part, so many girls wanted this part, but none of them got it but you. You are getting to play the part of that famous girl who got kidnapped by the Take Back America-ers but unlike any other girl over all these years they've done this, this girl escaped. No matter what they did to her, no matter what she saw happen, she did everything right for a really long time. And when this girl *did* escape, it fired up all the right people, all over the world. Everyone got together, and all of those other BK girls she had to leave behind when she escaped, well, they got set free, too.

My BK girls.

I never say it out loud. Not even to the other BK girls here who really seem like friends to me. I just can't know if they really *are* my friends. Thank you, Dad, for all the books, I know how these things go, it is way too easy to trust the wrong person.

I can't trust my BK girls but I love them. I love them so much. They see me and I see them, even when we can't cry even one single tear.

BK girls. BK is for Boko. As in, those Boko Haram guys who stole those girls.

Yeah, I know. Can't happen here. This is America.

Right. Here I am.

Here is my word. I am telling you, it *is* happening here. It is happening to me.

I bet for the future movie, you want every sick detail. You want the rape-marriage parts and the brainwash parts and all the ways they hurt us while they're telling us that we're saved, and that the babies they take are the chosen warriors, and that Out There, everything is Godless. Sorry. Not enough paper. Not for all of that.

Hand shaking again. Sorry. Worse mess than before.

I was almost fourteen when those Boko Haram guys kidnapped those girls from their school and made them into slaves. It was horrible, they made those poor girls convert and marry them, and I remember thinking how I was the same age, but totally grateful I lived in America.

I remember how those kidnapped girls were all over the news. I also remember that even though the whole world was upset, those girls stayed missing, mostly. Missing or dead. The whole world being upset, didn't change a thing for them.

No internet or cell phones here. None I could get to in a million years, anyway. But in this one single way I'm glad. Because I'm really, really scared that if I searched on those girls, I'd found out they're *still* mostly missing or dead. Or worse, that those terrorist guys are all still doing what they do and most of the world has long since forgotten those girls, everyone busy with dealing with something else.

Or maybe just keeping their heads down. Hoping they won't be next.

In this movie I'm starring in, playing the part of this kidnapped American girl, I'm going to make sure that in the end, every last girl is found. Here and over there. I'm going to make people want to do more than just be sad and move on, forgetting that me and my BK girls ever existed.

Those are my words for the end. The ones I say at night, before I go to sleep.

Here I am. Already at the bottom of this second side, down in the grass beneath the little lambs' feet.

I'll fold this sad piece of paper into a tiny strip. I'll stuff that strip back through the hole in the hem of this awful nightgown, and I'll pretend to wake up and ask to go pee. At the five-month mark, you can get away with that.

Are you reading this? If you are, you'll know I played this part of mine perfectly—the girl who did not get scared of her words. She did not burn them or stuff them in the muck.

You will know that me and my BK girls existed. That all of this really did happen. Because here, in the beginning and in the end, these words are mine, and I will believe that you will hear them. I will believe you will never forget.

• EVIDENCE • Redacted • 2/10/21 •

ISN'T LIFE GREAT?

Don D'Ammassa

Alice needed to go shopping. She hated the thought of it, but they were out of milk and bread and low on just about everything else. It was pointless to make up a list in advance because you could never predict what would be on the shelves and what would not. There hadn't been any lettuce since the autumn, and it had been months since she had last seen ground beef or bacon. Alice made a short list anyway, if only to delay the moment when she would have to go out.

She was dismayed to discover that her car had less than a quarter of a tank of gas left. Ever since the invasion of Iran, gas had steadily increased in price almost from day to day. The last time she had added any—she couldn't afford to actually fill the tank—it had just passed ten dollars per gallon.

The house next door was still empty. The gay couple who had lived there were now confined to the state's newest Behavioral Correction Facility. At the first corner, she turned left even though the grocery store was to her right. The more direct route would take her through one of the so-called Patriot neighborhoods and without the appropriate flag-embossed sticker, she'd be taking too great a chance. One of the neighbors had decided to risk it two weeks earlier and she'd been dragged from her car, beaten and raped. The police had admonished her for provoking the assault.

She threaded her way through Loyalist neighborhoods until she reached the main road. There was a grocery store there, but the placard in its window was Patriot rather than Loyalist and they would not have served her. There were more pedestrians here and most of them were armed, a change that had followed the Open Carry Executive Order. There were new posters on the telephone poles proclaiming major advances in the Pacific War. Everyone knew that South Korea had fallen and Japan was suing for peace, but it was considered seditious to admit it openly.

She passed the closed fire station—budget cuts had been deep this year—and the new police compound with its expanded detention area. She wondered if Old Mrs. Grant had been able to get her granddaughter released. Tiffany had been held there for six months without a hearing, and that had been last year. The courts were backlogged and since the President had suspended habeas corpus—not to mention posse comitatus—the number of pending cases had increased by an order of magnitude.

A small military convoy rumbled past as the armed guard checked her plate number against his list and let her enter the parking lot. Alice carefully engaged the alarm and got out, tightly clutching her handbag. There were so many homeless people nowadays, and many of them survived by purse snatching and even more violent assault. She walked briskly to the door, passing the newspaper vending machines, which were naturally quite empty. Both of the city's dailies had been shut down for sedition two years earlier, and the government news sheet that had replaced them had not shown up for a couple of months.

There were a dozen or so other shoppers. There was no conversation and no one initiated eye contact. Alice took a carriage and headed for the produce section. This was always the least well stocked. The repercussions from the mass arrests of migrant workers had been dramatic and enduring. Almost everything available here was locally grown, and it was too early in the growing season for there to be much that hadn't come from a greenhouse. Still no lettuce, although surprisingly there were some carrots. Alice took two packages, which was the per-customer limit.

There was ample milk and other dairy products, thanks to the large concentration of dairy farms nearby. Orange juice had disappeared long since but there was still apple and grape, though they were very expensive. She chose a few other items but avoided canned meats. The scale-back of FDA regulations had led to a rash of illnesses and even a few deaths over the past two years and almost no one ate anything that wasn't thoroughly cooked. Their water purifier was broken again, so she picked up some bottled water.

She stopped to read the bulletin board. There was another voluntary immunization clinic coming up. Alice wondered how many people could afford to pay the five hundred dollars per child expense even if they wanted to. The World Health Organization had been subsidizing distribution of vaccines until the United Nations was ordered out of its New York City headquarters. They were now in Geneva. As far as Alice knew, the US was still a member but a new ambassador had not been named after the previous one's resignation.

The cashier was new, but Alice couldn't remember ever seeing the same person at the register even twice. The adjusted minimum wage was so low that no one could actually survive now that food stamps were no longer distributed. The total was higher than she had expected. The sales tax had been raised again, and the special temporary border security tax supposedly financing the southern wall was still in force.

Alice loaded the groceries into the trunk so that they couldn't be seen by passersby, then crossed the street to the coffee shop that had replaced the now defunct Starbucks. The new place only served Christians, but she had a forged Methodist Congregation member card. She ordered a latte but drank it quickly because the two armed men sitting at the next table were openly ogling her. The adjacent park had disappeared under enormous piles of coal. The Coal Employment & Enhancement Act had required all municipalities above a certain population size to purchase coal on a sliding scale, even if they had no facilities that could make use of it.

She heard gunfire on the drive back, quite a lot of it, and breathed a sigh of relief once she was sure it originated nowhere near her home. A police surveillance drone flew overhead while she was unloading the car. It hovered for a few seconds, but the operator never challenged her. Even so, she was breathing heavily when she was finally inside the house.

Bob got home a half hour later than usual. He carpooled part of the way and walked the last two miles, following the discontinued bus route and crossing the now abandoned Amtrak right of way. There used to be a shorter way but the bridge over the river had been closed for safety reasons the previous year and both ends were blocked by barbed wire barricades. He worked for a small manufacturer who relied on government military contracts, so his job was safe enough, although he hadn't had a raise in three years and his benefits package had been dramatically reduced.

He waved a greeting, obviously tired, and turned on the television. The government channel came on first, by law, but it was not yet mandatory to watch it and he switched over to one that featured vintage television shows. Alice brought him a beer, the only actual luxury they allowed themselves.

"Hard day?" she asked.

"Yeah. We lost two people today. One of the supervisors was arrested for disturbing the peace. He got into an argument in a bar about the suspension of the Supreme Court. And Fred Nashawaty is going to be deported."

Alice frowned. "But Fred was born here, and so were his parents."

Bob nodded. "His grandmother was an immigrant, and naturalized, but she came from Syria. She was Christian, but under the Terrorist Association Act, her citizenship was retroactively revoked. All of her descendants are technically illegals now."

"That's awful!"

Bob shrugged. "Fortunately, if that's the word for it, business is down a bit. NATO members are no longer buying military parts from us." The President had withdrawn from NATO when it refused to join in the Iranian War. "If the trend continues, they'll cut back our pay in accordance with the Defense Wage Adjustment Act."

"I wish Congress would stand up to the administration more often. That was a horrible law and you could tell they didn't want to vote for it."

"Well, after what happened after the midterms, what do you expect? A third of the Senate and a quarter of the House all arrested for Disloyalty under the Domestic Security Executive Order."

The doorbell rang. They both stiffened, then Alice started for the reinforced closet that was the closest they could come to having a safe room. Bob retrieved his handgun from inside a vase and cautiously went to the door.

"Who is it?" he called out.

"Olsen Letter Delivery." Bob had never heard of them, but ever since the Post Office had been abolished, numerous small delivery services had sprung up.

"Leave it on the doorstep."

"You have to pay for it first."

Bob opened the peephole and looked out. A tired-looking man in a uniform stood just outside. "Who's it from?"

"City council."

Bob swore. It was against the law to decline to accept any governmental communication. "How much?"

"Two dollars." Bob swore again, but he extracted the bills from his wallet, unlocked the door cautiously, and traded it for the thin envelope. The delivery man turned back toward the armored van that awaited him, a body armored sniper in the roof turret.

The letter was routine and really didn't apply to them, since they had no children. Home schoolers were now required to include certain subjects in their curricula that had been optional previously. Following the privatization of all public schools, a very large number of parents had either chosen to take over the job themselves, or had been forced to because they could not afford the high attendance fees required by the Charter Network. The new requirements included Revised American and World History, Understanding Climate Variations, Creation Science, and Philosophy of Government.

Bob tossed it into a wastebasket.

After dinner, Alice turned on their aging computer. She rarely used it anymore. The Digital Priority Act had allocated so many resources to corporate users that it took as long as ten minutes to load some sites. The Pornography and Fake News Control Act had installed filters so stringent that many innocuous sites were no longer even accessible. She did most of her clothes shopping online, but even that had become less viable since the government had decreed that sales of used items were illegal unless the item in question was no longer available from the original manufacturer.

Much to her surprise, she had one email. Most of her friends no longer used electronic communications because Homeland Security monitored it tightly and had a rather all-inclusive definition of what constituted a domestic threat.

The message was from her mother. Alice's sister Paige had been indicted for murder following the discovery of her illegal abortion, even though doctors had determined that the fetus was non-viable. The message was terse and neutral in tone because it was not a good idea to be known as having pro-choice inclinations, but Alice knew her mother had to be devastated.

She was on the verge of tears when she angrily turned the computer off. Tired as he was, Bob felt a surge of sympathy and went over to put his arm around her shoulders. She told him the news and the dam burst as she itemized every way in which the day had been horrible.

When she was done, Bob sighed. "Look at it this way, hon. We've pretty much sunk as low as a nation as it is possible to go. I'm sure brighter times are coming."

Bob was right. Less than an hour later, two Chinese nuclear devices detonated over the city and brightened up their lives dramatically, if rather briefly.

THE MEN WILL BE HUNGRY AFTERWARDS

Ray Vukcevich

At the Boy's House

The men will be hungry afterwards. She'll bring fried chicken. Everyone loves her fried chicken. Maybe she should poison it and kill them all. She absolutely did not just think that! La la la la. Poor little Mia. The child should have known better. This was all the fault of her parents. They should have made sure Mia understood the rules and the dangers in breaking them. This is no laughing matter! La la la la. Turn up the heat to sizzling. Good fried chicken is all about what you do to it before you drop it into the hot oil. If there is anything even remotely good about this situation, it's that her own son, Samuel, might come to realize the way of things and straighten up and fly right. The kids are only ten, she likes to tell herself, but still he needed to spend more time playing with the other boys and less time messing around on the computers with Mia. Now it's come to this. She must remember to save him a couple of drumsticks.

At the Girl's House

"The Fewer is an old meanie!"
   Just a tweet.

She hadn't even included a hashtag. She hadn't addressed it to @POTUS and she had certainly not addressed it to His personal account. But she had also taken no precautions to cover her tracks, which totally surprised her friends, because if anyone knew how to surf the dark net, it was Mia. It was like she was sending him a message, sticking her tongue out at the most dangerous man on the planet. That had turned out to be a serious mistake.

It was just a joke!

Okay, okay, but let's not do that again.

Everyone stopped laughing when the President's Patriotic Police in full riot gear swarmed in and arrested the entire town.

The Upshot

Fox sent in a team that was actually bigger than the whole town. There were cameras everywhere and people running all over the place managing cables and lights and shouting at one another. Unsmiling men in the black and silver uniforms of the PPP prominently displaying assault rifles stationed themselves strategically at every corner and in every business. Everyone worried they would fine the tunnel running from their church basement to the church basement of their sister city on the other side of the Wall, but so far, it had remained undiscovered. With any luck it would remain that way until after this was all over.

The men of the Town Council milled and muttered about at the door of the church like they were waiting to be invited inside.

Samuel and his father stood a little apart from the men. His father held on to Samuel's shoulder both to reassure the boy with his touch and to make sure he didn't bolt.

Samuel looked up at his father and asked, "It's just pretend, right? I don't really have to do it, right?"

His father looked around quickly to make sure no one had heard what the boy had just said. Then he leaned down to speak in a low voice.

"That might have been true a few days ago," he said. "We could have handled this if was just us and our so-called Political Officer. We could have bought him a few drinks, and no one would have been the wiser, but now it's gotten totally out of hand. You'll have to do it for the cameras, so all these people will leave."

Samuel looked around wildly like he was thinking of making a break for it. His father could feel him trembling beneath his hand on his shoulder.

"It'll be okay," he told the boy. "Look over there with the other women. Your mom. I think she made chicken. This will all be over in a flash and we'll be eating drumsticks."

Samuel looked over at his mother in the roped-off area for the women. She didn't meet his eyes. None of the women were looking at him, either. Some were looking up and some were looking down. They were waiting for the signal to go inside and sit down in the pews.

A moment later, a white woman in a fancy costume that made Samuel think of evil clowns stepped up and spoke to his father.

"I think we're ready to start," she said. She didn't look at Samuel.

His father pulled him forward and into the church. The men followed them in, and then came the women of the town.

The woman in the colorful uniform pulled Samuel away from his father and out of the way while the townspeople found their assigned places. Then she marched him over to his starting position just inside the door and in the middle of the central aisle between the pews.

"Okay," she said loudly. "Listen up!"

Everyone got quiet.

"Looks good," she said. "Get ready. Here we go."

A moment later, she shouted, "Action!"

Someone pushed Mia out from behind the curtain. You could see the big pushing hands dart back out of sight as the girl stumbled forward onto the stage where Father Diego usually stood to mechanically recite how they all had to try harder to make the President's plans work. It looked like Mia might fall, but she caught her balance and stood looking out at the town, all her friends, her parents, her neighbors, the cameras, the news crews, the police and their guns. She wore a simple white summer dress with a pattern of green and blue flowers scattered down the front.

She hesitated a moment more, but then, as instructed, she lifted her hands up to her chest and put her palms together as if in prayer.

She looked terrified.

The woman directing things gave Samuel a little shove from behind, and he moved forward down the central aisle toward Mia. On both sides, the townsmen had been lined up like a gauntlet. The women had been assigned places in the pews, and they all twisted around to watch him pass. The cameras and lights and soldiers made the place look completely alien.

It was very quiet. Everyone was looking at Samuel. He was having some trouble getting enough air into his lungs, but he kept moving. When he got to the front, he turned sharply to his left and moved to the stairs leading up onto the stage. He walked up them and then turned back and walked up to Mia. She turned to face him.

This was all so stupid, so terrifying, so adult. The future was a dark cave with teeth and tongue, and Mia and Samuel were about to be snatched up and chewed to bits and swallowed.

He could choose to simply not do this. He could grab her hand, and they could run out the back and into the desert. They could hide in the gullies and eat prickly pear cactus fruit and sleep with the coyotes and the roadrunners. Surely the strangers would give up and go home sooner or later. Samuel and Mia could slip back into town unnoticed, could get back to their old lives, and everything would be okay.

He looked into her eyes and she looked into his. He wanted to whisper that it would be okay, that it would be quick, that he was sorry, that he would always be her friend, but then he saw that there was a camera back there pointing right at his face. There would be another one behind him pointing at Mia's face. They did not want to miss one juicy bit of this. If he whispered his words at her, they would read his lips and make them start all over again. If he did it right the first time, it would be over. He wished he could tell her that it would be best if he just did it right the first time. The two of them would grow up. They would become outlaws together! They would ride horses across this desert and shoot arrows at the President's Police. Maybe they would get married and their children would never ever have to do something like this. Would she ever believe that he had had such a plan on that awful day? Her face was now completely blank like she had gone off somewhere else where things were not so bad.

It was time to do it.

He reached his right hand forward, low and with the palm facing up, as he had been instructed, and plunged it between her legs, pushing the thin fabric of her skirt back, too. He glanced down, as instructed, to check his position. Everything looked right. He grabbed at whatever was under there, her pussy, they said, and gave it a little squeeze.

THE ROAD SOUTH

Madeleine E. Robins and Becca Caccavo

How's it going?
Hello?
Emma?
Where are you?

      hey mama llama. sorry bout that, dead zone was extra dead
Dead, huh?
                              As a dog.
You're in Texas?
                        mexico. south-y

Where are you now?
    around guadalajara? at least the road signs have been saying so.
Stay away from the Mexico City sinkholes.
                       but moooommmmm…
I'm serious. There's rioting again.
                  yeah mom, i know.

How are you guys?

    good. alexis has a cold. all good tho long as the snow lasts
    we can just tow him behind us on skis lmao.

    crossed into guatemala last night.

    how are you? how's the school?

I'm okay. School's smaller than it was. Reika and her family left
for Canada. Rolling blackouts: Oakland City Council threatened to
sue the state. State laughed. The usual.

Not too close to the coast, are you?

    no we heard about the flooding. wanted to go thru tegucigalpa,
    but it's lakefront property now.

    how's mycroft?

Fine. Misses you. Hasn't been made into a pie yet.

    thank goodness for that.

That cat has 18 lives.

How are you eating?

    OK. we glean, run into farms where we get fresh food
    when we can.

    got plenty of canned and dried tho.

    we on that oregano trail

    **oregon fucking autocorrect

Now who's not funny?

So where are you, Emma-lem?

Lemma?

Dammit, Lem, say something.

    sorry had to take alexis to hospital

Is he okay?

    no. medico said he was sick before we left US so, you know.

    rest of us are okay

You staying in—where? until he's better?

hes not going to be getting better. i knew this would be hard, mom, but...

Jesus, honey. I'm so sorry.

i know mama
left him in central nicaragua
Need to get to cabo de hornas before spring tide get too high.
hope you have a map.

I might have to close the school.

what mom no

I might. No one has money. Tom Chun paid with a chicken last week. Good eating, but not good for taxes.

the school is your dream

And the city was poking around talking about licensing, anyway. They don't care, just want the fees. Which I can't pay.

what would you do?

I don't know, sweetie. Maybe move out to Redding with Uncle Lou.

and...the house?

It's just a house. You're not coming back from Antarctica.

but its our home

Sometimes you gotta let go.

I'm sorry. That sounded bitter.

Lem?
Please answer.
Emma
Please answer. Where are you. Are you okay?
Lem

im here i'm okay we got held up at border to panama

When?

thursday.
no, friday morning.

Are you okay?

yeah they were looking fr plagues n shit
we're okay Im okay.

Plague? I thought that was just in the north.

they're trying to keep it out out of here. had to wait
for blood tests

So you're not carriers. Well, that's a mercy.
Boiling the water?

oh absolutely, darling, just like at home.

Will you hate me forever if I say you could still turn around and
come home?

won't hate you…just won't turn around.
last boat to king george goes in november.

Will they let you in?

of course, without a doubt.

I wish there was something here for you.

i'm not going away from there, mom. i'm going
toward antarctica
school is still in session?

More like day care now. The older kids are all working.

older like how old

All the kids over 7 are working the Oakland garden.
Still have some toddlers and kindergartners. And runny noses!

sorry I didnt text yesterday got stopped in Pasto in Colombia
mom
mama
you are really really scaring me mom
mom please

I'm okay.

I have that bug that everyone's getting.

what? bug? which bug? are you okay now?

Don't freak out. It's not plague. Just fever and feeling tired.

And I'm better today.

What happened in Pasto?

roadblock looking for contraband.

they didnt know what to make of the reverse

osmosis machine lmao

held us over night on the good

side though—FINALLY A SHOWER

But you're okay? Where are you guys now?

in ecuador been trading goods and art and stories.

its beautiful here. so green

I remember green. :)

When I was a kid there were trees and whole hills of yellow flowers
in the springtime. I'm sorry you didn't have that.

What did you trade?

some books some old tech just stuff. some ska-doodles

No medicine, I hope.

no mom im not dumb

Have you been in contact with the settlement?

ya via radio twice a week

How are things there?

Mom its amazing. the excavation sites—theyve found the first
sign of a city under the tundra! The hydroponics are in their third
harvest. The research station has launched a low-orbit seeding
platform—makes me feel like we have a chance.

Humanity, that is. and us guys in the van, too

It's good you're going.

that's the first time youve said that mama, whats going on?

Feeling a little blue. I haven't shaken this virus.
Had to close the school. Can't keep up with the kids.
                    but you're okay right? you've kept the gaerden going
                              and have been eating ogod food?
                         wait no! closed school for good?
It was going to happen.
                         so what are you going to do…go to reading?
I don't know. When I feel better I'll make a plan.
                    im sending you healing love. i love you mom, so much.
Me too, you.

        GREETINGS from catacaos peruuuu! remember miss lang from
                              4th grade she would love it here
Why?
               its beautiful…it looks like every photo she had on the
                    walls of the classroom. the marketplace is insane
Insane?
                                        so much beautiful fruit
Sounds delicious.

                                        hey, mamallama
Hey, honey.
                                   you still in oakland?
I am. I'm afraid
                    wait afraid of what is everyrhing okay?
Sorry, I got interrupted.
I'm afraid Mycroft is gone. He got out the window
last Wednesday and hasn't come back.
                    no, mom, he could still come back
I hope so, Lem.
                              so its just you?

Actually, no. Hua Tran and Luke moved in last week.
They lost their apartment and I needed some help. So.

what do you need help with.

I haven't been well.

mom what kind of bug is this? you've been sick for weeks.

Nurse thinks its one of the tick-borne ones. Bourbon or Heartland
virus. Can't afford tests, no retro-virals work on it. Don't fret. It'll
work itself out.

Looks like gardening isn't so healthy after all.

we stopped to work at a beautiful farm for a few days
so glad i took spanish—but here they talk mostly quechua.
on road south today. i'm learning so much, mom, every second.

had a close call today

What does that mean? Lemma!

were okay now
got stopped on the road by a local gang
they took most of the food and kaila's and stephen's tablets
didn't find the trap door to the emergency food and money

What happened? Were they armed? Was anyone hurt?

tbh, mom, they just wanted stuff we handed it over
everything was fine we were amicable, given.
i bought this phone in cajabamba

Were you frightened?

Lem?

ummmm…i was fucking terrified but played it
super cool considering
guns and screaming—
we're lucky only stephen got pistol whipped

Oh, God, baby. I want you home Now.

its ok mom nothign i havent seen in the bay tbh i just never told
you

we're more than half way there mom

and we're okay it was not fun but we got through it

I didn't think you'd turn around. But

I hate having you so far away.

i miss you too. i love you.

heading for argentina, then into chile. figure we've got about

10 days til punto arenas then another few days to

get to cabo de hornos

So in two weeks you'll be on King George Island.

yeh punto arenas is our last big city

we'll be there in time for spring

Spring in Antarctica. Wow.

antarctica isnt what it was back in the day mom

I know.

Listen, Emma-lemma: you may not hear from me after you get
there.

what? no, mom, the settlement has net amd cell reception

we can video-chat

mom

mom you there?

I'm here.

what did you mean before?

Before?

Oh. Nothing.

If I go to stay with Uncle Lou, I don't know what the cell service
will be.

mom you live in america. even when there's no water or food or

governmentthere will always be internet and cell service

I just didn't want you to worry. If you didn't hear from me.
im not worried that, i know that woudlnt happen
Where are you now?
left villa carlos paz this morning. heading back to highway.

Mycroft came back!
He wandered in this morning looking like he
had slain a dragon and could eat a horse, but
he's still alive.
YES!! i told you!
i fell in love with a puppy yesterday
that wandered up to the van
his eyes gave me the same feeling your hugs do
Are you going to bring him to the settlement?
i wish.
I can't imagine you without a pet.
i'm saving the world for all the pups out there, mom

puntas arenas by tomorrow morning
coastal route is flooded so we're going the long way
How're your supplies holding up?
we bought more fruit and stuff
haven't used the antibiotics since alexis
its only a few more days til we get there

mom we're on the boat! the water is so blue.
we got to cabo de hornos and for once everything went
just the way it was supposed to
loaded all the supplies we had left and now im on deck
watching chile vanish

its gray and blue here they may call it spring
but it's hot as hell!
mom i know me going was hard for you. it was and is for me too,
all the time.
but i'm so excited to get there and start creating and living my
purpose...in *antarctica* you know? ive always been obsessed
with the place
kay is already plotting data for the settlement long
distance. we have the chance to save the planet. its terrifying and
amazing

I hope you can.
of course we can mom! the planet is being saved right as we
breathe
I'm proud of you.
Remember.

be proud of yourself. you created me.

mama we sighted the shore—king george. it's green, with gray
hills behind. and theres yellow flowers, mama. its so beautiful
youd love it. we're going to fix the world.

SKIPPY'S VISIT EAST

Michael Kandel

Skippy: How you doin', Doug?

Doug: Okay.

Skippy was happy because things were so quiet now after all the noise. When he went to visit his cousin in Green Wood, they didn't get into an argument once, and Doug didn't even frown. Well, maybe a little but not to notice. So he had made his peace. Skippy thought it was high time, too, after all the griping and groaning and yelling, which seemed never to end, this, that, over and over. As for Aunt Jade and her animals, now that the animals were gone, she didn't have to raise her voice anymore, did she. Skippy remembered how her voice went into your ear like a knife when she got outraged, which happened all the time, with the news every hour on the hour. Both of them, she and her son, yelling and scowling, well but now that it came, the worst possible thing, and did its work, the world didn't end, did it. Being angry does a number on your health, and if Aunt Jade didn't break into her great horse laugh anymore, she was taking fewer nervous pills, Skippy saw, and there weren't so many doctors she went to now, this speciologist and that. Of course there weren't many doctors now, period.

Skippy: How you doin', Aunt Jade?

Aunt Jade: I'm okay, Skippy.

High time life got simpler. Okay, war wasn't a picnic, war never is, is it, but hey you know who your enemy is, an enemy is an enemy, no two ways about it, whereas Skippy could remember how, before, no one was sure of anything because there were always a hundred opinions and people holding up signs on this side, that side, over and over. You didn't need to strain your head anymore, because there were no questions left, really, just answers, and those answers, thank God, were every one of them clear, to the point, and didn't have a lot of big vocabulary words. In school Skippy had always hated big vocabulary words and the people who used them like a club banging you down, stupid-stupid-stupid, into the ground. A person could relax now without sour brains in lab coats on TV giving their warnings in rocket science gibberish and pointing to their charts of doom-doom-doom.

Skippy: Nice day.

Doug: I guess.

Doug lucked out, and what a relief that was, because after the government torture he wasn't locked up because of his joining that religious group, which was really crazy. Millie saved him, a treasure that girl, using her personal connection to a big-dick billionaire in Connecticut. Okay, Calvin didn't luck out, because of his color and last name, which maybe wasn't his doing but hey folks, too bad, you can't have everything: look at the apartments and parking lots and playgrounds underwater now around Blue Lawn, and look at all the cancer. A person, in Skippy's opinion, should step around the downsides the way you step around dogshit on the sidewalk, when there used to be dogs. A person should think positive. It's good for your ticker, they say, because there's so much to be thankful for, when you stop and think about it. Like for example: no more drug addicts with tattoos on their necks and corks in their earlobes. No more homeless who stink like year-old cabbage and hold out their paper cups as if it's your fault and not theirs. No more of those annoying reservation casino Injuns or those cabbies in turbans, with brown teeth and reeking. Mexicans, Jews, Arabs, Japs, Pakis, and queers all history.

Skippy: Anything up, Aunt Jade?

Aunt Jade: Not really.

To add to the thankful list: no more ton of leaves to rake and bag every November. There's not a tree left standing now, if you don't count the few scraggly dwarf pines at the edges of the sumps, looking more dead than alive these days after the Chinese blight, or the Saudi blight, whichever it was, or maybe the radiation did it, but hey who cares. What's past is past and not important. Skippy always hated history in school, American history, world history. They don't do that now, or civics or current events, either, because education has got a whole lot more comfortable and positive, high time, too, not just in the heartland but on both sour coasts.

Skippy: Hangin' in there, huh?

Doug: Yeh.

Skippy: That big scar there don't hurt you?

Doug: Nah.

They used to play, all four of them—Skippy, Doug, Millie, and Calvin—king of the hill on the steep landfill slope in the bird sanctuary north of White Shore, when there were birds and when there was air you could breathe without any protection, in the good old days before politics got in the way of everything. Kids laughing like crazy and never getting hurt. You fell, you rolled, you got up again. Aunt Jade would cook chili con carne for them in the evening, back when there was meat. God, it smelled wonderful. Or they would go hide-and-seek in the cemetery at the town border, among the old tombstones in languages no one could read anymore. Best friends every summer, for years. Of course today kids are a whole lot safer, after the militia guys took out all the terrorists, immigrants, and reporters with their semiautomatics and after the razor wire walls went up in every direction. Skippy sleeps with a Glock under his pillow and thinks of that familiar lump near his head as insurance. He doesn't need it of course but you never know and why take a chance.

Skippy: Great to see you, Aunt Jade.

Aunt Jade: Great to see you, Skippy.

At night, over his head when he gets home, in every room hangs a big color glossy of our shepherd, who is kind of like a father ten or a hundred times your size, and at the same time kind of like a buddy, who's just your size. Our shepherd is no-nonsense and down-to-earth, and if he's a badass sometimes, hey he's a badass there to take care of you when you need taking care of. Skippy sees no pictures of our shepherd in Aunt Jade's place, but he understands that it might be asking too much of her to put one up, time has to pass and wounds have to heal. He doesn't like to come east anymore, to tell the truth, this is uneasy, treasonous country, where sadness and hate hang in the air like smoke that won't go away, smoke on top of all the other crap a person needs a mask for. But this is his only family now and he feels drawn, probably on account of all the memories.

Skippy: Bye, Doug.

Doug: Yeh.

They used to go fishing, back when there were fish. Skippy never cared that much for fish, he was a meat guy, a juicy beef guy, but there was something wonderful about being on the water or in sight of it. The water made you feel clean and open and free. Now of course the water is nine-tenths scum and the permits cost so much. Skippy once reeled in a shark, and everyone was cheering. He was maybe ten then. Not a big shark, just a mud thing, maybe two feet long, ugly and thrashing all over the deck, but the fishing people slapped him on the back like he was a hero and had won first prize. He's choking up now, on account of that memory. He has to swallow. It will pass, in a minute. Take a deep breath, Skippy, as you wave, leave, go out the door, walk to the road, and turn west. The armed guardian drones above you will comfort you and lead you in the right path for our shepherd's sake. See, it was only a minute. Skippy feels better already. He's okay.

DESIGNED FOR YOUR SAFETY

Elizabeth Bourne

From: Sophie Goldstein

To: Emily Wilson

Date: July 12, 2020

Subject: Got it!!!!!

OMG I got the job! I'm so happy! I start at Patterson, Perkins, and Keller next Monday. It's temp—the paralegal I'm replacing is on sick leave. Man, I can't believe how many people are sick. It's a little scary.

I wanted to meet up with Krystal and Jennie at this 90s bar to celebrate my new job, but the mayor asked people not to "gather in public spaces." So I'm buying champagne and we're celebrating at my place.

Anyway, the law firm is in this green building called The Muir. Hopefully, I'll have a real office and not be in a basement hole like the last place.

Tell me more about Liam. He sounds gorgeous.

Ta!

Sophie

From: Sophie Goldstein

To: Emily Wilson

Date: July 19, 2020

Subject: Here I am—employed!

Sorry I didn't email sooner, I've been crazy busy at work. So many people are out sick everyone's doing OT to keep up.

Disappointing that Liam didn't show for your date, but prob just as well. Maybe you can hook up when he gets better. I guess this flu is everywhere. They say Patient Zero was located in some Chinese town called Yiwu, so I guess it's the Yiwu Flu. Gives me the shivers.

On to my office. It's on the 14th floor and I have a view! It's only houses, but daylight! You'd love this place. It's one of five Core Green buildings: The Carson (Denver), The Gore (Portland), The Abbey (SF), and The Muir (Seattle). Company headquarters are in The Roosevelt (Omaha). This building's The Muir, and it's SUPER crazy green.

Three of us newbs got an orientation Monday morning. The building is 100% off the grid. It generates its own power (solar), collects rainwater, and recycles gray water through a swamp filtration system on a terrace off the 6th floor.

Everything is software-controlled. Heat, windows, shutters, and lights. There's a rooftop garden with a barbecue pit, hangout spots, and a greenhouse growing vegetables that management gives to the local food bank.

OMG composting toilets! I thought they'd be gross, but they're OK. Everything flushes down to the basement where it's composted. Some is used on the gardens; the city picks up the rest. We DID NOT tour the basement, thank God.

The tour ended on the roof above the 22nd floor with a fantastic view of Rainier. Our guide gave each of us a roof-grown vegetable as a gift. A beautiful ripe tomato is sitting on my desk, I Instagrammed it. I could have it for lunch, but all I can think is that it grew in poo, so maybe I can't.

I know, you're rolling your eyes, but you were the one into WWOOFing, not me. Oh, and there's no parking garage; instead, bike racks are lined up under a beautiful big tree in this park-like area out front.

This morning, two people collapsed on my bus. I freaked out! We had to wait for an ambulance to take them to the hospital. I'm glad I was wearing the face mask dad gave me. I don't care if I look dorky as long as I don't get sick.

Stay healthy! Wear a mask!

Hugs

Sophie

From: Sophie Goldstein

To: Emily Wilson

Date: July 22, 2020

Subject: See you in October?

It's Overtime Saturday! I'm scheduled for Sunday, too. If this keeps up, I'll come see you in October. My 90-day gig here will be over then, and with all this OT, I'll have extra money in the bank. Let me know dates, and I'll look for cheap flights because that's why God made credit cards.

Mom says my brother Jack drove down to Portland today because his GF is sick, and her family's in Hawaii. I hope she's ok.

Hugs,

Sophie

From: Sophie Goldstein

To: Emily Wilson

Date: July 22, 2020

Subject: Hilarious!

You won't believe this, but the building locked itself!

I was working with Peter, one of the associates on this case, when the building announced, "This is an emergency. For your safety, the building has gone into lockdown. Please gather in the atrium where Core Green personnel will give you further instructions." All this in a British accent. Why British?

Anyway, the outside doors self-locked; the magnetic locks are controlled by the building's software. And the exterior shutters closed up to the 11th floor. Why 11? Why not 10, or 6, or 3?

The hilarious part is there is no emergency, and there's no building personnel on site (weekend!).

I took the stairs down to the atrium. Below 11 the stairwell lights turned on as they sensed me, so it's not dark (if we don't move, the building turns the lights off until we wave our arms telling it we're still there). It's creepy to see a wall outside the windows.

Everyone who came in today hung out in the atrium, waiting. When nothing happened, a couple of guys tried to force the doors with a crowbar they found in the basement—no luck. About 30 of us are stuck.

OMG, Mr. Jeffers, who's the lead attorney on the case I'm working was SO PISSED! He called the building manager, shouting at him over his phone. I couldn't help but hear.

The manager said the weekend guy is sick, but he'd call Core Green Omaha to find out what happened. The building only locks down if it loses contact with the central computer, like in a terrorist attack.

In the meantime, the manager promised someone will get right on it, if not today, then first thing tomorrow. So who knows? I may be sleeping under my desk tonight, an adventure for sure.

About Peter. He's been out of law school for a couple of years, no GF. Really nice guy. He has these amazing brown eyes, not handsome exactly, but did I mention the amazing brown eyes? Since we're locked in, who knows what could happen? ;D More later.

Sophie

From: Sophie Goldstein

To: Emily Wilson

Date: July 24, 2020

Subject: Freaking out

I'm still in the building. Unbelievable. No one showed up Sunday.

This morning, people came in to work, but couldn't get in. We saw them from the roof. They hung out around the tree where the bike racks are, waiting for the doors to open. We yelled down, they yelled up. Eventually, word spread. Everyone's gone now.

Mr. Jeffers called the building manager again, but his wife said he's sick and can't come to the phone. So Mr. Jeffers called a meeting. We met in the atrium.

Turns out 35 folks are stuck here. We exchanged cell numbers and emails. Everyone's mad. People have families they want to get back to. Betsy, who also works for Patterson—her ex called early this morning. Their daughter's sick and he took her to the ER at Harborview. She freaked out, and I don't blame her. I'm freaking out too.

Mr. Jeffers met separately with Livia Trujillo. She's a senior scientist at Kindness Labs, and the only other manager here. Kindness is on 18, and they're a cultured meat co., you know, the stuff grown in a vat.

The two of them came up with a plan: call the cops and get a helicopter to pick us up from the roof (fire ladders reach ten floors up, and the building locks through eleven "for security"). In the meantime, Mr. Jeffers will keep calling Core Green. Someone has to answer.

I saw on the news that things are bad in Chicago too, and there's rioting in Boston, Atlanta, and Dallas. Nebraska declared a state of emergency Saturday; that must've triggered our lockdown. The talk on my newsfeed is that Washington state will declare a state of emergency tomorrow.

Jesus. I can't believe this. Stay healthy out there, and let me know what's happening where you are. We'll have some real stories to tell when this is over.

I'd kill for a shower.

Love, Sophie

From: Sophie Goldstein

To: Emily Wilson

Date: July 25, 2020

Subject: Really stuck

The governor declared a state of emergency. The police turned our call over to the National Guard, and they said that as long as none of us are sick, we're better off where we are. That we're lucky. They'll pick us up in two weeks when things settle down. I spent the morning crying. I'm really scared.

The NG are going to air-drop food to the roof. Someone has to organize food, there are 35 people to feed. Mr. Jeffers volunteered, but Livia said she's used to doing calculations for the meat vats, it's best if she does it. I don't think Mr. Jeffers likes her.

Peter's going to help Livia while I stay with Betsy. Her daughter isn't doing well. She keeps calling the hospital, running her phone down, and then she has to borrow my charger. The line is always busy. It's really hard to be calm and comforting when I'm so scared myself. Mom hasn't heard from my brother since he left for Portland.

At the evening meeting, Livia told us she reached someone at The Carson in Portland. People are stuck there too, one of them is IT, and she hacked into Core Green's management files. The building maintenance software has a really strong firewall; she can't get through, so no way to undo the lockdown. Livia said we should harvest the roof-grown vegetables; we can eat those. I guess I better get over the poo factor.

I'm sorry you aren't feeling well. Call me, okay? It sounds like a cold. My mom texted my dad's sick. She's going to look after him at home because the hospitals are terrible. On the news they showed people lying on stretchers in the corridors, doctors as sick as their patients. Mom promised me she'd wear a face mask. I hope that helps.

God, I can't wait to get out of here.

Thinking of you,
Sophie

From: Sophie Goldstein

To: Emily Wilson

Date: July 27, 2020

Subject: Get better!

It was great to talk with you! I'm glad my "adventure" is a distraction. Colds are awful, and I'm super glad it's nothing worse, but probably not as glad as you are! LOL! What a relief!

On the emergency channel the National Guard advised healthy people in non-essential jobs to leave the city. Krystal texted, she's joining her parents at their place in Moclips on the coast. Jennie's going with her.

Yesterday Livia and Mr. Jeffers handed out key codes for all the offices in the building. We split into 16 teams of two. I wanted to be with Peter, but I was paired with Eddison, a real estate broker working at Cromwell & Reed. We were told to collect stuff—food, medicine, clothes—that kind of thing.

Eddison and I were assigned the 6th floor, which is where Cromwell & Reed's office is, along with four other businesses. We found food in all the kitchens—some gone bad, but there were canned goods as well, and they all had aspirin and Tylenol and bottled water and pop and coffee.

We also grabbed gym bags with workout clothes and toiletries, and lots of office sweaters, and some women had tampons in their desks, thank God! I kept some for myself. Then we piled everything in front of the elevator for collection up to Kindness Labs.

I found seed catalogs, a gardening book, and seed packets in one office. Mostly flowers, but some vegetables, too. He (the name on the door was Drew Nguyen) had a windowsill garden with an ornamental orange tree and a bunch of wilted pot herbs. We took those, too.

Some of the lobbies had comfy, comfy couches. I've been sleeping on the floor in the Patterson office, I think I'm going to move my stuff down to Eddison's floor, and see if Peter will come, too. There's no reason for us to stay in the Patterson offices, not when other places have nicer sofas to sleep on!

The haul got sorted in the Kindess Labs conference room. In addition to the rice, canned meat, and cheese that the National Guard gave us, we have tons of snack food, pop, and coffee. Most offices had a few canned goods, tuna and chili and things like that.

Every office kitchen has a coffee pot and a microwave so cooking isn't a problem, and there's the rooftop barbecue. We found tons of Tylenol and Advil. People had prescriptions stuffed in their desk drawers—anti-depressants, pain killers, allergy pills, and insulin. Most places had earthquake kits with bandages and anti-bacterials. I kept my private stash of tampons, peanut butter, and chocolate secret.

Tomorrow, Livia's handing out work assignments. The building does a lot, but it doesn't clean itself, or add chemicals to the composting vats. Lightbulbs need changing, and all the other work normally handled by maintenance needs doing.

Let me know how you're feeling. I can't believe I'm stuck here for two weeks!

Love you and get better soon.

Sophie

From: Sophie Goldstein

To: Emily Wilson

Date: July 31, 2020

Subject: Dad

Mom called. My dad didn't make it. When the National Guard picked up his body, they put mom on a bus going to the Kitsap Peninsula. She emailed me from home right before she left, said she'd send an address as soon as she had one.

That was two days ago. I haven't heard from her, or from my brother, or any of our friends.

I can't believe dad's dead. Folks in here are really depressed. Everyone knows someone sick, everyone knows someone who didn't make it. Livia's offering antidepressants to those of us who've lost family members, but I refused them. I need to feel what I feel. I have to be strong so I can find mom when we get out.

My "job" is bringing clean compost to the roof where we're making more vegetable gardens. Work keeps my mind off things, also I'm getting really strong. Livia rations food as if we'll be here for months, so I've lost weight too. Fortunately, she doesn't know about my stash.

Mr. Jeffers says she's crazy because we're only here for a week. The NG said so. He stays in his office working on the case. People don't like that he won't pitch in, but I'm going to believe he's right because the idea of being stuck here for months, I just can't.

Anyway, because everyone is so down, we had a barbecue with cultured meat. Livia's very proud of it, but Peter wouldn't eat any. He called it Frankenmeat. In the end, she left him alone saying, "More calories for the rest of us." Then her lab guys, Joey and Darryl, grilled up small burgers for everyone, and we split two bottles of wine. So many offices had liquor in them, we have quite a bar.

The vat meat wasn't terrible, but it wasn't hamburger. Chewy and dry, but it's been so long since we had any meat not from a can, and like I said, there was wine.

While we were on the roof I noticed the downtown buildings still have lights on. Eddison said that was automatic systems doing their thing, which bummed me. Peter and I did move to Eddison's floor, and a girl named Julie from a CPA firm joined us. She's nice.

We're not the only ones. Everyone has moved into empty offices, mostly on floors with unshuttered windows. It's kind of like having your own apartment. Each company has a kitchen, and you can make a bed out of sofas. Every floor has two bathrooms, men and women, not that it matters anymore. There's hot water so washing is awkward but possible. It's not terrible, which shows how my standards have dropped.

Hey, as soon as you're feeling up to it, please ping me. Did I miss your call yesterday, or maybe you were out? Have you left Chicago?

Let me know what's going on, okay? I'm worried about you. One more week!

Love,
Sophie

From: Sophie Goldstein

To: Emily Wilson

Date: August 1, 2020

Subject: Peter

Last night, Peter and I slept together. OMG, I'd forgotten what happiness feels like! He's such a great guy. We had dinner with the group, then Peter took a bottle of wine from his private stash, and we went down to three, to one of the Core Green conference rooms to talk.

It was quiet. Peter played a sound file on his phone of night noises—crickets and frogs and a distant thunderstorm. I imagined us sitting around a fire. I could practically smell the smoke. Then he kissed me.

Things went from there.

We showed up for breakfast rations holding hands, so we're officially a couple. Be happy for me! It may not last, but for now, it's nice not to be alone.

<3

Sophie

From: Sophie Goldstein

To: Emily Wilson

Date: August 6, 2020

Subject: Fires

The NG set the hospitals on fire, at least that's what we think happened. It started this morning with Harborview, which is just a mile west of us. I was throwing compost into one of the new raised beds when Peter shouted to look. The whole building was ablaze.

Then Swedish General went up, then Virginia Mason. Everyone came up on the roof to watch. We could hear the roar. No one even tried to put the flames out. The smoke smelled like chemicals and meat. Betsy screamed, then ran for the edge, but Darryl grabbed her. A lot of people were crying. We were all wondering the same thing: who was inside?

When the smoke got really bad, the building started closing all the shutters, and Livia yelled we had to go inside. As we herded down the stairs, she kept repeating, "It's containment. It's a safety precaution. It's just containment."

When I went to the bathroom, there was ash in my hair and on my face. I threw up.

From: Sophie Goldstein

To: Emily Wilson

Date: August 8, 2020

Subject: <No subject>

No one is coming for us.

From: Sophie Goldstein

To: Emily Wilson

Date: August 9, 2020

Subject: Done

I have to stop fooling myself. You're dead. My parents are dead. My brother's dead. I thought I'd feel sad, but mostly I'm angry. Angry that I wasn't with them. Angry I'm trapped in this stupid building. Angry at the people here for not trying harder to get us out. Peter says it's better to be angry than sad. What good does feeling sad do?

So why write to you? Because it makes me feel better. Because I think there should be a record for when things are back to normal. The building won't fail. It will store these emails as long as there's sunlight.

Livia thinks we can manage for a long time with the roof garden and her meat lab, as long as everyone works together. The real message is that she controls the food. Go along with Livia, or don't eat.

Julie moved out today. She's moving into a marketing company on 17 called BetterU. Terry, who worked PR there, asked her. She said it's because the shuttered windows are too depressing. I think it's because we're anti-L. Julie didn't want any part of that. Better Terry than trouble with L

I hope you're okay.
Sophie

From: Sophie Goldstein

To: Emily Wilson

Date: August 11, 2020

Subject: <No subject>

Yesterday while I was working with Peter and Helen (an older woman with a private banking firm) on the roof garden, a caravan of three pickup trucks and a red station wagon spotted us as they drove west on Madison. It was a group of ten, maybe twelve people. We ran to the roof's edge yelling, hoping they could help us. They tried to break open the doors. Fail!

Then one guy climbed the tree out front. He crawled out on a branch to reach the 6th floor terrace where he tried to force the shutters open. He couldn't. After he climbed down, they took out their guns and shot at us. WTF! That was the first time I've been glad the building's secure.

They hit Peter in the shoulder. Helen and I took him down to 18. Livia has the medical supplies in a sterile lab. After we told her what happened, she took Joey and Darryl up to the roof to "assess the damage."

Peter's shoulder was a bloody mess. Helen thought maybe they bullet shattered the bone. There's no exit wound, so the bullet's still in there. She cleaned it really well, even though Peter hurt so bad he was screaming. But she had to. What if it got infected?

I helped with the bandages, then we made a splint following the directions in one of the earthquake kits. I gave Peter an oxy scrip that belonged to Ruby Johnson, whoever she was, and then I settled him to sleep in our room. I'm frightened. If we don't get help soon, he could be crippled. He could die.

That night, L called a meeting in the atrium. She told everyone about the shooting, and that the building had protected us. Feelings were mixed. I mean, yay we didn't get killed or kidnapped, but boo, if they can't get in, then we can't get out.

Sophie

From: Sophie Goldstein

To: Emily Wilson

Date: August 16, 2020

Subject: <No subject>

We've been trapped here for a month. Things are not good. A couple of days after the hillbillies, Betsy jumped off the roof. A garden gnome that I used to think was cute held down her suicide note.

She couldn't live knowing her daughter died alone, crying for her mommy, not understanding why she wasn't there. Betsy's body lay on the street for two days, then it was gone. I don't know which was more upsetting, that she killed herself, or that her body disappeared. Animals? People? What happened? We'll never know.

Mr. Jeffers is also dead.

L says it was a heart attack. I call BS. I saw him every day, putting together stats for him. He was fine Monday evening when I brought his rations. I ate with him, and we talked about the case. He said he was out of coffee. I promised to bring some in the morning.

I found him when I brought the coffee. It was awful. I collapsed, weeping. Peter came looking for me when I didn't show for work. Mr. Jeffers' arms were bruised. How did that happen?

Eddison and I told L that Peter needed more antibiotic ointment. When she ok'd that, we went to the med lab. Once we were in, we searched all the drawers. The insulin was gone.

I think L, with Joey and Darryl, or maybe Lee who's her new ass kisser, I think they held him down, then injected him with insulin causing a heart attack. I can't prove it, but that's what Eddison and I think. Peter says we're nuts, and that I've read too many mysteries.

L called a meeting in the Atrium after rations. She said that while these deaths were terrible, they improved our chances for survival—it means more food for the rest of us. She argued there wasn't enough for everyone to make it over the winter.

Total bullshit.

The gardening book I found says you need 200 square feet to feed one person, and that's not taking into consideration our amazing compost. It may be gross, but the plants love it.

Eddison and I measured out the new garden area on the roof (including the greenhouse) while Peter did the math. We have just under 7,000 square feet. That's enough for 34 people. And we still have a lot of canned food. We could make it.

I don't want to live like this. I don't want to live with people who think like this.

From: Sophie Goldstein

To: Emily Wilson

Date: August 9, 2020

Subject: <No subject>

What did L do with Mr. Jeffers' body?

From: Sophie Goldstein

To: Emily Wilson

Date: August 21, 2020

Subject: A way out

I found out what happened to Mr. Jeffers. While I was carrying buckets of compost for the garden I got to know this guy Brandon. One of his jobs is monitoring the compost vats. He adds chemicals and makes sure they're turning and stuff like that. He told me L added Mr. Jeffers to the vats.

OMG I felt sick. If that doesn't prove she killed him, I don't know what does. Brandon wept when he told me. He said he couldn't stop thinking about it, and felt like puking every time he went into the basement. He's a good guy, so I suggested the four of us—Peter, Eddison, Brandon, and me—hold a wake for Mr. Jeffers. Eddison pulled out Scotch from his private stash. We all got drunk.

Peter and Brandon tossed around ideas about escaping. A lot of them were dumb—make parachutes, jump from the roof into the tree—stuff like that. Then Peter had an idea that could work: start a fire.

It makes sense. The building's programmed for our safety, which means if there's a fire, the doors unlock so we can get out.

The more we talked, the more we wondered why no one thought of this before.

Tomorrow, after we finish our work assignments, we're going to collect paper. The cleaners came in on Sunday nights to clean up for Monday; the trash is still there. We should be able to get enough scrap to start a bonfire, then the sprinklers will come on, the doors will unlock, and out we go.

Peter and Brandon said since this was their idea, they'd start the fire, and keep it burning until we tell them the front door releases. So tomorrow may be the day we leave!

From: Sophie Goldstein

To: Emily Wilson

Date: August 25, 2020

Subject: <No subject>

I hate this building. Peter's dead, and so is Brandon. The building killed them. L insisted I take antidepressants, but I've stopped them. Maybe it'll help if I write it all down.

We decided to set the fires on the 3rd floor in the four Core Green conference rooms. We spread out paper under the conference room tables so the sprinklers or the foam wouldn't extinguish the fire before the doors unlocked.

Once that was done, Eddison and I stood by the stairs. Our job was to keep people out when they came to investigate, and let Peter know when the doors unlocked. Peter and Brandon lit the fires. The fire alarm went off as planned. Then the building said, "Gas fire suppression activated. You have one minute to exit." Eddison freaked, screaming at Peter and Brandon to come out.

I don't think they heard us. I don't think they understood the danger. When the fire door auto-closed, we grabbed the handles to keep it open, but the metal turned red hot, burning us. I guess it's wired to do that so you can't hold the fire doors open. When we let go, the doors locked with Peter and Brandon inside.

L came running down the stairs, with Lee and Darryl behind her. Eddison told her our plan. She was furious. Of course we didn't know. How could we know? She's never shared the building manual. Everything she knows about the building, she's kept secret.

They waited with us. After half an hour, the building told us the fire was suppressed and the room clear. The handles cooled. The doors unlocked.

Peter and Brandon lay just inside. They used the sling from Peter's shoulder to insulate the handles, but they couldn't force the door, not after the building locked it.

L said the building uses a gas suppression system during lockdown. Carbon dioxide, which is very green. She added, "Next time you have an idea. Don't be stupid. Talk to me first."

I lost it. I lunged for her. Eddison grabbed me, dragging me away. While I was still screaming, calling her a murderer, a bitch, she told Lee and Darryl to take the bodies to the composter. Then as she walked upstairs, she said, "I'm sorry. I really am. I'll send Julie down with burn cream for your hands, and something to calm down Sophie. Everyone who dies means more food for the survivors."

I hate her.

From: Sophie Goldstein

To: Emily Wilson

Date: August 30, 2020

Subject: <No subject>

It's been a week since Peter died. Terry, Julie's BF, took me aside for a talk. L must've put him up to it, thinking he's a friend. He explained something had to be done with the bodies. It would be worse to throw them off the roof, and the building has no cold storage. Composting is the logical choice.

It will be at least three months before compost made from their corpses is useable, so it's dumb for me to starve myself now. And my grief is upsetting people. I'm not the only one who's lost a loved one.

I was polite. I said thank you for your concern, then walked away. I do a lot of walking now, up and down the stairs, into all the dark offices. Step, step, step, light, light, light as I go forward, behind me it's dark, dark, dark as the lights go off.

I'll eat my private stash until it's gone. I'm not sharing their food. I'm not working their jobs. Fuck them. I don't care. I'd rather be dead.

From: Sophie Goldstein

To: Emily Wilson

Date: September 6, 2020

Subject: <No subject>

It's been 15 days since the fire, days of walking the dark floors, 3 - 11. At first, I was moving just to move. Then I got curious about who the people in all these offices had been. I started poking around, looking at the photos on their desks, the books on their shelves.

My first find was a bottle of Scotch on seven, hidden behind a Webster's dictionary in a bookcase. I gave it to Eddison.

I went back to see what else was out there. It felt like a treasure hunt. I learned people on the daylight floors use the dark floors to hide their stashes.

In the GBH Capital offices on four I found a stack of *Juggs* and *Asian Fever*. Gross. Also on four, in Jennie's Fine Foods I found a gun and a box of ammo along with a case of tuna tucked under a couch. I took the gun and ammo, left the tuna. On ten, in the *Salish Sea Weekly*'s offices I found birth control pills and weed. Sweet!

Someone working for Loan Care hid a case of Soylent in their server closet. I tried one. It tasted like pancake batter, so not terrible. When I told Eddison, he rolled his eyes and called it "food for techies who hate themselves," so I left it.

The prize was on nine, in the Adventure Gear lobby. Sure, all the energy bars had been taken, as well as the dried food and freeze-dried coffee, but laid out in a display case was a climbing harness, blue rope, pretty, anodized metal things I didn't recognize, and carabiners. There was also a book on climbing on the coffee table.

No doubt back in the day when we expected to be rescued, no one wanted to break the display. Since then, whoever went through this floor had forgotten it, if they even noticed.

I used a chair to break the glass, then I shoved everything into an Adventure Gear backpack. When I got home, I left a note for Eddison to come see me. We have to do this together.

From: Sophie Goldstein

To: Emily Wilson

Date: September 7, 2020

Subject: <No subject>

It's dangerous, but Eddison agrees it could work. The climbing rope is 60 meters. That's almost 197 feet. We estimated ten feet for each floor, more than enough to get us from 12 down to the 6th floor terrace, and from there, to the tree.

We'll need to break a window. There might be an alarm. The shutters might close. The windows might not break. The building protects itself.

We decided to test the windows in my old office on 14. No one lives in the Patterson offices anymore. If we're discovered, Eddison will say I lost it, and he tried to stop me. That settled, we went upstairs. We hit one of the two windows with an end table. Even double paned, they broke easy, and no alarms. But the shutters closed. That freaked me out.

We broke the other window, timing it. The shutters close in one minute, 20 seconds. By 43 seconds, the opening is too narrow to get through. 37 seconds to escape. We'll have to move fast.

There's only one climbing harness. Eddison insists I use it. He's stronger than me, and figures he can jury rig something with a couple of belts. He'll wear gloves and slide down if he has to.

Should we risk it? Here, we have heat and light and water. Even if rations are cut, probably we can survive the winter. Then what? How long will we stay in this stupid building, hoping civilization will magically reboot?

Outside, we can find people. Not everyone will be like the hillbillies. We can stay in empty buildings, and get canned food from supermarkets. We have a gun. We even have a place to go, Krystal's cabin at Moclips. If we grab bikes, we can get there before winter. It's less than 200 miles, down to Tacoma then across the bridge.

We're going to do it. It's dangerous. We could die—neither of us are climbers—but we can't stay here. We just have to get to the terrace, from there it should be easy. If the hillbilly could climb down the tree, then so can we.

Eddison will bring our rations soon. We're going eat and study the climbing book until everyone's asleep, then we'll go. Wish us luck.

EXTREME BEDDING

David Marusek

I went to the office the other day and found a terrorist sitting at my desk.

"What the hell?" I said.

My boss came over and pulled me aside. "Why don't you sit at Marilyn's desk today?" she said. Marilyn was away on leave.

"Because I prefer to sit at my own desk," I replied. "But I can't because *there's a terrorist sitting at my desk.*"

My boss threw up her hands. "What can I do about it? We all have to pitch in and help out in difficult situations, don't we? Of course we do. Around here the real work is teamwork. So try to be the solution, Bob, and not the problem."

So I sat at Marilyn's desk that day. The sky didn't fall, and the next day the terrorist was gone.

At first I felt a little sheepish about all the fuss I had made, but then I noticed that my Post-it notes were rearranged on my computer. And the cap of my favorite ballpoint pen had chew marks all over it.

Who does that? Who rearranges and gnaws on people's things like that?

Worse, there were cigarette ashes on my keyboard.

Ashes? Really? Who smokes cigarettes anymore? And in a smoke-free building!

But when have you ever known a terrorist to follow the rules?

That afternoon, when my boss walked by my desk, I stopped her and asked why the terrorist couldn't have used Marilyn's desk instead of mine. She didn't even slow down but rolled her eyes way back in her head. Made it seem like everything was my fault.

Right before five o'clock, my girlfriend texted to tell me she had an unexpected open house and not to wait dinner on her. This was the third time this had happened this week. The real estate market was on fire, and my girlfriend worked around the clock.

So I stopped at the supermarket on the way home to pick up some take-out dinner. But the front doors didn't slide open for me, and the aisles inside the store were dark. There was a big sign in the window that said:

CLOSED BECAUSE IMMIGRATION

"Oh, for crying out loud!" I said. "Closed? Really?"

I made myself a frozen pizza at my girlfriend's apartment and afterwards watched some TV while I waited for her. The news was all about a terrorist plot at a train station in Europe. I was grateful that at least the terrorist at my desk hadn't blown himself up.

Another news story reported on the president's speech at a victory rally in an Air Force hangar. The Air Force was rolling out its new drones with bombs so smart they could pick out a single terrorist in a crowded football stadium. The president declared that America was wonderful. America was just incredible. And *that* was why terrorists were blowing themselves up big league.

I must have dozed off because I woke up when my girlfriend came in. It was quite late, and she was tired and cranky. Turned out, her prospective buyers were terrorists and they made her show them, like, a dozen different listings.

"They had all of these unreasonable demands," she complained. "Everything had to be just so."

But the terrorists eventually saw something they liked and made an offer, so things turned out well and good at the end.

The next day, as I was riding the train to work, I received a blast text from the office. My boss instructed everyone not to come into work; the office was closed, permanently, due to abortion. She thanked us for our years of service and sent us her best wishes.

I was stunned. I was unemployed. Again! I got off at the next station and took a return train home.

When I got to the apartment, wouldn't you know it, there was a terrorist in bed with my girlfriend.

I lost it completely then. "Get out!" I screamed at them. "Both of you! Get out!"

The terrorist only smirked and flicked cigarette ash on the sheets, and my girlfriend said, "Someone's forgetting whose apartment this is."

Now I live in a motel, not far from the fulfillment center where I work. I get weekly rates here, with cable TV, wi-fi, air, and pool included. It even has maid service, so I suppose things could be worse.

I work the night shift packing cartons. Basically, the robots bring me stuff, and I put it in cartons.

I sleep during the day. Or at least that's the plan. Lately, the minute I close my eyes, they pop right back open and I lie there, sometimes for hours, staring at the ceiling. Weeks have passed since I've gotten a good day's sleep. It's wearing me down.

But this morning I received an encouraging bedtime tweet from the president: *America has the best sleep. It's world-class sleep, what can I tell you. Our sleep ranking is huge, believe me.*

His words help a little and I drift off, only to bolt upright an hour later with a galloping heart.

Why are things so screwed up?

I lie there, powerless against exhaustion, as I try to figure out how in the hell we got ourselves into this mess in the first place. Was it something we did as a nation or something we failed to do? Are we the victims here, or is all of this our own damn fault?

In desperation I cry out, "When, oh when, will this nightmare end?"

Under my bed, someone yawns and says, "I don't know for you, my friend, but for me when you do something about the snoring. Sad (or Sick)."

ABOUT THE CONTRIBUTORS

K. G. Anderson has published short fiction in *Second Contacts, Triangulation: Beneath the Surface,* and *The Mammoth Book of Jack the Ripper Stories.* She is online at writerway.com.

Elizabeth Bourne has published short fiction in *Clarkesworld, Interzone,* and *The Magazine of Fantasy & Science Fiction.* She is currently at work on a novel.

Richard Bowes is the author of *Minions of the Moon, From the Files of the Time Rangers,* and *Dust Devils on a Quiet Street.* His fiction has been honored with the Lambda Award, the International Horror Guild Award, and the World Fantasy Award.

Scott Bradfield is the author of *The History of Luminous Motion, Animal Planet,* and *What's Wrong with America.*

J.S. Breukelaar is the author of *Aletheia* and *American Monster.* She has a website at thelivingsuitcase.com.

Jennifer Marie Brissett is the author of *Elysium, or, The World After.* She is working on her second novel. She can be found online at jennbrissett.com.

Becca Caccavo is currently a college undergraduate. This is her first published work of fiction.

Don D'Ammassa is the author of such novels as *Haven, Scarab,* and *Multiplicity,* as well as having written encyclopediae of adventure fiction, fantasy, and science fiction. A longtime reviewer for *Science Fiction Chronicle,* he continues to publish reviews online at dondammassa.com.

Stephanie Feldman is the author of *The Angel of Losses.* She has sold essays and stories to *Electric Literature, Forward, The Rumpus,* and *Asimov's.* She can be found online at stephaniefeldman.com.

Eric James Fullilove's novels include *Credible Threat, Narcolepsy,* and *Circle of One.* Born to a literary family, his grandmother, Maggie Shaw Fullilove, wrote for *The Half-Century Magazine,* and his uncle, J. B. S. Fullilove, published fiction in *Weird Tales.* Eric can be found online at ericjamesfullilove.com.

Ron Goulart is the author of dozens of novels, including *After Things Fell Apart, Calling Dr. Patchwork,* and the Chameleon Corps books. He has also written extensively about comic books and dime detectives, including the recent volume, *Alex Raymond: An Artistic Journey.*

Eileen Gunn's short fiction has been collected in two volumes, *Stable Strategies for Middle Management* and *Questionable Practices.* A former director of advertising for Microsoft, she maintains a web site at eileengunn.com.

Leslie Howle attended the Clarion West Writers Workshop as a student, then wound up working as its director for more than twenty years. Formerly the education and outreach manager at the Science Fiction Museum and Hall of Fame, she is currently teaching digital film making to teens and working on a novel.

Matthew Hughes's many books include *Fools Errant, Hell to Pay,* and *Template.* He is online at matthewhughes.org, where "Loser" first appeared.

Janis Ian is a singer, songwriter, producer, writer, and occasional actress. Her recent books include an award-winning autobiography, *Society's Child,* and a book for young readers, *The Tiny Mouse.* She has a website at janisian.com.

Michael Kandel's novels include *Strange Invasions, Panda Ray,* and *Captain Jack Zodiac.* In addition to his own writing, he is also an accomplished translator and editor.

Thomas Kaufsek has published reviews and short fiction in *Science Fiction Eye, Infinity,* and elsewhere. He works as a copyeditor and has been true to his resolution not to have his own web site.

Paul La Farge is the author of *The Artist of the Missing, Luminous Airplanes,* and most recently, *The Night Ocean.* Check out paullafarge.com for more information, before it disappears.

Yoon Ha Lee began publishing fiction while still a college undergraduate. For more information, including news about the novel *Ninefox Gambit,* visit yoonhalee.com

Michael Libling has published short fiction in *Realms of Fantasy, Asimov's, F&SF,* and elsewhere. His debut novel is due out soon. A former newspaper columnist and talk radio host, he blogs occasionally at michaellibling.com.

Heather Lindsley has published short fiction in *Asimov's, The Magazine of Fantasy & Science Fiction,* and *Brave New Worlds.* She has also published and directed a variety of plays, a list of which can be found online at randomjane.com.

Barry N. Malzberg is an author, editor, and critic perhaps best known for the novels *Herovit's World* and *The Men Inside*, and for his nonfiction collection *Breakfast in the Ruins*.

David Marusek's novels include *Counting Heads* and *Mind Over Ship*. He won the Theodore Sturgeon Award for his story "The Wedding Album." According to marusek.com, his latest novel, *Upon This Rock*, has recently been published.

Lisa Mason has published ten novels, including *Arachne, Summer of Love*, and *The Gilded Age*. Her short fiction has appeared in *Omni, Asimov's, F&SF*, and various anthologies. A full list of her works can be found at lisamason.com.

Mary Anne Mohanraj has founded and edited three magazines, including *Strange Horizons*. She's published a dozen books, including the Lambda-finalist, *The Stars Change*, and writes for George R.R. Martin's Wild Cards series. She's online at maryannemohanraj.com.

James Morrow's novels include *Only Begotten Daughter, City of Truth, Towing Jehovah*, and *Galápagos Regained*. He can be found online at jamesmorrow.info.

Ruth Nestvold has published stories in such markets as *Asimov's, F&SF*, and *Strange Horizons*. In 2007, the Italian translation of her novella "Looking Through Lace" won the "Premio Italia" award for best international work. She maintains a web site at ruthnestvold.com.

Deji Bryce Olukotun is a technology activist who focuses on cybersecurity and freedom of expression. He has published two novels, *Nigerians in Space* and *After the Flare*. He can be found online at returnofthedeji.com.

Marguerite Reed recently published her first novel, *Archangel*. Her bio online at margueritereed.com spells out some of her real-life efforts for change.

Robert Reed is the author of *The Memory of Sky, Down the Bright Way, An Exaltation of Larks*, and many short stories. He can be found online at robertreedwriter.com.

Madeleine E. Robins is the author of *The Stone War, Point of Honour*, and *Petty Treason*, as well as a score of short stories. She lives in San Francisco and currently works at the American Bookbinders Museum.

Jay Russell's novels include *Celestial Dogs, Burning Bright*, and *Brown Harvest*. His short fiction has been collected in *Waltzes and Whispers*. He teaches writing at St. Mary's University.

Geoff Ryman's novels include *The Unconquered Country, Was, Air, 253*, and *The Child Garden*. He is the administrator for the Nommo Awards for Speculative Fiction by Africans and his interview series *100 African Writers of SFF* is appearing in *Strange Horizons*.

James Sallis has published more than a dozen novels, including *The Long-Legged Fly*, *Drive*, and *Willnot*. His nonfiction books include *The Guitar Players* and *Chester Himes: A Life*. His website is jamessallis.com.

J. M. Sidorova published her first novel, *The Age of Ice*, in 2013. Her short stories have appeared in *Albedo One*, *Asimov's*, *Clarkesworld*, and other magazines and anthologies. She has a website at jmsidorova.com.

Brian Francis Slattery is the author of *Spaceman Blues*, *Lost Everything*, and *Liberation*. He's also a frequent contributor to Bookburners. He can be found online at bfslattery.com.

Harry Turtledove has published more than four dozen novels, including works of fantasy, historical fiction, and stories of alternative history such as *The Guns of the South* and, more recently, *The House of Daniel*.

Deepak Unnikrishnan won the Restless Books Prize for New Immigrant Writing for his first novel, *Temporary People*. "Birds" is excerpted from this novel.

TS Vale (tsvale.com) is one of the pen names of an awarded author who's loved and practiced "writing" her entire life. TS wrote her first published novel, *Buck*, at age 16. The novel remains on certain banned and challenged book lists.

Leo Vladimirsky works in advertising and has created campaigns for clients like IKEA, YouTube, L.A. Tourism, and XBOX. His fiction has been published in *The Magazine of Fantasy & Science Fiction* and *Boing Boing*. He recently finished his first novel, *The Horrorists*. You can find his work at leovladimirsky.com.

Ray Vukcevich is the author of *The Man of Maybe Half-a-Dozen Faces*. His short fiction has been collected in *Meet Me in the Moon Room* and *Boarding Instructions*. Read more about him at rayvuk.com.

Ted White has been publishing science fiction stories for more than fifty years. His novels include *The Jewels of Elsewhen*, *By Furies Possessed*, and *Phoenix Prime*. He is also a veteran music journalist and magazine editor who spent many years editing *Amazing*, *Fantastic*, and *Heavy Metal*.

Paul Witcover is the author of *Waking Beauty*, *Tumbling After*, *Asylum*, *The Emperor of All Things*, as well as a collection of short stories, *Everland*. His digital home is at paulwitcover.com.

N. Lee Wood has published seven novels, including *Looking for the Mahdi* and *Faraday's Orphans*.

Jane Yolen's 365th and 366th books are coming out in 2018, so reading a book of hers every day is possible even in a Leap Year. Among her many awards and honors are two Nebulas, three Mythopoeic Society Awards, the Jewish Book Award, six honorary doctorates, and a Skylark Award that set her coat on fire.